The Standard

The Standard

John Reinhard Dizon

PART ONE: The Pledge

Chapter One

Captain William Shanahan always thought of himself as the gold standard of the SAS. He considered himself the prototype of what every secret agent in MI6 should be. At six-foot-two, two hundred and ten pounds of surgical steel and sex appeal, he was the ladies' pet and the men's regret. He had religiously followed a rigorous training schedule and personal diet over the course of his lifetime that gave him an imposing athletic build featuring a washboard waist and perfect musculature. Whenever he had any concerns or doubts about undertaking a difficult assignment such as this, one look in the mirror quelled his apprehensions.

He had arrived at Craigavon two days early in order to brace himself for the task ahead. Craigavon was one of the most refreshing outdoor venues in County Armagh, a place where one could be forgiven for thinking they were still in the United Kingdom and not merely in Ulster. He spent his first day at the Craigavon Golf and Ski Centre, savoring the perfect spring day as he mentally rehearsed this juncture in the mission ahead. He played eighteen holes and tallied a decent score which he conveniently excused for the preoccupying distraction.

The next day he divided between a morning at Tannaghmore Gardens, where he spent time watching mothers and children at the petting zoo before wandering around the botanical areas. He had been motivated by a lifelong desire to have a family, a wife and children of his own. MI6, the Secret Intelligence Service, had been his universe for nearly two decades. He had worshipped at its altar, been one of its most devoted acolytes, and gave it place over his life. After this job, he would call in his markers and get the desk job. After this he would find a wife, reclaim his life, and live happily ever after.

That afternoon he drove over to the Craigavon Watersports Centre where he rented out a canoe and leisurely coasted around the Craigavon Lake. It had been an idyllic forty-eight hours that recharged his batteries, helped him clear his head and focus on the task ahead. He loved the outdoors, it helped remind him that there was a loving God Who loved mankind and brought His people to peace and goodness beyond the valley of death. It helped remind him that they were the white knights fighting the good fight, although it seemed his hands got dirtier and dirtier as the fight wore on.

He enlisted in the service in order to take part in Operation Desert Shield in 1991, and when it escalated to Desert Storm, he volunteered for the Special Air Service. He served with them for his first tour of duty before being transferred to the Special Boat Service. He spent his second and third tours with the SBS before being dispatched to Afghanistan for a fourth tour. It was during that time he was offered and accepted a position with MI6. It was then that he could look back and say he had sold his soul in the process.

Yet there was that deep, dark recess inside him that would always question who his soul had belonged to in the first place. It was there on his birth certificate, the fact that he had been born a Catholic, to a Catholic father and a Protestant mother. In England and almost anywhere else abroad, it made little or no difference. In Northern Ireland it was like a scarlet letter, a birthmark he could never erase. Despite the fact his father had converted to the Protestant faith, and that his parents lived in East Belfast, the hospital officials had record of his Da's birth certificate and dutifully traced the lineage onto his son's record. William Shanahan was forced to deal with it all his life, hiding it as best he could and backing down all who challenged it when it came out.

He was a proud citizen of the realm and enlisted in Her Majesty's service as soon as he came of age. His service record spoke for itself and he was decorated numerous times for bravery. His parents died while he was overseas, erasing even more of his past as he continued his journey towards self-fulfillment. He had reached a turning point in his career, the juncture where a coveted desk job was now within his reach. He had proven himself as a soldier, as a commando, and as an undercover operative. If he successfully completed this one last mission, his next place of employment could well be on Downing Street in London. He might have finally found his true station in life.

His parents had compensated him well for the stigma of their mixed marriage. He was a very handsome man with thick blond hair, piercing blue eyes, a perfectly chiseled nose, Cupid's bow lips and a granite jawline. He could easily run ten miles, swim a mile at full speed, and held a black belt in Tae Kwon Do. He maintained a perfect tan throughout the year and never failed to catch the eye of beautiful women who could not take their eyes off his chiseled abdominals.

He had also been a grade-A student, having earned an associate degree in economics. He was earning a Captain's wage in the military and had managed to save almost half his earnings over a twenty-year career. Once he was given a coveted position at SIS[1] at 85 Albert Embankment, it was a hop, skip and jump from Central London to Downing Street. He knew lots of guys who had made the grade, and he had no doubt he would be one of them.

He knew there was a defining moment in every man's career, beyond the battlefield heroics that set a commando apart from the rest. The move from the SBS to MI6 had set the stage, and now his time had come at last to truly break away from the pack. They had offered him this mission, and he accepted it without reservation or question. His mentors told him that this was a top secret assignment that many above his station would have given their eyeteeth for. They told him to take it and run, not to dare look back, and sink his teeth into it and take everything he could from it. Few got such an opportunity at this

---

1. Secret Intelligence Service

stage of their career, and he would forever regret it if he did not make the most of it.

He spent the afternoon canoeing and had a sumptuous supper at a classy restaurant, treating himself to filet mignon and a baked potato with a vintage Merlot. He flirted with his sexy auburn-haired waitress and even got her phone number, but knew he might possibly never return. He knew that somehow he would marry an Englishwoman in London, a woman of noble lineage or at least a wealthy background. Marrying an Irish lass could very well be a heavenly thing, especially in the case of a woman like this, but life was lived only once and one had to make the very best of what it had to offer. After dinner he wandered around town, collecting his thoughts and enjoying the rural domesticity of Craigavon before turning in for the night.

He drove from Craigavon to Maghaberry HMP[2] the next morning after a fitful night of sleep, and the ride along M1 was windswept and slick from a light drizzle that had descended overnight. The weather had turned gray and dismal, and he felt somewhat blessed by the quality of the climate he took advantage of the day before. He expected it to be a harbinger of the luck he would anticipate in the days ahead. No matter what came his way, he fully intended to capitalize on his momentum and press irresistibly towards his goal.

The prison complex could appear as an industrial park to the unknowing. It was only when one approached the front gates would they realized they were entering into a different world.

Just as any other prison, the blue signs with their crude printing gave fair notice of what was to come. Shanahan drove to the gate and handed his papers to the guard, who gave him directions to the parking area where he would begin his guided tour of the facilities. He was hoping it would end in the cell of the man he was scheduled to interview.

---

2. Her Majesty's Prison

He was well-dressed in a metallic gray suit, midnight blue shirt and pastel tie, his boots shining as mirrors as he strutted along the pathway to the series of checkpoints leading to the maximum security area. He did his best to hide his contempt for the brutish guards who completed their rubdown search as their drug dogs watched languidly. He protested mildly as his personal items were collected in a basket, but the captain of the guard assured him it was a mandatory procedure.

"I'm not pleased at all with the arrangement," the captain informed him as he escorted Shanahan through a corridor of steel doors that could only be opened electronically by guards at protected stations. "I don't like you being in a cell by yourself with a bastard such as that. It was arranged by forces beyond our control, and if anything goes wrong I hope to God they are prepared to accept the consequences."

One of Shanahan's redeeming qualities was his reluctance to boast. He wanted to tell the ruffian that he had survived a thirty-man siege of his position alongside two wounded comrades in a shack in the mountains of Kandahar in Afghanistan. He wanted to tell him about fighting off a pincer attack by two squads of ex-Republican Guards in Fallujah over in Iraq. He wanted to tell him that he was willing to lock himself in a cell with the man and four of his best, to see who would remain standing.

"Let me remind you," Shanahan said before two guards prepared to allow him access to the metal door at the end of a narrow, poorly-lit corridor. "This is a top secret interview. If you have any eavesdropping devices in the cell I strongly suggest you turn them off lest you be in violation of Her Majesty's laws."

"We've been well advised," the captain growled, ordering his men to open the door and permit Shanahan entry.

Shanahan entered the small cell, where a chair had been placed a couple of feet from the entrance. There were pictures, posters, a Union Jack and a Red Hand of Ulster banner along the walls. There was a small table by the wall next to which sat a small chair, and beside it a tiny bookcase holding about a dozen books. The King James Bible and a scented candle sat atop it. On the metal cot laid the sole occupant of the cell, who rose lazily and stood to face Shanahan.

"Right on time, I like that. Have a seat."

"Captain William Shanahan, Military Intelligence," he introduced himself.

"Jack Gawain. My pleasure."

Gawain stood 5'9" and weighed one hundred eighty pounds. Although he was fairly smaller than Shanahan, he was thickly muscled which suggested a lifetime of powerlifting. His black hair was trimmed, his skin was pasty from lack of sunshine which accentuated his coal-black eyes. His eyes brimmed with energy as he stared at Shanahan, his lips curling just short of a perpetual smirk.

"I trust you were informed as to the nature of my visit."

"West Belfast?"

"I beg your pardon?"

"West Belfast. You were born there. I'm sure you moved to the East Side at one time or another, then the UK for a short time before or after you enlisted. You never lose the accent, you know. It's kinda like a coal miner, once they get the soot in their skin it never comes out."

"Just like they'll always know you're from Ulster to the day you die," Shanahan replied curtly.

He knew this was coming and did all in his power to avoid it, but he took an immediate dislike to the man. Gawain was everything he remembered about the street punks in East Belfast, from the cocksure sneer to the Scottish accents. He remembered the horror stories of what had happened to his relatives on the West Side, how the hooligans in the street would watch his face when they told their stories, searching desperately for a flinch of emotion. It was the same way Gawain was studying him, and it made him want to bash his face in.

"I must say I always envied you fellows who took the plunge," Gawain lit a cigarette without offering one to his visitor. "It was the best thing, the noble thing to do. It truly changes a man's character, and you certainly are a perfect example of that."

"I'm sure you had plenty of chances," Shanahan was brusque. "The Constabulary, the reserves, the Army...but you chose your own path."

"And so I did," Gawain blew a stream of smoke to the side. Shanahan noticed his fingertips lacked the tobacco stain of the typical chain-smoker, and his nails were well trimmed. "For Queen, God and country, though not as traditionally as you."

"I'm sure you and your colleagues thought so. Yet here I am, and there you are. So, putting all that aside, now is your chance to make amends."

"And what makes right and wrong?" Gawain narrowed his eyes. "The victors are the ones who write history, yet the revisionists rewrite the history and put a different spin on it all. Do y'think those ragheads demonstrating in the streets of London are going t'let matters rest twenty years from now? Right now, whatever medals you've earned make you a hero of our nation. How will it feel once you've retired and they start mocking your efforts as a criminal attack on the Iraqi people? I think you may get an idea of how I'm feeling right now."

"Sorry to differ, but I was part of an international campaign against a criminal regime," Shanahan said blandly. "You were part of a vigilante organization that murdered civilian relatives of organized criminals. Not to mention the blackmarket operations you masterminded after the so-called hostilities ended. Perhaps the Iraq War will be white-washed and reinterpreted in generations to come, but yours was an illegal enterprise from start to finish."

"And who do you think it was that gave us the power, Captain Shanahan?" Gawain grinned wickedly. "Do you think for one minute that it wasn't the PSNI[3] or the British Army standing by while we stood up for them in the line of fire against the IRA? We have our share of KIA's, and our share of martyrs. You can sit there and gloat while I sit here as a prisoner of war, but the day will come when you are as old and weak as the tea we're given here daily. The day will come when those Paki kids are pissing on your porch, blowin' their nose on

---

3. Police Service of Northern Ireland

the Union Jack on your front lawn and there won't be a feckin' thing you'll do about it."

"All you're doing is changing the cast of characters," Shanahan shrugged. "Five years ago you would've been talking about Catholic weens doing such things. All you've done is set your sights on different game."

"And what'll it be for you, Captain Shanahan?" Gawain's gaze bored into his eyes. "Maybe this is the pot at the end of your rainbow, but do you think varnish lasts forever? It'll never erase that accent, nor will it change the mark of the papists on your birth certificate. Sure, and you'll get that promotion, find a flat not far from Downing Street, but will it ever erase the stigma your missus will always endure, or your children, for that matter? You'll always be a West Sider, Captain, no matter how far ye move away to escape it."

"You know this is a one-time offer," Shanahan cleared his throat despite his best efforts. "The offer expires once I walk out that door. I'm interviewing candidates on a very short list, and when I'm gone you'll never hear from us again."

"Pray tell," Gawain clasped his fingers. "Who do I have to kill? I'm here for a triple life sentence. Does your Government think it more expedient to have me done on the field of honor, and give me a proper sendoff thereafter? I would think someone who has sent over thirty IRA men and their confederates to hell deserves as much."

"According to what I've heard, there were a number of women and children that were unaccounted for at your trial," Shanahan could not restrain himself. "Even in a traditional war scenario, most of what you did would place someone before a firing squad."

"Let me ask you this, Captain," Gawain leaned forward intently. "You won your medals by saving lives against impossible odds. Why don't we change the channel and take a peek at an East Sider fighting off ski-masked IRA riflemen, with his screaming wife and children huddled about him. It's the same game played on different sides. You wear your medals with pride, and though mine are invisible, so do I."

"Like I said, Gawain," Shanahan rose from his chair, "it's a one-time offer, and if you won't take it I've other fellows to talk to."

"You didn't tell me who I had to kill?"

"What does it matter," Shanahan would regret having lost control, "to a murdering bastard like you?"

"You've got a point," Gawain chuckled. "No matter who you've singled out, I'm certain it will be far better than sitting around here."

"Good," Shanahan rapped on the door, resulting in the door being yanked open immediately. "We'll be in touch shortly."

"To God and Country," Gawain called behind him as the door slammed shut.

Shanahan would drive back to Craigavon and drink a large volume of Irish whiskey at the nearest hotel before spending an inordinate time in the shower to wash the psychological stench away.

Chapter Two

Rise of the Hacker

Shanahan flew from Belfast International Airport to Heathrow Airport in London the next morning. He had been summoned to a briefing by Colonel Mark Shaughnessy, the legendary SAS veteran who was now a key figure on Downing Street. The meeting was being held at the SIS Building, the ziggurat-shaped structure at 85 Albert Embankment near Vauxhall Bridge on the River Thames. Shaughnessy had been in the game most of his life, finally securing a desk job after undergoing hip replacement surgery. Though he walked with a cane, he was still an imposing figure and Shanahan considered it an honor to meet him.

"I'm glad you were able to successfully interview the prisoner and decide for yourself whether he is what we're looking for," Shaughnessy disclosed. Shanahan was seated across from him in his plush yet conservative office, comfortable in the overstuffed leather chair.

"I just connected the dots on this one, sir. My orders were to interview the subjects in order from top to bottom of the list and cut a deal with the first to accept."

"Your perspective, Captain?" the 6'4", 300-pounder leaned back in his heavily-padded swivel chair.

"I was given a dossier on the subject. It confirmed my opinions after the fact."

"Well, what of it?"

"May I speak freely, sir?"

"By all means."

"This fellow is scum. I think he is right where he deserves to be for the rest of his life. If anything goes wrong with this mission, I believe we will have no one but ourselves to blame."

Shaughnessy allowed himself a laugh before folding his hands atop the enormous mahogany desk.

"When you've been in this business as long as I have, you start realizing the truth of the saying that the scum does indeed rise to the top. The ones who make it past the local police and earn the attention of the special operations units are usually the worst of the worst. For this particular assignment, you are going to need someone readily identifiable within the low-life community. This fellow is made to order."

John Oliver Cromwell Gawain was the youngest of four children born to a working-class family in East Belfast. His father was a known and respected member of the Ulster Defense Association. After a drive-by shooting in West Belfast when Gawain was six, the Official IRA mistakenly identified his father as the gunman. They ordered that his death be made a warning and an example to others. A hit squad was sent to the Gawain home, and his father was shot to death after his mother was raped and strangled before the entire family.

They said Gawain lost his soul that night. The personable, spirited young boy became a troubled youth when he and his siblings were separated and parceled out to foster homes. He became obsessed with fighting, spending his time at youth centers finding others to wrestle and box with. When the center closed he spent the nights with street gangs, and when he rose to leadership he started skipping school. He took a fancy to the Apprentice Boys, a junior paramilitary force whose regimentation bringing out the best in him. His foster parents began treating him much kinder and gentler once they found he was under the tutelage of the UDA. When he reached his teens, the top guys began grooming him for full membership.

After a stint with the Ulster Young Militants, he was reassigned to C Company of the 3rd Battalion of the Ulster Freedom Fighters under

Johnny "Mad Dog" Adair. The UFF leadership liked the young man and predicted great things for him. After the Good Friday Agreement of 1998 went into effect, Gawain was given charge of his own platoon. They promptly cornered the local market in bootleg cigarettes and drug trafficking, and more and more leaders turned to him for his ability to move merchandise and turn quick profits. Gawain soon became one of the biggest dealers on Shankill Road, which caused him to run afoul of the Continuity IRA.

After the GFA ceasefire, the Continuity IRA and the Real IRA remained the only splinter groups active in Ulster. The conflict had shifted from political to mercenary issues as both sides sought to take control of the local black market. The UDA and its offshoots engaged in fierce warfare with the IRA factions throughout the streets of Northern Ireland. Gawain soon established a reputation as one of the most hated and feared Catholic killers.

"So why do they call him the Hacker, is he good at computers, that sort of thing?" Shanahan wondered.

"Not quite," Shaughnessy frowned. "He has a reputation for beating his victims during interrogations with the backs of his blades. When the handle shifts in his hand, either accidentally or on purpose, he winds up hacking into his victims. It leaves most of them grievously wounded, maimed or dead."

"Wonderful fellow," Shanahan was curt. "Sir, you know I come from an Irish Catholic background. I'm not sure I'll be the right man for this assignment."

"It's part of what makes you just right for the job," the Colonel reasoned. "This fellow is sublimely clever and intelligent. He is arrogant and calculating, the textbook definition of a ruthless opportunist. The greatest danger would be for him to cast you under his spell. I am quite confident that would not be the case here."

"Impeccable logic, sir," Shanahan did not want to offend. "Who might be waiting for us at the other end of this viper's nest?"

"This fellow," Shaughnessy slid a second dossier over to Shanahan. "Enrique Chupacabra, real name Muniz. You talk about slimebuckets, this fellow is one of the worst you'll find. He's from Medellin in Colombia, one of the top enforcers in the Medellin Cartel. This is the conundrum we are faced with, Captain. Chupacabra and his gang have been converting large sums of cash into gold bullion all along the cartel's international network. We are talking about a territory that extends from South America to the Canadian border. I'm sure you've been reading the papers about a proposed global shift to a gold standard economy. The Prime Minister is quite certain these fellows intend to gain some serious leverage in this matter."

"So the PM wants me to toss that shitebag over at Maghaberry into his path to keep him from buying up too much gold," Shanahan deduced.

"It gets a tad more complicated than that," the Colonel explained. "Chupacabra is just a puppet on a string at this level. Neither he nor the people behind him have the brains or the resources to play this kind of game. There is someone above them giving the orders, and we have to find out who it is."

"And if we create a train wreck, maybe someone pops out from behind the curtain to clean up the mess," Shanahan was sardonic.

"Captain, let me be more precise and to the point," Shaughnessy leaned back. "You were highly recommended for this assignment. You've got an excellent service record, you're very well-liked and respected. You're known for your intelligence, courage and natural ability. As much as we hate seeing men like you leave the field, we all know that the desk job is the big prize in this line of work. Men like you, who accomplish so much in Her Majesty's service, are well deserving of it. However, it's going to take one last push to get you to the next level. I would be more than glad to provide it. Yet the stakes are rather high, from both our points of view to those of the Prime Minister and the Crown. Let us approach this assignment with all due care, and avoid being overzealous or presumptuous. We cannot let this great opportunity degenerate into a crisis that could jeopardize our nation."

"You are absolutely right, sir," Shanahan quickly deferred to his superior. "I have no reason not to keep all things in perspective. How are we to approach this matter?"

"Chupacabra's weaknesses are common: sex, liquor, drugs and gambling, the fatal Four Horsemen," Shaughnessy explained. "We believe the chink in his armor is the gambling. He likes participating in high-risk games at high-profile events, loves being seen in public. It's the only time anyone can actually get near him. Even in public, he travels with anywhere from six to twelve armed guards. He's been known to rent entire penthouse suites to ensure his privacy and charters his own Lear Jets. He always has a beautiful woman as a companion, but treats them like pets so they provide no way to get to him. His role is as a troubleshooter and an emissary, if you can call it that. He eliminates congestion along the drug pipeline and sits down with rival connections as necessary to make sure things flow smoothly. When he gets involved, it usually means someone is going to die. He operates along the East Coast, the Caribbean and the Gulf of Mexico, and spends most of his time between New York, Miami and Houston. They call him in once a month, and he'll spend a weekend in Medellin before he's back on the circuit."

"Are you planning to have Gawain liquidate this fellow?"

"What we're planning to do is have Gawain draw Chupacabra offsides," Shaughnessy said flatly. "Chupacabra's a loose cannon. Apparently he's got some big backers in the Cartel who've been keeping him from getting knocked off. He's already killed a mayor, a congressman, a sheriff and a couple of police officers. He was looking at a governor one time before the Cartel made him back down. Our contacts in the States tell us that one more major slipup may be just enough to put him in a pine box. Hopefully Gawain will do the trick."

"Why aren't the Americans doing the heavy lifting here?"

"Frankly, we can't take a chance of them going to sleep at the switch," the Colonel replied. "They're in the middle of a major political transition and are going to be more concerned with who has the power before they get focused on the economy. Unfortunately, the Crown doesn't have that luxury. If there's some kind of conspiracy going on between the drug cartels and one of the terror networks like Al Qaida, or even some rogue nation like Iran or North Korea, a disruption of the gold standard system could plunge us into a Depression."

"I hate to think that such a scenario could be directly impacted by my success or failure," Shanahan was hesitant.

"Not entirely, but if we can find out what the drug cartels are up to in buying up all that gold, and what their agenda is, it will have a significant effect on the shape of things to come," the Colonel assured him. "Your mission is to report to our people in Montreal where Gawain will also be brought for briefing. They will prepare you for your rendezvous in New York where Gawain will be put into play against Chupacabra."

"How will I go about this?"

"We've provided detailed instructions," Shaughnessy pushed yet another folder towards Shanahan. "There's contact information along with travel accommodations, maps of the areas you'll be working, everything you need to know. Your plane leaves tomorrow morning. Gawain will be brought to Montreal for the briefing at a time and place to be determined."

Shanahan returned to his vehicle and headed back to the Hotel Europa, psyching himself to once again face this man he loathed.

Only this time, Jack Gawain would be a free man in her Majesty's secret service.

Chapter Three

Days had passed since the release of Jack Gawain from Maghaberry HMP and his briefing by Captain William Shanahan and other agents of MI6 in Montreal, Canada. The legendary Canadian city became the meeting place of yet another group who would be establishing the groundwork for the global catastrophe to be known as Operation Blackout.

The speech by Tea Party Chairman Paul Wallace in New York City was the trigger the attendees of the meeting had been awaiting. The meeting was confirmed by cell phone and e-mail shortly after the nationally publicized press conference held by the Tea Party. Though the speech had tremendous ramifications for governments and financial institutions around the world, it was of vital importance for this particular group.

Wallace had announced that the Tea Party would use its national influence to urge Republican leaders to take immediate steps in initiating a long-awaited return to the gold standard by the United States of America. The grand strategy was to appoint a Gold Commission that would supervise the linkage between the dollar and the Federal gold reserve. It would be a last-ditch effort by the government to restore balance to the Federal budget in the face of a worldwide Depression.

"The creation of a Gold Commission will provide us with a cornerstone in establishing a worldwide gold standard in this new century," Wallace declared before the world press in a speech held at a conference room at the New York Stock Exchange. 'It will restore the financial security and economic independence of the American people and the global community. It will liberate us from the insolvency of the paper dollar foisted upon us by financial wizardry and banking conglomerates. It will return the control over our economic future from Wall Street to Main Street across the country. It will save our Social Security system, restore fiscal control over State budgets across America, bring a halt to energy prices and restore price stability to the stock market. It would ensure the financial stability of our middle class, end the Great Recession, and guarantee us a four percent annual increase in national economic growth."

He urged Congress to unite behind Republican and Tea Party leaders in their efforts to pass legislature restoring the gold standard and creating a Gold Commission. Only a concerted grassroots movement by the American public, he insisted, could counter the effects of an impending global depression that could lead to the financial destruction of world governments in months to come.

"I am glad you were all able to take time away from your busy schedules in order to attend this meeting," the tall, portly man came to the fore of Le Lutetia conference room at the luxurious Hotel de la Montagne in downtown Montreal. They were afforded cocktails at the private bar before being seated to watch a videotape of Wallace's speech. "I will introduce each of our honored guests, going from right to left, so that everyone will be acquainted with one another. I would ask that each of you provide any additional comments upon introduction that will enlighten us as to the intentions of the sponsors you represent."

"I am Amschel Bauer," he continued. "I am an investor in gold bullion. I represent a network of what you might call billionaires with interests throughout Europe and the Middle East. As you can see from the video, this so-called grassroots movement threatens to change the face of international commerce and finance across the globe. My associates believe that, by means of a coordinated effort of our own, pooling our resources, we can sabotage these plans and capitalize on a financial collapse that can and will earn us mastery of the world economy."

"First, let me introduce our guest host, Nathan Schnaper. He is the one who so graciously coordinated our meeting today. He is the chairman of what might loosely be considered the Commission of the Canadian Syndicate. Although most people believe that organized crime has been eliminated in Canada, his associates in Montreal, Toronto, Vancouver, Edmonton, and other major cities would think otherwise." Schnaper remained silent, raising a hand in salutation.

"Next is Tony Ramos, the president of the Mara Salvatrucha, or MS-13, in Los Angeles. The MS-13 is a transnational organization that supervises drug traffic from California to New York in conjunction with their associates throughout the Caribbean and along the Mexican border." Ramos greeted them in Spanish before lighting a cigarette.

"To his left is Alberto Calix, *el patron* of the Mexico City drug cartel. Mr. Calix has worked miracles in uniting the various factions throughout Mexico, bringing peace to the underground network and earning the cartels billions of dollars in the process."

"I am very glad to be here," Calix gave a gold-toothed grin.

"We also have with us Ernesto Guzman of the Mexican Mafia. Mr. Guzman is a Filipino national trained by the CIA in his homeland and has provided the MM infrastructure with a wealth of knowledge along with his capable leadership. He operates throughout South Texas and will be making a vast contribution long with his connections in the weeks to come."

"Seated to his left is Julio Cruz, representing the Cuban Syndicate operating out of Miami. Mr. Cruz's associates have established a confederation of dealerships who have established control over a large portion of the southeast coastline and, in doing so, holding a monopoly over most of the Caribbean drug trade."

"Next we have Enrique Chupacabra, who represents the Medellin Cartel in Colombia. Mr. Chupacabra oversees the daily operations of the cartel from LA to New York, and ensures the supply of narcotics from South America to dealerships throughout North America."

"Finally we have William Bruce, who speaks for the European Council. The Council is another confederation of organized crime groups from the United Kingdom to the Mediterranean. Ironically, it is the Council of Europe itself which is the archenemy of Mr. Bruce's associates. They feel it is in their best interests to establish ties with their counterparts in the Americas to provide alternative trade routes in expanding their operations."

"A pleasure to be here," William Shanahan greeted them. MI6 had set up a cover in conjunction with EUROPOL, establishing a bogus network across the Continent. They had been working Bauer's connections for months and finally convinced them of their legitimacy, leading to Shanahan's invitation to the meeting.

"The Council calling itself the Council," Alberto Calix chuckled. "Excellent idea. I'm going to approach my partners about renaming ourselves *Los Federales*." The others joined him in raucous laughter.

"Gentlemen," Bauer called their attention. "As you have seen and heard from the broadcast, the gold standard will redefine the international banking community and reset the balance of economic power across the globe. Unlike the current electronic system, this new structure will be based on material wealth as opposed to values existing only in cyberspace. Therein lies its weakness. Before we could deceive and manipulate cybersystems into redistributing assets, only once the theft was detected it could be restored once the error was found. Now, once we buy, steal or destroy the physical asset, once it is gone, it is gone."

"If that is the case, why would anyone think of destroying gold?" Calix insisted. "Anything can be stolen, given the time, place and opportunity. Like you said, once it's gone, it's gone."

"Perhaps not destroying it," Bauer replied. "Let's say making it irretrievable or unusable to the competition. If we have access to our assets and the competition does not, then we are the ones with the power at that given time."

"How do we end up with more money on the table than any of the world powers?" Schnaper squinted.

"The world debt of the United States in sixteen trillion dollars," Bauer pointed out. "This is sixteen thousand billion dollars. If, my friends, we can accumulate sixteen billion dollars of gold in sixteen thousand isolated, fortified locations around the planet, we will have enough to match the amount owed by the richest country in history. At that point, if we can seize or freeze the assets of any one or all of the G8 nations, it is easy to see that we become the most powerful financial conglomerate in the world."

"I am beginning to think your vision is impairing your judgment, my friend," Cruz shook his head. "Let us say that, in fact, my associates and I actually did have sixteen billion dollars in assets. If we were to consolidate all of these assets and convert them to bullion, our business would come crashing down around our heads. It takes money to make money, and cashing in one's chips means they are leaving the game. We cannot afford, nor do we wish, to sell everything in order to participate in this scheme. And even if we did, this would be but one-sixteenth of your billions. I do not see nine hundred and ninety-nine other men sitting in this room."

"Excellent point," Bauer agreed. "Let us look at it from this perspective. Once the gold standard is established, then the entire debt system would have to be recalibrated. Either the value of gold would have to be increased or the total debt be reassessed. This is why the Americans moved in and quashed the real estate predators throughout the country. You cannot hold a man to a two million dollar debt if the home he has borrowed against is only worth two hundred thousand. If the total gold assets of the international market is only nine trillion, then not only will the value of our gold increase but the world debt will decrease. It is during this reshuffling and reorganization when we strike."

"Tell us of your plan," Guzman chewed his gum furtively. "Let us know how you intend to make all this happen."

Bauer then proceeded to explain a grand strategy that would leave them with gold in their hearts, souls and minds.

As Shanahan returned to the lobby nearly an hour later, he found Jack Gawain holding court amidst a group of bodyguards waiting outside for their own charges. Gawain was in the middle of a story and it seemed the others were having trouble maintaining their composure.

"So, the fellow can hear the police breaking down the door with the battering ram," Gawain explained, "and the lass is yelling at him, 'Take it out! Take it out!'.Now, he keeps on trying to tell her, 'You have to calm down, girl, your arse is locked tight. If you do not calm down it will not come out!' "

Shanahan remained at a distance, watching in bemusement as one of the gunmen wiped tears of laughter from his eyes.

"Well, at that point, the peelers came crashing through the door, grabbed Jimmy and smashed his face against the wall," Gawain continued. "The girl lost it at that point, and she threw open the patio door and went running out into the back yard across the lots. There you have it, a naked lady running off dressed only in her high heels, with a horse's tail sticking out of her arse."

"*No mas, no mas!*" one of Julio Cruz' gunmen seemed about to wet his pants as he shook with laughter.

"Now hold on," Gawain insisted. "Here's the kicker. She runs off, but the back yard seems to be deserted behind her. Only a few moments later, a couple of boys come running out of their house chasing after her with a lasso."

"Charming," Shanahan strolled up to them. "We'd best get a move on, we've got a plane to catch. There's some serious digging to be done ahead, and it's said that the early bird gets the worm."

The two of them bade farewell to the gunmen awaiting their charges' emergence from the conference hall. They walked together in silence to the elevator, and continued thusly to the crosswalk leading to the parking garage. Only when they reached the other side, Gawain signaled Shanahan to a halt.

"Come now, quit screwing around," Shanahan was irritable. "Did I not tell you that we have to be at the airport for the first flight tomorrow?"

"Hold on, Gummo," Gawain nodded to the lower level across from them where Julio Cruz and his gunmen were getting into their rental car. He brought out a disposable cell phone and watched the vehicle as it prepared to drive off.

"What in bloody hell are you on about?" Shanahan insisted.

"Just watch, boyo," Gawain insisted.

Shanahan continued to watch, and at once his impatience turned into astonishment as the rental car erupted with a deafening roar. The explosion was so powerful that it tore a huge chunk of concrete out of the garage wall, sending it crashing to the street as bystanders fled to safety. Shards of burning metal and glass were as shrapnel gouging into everything in its path. Shanahan gazed in awe as smoke and flames belched from the vehicle with no sign of survivors.

"There ye go," Gawain grinned wickedly, dropping the cell phone over the rail to where it shattered on the sidewalk below. "I'd say we won the first round. On to round two, then. Off we are."

Shanahan was torn between the need to flee the approaching police sirens, and an urge to hurl Gawain over the ledge from the fourth floor of the garage. He reluctantly chose the latter, trotting down the stairwell with Gawain close behind as they hurried into their rental car and sped away from the scene of the impromptu assassination.

Chapter Four

They arrived at Newark International Airport that evening, and William Shanahan was as edgy as Jack Gawain was nonchalant. Neither of them exchanged small talk, and it was almost as if they were conversing via telepathy as they were loathe to be the first to break the ice. Yet they could not help being impressed by their first visit to America. When one stopped at a store window the other would step inside if equally impressed, otherwise they kept moving. When they arrived at length at Ruby Tuesday's, they shrugged and nodded and went inside. Inwardly they both felt childish about how they were acting. Yet Shanahan felt as if he was being forced to consort with a thief and a murderer, while Gawain felt slighted by having to deal with a pogue.

They ordered drinks at the bar and were immediately taken in by the wide-screen plasma TV. Gawain quickly lost interest and began looking about at the crowds passing by and people walking in and around the lounge. At once he saw a couple of lovely stewardesses coming into the area and taking seats at a table in a far corner.

"I'm going to go over and see if we can sit with them," Gawain decided.

"Sure you will," Shanahan grunted. "Go on and try your luck."

Shanahan watched on his peripherals as Gawain walked over and introduced himself. He was still bent out of shape over the series of events from yesterday. He had not yet contacted Downing Street and was greatly concerned as to how MI6 was going to react. Shaughnessy would undoubtedly ask what motivated Gawain's terroristic attack, and Shanahan had yet to figure that one out or pick Gawain's brain for it. He had never seen anything as erratic or irresponsible in his life, and fully intended to regiment this operation as soon as possible.

To his surprise, Gawain came over with a big grin on his face.

"It's fine with them, let's go and join them."

Shanahan dutifully followed Gawain to the table, both of them having collected their drinks as they went. He was at once taken aback by the stewardesses as they drew nigh. The statuesque blonde was something of a Nicole Kidman type who Shanahan thought the most striking woman he had ever come across. The auburn haired woman was not as gorgeous but had a sensuality that seemed to have an aura about it.

"William, this is Morgana and that is Fianna," Gawain made the introductions. "Ladies, this is my associate, William. We are traveling on business on behalf of Universal Exports out of London."

"Nice to meet you," they had grins on their faces.

"The girls work for Aer Lingus," Gawain explained. "They say they're back and forth between London, Scotland and the Republic all the time. I thought it was pretty poor luck that we hadn't come across each other sooner. Now's a good time as any, I always say, and if anything happens again like yesterday, at least we have a couple of angels on hand to escort us."

"Okay, I'll bite," Morgana rolled her eyes, still smiling at William. "What happened yesterday?"

"Well, we just happened to be on the way back to our motorcar when this explosion of sorts went off in the lot across the street from where we stood," Gawain explained. "William was quite calm, but I had never had such a fright. Can you imagine, I'll bet you saw on the telly about it being drug dealers up there in Montreal. I was beside myself for most of the afternoon. I says to William, here am I on my first business trip and they send me on to the middle of a war zone. I certainly hope such things are covered by workman's compensation."

"Were you actually there when that happened!" Fianna's eyes widened as William just managed to stare at Gawain in disbelief. "My goodness, what a sight that must have been!"

"You know, I'm about to tell all about it, but I think they're playing our song there, aren't they?"

"What?" Fianna glanced around. "That's just the muzak playing from behind the bar."

"And you've never danced muzak?"

Gawain shifted his eyes towards William and Morgana, and Fianna flashed him a knowing smile as she accompanied him to the open space beside an empty entertainment dais.

"So how are you feeling?" Morgana grinned at William.

"I'm just fine, thank you," he replied, then leaned slightly towards her. "Say, not to appear boorish or anything, but I seem to be missing something here. Everyone seems to find something to be funny that I'm not catching onto."

"Well," she tried to look serious, "he said you only had three months to live, and it would be kind of us to have you two sit with us."

"He said…" William squinted in astonishment, then looked over at Gawain and Fianna dancing. He looked back to Morgana, then broke into a big smile. "He certainly is a piece of work, isn't he?"

"It was quite an unusual pick-up line," her laughter tinkled like chimes. William had been struck by the Irish thunderbolt, and he could not remember the last time he felt so tentative. "You don't look very sickly, and you don't seem very sorry for yourself."

"Well, I try to reserve my pity for him," William replied. "He is a bit sick in the head, don't you know."

"I just love those accents," she smiled. "It's not just more of your come-on, is it?"

"Actually we're both from Belfast. Or at least that's what he told me."

"It doesn't seem like you two have been working together long," she mused.

"How about you two?" Shanahan nodded towards Fianna, who was now doing the twist with Gawain along with a muzak version of 'Peppermint Twist'.

"We got out of training at the same time and got assigned to the same schedule," she sipped her drink. "We decided to room together, so we got an apartment near Soho in the Village. Our supervisor sees to it that we get booked on the same flights, so it works out great."

"Say, lad," Gawain led Fianna back to the table, "the lass says they haven't had anything to eat this after. Whyn't you break out some of that big money of yours and treat us all to lunch, then? I'm sure I could use a bite myself, and we wouldn't want this other lovely lady to waste away either."

They headed over to Phillips Seafood in Terminal A, where the girls insisted on crab chowder while the men decided on the lobster bisque. Gawain got Shanahan to spring for margaritas, then a second and finally a third round before both Shanahan and Morgana decided enough was enough.

"We've got a flight to London in the morning," Morgana explained. "I hate to be a party poop, but if we have a couple more we're liable to get dumped out somewhere in Jersey and not know the difference."

"I'll take the cabbie's license plate number, to be sure, and if he attempts such a thing, we'll find him and give him a good thrashing," Gawain insisted.

"Oh, and isn't this a mean one!" Fianna giggled, squeezing his arm. "And a big strong fella, to boot. You'll keep him out of trouble, won't you, Bill?"

"William," he gently corrected her. "I'm not sure anyone can keep that fellow out of trouble, but you're certainly welcome to try."

"Well, you just make sure he doesn't blow up any more airports," Morgana playfully slapped William's forearm as he broke a cold sweat.

"Um, I'll—I'll do my best," he managed.

William had had trouble throughout the day reconciling the murderous beast he knew to the joking, free-spirited chap that was making such a great impression on the ladies. He told great yarns, had a witty remark always at the ready, and generally came across like a mischievous kid brother. William spent most of the afternoon deconstructing and reconstructing his image of Gawain while simultaneously trying to keep from being overwhelmed by the voluptuous Morgana.

They finally escorted the girls to the taxi stand and said their goodbyes, Gawain managing to get a business card along with a kiss from Fianna while William and Morgana shook hands.

"Well, then," William smiled broadly, "I don't doubt that those two will be seeing each other again fairly soon. Perhaps we might tag along and keep them out of trouble."

"I thought you said you wouldn't be up to that," she teased him.

"In that case, maybe I'll come along to keep you out of trouble."

"Think you're up to it?"

"You betcha."

"That's the boldest thing you've said all day," she ran her finger fleetingly along the lapel of his suit jacket.

"I didn't want anything to spoil the moment," William gazed into her eyes.

"Which moment was that?" she smiled.

"Hey, Mor, the cab's here," Fianna called as Gawain playfully shook her shoulders.

"Mor?" William kidded her. "I like Morgana better."

"Yeah, a ladies' man like you," she chuckled. "You'll forget my name by the time you get home."

"I'm pretty sure I'll be saying it in my sleep," he gently kissed her hand.

He walked behind her, marveling at her stunning figure as they came over to the cab where Gawain was trying to pull Fianna's shoe off. He got one last kiss from her before Morgana slid in alongside her before the taxi whisked off towards the highway.

"You owe me one, don'tcha, boyo?" Gawain waved at the cab.

"As you see it," Shanahan replied tautly. He was able to hail another cab that picked them up, and they clambered into the vehicle en route to their next destination in this surrealistic voyage.

Reservations had been made for them at the Surrey, one of the luxury boutique hotels on East 76th Street near Central Park. Shanahan had picked up their Mercedes Benz 550i at the Hertz rental office, and they negotiated the traffic crawl back to the East Side of Manhattan where they parked on the roof of a garage not far from the hotel.

"Okay, look," Shanahan walked across the roof to the elevator along-side Gawain. "Obviously they haven't pulled the plug on this operation over that stunt you pulled. Perhaps you can give me an inkling of what was going on inside your head?"

"Let's get something straight here, lad," Gawain grinned tautly. "If I wanted to get myself killed I could easily have had the deed done in prison. Your people gave me a chance to walk away as a free man, and I don't intend that to mean a dead one. Your Boy Scout mission may take priority with you, but my life comes first for me. If you want me in on this job, it's going to get done right. Right now, Cruz' people knows that he got car-bombed, and Chupacabra just happened to be at that same meeting. The Cuban Syndicate must be thinking that the Colombians ordered the hit on Cruz. When word gets out, which it has by now, the Cubans are calling the Colombians to see about going to war. Of course, the Colombians won't know a thing, and they'll call Chupacabra to find out what's up. Now, your people told us that they're already looking at him. If they're as pissed at him as they've let on, then he'll be looking over his shoulder after this, right?"

"Okay," Shanahan conceded. "So?"

"C'mon, boyo," Gawain smirked. "Of all the people at that meeting, you've got to be the least suspicious. Those spics are on the watch for one another, they are not thinking some poor bastards from the European Mob are coming all the way over here to start a gang war. Yet, tomorrow night, Chupacabra'll look across the table at the casino and see my happy face. Whether he checks with them or not, and whether believes them or not, he'll still be smelling a rat. I'll tell ye, fellow, that poker game is going to be the last thing on his mind."

"Where'd you get the makings for that bomb?" Shanahan demanded.

"Oh, some things from the hardware store. I'll show you how-to sometime."

"Suppose there had been women and children out there?"

"Aye, but there weren't, now were there?" Gawain smirked.

"All right," Shanahan growled. "I'm going to have to call London for further guidance. I want you to go back to the hotel and do not screw around. We have a flight to catch tomorrow to Atlantic City, and we've got to be sharp. I've got a very important connection to make while you're trying to fleece Chupacabra. You rest up, you psych up, you be ready. Got it?"

"You just be certain you're watching my back, Gummo," Gawain glanced at the printed directions as he headed for the hotel.

"It's a better view than watching the front of you," Shanahan retorted as Gawain shot him the finger before trotting down the stairwell to the street below.

Chapter Five

William Shanahan had awakened early that morning and walked over to Central Park for a run before heading back to the hotel for a shower and breakfast. It was a pleasant day and he would consider finding a nearby gym for an afternoon workout. He was able to recharge his batteries by working out, just as much as communing with nature did. He knew that they would be expected in Atlantic City tonight, and he wanted to be mentally, physically and psychologically wired to deal with the situation.

He was doing his best to marginalize his meeting with Morgana McLaren yesterday. Although she was the most beautiful woman he had ever met, he had to keep things in perspective. If he allowed things to run their course and things grew serious, he would be forfeiting his option to marry a woman of position in London. It might prove the costliest decision of his life, yet therein lay the conundrum. What was most important, money or happiness? He had no doubt that waking up every morning beside such a woman would be what every man would dream of. Yet, suppose she reached frigidity at forty? It would be the ultimate tragedy in having forsaken a lifelong quest for prestige and fortune.

The problem he had would be with Gawain. The murderous cur would be chasing after Fianna Hesher like a bitch in heat. Undoubtedly they would be setting up the double date, and anyone in their right mind would hardly decline the opportunity. Still, he realized he would have to do his best to keep his wits about Morgana lest he fall under her irresistible spell. He could wine and dine her, make out with her, possibly bed her, but never commit to her. If he did, his entire life plan could be derailed in one false move.

He was glad to have had the opportunity to take in Central Park, to breathe in the smell of trees, the grass and the bushes. He saw more than one lovely lass jogging by, and judging by the expressions on their faces he would have had no trouble catching up to them and introducing himself. He could have stayed with them until they tired out, then offered to buy them a fruit juice, or a soda, perhaps. One thing would have led to another, and he did have a marvelous hotel room to romp around in. It would have been a wonderful affair, if not for the damned mission and the damnable Gawain.

He generally had his pick of the loveliest women he came across, although none as wondrous as Morgana. Yet it always seemed to be the ones of means and privilege that eluded him. He had to focus on the fact that the success of this mission would earn him the opportunity of working on Downing Street, meeting the best people, going to the best parties and meeting the right women. No matter how dirty his hands might get or how his principles might be compromised, it was imperative that he keep his eye on the ball and make this happen for himself.

His feedback from MI6 was anything but encouraging. He called them at the break of dawn and reported what Gawain had done. They already collected their intel and pieced it all together but decided to wait for Shanahan's report before passing judgment. In their opinion, it was a good move by Gawain as it had the desired effect. The Cubans immediately suspected Chupacabra, and it took a great deal of persuasion by the Colombians to convince them they were not the perpetrators. MI6 insisted that the most important thing at this juncture was to have Gawain psyched up with full confidence that he could jerk Chupacabra's chain even harder at Atlantic City tonight.

Shanahan made it a habit to leave his cell phone at the hotel room when he went out on his runs. He refused to let anything interfere with recharging his batteries, and that included being roused from sleep. He knew he was a lethal weapon when he had worked out and rested, and the special care he afforded his perfect body was well worth the inconvenience his idiosyncrasies might cost his superiors. Besides, his general rule was that if there had been a train wreck there was little he would be able to do about it while asleep in bed or running in the park.

"Sir," the desk clerk seemed perturbed when he returned, "there have been a number of calls for you that seemed rather urgent. Do you not carry a cell phone with you?"

"Not when I'm jogging," Shanahan replied coolly. "They tend to be a nuisance."

"Captain Shanahan?"

He spun around to face a couple of plainclothesmen with the NYPD flashing badges at him.

"I think we were just talking about you," he remained nonchalant. "How can I help you?"

"I'm Lieutenant Martin, this is Lieutenant Lewis. We'd like you to come with us."

"Am I under arrest?"

"There's some very important people who need to speak to you. One of them just finished having a long talk with your people at Universal Exports."

"Well, in that case," Shanahan frowned. "I'd like to go upstairs and change. I won't be long."

"Don't be long, we've got a lot of straightening up to do," Martin allowed. The desk clerk was lingering about for some juicy gossip but a dark glare by Lewis sent him away.

Shanahan walked briskly towards the elevators, irked that he was being bandied about by a couple of cops. At once he suspected that it had to do with Gawain, and he cursed the stupidity of the Firm for bringing him in on this operation. Most likely he got fingered for the garage bombing in Montreal, and if anyone had been injured or killed by the blast besides the Cubans, it was probably going to take more than diplomatic immunity to get them off the hook. It would probably put Gawain back where he belonged, and Shanahan where he did not.

They rode in silence to the 32nd Precinct on West 135th Street, and as Shanahan looked out the window at the gang-infested East Harlem neighborhood he began second-guessing what this was about. He started to text MI6 but thought better of it. He was aware that the Salvadorans' tentacles reached into ghettoes throughout NYC, and thought perhaps the MS-13 had made a move that put them on MI6's radar. Whatever the case was, Shanahan would play it cool until he had all the details in order.

Shanahan was escorted into the main entrance of the precinct where he turned over his Glock-17 at the metal detector. It was returned to him at Martin's behest, and they led him past the booking area where strung-out hookers and crack addicts were being processed. One of them propositioned Shanahan, and it served to break the tension as one of the cops on duty gave her a gratuitous kick in the ass.

They led him down a narrow corridor where the holding cells were located, and into a room where five other plainclothesmen stood peering through a two-way mirror. Shanahan could not help but stare in wonderment at Jack Gawain sitting at a table on the other side of the glass.

"What in hell?" he managed.

"I'm Joe Bieber with the CIA office here in New York," the auburn-haired man dressed in a tasteful black suit stepped forth and shook hands. "It seems your associate made his privileged call to our office and gave them the number to Universal Exports in London. He was up to his neck in hot water and just managed to luck out by calling us. If our operator hadn't checked the number on a hunch, he might have been getting sweated as we speak."

"I'll tell you, I think a good sweat might be the best thing for him, only we've got a plane to catch in a few hours and it might put us behind," Shanahan said airily. "What has this fellow been up to, anyway?"

"I'll tell you what he did," one of the other plainclothes cops exploded. "He seriously compromised a sting operation we've been running for months! We've been trying to take those scumbags down before the DEA tried to horn in, and just when we're tightening the noose, that frickin' cowboy of yours comes running in!"

"What scumbags were you referring to?" Shanahan inquired.

"It seems your partner confiscated a handgun from a gang member just minutes before breaking through a door in a loosely-guarded crack house on 137th Street," Bieber cut in. "The best we can figure is that he was going to take the dealer out of the building at gunpoint and carjack his way out of there. The NYPD's undercover surveillance unit had no choice but to move in. All they found was a cell phone and a folding knife on him, along with $5,000 in cash he stole from the dealer. He wouldn't tell them a thing, and they were totally baffled until he made his call and got us involved."

"I'll tell you who would've got baffled if you hadn't showed up," a beefy cop in a dark gray suit growled.

"All right, then, how are we going to sort this out?" Shanahan asked flatly.

"For starters, you wanna tell us what that maniac was doing in there?" a blue-suited cop demanded. "He created a hostage situation, regardless of who was on the business end of the gun. Our guys could've wasted him right on the sidewalk if he didn't drop the gun like he was told. If we weren't on site, the 137th Street Gang would've done the job themselves."

"Uh, Mr. Bieber, can I have a word?"

"What? You think you're gonna keep us in the dark? We got that mick for armed robbery, possession of a handgun and kidnapping charges!" a hulking brown-suited cop exclaimed.

"Lt. Martin, I'll need to speak to the Captain in private," Bieber requested.

"Jerry, are you gonna let these limeys come up here and kick sand in our faces?" the gray suit was flustered.

"Look, Pete, we've had everyone on the horn from the Commissioner to the British Embassy," Martin explained as Shanahan and Bieber left the room. "They want the press to run this as a hopped-up crackhead trying to make a quick score. The narcs have to get our covers to make the dealers think our people were on surveillance trying to nail this guy. Dino, go on up to the squad room with these guys and help them work out the storyline. There wasn't any serious damage done, guys, let's just clean up the mess and get on with the job."

"I should've popped a cap in the bastard's ass to teach him a lesson!" the blue suit yelled at Shanahan before they closed the door behind them.

Bieber went back inside the room and asked Martin if he could bring Gawain to one of the holding cells. Martin complied, and within a few minutes Shanahan and Bieber joined Gawain in an available cell.

"Sleeping in late, eh, boyo?" Gawain chided, sitting casually on the worn wooden bench in the white cinder block room.

"This is one of our cousins from Langley," Shanahan introduced him, "Mr. Bieber has been wondering what in hell you thought you were doing out there."

"Where, with the peelers?" Gawain cocked an eyebrow. "I thought we were on a secret mission."

"I'm getting tired of cute, Gawain," Shanahan said tersely.

"Well, since we're all friends here," he smirked. "Look, Gummo, you give me this piece of plastic and you won't let me draw off it. You've got me going up against this major drug dealer in a high-stakes poker game without a dime in my pocket. You and your friends have got to be stupid, can't you see that when he takes one look at a wiseguy making his way on plastic, he's gonna smell a rat? I needed some big cash quick, and I merely looked about on the Internet for a bit to figure out where some was and how I could get it."

"So you go up to 137th Street and hold up a crack house in broad daylight?" Bieber could not help himself. "Where the heck do you come from?"

"East Belfast, on the better side of town," Gawain cracked. "You know, I've ripped off so many IRA drug houses I've lost count. Normally I've got folks who can tell me if I'm walking into a stakeout. I simply didn't have that luxury here."

"I'm thinking Chupacabra in Atlantic City tonight," Bieber surmised. "We've been watching him since that car bombing in Montreal yesterday afternoon. We had the Montreal police check the surveillance cameras at the hotel garage and run plate checks. We came up with a bunch of rental car license numbers, and a few of them turned up with bogus ID's at the rental offices. We're figuring there was a high-level summit meeting, and it was used as a subterfuge to lure Julio Cruz in for the hit."

"Not too shabby, these cousins of yours," Gawain nodded at Bieber.

"MI6 told us they have you two in-country doing recon on the Cartel," Bieber confided. "Frankly, we've got so much going on with Al Qaida that these guys have been slipping the radar more and more often. The Company's figuring you'll be doing us a favor by working the Cartel. Matter of fact, I'm going to give Jack here ten grand of pocket money. I'll write him a travelers' check so you can cash it at any bank. If there're any problems with the amount, just have them call our office."

"Lovely," Shanahan muttered. "He bungles an armed robbery at a crack house and gets ten grand for his troubles."

"Bungles," Gawain mocked him. "If it wasn't for the peelers wrapped around the place, I would've jacked a car, taken the bastard with me, and tossed him into that lake you were jogging around."

Shanahan cursed himself a fool for not having checked on Gawain before he went out. Gawain had obviously scouted him before heading out on his caper.

"Okay, fellows," Bieber handed Gawain a check and Shanahan a business card. "Keep us posted if you will, give us a call if you need anything. My boss is in contact with Shaughnessy on Downing Street, so we're all in the loop. There's a car downstairs that'll get you back to the Surrey. Good luck, gentlemen."

Once again the operatives left the building and returned to the hotel in stony silence. Shanahan was chafing to get back to his room and report all that happened, while Gawain was anxious to get his hands on ten grand in crisp $100 bills. It was going to be a long, icy ride to the airport, but neither of them could dwell on past incidents with the task at hand just hours away.

Chupacabra was one of the most dangerous men in North America, and he was probably not going to be delighted to see Shanahan or Gawain at their Atlantic City showdown just hours ahead.

Chapter Six

The Water Club on One Renaissance Way was one of the more prestigious luxury spots in Atlantic City. Located within walking distance of Snug Harbor, it was part of the Borgata Hotel complex whose casino was quickly becoming one of the world's most renowned. The Vista Room accommodations were made to order for well-to-do clientele, and both of the MI6 agents were greatly impressed by the luxury.

William Shanahan stood on the balcony of the deluxe suite, sipping a Jameson on the rocks he poured at the bar, savoring the view as much as the Irish whiskey. He had been in dozens of hotels whose lobbies were not as impressive as this room. He shook his head at bemusement over the private safe that was available in the rooms and ruefully considered the fact that Jack Gawain certainly had enough to store inside one.

As the mission progressed, he found it greatly disturbing that the previous episodes had adjudicated in Gawain's favor. He could not believe that they had glossed over a car bombing and an armed robbery in scarcely seventy two hours. This man was a walking shrapnel bomb that MI6 was undoubtedly eager to detonate right in Chupacabra's face. Yet they had no qualms about overlooking the enormous collateral damage such a man could cause. It made him step away and take a long look at who he was and what he wanted to become part of.

He had always been scrupulous to a fault. He always wondered if it had anything to do with his humble beginnings, those which even a man like Gawain was able to rub in his face. He wondered if he had programmed himself to operate at a higher level as well as a higher standard to atone for it. He considered the notion that he was compelled to be stronger, faster and smarter than the next fellow. It was likely that he demanded a stricter system of values and code of conduct from himself as well. It was causing him undue stress over the last few days because he could not rationalize what his superiors were condoning in the name of God and Country.

He knew that the armed forces operated in a gray area in this new century, possibly more so than any before them. They were fighting wars against armed civilians, combatants who could not legally be defined as such under the terms of the Geneva Convention. These were wars without rules, without limits, yet the armies of the world were being held to the standards of the law while the insurgents remained accountable to no one. When he joined the SAS, he was considered part of Special Forces whose assignments were to deal with these forces using unorthodox methods. These 'black ops' intensified with the SBS, and now with MI6 he was taking it to the civilian level. He was now dealing with the powers and principalities in high places, those who considered themselves beyond the law. The question was whether the 'good guys' had the right to operate beyond the law as well.

Even this was becoming an incidental as things progressed. He was starting to see that they would do as they saw fit regardless of right or wrong. His dissonance arose from the question as to whether or not he would blindly obey, or stand by as an observer as others broke the rules or followed illegal orders. He had already stood by and watched Gawain detonate his car bomb though unaware as he was. Yet he watched the powers-that-be compensate the man for the illicit funds he had tried to steal at gunpoint.

There was no doubt that they had sunk into a morass, surrounded by the bottom-feeders of the earth. It would take a man like Gawain to deal with them on their level. Shaughnessy had tried to explain it to him, and he could see everything clearly now. The question now was how it was going to change his own self-view, and most importantly, his esteem of the country he would sacrifice his life for.

He fixed himself a hot bath and slipped into it gradually, setting the water as hot as he could stand it. He vaguely considered the thought that he might be trying to scour his subconscious clean as well. He turned the TV on to ESPN, allowing a golf tournament to lull his soul into a more peaceful state. He would probably head down to Fornalletto's for their *lobster fradiavolo* with pasta, which would gird his loins for the night of drinking ahead.

He was discovering more and more that the underworld had the same standards of machismo adhered to by the military elite. The foulmouthed heavy drinkers were seen as the tough guys and hardcases, although most took caution when dealing with the strong silent type such as Shanahan. He hoped that Shaughnessy was accurate in predicting how the gangsters would assess him. He had no doubt that they would accept Gawain at face value, and if they did not, the moment of truth would have arrived.

His biggest concern was the scheduled rendezvous with their connection from the Sardinian Mob. This was easily the weakest spot on the ice they were skating upon, and if the veneer gave way at any point, lives could easily be at stake. He knew that the Sardinian Mob was a loose confederation of splinter groups arising from the multiple fractures suffered by the Sicilian Mob, and were about as unstable as the post-IRA groups operating in Ulster. If the cartels came across too many phony leads on the European side, they might be tempted to squeeze the truth out of him or Gawain.

He found it interesting that he was taking on the same paranoia that he was trying to foist on Gawain. He knew that the secure cell phone he had been given was virtually untraceable, yet the permeability of space satellite networks made all electronic communications suspect. He could not help but consider that if international financial institutions and military infrastructures were being compromised by hackers, how much easier could it be for them to intercept a phone call? To make matters worse, gangsters would most likely not be conversing in code unless an illegal deed was being discussed. Having to go through a third-party switch to tell the contact where to meet might well seem highly suspicious to an eavesdropper from a cartel.

He decided to wear his $1,000 forest green Armani suit along with matching tie and gold shirt. He had no idea how Gawain was going to dress and could care less. The game plan was for Shanahan to play it low-key and check out the different games before making the Sardinian connection. He would be getting a call within the hour, a specific text code indicating in what part of the casino he would be meeting the Sardinian. He checked his washboard waist in the gold-framed mirror as he got out of the bath, satisfied that at least he would be in the best shape of anyone engaging in this war of nerves this evening.

Enrique Chupacabra had flown in his Learjet from Montreal to New York that morning. He and his entourage checked into his penthouse suite at the Taj Mahal on the Boardwalk shortly afterwards. He retired to the bedroom with his newest gal pal Marilyn, and screwed her into the mattress for over an hour before exhausting himself. He then had supper brought up from Il Mulino, the exquisite Italian restaurant inside the casino building. They had dinner before taking a shower together, then he screwed her again before stepping back into the shower one last time. They were both dressed to the max when his bodyguards showed up at 7 PM.

Enrique Muniz had come up from the gutters of Bogota, Colombia, never having known his father and abandoned by his mother at six years of age. He was a scrawny kid who soon learned the advantages of fighting with weapons. He found that most kids did not have the guts to really use a weapon, and he seriously injured most kids who messed with him as a result. His weapons grew more deadly as he grew older, and by the age of thirteen he was nicknamed Machete after his weapon of choice. He stole a gun when he was fourteen, and no one messed with him after that.

He started a gang around that time that committed burglaries in town and robberies along the city limits. One of the drug dealers in town heard rumors about their ruthlessness, and hired them as enforcers and extortionists. Enrique, now called Chupacabra, killed his first man at fifteen and moved up in rank as one of the drug boss' personal bodyguards. He was then given a hefty weekly salary ($1,000 US dollars) as an assassin for *El Jefe*[1]. He remembered killing thirty men by the time he turned eighteen before losing count.

A bloody drug war cost the life of *El Jefe*, causing his gang to splinter and go underground to avoid vengeful hit squads. Chupacabra decided to cut his losses and relocate to Medellin, known as the exclusive domain of the most powerful drug lords in South America. It was not long before word got around that he was in town, and shortly thereafter he was brought to a meeting with Salvaje[2] Pulga. The beefy ex-wrestler was one of the wealthiest and most ferocious gang leaders in the Medellin Cartel, and supplied muscle to the other gangs in the cartel. After an evening of dining out and dancing, followed by drinking and gambling until sunrise, Chupacabra was hired as one of Pulga's personal bodyguards. It was not long before he rose to the lofty position of security administrator which he continued to hold.

Marilyn was a beautiful Cuban girl with honey-colored hair, green eyes and an upturned nose along with ruby lips that caused men's hearts to skip a beat. At 5'5", her hourglass figure was breathtaking, and together with the wiry, ruggedly handsome Chupacabra they made a remarkable couple. He wore a burgundy suit with a black shirt while she wore an exquisite ruby silk sheen evening gown with a slit that exposed her lovely leg. They rode in a white stretch limo to the Borgata and were afforded red carpet treatment by the doormen in exchange for $100 tips. She held his arm as they were led in by their six bodyguards who escorted them directly to the gaming tables.

Chupacabra headed directly to the $500 ante tables in the rear where he had occasion to play against movie actors, rock stars and other celebrities. His guards took turns standing at each corner of the ta-

---

1. the Chief
2. savage

ble while the other two were free to run errands at their boss' whim. Every now and again some hotshot wannabe poker stars would come up against him but he would raise them off the table when his mood darkened. Alternately, he was known to throw games against celebrities with whom he wanted to leave a good impression. Yet Chupacabra respected money and would never leave huge sums behind unless he was cutting his losses after losing a major showdown. He was known to be at his craftiest when on the losing end against expert players.

He was ahead by about $5,000 and in a good mood after winning a $7,000 pot, kissing Marilyn and cracking jokes with his bodyguards. Only he was somewhat surprised when he saw a somewhat familiar figure at the opposite end of the table.

"Hey there, Ricky. Fancy seein' you here."

Jack Gawain was dressed in black, wearing a leather jacket over an open-collar shirt and pants. A cigarette dangled from his lips as he sat down at the table, ordering a Bushmill on the rocks from a passing waitress.

"Jack Gawain, isn't it?" Chupacabra acknowledged him. "Good to see you. Ready to lose some money?"

"Well, you're lookin' kinda sheepish, and I've brought my shears, so let's have at it," Gawain shot back.

There were three other players at the table: a cowboy, a Saudi Arabian and a high-rolling executive. Gawain started off conservatively, throwing in four bad hands in a row, but suddenly hit two kings on top in a seven-card stud game and got vicious with a $1,000 raise. They all folded abruptly and Gawain cheerfully raked in around $2,000 for his troubles.

"Not bad for a fast hand, eh, Rick?" Gawain chuckled. "Beats the hell out of shoveling snow."

"That's Enrique, my friend," he replied pointedly, nettled by the oblique reference.

"I reckon you ain't gonna buy the next one, feller," the cowboy ventured.

"Wanna see?" Gawain smirked.

"Yes I would," the Arabian grinned back.

They went for another game of seven-card stud which appeared to be agreed upon by consensus. Gawain had a pair of deuces on top with a nine, going up against the Arab's pair of kings and Chupacabra's six thru nine of hearts. The cowboy had folded with a nine showing, so the slim chance of another nine appearing would do no good to anyone. Gawain raised $2,000 and, true to his word, the Arab would not back down. The bet was to Chupacabra, who was not going to toss a possible straight flush.

"Well, fellows, let's see who is going to serve me a plate of crow here," Gawain chuckled. "I've got five grand that says you two are standing on garbage."

"Pair of deuces?" the cowboy muttered. "Dude, you gotta be kiddin'."

"Gentlemen, please," the dealer reminded them to observe the protocol of the gaming room.

The Arab showed a king in the hole which gave him three kings. Chupacabra folded, indicating he had missed his card. Gawain giggled before tossing out a pair of aces and a deuce, giving him a full house. He eagerly raked in the pot which totaled almost twenty thousand dollars. Chupacabra sat back irritably, waving a hand at Marilyn who had whispered in his ear.

"Tell ye what, laddies," Gawain began sorting his pile of chips into his rack. "I'm gonna go take a leak, and I'll be back to give you a chance to get even if yer still here."

"I'll be looking forward to it," Chupacabra replied curtly.

Gawain headed towards the bathroom, then adjusted his path so that he was a distance behind Marilyn, who was en route to the ladies' room. He pulled out his cell phone and hit Shanahan on the top of his contact menu.

"Gawain here," he spoke up. "I think we're being compromised here. Do you have a disposal unit nearby?"

"What?" Shanahan insisted. "I'm in route to meet the Sardy. What kind of time do you have?"

"Hostile action imminent," Gawain advised him. "Have your people in the south garden in five minutes. Gawain out."

Marilyn came out of the restroom after having touched up her makeup. She was pleasantly surprised to see Gawain standing by the wall facing the doorway.

"Evening, love," he came forward. "Thought I saw you come through here. I figured you might be powdering your nose."

"You've been pretty lucky tonight," Marilyn smiled at the ruggedly handsome Irishman. "Congratulations."

"Aye, and hopefully it'll get better. Y'know, I think I've got a wee better kind of powder in my bag than you have," Gawain jiggled a gram bag of coke at her.

"Omigosh!" she covered her mouth as her eyes widened, looking about for onlookers. "Be careful!"

"Not to worry, darling. Let's step outside for a sec and we'll be right as rain."

It was Chupacabra's idiosyncrasies that often resulted in the breaches of security which had led to a number of his recent fumbles. He routinely allowed his entourage to indulge themselves in the plentiful supply of coke that was always at hand. Yet, in public, he insisted that they refrain, not accounting for the possibility of moderate addictions amongst them or the lack of willpower he himself possessed. As a result, Marilyn was eager to follow Gawain outside into the south garden where she could get a pick-er-upper to carry her for a couple of hours.

She followed him to a shadowy area by a stand of potted evergreens, and he handed her the gram bag.

"You'd best turn away from the joint, love, it's not hard to figure what yer up to," he suggested. He admired her lovely features and wished that she had chosen a better path in life than to have hitched her wagon to a falling star like Chupacabra.

Marilyn also thought well of Gawain, considering the fact that he was a handsome man with a certain swagger about him, though with a boyishness about him that many women found endearing. In a different place and time this chance encounter might have to amounted to something more, though in reality she would never indulge such a fantasy in leaving Chupacabra.

Gawain had been supplied with a wristwatch with an expandable titanium band that could be used for different purposes. In this case he extended it as a garrote, which he looped around her head before yanking with all his might, dragging her to the granite-paved walkway. Gawain was an extremely strong man for his size and she had no real chance at all to pull free. He continued pulling until he could hear and smell her bowels releasing in her death throes, and at once saw the rustling in the bushes where the MI6 disposal team awaited.

"Aw reet," he acknowledged, freeing his watchband from Marilyn's neck as the dark-clad men came from the bushes and shrouded her in plastic before pulling her back into the bushes from whence they came. He lit a clove cigarette and looked about nonchalantly before heading away from the casino building, along the walkway towards the street where he take a very short walk to the Water Club entranceway.

Chapter Seven

"He murdered a woman, sir."

"What? Shanahan?"

"The murdering psychopath killed a girl, sir. Strangled her right outside the Borgata Casino."

"Captain, you know the routine. Are you in public? Are you aware this line might possibly be compromised?"

"I'm in my room, sir. I request that Gawain be removed from this case and sent back to the UK, and I would gladly press charges in the matter."

"The *person in question*," Shaughnessy stressed, "will be debriefed by a member of our disposal unit. You will both be contacted shortly."

"Sir, if this sick butcher is not replaced, I request transfer to a different position in continuing this assignment."

"Negative, Captain, you will stay the course," the Colonel replied before a long pause. "I want you to know that the Firm is very pleased with how the case is progressing. The subject has been under observation and we have determined that the actions taken have been greatly distressing to him and has had a solid impact on his infrastructure. We will continue the next phase of the operation in Miami and expect the mission to continue to bear fruit."

"Shanahan out."

It was the confirmation of his worst fears. They had condoned an unauthorized assassination and an attempted armed robbery, and now they were overlooking the murder of a civilian. Even worse, they were taking the side of a convicted murderer against one of their top operatives. He had no way of rationalizing this, no way of coming to terms with what was happening. If there had been one person to blame this on: Shaughnessy, his superior, or even Gawain himself, it would have been much easier. Instead, it was those acting under the authority of MI6 who were sanctioning these things. It was being declared permissible in the name of God and Country.

Now that they had proven themselves to be as without scruples as Gawain, as hypocrites and liars, how could he even remain certain that they would honor their commitment to putting him on Downing Street? Suppose Gawain fouled this job up and it was declared a failure? Would William Shanahan become their scapegoat? Certainly not Shaughnessy, the living legend. It would be all too simple to pass the blame to him and plateau his career. This whole thing was slipping out of his grasp, he was losing control of his own destiny and there wasn't a damned thing he could do about it.

They were being given a couple of days for MI6 to adjust their game plan and decompress somewhat. The Firm would arrange for them to find lodging in Langley VA. They would be flying to Langley Air Force Base this evening on a chartered flight, and would be provided lodging at the luxurious Staybridge Suites. He remembered the old Irish saying: keep your friends close and your enemies closer. The CIA would now have this pair of MI6 operatives as close as they could get.

Enrique Chupacabra had flown to Puerto Rico that afternoon as the guest of Amschel Bauer. He arrived at Aguadilla Airport outside the capitol city along with a four-man entourage and was driven by limousine to the Horned Dorset Primavera Hotel. It was located along the exclusive west coast of San Juan in the suburb of Rincon where guests were afforded a breathtaking view of San Juan Bay. His bodyguards were reserved despite being impressed by the luxurious accommodating, largely owing to the fact that Chupacabra was in a foul mood.

They checked into their residences by noon, giving them all an opportunity to shower and change clothes before gathering at Chupacabra's suite. They fixed drinks at the well-stocked bar and sat out on the patio overlooking the bay, no one breaking the silence as Chupacabra finally came out and sat at the glass table shaded by a huge sun umbrella.

"Dirty bastards," Chupacabra cursed and swore as he took a long sip of his marguerite. "Somebody's trying to set me up. First they whack Cruz and his bodyguards in broad daylight with a car bomb, then they kidnap Marilyn right under my nose. They're trying to get me in a war with the Cubans, and even worse, they're trying to make the Cartel think I'm starting it! Plus they take Marilyn right in our faces! I still don't know how you guys let that happen."

"Come on, Enrique," his top gunman, Big Kenny, entreated. "I told you a dozen times, she went to the damn bathroom and didn't come back. We had our people bribe the casino people and they didn't find anything on the security cameras. These people were professionals, they probably checked out all the camera locations before they made their move. Look, she'll turn up one way or another, you know that. Either they're holding onto her and are gonna ask for money, or… "

"Or she shows up dead and they try to pin it on us," Chupacabra snarled. "Look, I want to call Salvaje and find out everything you can. He's my *padron*, he's not going to let me get screwed over by those other rat bastards down there in Medellin. You tell him we're down here with Bauer, getting all the information and advice we can before we head up to Miami next week. I want to be sure that those lousy Cubans don't have a hit squad waiting for us!"

"Don't you think maybe you should be making this call, Enrique?" Kenny asked quietly. "Suppose Salvaje thinks we're not showing him the right respect if I call."

"What did I just tell you?" Chupacabra was hot. "He's my *padron*, he knows how I hate talking on the phone. Plus he's old school, the hardcore guys always talk through a buffer. This way, if Homeland Security picks it up on that satellite tracking shit of theirs, we whack you and they got no evidence."

"Gee, Enrique, that's really making me feel secure about my job," Kenny was sarcastic.

"Hey, if we screw up the hit, maybe you can file for Workman's Comp," Chupacabra finally allowed a smile. "Okay, you guys go on and take a walk around, make sure everything's clear around here. Go on and make that call, Kenny. Once you get done, give Bauer a buzz and tell him we'll meet him at lunch in about an hour."

Chupacabra's bodyguards felt much better now that Enrique was back to normal. He had been in a dark mood since Marilyn went missing, and they knew by bitter experience that he was capable of anything when his paranoia set in. He had had more than one bodyguard killed as an example to others when they fumbled on the field, and no one was truly safe until the episode had cleared from Enrique's mind. Even though Marilyn was just a sex toy, someone had stolen something from him, and they knew he would not rest until he had avenged the insult.

At least now they knew he would be taking it out on someone else, and they would be more than glad to help him indulge his bloodlust.

Shanahan had been more upset about having to cut short his interview with his Sardinian connection when he got the call from Gawain last night. Emiliano Murra was a notorious *caporegime* of the *Codice Barbaricino,* a uniquely Sardinian bandit organization having no direct connection to the Sicilian or the Italian Mafia. He was a heavily muscled man, about 5'9" and 210 pounds, his upper body covered with prison tattoos which were visible on his neck and his left wrist. He had jet black hair worn in a ponytail, and his skin was pale as a result of spending most of his life hiding out from his enemies. His eyes were brimming with evil, as if he had become resigned to the fact that death followed his steps like a hound from hell. Shanahan had met many a man who had the million-mile stare of those who had looked into the abyss. The look of this man was something he had not yet seen.

Shanahan met him at the Gypsy Bar at the Borgata casino, and was mildly impressed that he came alone without bodyguards. Yet there was always the possibility that any one of a number of men, or even women, lounging around the area could have been assassins in wait for anyone to fall afoul of their leader. They introduced themselves by their first names, then retired to a corner table where they sat parallel to one another, both having a clear view of the bar and its entrance.

"My people are very interested in your proposition," Murra had a way of staring that was most unsettling. Shanahan, however, was certain that he could physically overcome the man so was not overly concerned. "We did some checking around and found that most of your connections are in the UK and France. That, of course, would justify your interest in making an arrangement with our organization."

"Well, we did some checking of our own," Shanahan replied. "We were somewhat pleased to learn that you had no direct connections to the Mafia. They're under a lot of pressure right now, just like their Yank counterparts, and they've got lots of people rolling over under threat of life sentences. We wanted to start fresh with organizations who weren't as well known to EUROPOL or the FBI, or Homeland Security or the CIA, for that matter."

"We find it amusing that the Mafia actually provides a cover for us," Murra sipped his Remy Martin brandy. "Most of the time, those incompetents at EUROPOL come looking for us and do not get much further than the local Camorra. We have actually seen reports indicating that they see us as little more than a glorified *borgata*[1]. As you can imagine, this suits us just fine. Those same reporting agencies seem to think that your people are little more than an exaggerated paramilitary gang yourselves."

"Our Council members are very pleased by that tidbit of misinformation," Shanahan smiled tautly. "It makes it much easier to move our cargo, and thereby make this entire enterprise less risky and more profitable for all of us."

"Tell me more about this adventure of yours," Murra was curious.

---

1. gang

"Very well," Shanahan produced a Blackberry which featured a map of North America and Europe. "We have a considerable gold shipment that we are planning to sell to the Cartel. We've gotten word that they are heavily involved in a gold investment scheme in light of the proposed return to the gold standard by the G8. We are looking for a middleman who can not only guarantee the safety of our merchandise, but can negotiate the transfer of funds and bullion between both parties involved. Of course, if this proves successful, we see no reason why you would not continue in this brokerage as we see our way towards future joint ventures."

"I like what I am hearing, Mr. Bruce," Murra lit a Tuscan cigar. "How much gold are we talking about?"

"These are twenty-five pound bars of pure gold," Shanahan replied. 'We have 5,800 of these bars, which weigh around sixty metric tons. We estimate that, once the value of gold increases according to the gold standard redefining the parameters of global debt, this amount of bullion may be worth as much as $100 million dollars. If you broker this deal for us, we will sell the bullion to the Cartel for $75 million, of which we will pay you ten percent as a commission fee."

"I cannot say that $7.5 million is chump change by anyone's standards," Murra exhaled a stream of smoke away from Shanahan. "However, in comparison to what the other parties—you and the Cartel—are making, it seems a paltry sum. Suppose you increase your profit by five million so that I can make an additional $500,000 on the deal. Plus, I would want to be able to charge the Cartel for my services on their behalf. This gives me $16 million for my efforts, which I think is reasonable considering the risks involved on my end."

"With all due respect, Mr. Murra, I don't want you to overestimate the risk on your part," Shanahan said pointedly. "We intend to parcel the bullion into two shipments so as not to compromise the entire fortune. Thirty metric tons is about what an average load of foreign-made vehicles consists of. If one of the shipments is lost, of course we would suffer a grievous loss, but it might well cost you the opportunity to work with us on future operations. Plus there would be no cost at all to the Cartel. Your people might do time for piracy or international smuggling, but it would hardly compare to our loss of thirty-five million dollars."

"So what is it you would have me do for you?" Murra wondered.

"We will arrange for your vessel to take possession of the first shipment of bullion in Belfast," Shanahan activated a Power Point presentation on the Blackberry. "Your people will get it to Montreal where Nathan Schnaper's people will transfer the shipment to the Bank of Montreal. Once it is registered and deposited, your fee will be electronically transferred to any location of your choice."

"And the second shipment?"

"Most likely from Larne, off the coast of Scotland, but we will confirm that once the first shipment has been registered and deposited."

"When do we start?"

"Very soon," Shanahan confided. "There is, however, just one more thing."

"Of course, there is always just one more thing," Murra allowed a humorless laugh.

"The man we are going to approach to make the deal with the Cartel is one Enrique Chupacabra, who just so happens to be playing poker here this evening," Shanahan said intently over the band music that was starting to play in the background. "Our sources reveal that Chupacabra's position within the Cartel is tenuous at best. He may be instigating a gang war between the Cartel and the Cuban Mob, which will prove extremely costly to everyone involved in this new network we are building. He might even be tempted to compromise one of our shipments if he has reason to believe the Cartel may no longer have need of his services."

"So do you want us to take care of this problem for you?"

"Let's just say that, if it becomes necessary to eliminate this particular risk, we might be able to suggest to the Cartel that your people may be available to take on the troubleshooting duties that are currently assigned to Chupacabra. This would not only put you directly into the Cartel's network, but increase your leverage and strengthen your position as our brokers in North America."

It was at that point when his cell phone went off, and Shanahan got word from Gawain that they were going to have to vacate the premises. Shanahan explained to Murra that an urgent matter had arisen that required his immediate attention. He assured Murra that he would get in touch by e-mail within the next forty-eight hours. The men shook hands and departed in opposite directions to minimize chances of being followed.

Shanahan found himself oddly intrigued by Murra. Of all the criminal types he had encountered, and even the non-criminals in the Firm, Murra seemed to be one of the few who did not have hidden agendas. He did not attempt to hide who or what he was. He also seemed to be genuinely tough, one who commanded respect without a gun in hand like Gawain. Shanahan was playing Murra, for certain, but he doubted that the Firm would be so stupid as to burn Murra and lose this invaluable resource within the European underworld. If he could help them pull off this sting operation and dispose of Chupacabra, Shanahan would surely be able to convince MI6 that the Sardinian Mob would be a tremendous ally indeed.

He resolved that, if he were to get his hands dirty, then the work product would be something worth the sacrifice. He would contact Murra tomorrow and coordinate their agenda, which might well greatly diminish Chupacabra's odds of survival in the days ahead.

Chapter Eight

Enrique Chupacabra met with Amschel Bauer shortly after noon and continued to be impressed by the man's panache. Enrique had always known that he and his associates had, in most cases, rose from the gutters of the world to carve their names in the sun. There were a scarce few who had been born to money and reinvested their fortune to harvest thousands of times more than those constrained by traditional ways and means of accumulating wealth. Amschel Bauer was one of this exclusive breed.

His father, Abraham Bauer, was a Russian Jew who migrated to the Brighton Beach district of Brooklyn NY with his family in 1954. Bauer, a Hasidic Jew, married a Sephardic Jewess named Rachel Roth. He started a family and opened a pawn shop which specialized in buying and trading gold and antique coins. After the birth of his fourth child he opened a second shop, and after the eighth son was born he opened a third shop. He opened the last of his shops in 1974, the year Amschel was born. By this time, his oldest son was running the original shop and the second store, while his second oldest was managing Bauer Pawn Shop #3. Abraham devoted his energies in building Shop #4, which he would make the most profitable of all before turning it over to his beloved Amschel.

Amschel exhibited great intelligence at an early age, outplaying his older brothers in chess when he was six years old. Abraham brought him to a local *yeshiva,* where his IQ was registered at 160. The boy's extraordinary propensity for mathematics prompted Abraham to hire a tutor to work with Amschel after school. By the time he reached sixth grade, his math teacher declared there was nothing more he could teach the boy. He gave a personal recommendation to have him enrolled at Yeshiva Lomza Petach Tikva Israel, a school for gifted students on Parkville Avenue.

Despite Abraham's fervent wish for Amschel to go on to University and become a rabbi, the youngest Bauer headed directly to Wall Street after graduation in 1991. He found a mentor at the brokerage firm of William and Hanau, where Hyman 'the King' William took the brilliant young man under his wing. He taught Amschel the nuances of corporate raiding, finding which businesses facing bankruptcy could be purchased and its assets sold for maximum profit. Bauer amassed a small fortune in a short time, yet turned his attentions back towards the family business.

He inherited his father's love for gold, Abraham constantly reminding his son how many of their relatives in Israel survived the Holocaust with the gold they had hoarded over the years in case of catastrophe. Regardless of economic disaster, political adversity, racial or religious persecution, gold spoke and others listened. Yet Amschel also developed a deep respect for the 'white gold' that pulsated through the veins of the East Brooklyn community and made some wealthy beyond imagination: narcotics. He began to nurture a dream of siphoning the profits from drug trafficking into the purchase of bullion, and soon began to put a lifelong project into action.

Amschel discovered who the biggest dealer in Flatbush was, and soon established contact with Nikolai Biden. He arranged a meeting with Biden in Bensonhurst, where they held their entire discussion in their native Russian at an elegant Jewish restaurant. He explained in layman's terms the magic of insider trading, guaranteeing enormous profit by investing in stock according to the rise and fall of a company's fortunes. Amschel proposed that Biden provide him with information about businesses that were on the verge of bankruptcy. He could invest large sums of drug money and buy up the stock as it plummeted on the market. From there, Amschel's raiders could move in and make counteroffers that would place the companies on the verge of miracle recovery. Once the stock began to soar, Amschel would sell it all before withdrawing his support and allowing the businesses to collapse. On the verge of liquidation, they would clutch at any straw that Amchel's wolf pack offered before devouring the businesses entire.

Biden was hesitant but the first couple of million dollars sold him completely. His gang began targeting companies, then corporations, whose owners and managers had developed serious drug habits and would do anything for Biden to open his spigots. Biden preyed on their addictions and gave Amschel the keys to the kingdom. Eventually Amschel arranged for a meeting between Biden and Hyman William, which enabled him to put his master plan into action.

Amschel contacted the FBI, requesting immunity in exchange for information on 'King' William's insider trading activities. After picking up $100,000 in cash from Biden, he notified the Feds about the impending deal. They nailed the conspirators on a wiretap, and Amschel walked away with the cash after William and Biden were arrested for securities fraud. Biden had William killed in prison, and was assassinated by the Russian Mob in order to cover their tracks during the Federal investigation.

From there, Amschel relocated to Canada to avoid further investigation by the Feds and, in time, made contact with Montreal Mob boss Nathan Schnaper. It was there that Amschel learned the fine art of money laundering, assisting Schnaper in reinvesting racketeering profits. His intricate real estate refinancing schemes made Nathan and Amschel multi-millionaires, and they next focused their attention on using drug money to purchase bullion. The proposed return to the gold standard was a magic moment in time, heralding the birth of Operation Blackout.

"You remind me of myself when I was your age," Amschel admitted as he and Chupacabra had lunch on the grand patio of his residence overlooking San Juan Bay. The aquamarine waters extended as far as the eye could see, from the sun-drenched, palm-studded golden beaches to the pale blue skies whose majestic clouds intermittently veiled the brilliance of the majestic autumn sun. "Industrious, enterprising, yet aggressive and opportunistic. I recognize those who are quick to recognize a chance to turn a profit, but neither reckless nor avaricious. You have not gotten to where you are by being wasteful or wanton with the property and assets of others, Enrique, and neither have I."

Chupacabra's bodyguards enjoyed their lunch beyond earshot of their host, and ate quickly in order to assume positions along each point of access to the second-floor dining area. Big Kenny stood at the top of the masonry staircase rising from the tropical garden, deterring anyone who seemed as if wishing to intrude on the privacy of Enrique and Bauer in the near corner. Chupacabra feasted on a breast of duckling with bay leaves and raspberry sauce over basmati rice, while Bauer sampled the lobster medallions in beurre-blanc sauce over asparagus.

"I must admit, Amschel, I like your style," Chupacabra complimented him. "Up in Montreal, here in Rincon, you know the best places, the best food and wine, the finer things in life. You find so many guys in this life of ours who can't escape their past. Back in Medellin, you see gang leaders worth millions of dollars hanging out in the same dives from back when they were selling weed in the ghettoes. You got to keep evolving, improving yourself, getting bigger and stronger, or you go flat and get flattened."

"I want you to know that I don't believe you had anything to do with that car bombing in Montreal," Amschel looked at him intently. "I know there has been a lot of electronic correspondence over that episode. I myself, along with Nathan Schnaper and our associates, believe that you are innocent and that someone is trying to set you up."

"Who would do such a thing, Mr. Bauer?" Chupacabra dipped a piece of exquisite garlic and herb bread into his raspberry sauce. "Who would want to accuse me?"

"Somebody who wants you replaced," Amschel sipped his white wine. "It is well known that you are the troubleshooter for the Medellin

Cartel. Your name is feared among your associates because you zealously protect the business entrusted to you. If a guardian such as yourselves is removed, it makes it that much easier for someone of lesser talent to take your place. Those who would not have previously dared to cheat or steal from the Cartel could possibly take advantage of the new opportunity."

"Who, Mr. Bauer?" Chupacabra insisted. "Who?"

"I don't know, Enrique. But I intend to find out," Bauer replied. "You see, Operation Blackout is a chance for immortality for all of us. We can transcend the New World Order of the Zionists, the Muslims and the Christian nations of the earth. We can become the kings of a new dynasty, establishing absolute control over the international economy. I intend to make that dream a reality, and I know that a man like you can become the protector of our realm. Join me in this, and I will personally uncover this conspiracy against you. Together we will eliminate those who would subvert our plan to control the wealth of the nations."

"Sounds good to me," Chupacabra sipped his wine.

"How do you like it?"

"Excellent," Enrique sipped, swirled and savored.

"Montrachet 1978, delivered from the Domaine de la Romanee-Conti vineyards in Burgundy directly to Nathan Schnaper's mansion in the Westmount area of Montreal. We will have finished a bottle of wine with our meal that costs twenty-four thousand dollars. One bottle worth more than 80% of the world population earns in one year. One bottle that costs over one hundred times what this hotel tab will have cost. Yet it is the wine that makes the meal, not the other way around. No matter how exquisite the dinner, it is always about the wine. And so shall it be with us. The others will provide the banquet, but we will bring the wine."

"I think it's more about you bringing the wine and me protecting the bottle," Chupacabra speculated.

"Precisely, my friend," Bauer smiled. "With all due respect, and not to impugn your brilliance in your field of expertise, I want to bring you into my mind, and that of my associates. Do you, but chance, know what a milliard is?"

"What's that, like a duck?"

"A milliard is a billion dollars," Bauer leaned back in his seat, his receding red hairline gleaming in the sunlight. "At our meeting the other day, we were discussing the possibility of amassing one thousand milliard in bullion. This translates into a quadrillion dollars. If, in fact, we were able to accumulate this, it would be but a tenth of the gold held by the Federal Reserve and the Bank of International Settlements. What we have to do is deprive our competitors of their reserves by any means necessary."

"How can we do that?" Enrique's eyes widened.

"This can only be accomplished by preemptive military strikes against our competition's supplies. This is the wine I will bring to the banquet. The banquet is all the remaining gold in the world left in our possession. This, Enrique, is what I will ask you to protect."

"You got it, Boss," Chupacabra shrugged. "I may work for the Cartel, but they're hanging me out to dry. You watch my back, and I watch yours. If you keep them from taking me from behind, I'll use everything they give me to protect you before them."

"This is a very important day in the history of the world," Bauer reached over and shook his hand. "In the next couple of months, we will accomplish things that will make all of mankind stand in awe."

Chupacabra had no doubt that Bauer had become his savior, and in turn he would act as the rock upon whom he would build an eternal empire.

The future, he knew, was now.

Joe Bieber met with Shanahan and Gawain shortly after they arrived at the Staybridge Suites in Yorktown. They opted for dinner at the Riverwalk Restaurant, an elegant dining spot overlooking the York River. Its large paned windows provided a panoramic view of the riverfront, the well-furnished dining area enhancing a memorable dining experience.

Shanahan had ordered the grilled beef tenderloin and shrimp with au gratin potatoes and steamed vegetables, while Bieber enjoyed a thick pork chop with cheddar potatoes and sautéed onions. Gawain happily munched on a meal of sautéed shrimp, scallops, mussels and clams over linguini with a roasted tomato marinara. They exchanged pleasantries about their travel accommodations and anecdotes about the day's events before getting down to business.

"Gentlemen, as I'm sure you have been informed by your superiors, there is a great concern over the political turmoil impacting certain countries as of late," Bieber began. "There is also apprehension over other countries outside of the international banking community. They may be taking drastic steps to ensure their positions during the financial revolution ahead."

"Our people indicated that we may be looking at two different groups," Shanahan noted. "Al Qaida has instigated revolutions in Pakistan and Iran. Both nations are perceived as nuclear threats to both our countries. The President and the Prime Minister have issued statements to the people of both lands to carefully consider who they are entrusting these weapons of mass destruction to in the months ahead."

"That's what we always say back home," Gawain said through a mouthful of shrimp and linguini. "Give a Paki a gun and he'll stick up your grocery store. Give him a nuclear bomb and he'll stick up your country."

"Your friends at home might also say that birds of a feather flock together," the athletically-built Bieber's gray eyes simmered. Both Shanahan and Bieber were dressed in black designer suits while Gawain picked out a silvery silk suit at a local haberdashery. "As we speak, the only nations on earth not connected to the central banking system are Cuba, North Korea and Iran. These nations have suffered under international embargoes for a number of years, so a switch to the gold standard may leave them bankrupt. These may be desperate nations in the times ahead, and they may resort to desperate measures. This is what the UK and the USA are faced with."

"Considering the Pakis and the Iranians are halfway around the world, it will take either a missile strike or a smuggled bomb to do the damage," Shanahan gave Gawain a withering stare as he drained his glass of Pinot Grigio in one gulp and quickly refilled his glass to the brim. "Of course, they face the prospect of a devastating counterstrike, but fanatics aren't necessarily concerned about collateral damage on their end."

"Precisely," Bieber nodded. "If you look at this as a Venn diagram, Iran is the one nation which resides in both circles. Recently the Supreme Leader Ayatollah has fallen ill. His acting representative, Saddam Al Varka, has strong ties to Al Qaida and may well use his temporary powers to make a move that the Ayatollah will be unable to undo. He has already initiated serious discussions with North Korea to acquire a missile launching system. Both the US and the UK have given both nations strict warnings, to no avail."

"Worst case scenario?" Shanahan postulated.

"I'd say that they drop the missile on Downing Street and the smuggled nuke on Shankill Road," Gawain cracked. "I'd be looking for a new place to live and you'll be looking for a job."

"We think they may be looking in places besides London," Bieber was not amused. "New York, Frankfurt, Zurich and Paris round out the list as the top five central banks on the planet. Of these, London, New York and Zurich are the world centers on gold bullion market. A nuclear strike on New York would mean the destruction of Wall Street, which would be a paralyzing blow to the global economy. This does no good to anyone. Destroying our reserves in Fort Knox, West Point and Denver would be just as self-defeating, though if they wanted to deny our access they would target Fort Knox. It has over twice the amount of gold than that stored in either of the other facilities."

"Isn't there a military installation at the fort?" Shanahan wondered. "Wouldn't the governor be able to call out the National Guard, or even declare a state of martial law in the area in case a threat was detected?"

"The downside would be for Al Qaida to make a bogus announcement to draw our forces offside or incite a public backlash in case of overreaction," Bieber pointed out. "Our government has resolved not to allow the threat of Al Qaida to deprive our people of their pursuit of happiness. Even the threat of a low-intensity nuke will not change our strategy. Instead we'll be focusing on possible points of egress for terrorists to bring a WMD into the States."

"Say, boyo, how about another bottle of this stuff?" Gawain held up a bottle of the 1995 Drouhin Chassagne Montrachet Marquis de Laguiche. "Or perhaps two, an extra bottle for my friend here."

"I'm quite fine, thank you," Shanahan assured the waiter.

"Well, then, I'll drink his, go fetch it anyway," Gawain insisted.

"Where were we?" Shanahan managed a smile. "Uh, yes. You are aware, Joe, that we are here in the States on assignment to infiltrate the smuggling network along the Eastern US seacoast, and harass and interdict its operatives as best we can. I'm not sure what use we would be in attempting to intercept a team of smugglers trying to bring a nuke into the States. If we happened to catch wind of such of an operation, it would take first and utmost priority. Other than that, I don't know what kind of help we could provide."

"We're thinking perhaps Mr. Gawain would be of most usefulness is a possible scenario," Bieber revealed. "As you know, this current Administration has become unduly encumbered by civil rights issues surrounding interrogation procedures of those who have declared war against our people and, technically, have no Constitutional rights. If we were to capture terrorists on our borders who have information that could lead to the capture of nuke smugglers, obviously there would be a serious time constraint involved. Bringing someone like Mr. Gawain in could mean saving hundreds of thousands of lives."

"You mean like making 'em talk?" Gawain nibbled on a piece of garlic bread. "Well, put it this way, I haven't come across nary a one I could not make talk."

"Of course, we would not think of contacting you unless we were absolutely certain we had an accomplice in custody," Bieber assured them. "We'll be working out the fine details with the Firm, and should a situation arose, we would be contacting them directly before seeking your assistance."

"I don't anticipate a problem should the need arise," Shanahan replied half-heartedly. He knew that Bieber was soliciting them, or, more precisely, Gawain to commit acts of torture for him. He would most certainly be confirming this with Shaughnessy, yet he was getting a sinking feeling that MI6 had already agreed to this heinous arrangement.

"Good. Gentlemen, I have front row and balcony tickets to the Kimball Theatre in Williamburg, which is about fifteen miles from here. Should you choose to indulge yourselves before your flight tomorrow evening, just call our number and we will make arrangements," Bieber offered good-naturedly. "I'm afraid I won't be able to attend but we remain available if there's anything you need."

"I'm quite done here myself," Shanahan touched a napkin to his lips, declining the waiter's offer of dessert and coffee. "Gawain, please do indulge yourself. I'm sure the dessert menu is scrumptious. Joe, I'll be calling you tomorrow, and hopefully we'll see you before we leave."

"Excellent," the three men shook hands before Bieber and Shanahan took their leave. Gawain bade them farewell before ordering a French silk chocolate pie and espresso. He was not sure exactly what those two had in mind, but he intended to thoroughly enjoy every moment before the day of truth arrived.

Chapter Nine

The magnificent view of West Palm Beach was one of the most exquisite in the country, and it was best afforded from the majestic surroundings at the Brazilian Court Hotel and Beach Club. It was a favorite choice of many of the rich and famous who vacationed in the exclusive community, and the golden-upholstered Café Boulud provided the finest of French cuisine to those who expected the best.

Among those was Sheik Mandhur Mohiuddin, one of Al Qaida's top operatives. Mohiuddin's brother Mahmud was an executive vice-president with Freyssinet Saudi Arabia, a leader in the nation's pre-stressed concrete construction trade. The Mohiuddins were Salafi Muslims, and Mandhur left the company in order to pursue a degree in Islamic studies with Mahmud's blessings. He graduated from Imaam Islamic University in Riyadh, and shortly afterward made contact with Al Qaida.

Al Qaida conferred the title of Sheik onto Mandhur, and soon arranged for his employment at the Islamic Saudi Academy of Washington. As an associate professor, he provided the use of his luxurious apartment in Alexandria VA for gifted students who he tutored for membership in Al Qaida. Over twenty-four of his prized pupils quit school and were sent to Al Qaida training camps from the Middle East to Africa. Only a Congressional investigation resulted in accusations that Al Qaida was sponsoring *madrassas*[1] through the Academy, and Mandhur returned to Saudi Arabia shortly thereafter.

He had been entrusted with a sacred mission by the Military Committee, and took command of Al Qaida's cell at Khartoum University. He was in charge of insurgent operations throughout Sudan, and only left after the Sudanese government allegedly put a bounty on his head. He was now working throughout the Middle East and only came out of hiding for important negotiations such as this.

The Sheik met with his North American connections that morning at the Bohlud. They ordered brunch under close watch by aneight-man team consisting of two gunmen accompanying each man. The unobtrusive wait staff were accustomed to such meetings and made sure to seat new arrivals at tables out of earshot to ensure the privacy of these guests.

"Nice place," Johnny Carmona sniffed as he forked his grilled Spanish octopus. He was a swarthy Cuban with thick black hair, a silvery gray suit and a black shirt. "Look, I just want everyone here to know that my people are satisfied that no one at this table had anything to do with what happened to Julio Cruz. I'm here to resume business as usual, and I come here with full authority of our leadership to make a decision on your proposal today."

"Glad to hear it," Ernesto Guzman spoke up, his beady black eyes gleaming against his orange-hued skin. "My people want to be sure that everything is being done to avoid another gang war. I'm sure that Alberto feels the same way. Greed is no good. It's an infectious disease that kills. There's more than enough for everyone, and both Alberto and I have learned that the hard way."

"That's for sure," Alberto Calix said gruffly. His Mexican Cartel and Guzman's Mexican Mafia had been engaged in a vicious border war that cost the lives of nearly 1,000 people. It cost both groups millions of dollars in resources that were lost, destroyed or captured by the DEA and the *Federales*. The truce between the rival organizations helped

---

1. radical Islamic schools

them recoup their losses and nearly double their profits over the past year.

"As you all know, this meeting was coordinated by Amschel Bauer for the purpose of coordinating our efforts as Operation Blackout enters its second phase," the Sheik looked at each of the men at the table. "I'm sure that everyone is aware that all of our associates are well into the task of laundering their unreported assets by converting them into bullion. We are aware that a certain amount it required to continue business as usual, but the reports we are getting indicate that everything is progressing well. Now is the time for us to begin planning how we are going to paralyze our competitors' gold supply once the gold standard is restored by the central bank network around the globe."

Enrique Guzman suddenly realized how deeply Al Qaida was involved in the operation. From what he understood, Bauer and his people had connections to Al Qaida, who were playing a peripheral role in the operation. For the Sheik to have mentioned 'reports we are getting' told Ernesto that they were directly linked to the network. Whatever was going down here was coming under the direction of a vested partner in this enterprise.

"You know," Carmona had also picked up on it, "if Homeland Security gets the idea that any of us are directly linked to Al Qaida, the pressure on us is going to double. There's already talk of deploying troops on the Mexican border once they're brought home from Iraq and Afghanistan. If they start conducting naval exercises in the Caribbean, we're not going to be able to bring shit through there. It's going to make us entirely dependent on Alberto's people, and who do you think they'll be after next? It's the process of elimination, *amigo*. If they close down Alberto and Enrique, next they move against the Salvadorans and the Colombians. Getting involved with you is going to be very dangerous."

"We're not asking for a commitment," the Sheik replied. "All we need for you to do is arrange security for two transports to be moved across the border within the next couple of weeks. One will come by land, the other by sea. One of these shipments is a decoy. The other one is a bomb which will result of the paralysis of fifty percent of America's gold reserves stored at Fort Knox."

"You gonna bomb Fort Knox," Guzman shook his head. Like Carmona, he had barely touched his smoked duck *marbre*. "This gonna be as bad as 9/11. They gonna come at us with everything they have if they even suspect we had anything to do with it."

"Two million dollars apiece, the funds to be transferred in each of your names in Swiss bank accounts," the Sheik assured them. "Our people will be bringing the transports in private vessels arriving from Honduras to ports in Mexico and Cuba. Our connections in both governments will make the best arrangements possible for your people to provide escort for our agents. Once our transports have crossed the US border, we will consider your mission accomplished and your payments electronically processed on demand."

"That puts a lot of cash back on the street," Calix sucked his gold teeth pensively as he took a break from his burgundy escargots.

"So you're telling me that all I have to do is escort your boat across the straits into the Keys, and I score two mil." Carmona reiterated.

"If you consider getting through the Navy, the Coast Guard and Homeland Security's satellite tracking systems all in a day's work, I salute you, my friend," the Sheik raised a wine glass to him.

"We won't even know who's got the bomb," Guzman pressed for more details.

"This is extra insurance on your end," Mohiuddin pointed out. "If your men are captured, even under torture they will not be able to confess that they knowingly brought a bomb into the country. Plus they will be under much less pressure if they convince themselves that they are the ones bringing in the decoy."

"What good is the decoy going to be once we bring it in?" Calix asked.

"Our people will notify Homeland Security, the FBI and the police that it had arrived," the Sheik smiled. "It will deceive the Americans into thinking they have foiled our plan, and give the actual transport a greater chance of arriving unnoticed. Plus, keep in mind that the

Americans are expecting an attack on a major city, not a gold reserve. Just as Amschel Bauer has said, this is a financial assault unprecedented in the history of mankind. Nations throughout history have always destroyed their enemies' armies to capture their riches, never the other way around."

"Now, suppose the international financial community, as you call it, decides not to go for the gold standard option," Guzman posed. "Maybe you knocked out the gold supply, but they'll just print enough money to cover their losses."

"Not to worry, my friend," Mohiuddin assured him. "Al Qaida has its ear in many doorways. We are quite certain that OPEC is going to force the decision anytime soon. They are not going to allow the Christian nations of the world and their Zionist allies to usurp absolute control of the world economy without them having any say whatsoever."

"It's bigger than all of us, guys," Carmona shrugged. "Count me in."

"They're coming after us one way or another," Calix agreed. "Plus we got the gold, and maybe they won't. Even if it fails, we still got a helluva lot of gold. I'm in."

"The way I see it, if Mandhur succeeds, he knocks out all the gold the USA needs to legitimately finance the Navy, the Coast Guard and Homeland Security's satellite tracking systems he was talking about," Guzman was reluctant. "It's worth a shot, I'll take it."

"Excellent," the Sheik clapped his hands. "Gentlemen, history will be made when our mission is completed. 9/11 will fade in comparison to what we will accomplish. You are to become part of history, this I guarantee."

They all secretly hoped that their organizations would not also become history in the aftermath.

"There is no question that OPEC will not allow itself to be marginalized as the G8 nations seek to redefine the financial standards of the world market," Sheik Mahomet Farhat's pronouncements were broadcast throughout the world media shortly after the Palm Beach meeting between Al Qaida and the drug cartel. "It is almost as if the Western nations fail to realize that, if we were to call in the debt owed for the petroleum we have supplied just this past year alone, it is quite possible the gold supply of the nations might be seriously depleted. Let there be no misunderstanding, we are part of a world community that shares its resources, giving what we have in exchange for what we lack. We do not in any way intend to threaten those who so generously contribute to the improvement and betterment of the Arab nations. Nevertheless, we will not stand by in wonderment as the standards of international finance are reassessed. We insist that we be given a voice in this discussion and, if there is a return to the gold standard, we demand there be a transparency of procedure so that our interests are not only respected but satisfied."

"There you have it," Salvaje Pulga said in Spanish to his Salvadoran counterpart, Tony Ramos. "This is going to happen. The world is going to be forced into this gold standard, and we are going to have no choice in the matter. We have put together $500 million of bullion together. Have you done what you said you could do?"

"$500 million is not a billion, my friend, it is only half," Ramos said as he peered out the window of the Sofitel Bogota Victoria Regia hotel in the Colombian capitol. "I will admit, that is just about what we were able to put together. Like you say, win or lose, we have put away quite a bit of gold for a rainy day."

"The millions and billions is not why I had you flown over here," Pulga leaned over their table at the prestigious Basilic Restaurant. He had brought a laptop where he replayed the video of Sheik Farhat's speech, and it was quietly taken away by one of the gunmen who cordoned off their table in the elegant restaurant. "My concern is the man who I took in as a son, the man I empowered to watch over our empire, the man to whom I gave the keys to the kingdom. My friend, Enrique Chupacabra, is being perceived as a risk to the organization I represent. If he fails in his duties, as you know, there is no option to resign or be replaced. If he fails, as his *patron*, it will be my duty to the cartel to remove him from his office."

"And so you wish to delegate this responsibility to us," Ramos nibbled on a piece of Raclette cheese. "This is not going to be a simple task. Chupacabra is feared and respected all over the East Coast. Even though many people feel he engineered the assassination of Julio Cruz, the word is out that the Cubans had long suspected that Julio was skimming. Many people believe that Enrique was acting on your orders, by request of the Cubans."

"These are the opinions of cowards afraid of another drug war!" Pulga slapped his palm on the table. "We gave no such order! If he took it upon himself to whack Cruz, or even worse, took a contract from the Cubans to do so, he is putting himself and our cartel at a risk that he has no right to chance. Ramos, my friend, if Chupacabra makes one more false move, we are willing to pay you a million dollars to end his life."

"It makes no sense, my friend," Ramos debated. "If his people learn that Salvadorans have come to any town he is in, they will immediately suspect the worst. Besides, suppose he has put together a gang of his own in an attempt to seize power in the US? I'm not sure our people want to be caught in the middle of such a thing. You may end up having to clean up your own house in this matter."

"Our airport spies found out that he recently flew up to Montreal," Pulga fumed. "What in hell was he doing in Montreal, watching hockey? He was up there making a deal with Nathan Schnaper!"

"So what's wrong with making a deal?" Ramos sighed. "What's ever been wrong with making a deal? You fly off the handle, Salvaje. Enrique is a good earner. You can whack a man, but you can't bring him back from the dead. Remember that."

"All right, then," Pulga growled. "What about the transports from Al Qaida?"

"Piece of cake," Ramos nodded, sipping a glass of wine as they indulged in a wine and cheese buffet. "We'll be taking the cargo off your hands along the Golfo de Fonseca at Amapala. They're paying pretty good money to deliver a couple of shipping containers."

"I'm thinking there is more to these containers than meets the eye," Pulga lit a Marlboro. "How much are they paying you to deliver the boxes?"

"A mil. And you?"

"Same amount. That's a lot of money for a couple of boxes. I'm thinking terrorist attack."

"So give it back, Pulga. I'm sure they'd give it to us to figure a different way across Guatemala."

"We are in such deep shit with the Americans already, it won't make a difference what we move. Another shipment of coca, a nuclear bomb, they're putting our top guys away for life one way or another," Pulga shrugged. "Maybe this teaches the *gringos* some respect. You know, during World War II, the US Government reached out to the Mafia to help stake out the New York waterfronts for Nazi saboteurs. Maybe this is what will happen for us soon. If Al Qaida kicks them in the balls again, maybe they reach out to us."

"Sounds like you've been doing a lot of reading, Pulga," Ramos chuckled. "And wishful thinking. They accuse us of destroying their society and culture, despite all their political corruption, the pornography, the homosexuality, child abuse, violence in the media. All we do is give them a little boost while they indulge themselves. I always ask myself: what difference would it make if there was no cocaine in America? I answer: very little, my friend. Very little."

"Maybe they will come to realize this, and maybe we won't think we are such bad guys once Al Qaida strikes again," Pulga replied. "We hope, we watch...and we deliver these shipments and see what happens."

The Colombian and Salvadoran gang leaders raised their glasses, toasting what they anticipated would be a whole new era of relations between America and the drug community of the southern hemisphere.

Chapter Ten

It was the morning after the meeting with Bieber, and Shanahan was preparing for his morning workout at the on-site health and fitness center. He had taken in a late movie at a nearby theatre, though it was hard to focus on the flick as his mind continued to race a million miles an hour. Now they were considering having him bring Gawain out to torture suspected terrorists captured along the Mexican border. This was an outrage being sanctioned by the British government, yet there was nothing he could do about it. He was being used as a pawn by not only his own government but the Americans as well. He could not see a way around this other than to resign, but he was now immersed in a game where the fate of the Free World could be at risk.

He knew that the US and the UK were not always straight with each other, and only provided information at their convenience. The Americans might well know who was involved in Al Qaida's plot, and was only waiting to close the trap before bringing in Gawain. He just wondered if MI6 would give it precedence over the psych job they were doing on Chupacabra. Would they pull Gawain away from the game if the Yanks nailed the terrorists who had the intel? More than likely. It was bigger than Chupacabra now, and it was a CIA agent who hinted at it. His own people at MI6 had not even called to confirm it.

It occurred to him that MI6 might or might not know about him meeting with Bieber. He got no advance notice from Shaughnessy about it, which would have meant that anything Shanahan agreed to did not reflect the official policy of the British government. It was looking more and more as if MI6 was acting as some sort of artificial providence, assuming the role of a distant deity who often let its acolytes work things out themselves.

To report or not report, that was the question. If MI6 ordered him to stay out of US affairs, then the CIA would lose their option of having an interrogator as diabolical as Gawain at their disposal. He was not sure that he would want to be the one to take that off the table. He decided he would wait to see what Shaughnessy would say, if anything. Perhaps if Shanahan said nothing and something did happen, the UK would have truly known nothing if the affair went public. Again, Shanahan would be hung out to dry, but the US would be spared another 9/11. That should be enough to put him on Downing Street in any event.

His cell phone went off and he figured he had better take the call. He had just showered and put on his workout suit, and was almost on his way out the door.

"Shanahan."

"Morning, boyo. We've got company, I'll meet you in the lobby."

Shanahan cursed as Gawain hung up. He had successfully avoided this fellow at every turn, but when he tossed out these curve balls it was impossible to predict where they would land. He just hoped the rogue had not done anything stupid, but he knew that was too much to ask for. He decided on going down dressed as he was, so if Gawain was merely indulging his stupidity, he could go on about his workout as if nothing happened.

He stalked impatiently into the lobby and was astounded by the sight. He saw Gawain holding court in a luxurious armchair, dressed in a gray blazer with black shirt and pants, amiably chatting with Morgana McLaren and Fianna Hesher.

"William!' Morgana seemed delighted. "How nice to see you again!"

"The pleasure is all mine, my dears," Shanahan came over and kissed their hands. "Were you staying here in town?"

"No, as a matter of fact, we just got back from London and Jack called me on my cell phone," Fianna revealed. "He told us you two would be here until tomorrow so we decided to come out. We get to ride free, you know."

"That's just deadly," Gawain smiled. "So do we. Matter of fact, we're off to Miami this weekend for the World Domino Championship games. I won a lottery of sorts, and they're having me compete."

"Gee, that's great," Fianna was wide-eyed. "You must be really good. Did you learn to play in Belfast?"

"No, that was in Maghaberry Prison when I was a ween. My mum couldn't find a suitable babysitter, so that seemed the best place at the time," he replied as the girls giggled and shook their heads. Shanahan's head was nearly reeling at the things that were coming out of Gawain's mouth.

"Say, have you girls had anything to eat yet?" Shanahan offered.

"I think I'd like a cup of coffee," Morgana replied. She wore her long blonde hair loose and it spilled thickly over the shoulders of her black blazer. Her black skirt accentuated her lovely white-nyloned legs that Shanahan struggled not to gaze at. Her emerald eyes were almost mesmerizing, her bright red lips as cherries on a tree. He was still piqued by Gawain but found his defenses melting as if bathed by the sun.

"Say, why don't we have a look around," Gawain jerked a thumb at the outer walkway. "We can get a breath of air and watch these tourists gatching about the property."

"Sure," Fianna hopped up, dressed as fine as Morgana in a tan suit, her long auburn hair pinned back in a ponytail. "Okay, you guys, we'll be back."

"Stay out of trouble, Jack," Shanahan managed.

"Can you imagine?" Gawain made a face, causing Fianna to bust out laughing as they went on their way.

"Is something bothering you?" Morgana wondered.

"No, no, not at all," Shanahan recovered. "Would you like to walk? I was on my way to the gym before he called, as you can see I'm not quite dressed..."

"Well, I wouldn't want to put you off your schedule," she insisted. "I can do some sightseeing and meet you back here…"

"Nonsense, girl," he got up from his chair, holding out his hand to help Morgana up. "What I would really like to do is go up and change. I would feel terribly uncomfortable walking about in a workout suit with you looking as splendid as you do. Would you be so kind as to accompany me back to my room, I'll be changed in a jiffy."

"Well…" she mused. "I'm not sure going back to your room is such a great idea. We hardly know each other."

"No, no," Shanahan held up his hand. "Please. I meant no disrespect. I simply did not want to leave you alone here in the lobby. The suite's quite elegant, not the type you see in the movies. I thought you might enjoy poking about, and I'm a very quick dresser, by the way. I'll have changed clothes before you can say Superman."

"Okay, Mr. William Shanahan," she smiled impishly. "Lead the way. You're on your honor, you know."

He escorted her to the elevator, and they took the ride in the seemingly motionless elevator to his upper-level suite. He opened the door with his card key and held it for her, reaching in to switch on the light as she entered the spacious, luxurious suite.

"How nice," she said as she glanced around at the stone-veneer table and the kitchenette adjoining the parlor area dominated by the extra-large sofas and the wide-screen plasma TV. "You two certainly are traveling in style."

"The company's been doing well as of late," Shanahan agreed. "There's fruit juice at the bar, go on and have whatever you like. I'll be out in a minute."

He slipped into the bedroom and pulled off his sweatsuit, thinking of showering just in case but chided himself after having just taken him morning shower just a short time ago. He was a fastidious man and stepped into the shower to rinse off before changing as a rule. He did not want to keep a woman like Morgana waiting, however, so plucked a beige suit and white silk shirt out of the closet and began hunting for his dress shoes. Suddenly he felt eyes on him and whipped around.

"Whoops, sorry, I'm lost," Morgana smiled sheepishly, taking a long look at Shanahan clad only in his briefs, admiring his long-legged, tiger-muscled build and his tanned, flawless skin, the washboard abdominals as armor around his slender midsection.

"Be right with you, love," he swiped the trousers off the bed and swiftly hopped into them.

"Nice bedroom," she grinned saucily before sauntering back to the living room.

He dressed hurriedly and met Morgana in the dining room where she was sipping on a mango juice bottle, absently flicking through the channels on the flat-screen TV.

"Would you like to stay and watch something?" he asked. "I can order breakfast if you like."

"Don't you want to see what Fianna and Jack are up to?" she switched off the TV. "If they haven't gone back to his room, they could be getting into a lot of trouble."

"My god, you're right," Shanahan muttered. "All right, dear, off we are."

"I'm only kidding, silly," Morgana tugged his sleeve as he opened the door for her. "Are you always so serious?"

"No, why, not at all," he recovered. "I'm just a bit out of sorts, you see. I just awoke about an hour ago, dressed in sweats on the way to the gym, and now I am here on the way onto the town with the most beautiful woman in Yorktown. You simply can't expect me to be on my game in a couple of shakes."

"Sorry to have shaken you up, Mr. Shanahan," she gazed into his eyes before he patted her back, resting his hand on her waist as he escorted her to the elevator.

When they got to the lobby, they walked out onto the patio area overlooking the garden leading to the street level. They watched Gawain and Fianna furtively hopping back from the concrete ledge, the buxom lass holding a bunch of grapes. Shanahan and Morgana peered down to the garden, where a tourist wearing a cap looked up and yelled something at them before continuing on his way.

"That's five-ought, love," Gawain nudged her. "You'd best try and catch up."

"You can make it fifty to one," she retorted. "I'm not going to throw grapes at people."

"Well, you know what happens if you lose," he reminded her slyly.

"Don't hold your breath, mister," she shot back.

"Oh, my," Shanahan pinched the bridge of his nose. "Wouldn't you know."

"Fianna!" Morgana was exasperated. "What are you doing?"

"You're the one who left me with this crazy man!" she protested.

"I'll fix you," Gawain ducked down to pick her up, and Fianna bounced a grape off his nose. He lurched towards her as she squealed, dropping the grapes before he laughingly stopped to pick them up.

"Perhaps we can find a museum hereabouts, stop by and have lunch," Shanahan suggested.

"And do what, have you stand as an exhibit and pose for the tourists?" Gawain snorted. "Surely you can come up with something better than that."

"I'm pretty sure there's a Busch Gardens not far from here," Morgana mentioned. "I saw a brochure on the plane over here."

"All right, then, that sounds like a winner," Gawain agreed before pitching the grapes over the ledge. They heard a group of tourists yelling from down below as he grabbed Fianna's hand and ran with her back to the lobby.

Back in Belfast, a group of four hard men made their way down Great Victoria Street in the downtown area to the fabled Crown Bar for a meeting that would have great effect on the MI6 operatives in Yorktown. They looked like the paramilitary types that ruled the neighborhoods along the East and West ends, and pedestrians gave them ample space as they barged into the bar and peered about. They spotted the private booth where the appointment was set, and pulled open the door to introduce themselves to the patrons within. Two of the men, leather-jacketed Sardinians, silently rose from the table and pardoned themselves as their leader motioned for the hard men to take a seat.

"I'm Jimmy Burke," he shook the Sardinian's hand. He was a blond man with icy blue eyes, a thin mustache and a wiry build. "These are my associates, Edward, Kevin and Danny."

"My pleasure," Emiliano Murra smiled, sipping a glass of spring water. "Pleasant little town you have here. I find it hard to reconcile the images on the television with what I've seen here so far."

"You can rest assured that things tend to pick up in the local neighborhoods when the sun goes down," Burke allowed a smile. "You probably have places of your own in Sardinia where people mind their own business after dark."

"More than our share, my friend," Murra nodded. "So. How close are we to finalizing our arrangement?"

"Ready when you are," Burke replied as the waitress came into the cubicle to take their orders. Danny got up and ushered out of the room, ordering three pints and handing her a L100 note. "I'll send you an e-mail as soon as we get confirmation your people are in harbor. We'll be ready to load your vessel for transport to Montreal as soon as possible."

"That is thirty tons of cargo," Murra pointed out. "I've been informed that once our first ship has left port, you'll be heading to Larne and be standing by to deliver the next thirty-ton shipment."

"If you've got your ship along the harbor, we'll be ready to load as soon as we get word from Montreal that the first load has been transported," Burke sat back in the booth. "Everything happens simultaneously. When we get confirmation from Montreal, we signal your people to bring the ship into Larne to pick up the next container. As soon as we do, our people electronically transmit your first payment. Once the second shipment arrives and gets unloaded, we transmit the balance. It runs like clockwork, our people are the best in the business."

"No doubt about it," Murra agreed. "We've done some checking around, and your references are quite solid. Of course, Mr. Chupacabra's people are in place to accept the delivery in Montreal."

"I doubt very much that anyone less than Chupacabra will be onsite to make sure that kind of cargo is being handled very carefully," Burke assured him. "Just as I doubt just as much that he'd stop off for a pint and keep your people waiting."

The men laughed heartily as the waitress brought in the trayful of pints.

"I hope you and your friends are thirsty," Burke toasted him with a Guinness. "I don't know if you've heard much about Irish hospitality down there in Sardinia, but if you haven't, you're in for an experience, my friend."

"I'm afraid you haven't heard much about night life in Sardinia," Murra toasted them back. "Here's to our good fortune, $100 million of it."

And so they concluded the business portion of their meeting, which would set off one of the biggest gold smuggling operations in North American history.

PART TWO: The Turn

Chapter Eleven

The World Domino Championship was being held this year in Miami for a million dollar prize to the winner. It was more than had ever been offered before, but ESPN had gambled on its success with minority groups across the country with whom the game was more popular than poker. The number of participants was far greater than ever before, and ESPN set up elimination tournaments as qualifying rounds in all fifty states. From there, they cut the number of states to twenty-five for the quarterfinals, and twelve states for the semi-finals.

Two of the twelve finalists were Enrique Chupacabra and Jack Gawain. Both the Chupacabra Gang and MI6 had hunted down ringers and bribed officials to get both names onto the final roster. Gawain and Chupacabra's lookalikes were excellent players, and in the games they lost they either got to the officials or paid off the winners to allow them to move onto the next round. Gawain and Chupacabra's photo ID's were verified by the officials at Miami, and the champion was to be determined by the following weekend.

MI6 had brought the operatives into Tampa that weekend in anticipation of the game the following Saturday. Both Gawain and Chupacabra were playing under assumed names to avoid publicity and detection by rivals and enemies, so Chupacabra was unaware that he would be facing Gawain in the final game. MI6 also ordered their operatives to keep a low profile so as to make a maximum impact on Chupacabra at the game.

Chupacabra had flown up to Montreal the night before to supervise the transportation of the smuggled bullion from Belfast. A dozen men from Nathan Schnaper's gang arrived in an eighteen-wheeler and had the containers transferred from the Sardinian freighters to the trucks as they arrived. Within twenty-four hours both transports were driven to a warehouse owner by the Montreal Mob, and Chupacabra arrived at Amschel Bauer's downtown to report the mission accomplished.

"Now for our next step," Bauer leaned back in his chair as he faced Chupacabra across the glass-topped desk at his luxurious penthouse suite. "I wish to sell the bullion to your Cartel in exchange for cocaine of equal value, or for cash and product as they prefer. It will provide us the opportunity to sell the cocaine and invest the revenue in more bullion. We have already set up the pipeline from Europe, it has been tested and it works. As we speak, the governments of Russia, China and Iraq are buying up huge quantities of gold on the open market in anticipation of the switch to the gold standard. I am expecting you to do whatever you can to convince your superiors of the wisdom of purchasing our bullion while it remains available."

"How much are we looking at?" Chupacabra wondered.

"Seventy million dollars," Bauer replied. "We are giving it to you at a ten percent discount on its current market value, but we are expecting to recoup that amount with whatever cocaine your superiors throw into the deal. You would want them to realize that, though they probably have more product than cash to dispose of, it is far easier to move cash than narcotics at this time. We would suggest ninety percent cash and ten percent product, but of course that will be up to them to decide."

"Seventy million," Chupacabra shook his head, slapping his hands down on the armrest of the transparent plastic chair. The white upholstery and furnishings of the suite, enhanced by the glass and plastic, gave a subliminal impression of being one with the clouds outside the window. It was the kind of luxury a man like Bauer was accustomed to, and one that Chupacabra expected to enjoy someday soon. "That's a big number for a man like my boss. It's almost six months' profit for some of our biggest dealers. I'll talk to him, see if I can get him to move on it. Like you said, if this is a secure pipeline, we can keep siphoning gold out of Europe until they change to the gold standard. It may be worth double that amount when it happens, who can say?"

"You have a clear vision of the future, my friend," Bauer smiled. "I am certain that you will guide your superiors to your level of clairvoyance."

"That's going to be the trick, Mr. Bauer. I will guarantee that I'm going to make every effort to make this happen."

Chupacabra left Bauer's office shortly thereafter, making his travel arrangements and girding himself for the task of convincing Salvaje Pulga to loosen his purse strings. That, he knew, was going to be a prodigious and unenviable feat.

Emiliano Murra flew to Miami that Thursday to meet with the man he knew as William Bruce. He made his eight million for the Sardinian Mob just days ago as commission from who he perceived to be the European Mob Council. If the Medellin Cartel agreed to purchase the bullion from Bauer and his Montreal associates, he would be collecting eight million from them to transport the gold from Montreal to Colombia. The Sardinians were very pleased with the way things were going, and expected to be doing business with the Council again in the very near future.

Shanahan and Gawain had been booked at the exclusive Shore Club Hotel on Collins Avenue along the oceanfront. In order to minimize friction between the operatives, they were booked on separate floors and required to check in twice daily by cell phone with Downing Street. Once again Shanahan found himself in the lap of luxury as he soaked in the tub in the Mexican sandstone bathroom. He gave himself plenty of time, indulging in his Continental breakfast brought to his room before going downstairs to meet Murra.

They met at the SkyBar, its tropical surroundings enhanced by the cobalt walls, fountains and pergolas making it seem as if they had come across a mystical cave in an exotic jungle. The men shook hands after they spotted each other inside the lounge, and both asked for fruit juice as the waitress promptly took their orders.

"You know, it is really nice when things go as smoothly as this job did," Murra said airily as he leaned back in his chair at their table facing the doorway. "There were no problems or delays, your people unloaded the containers in a timely manner, and the payment was made electronically as soon as the customers in Montreal took possession. You know how it is in this business, William. There are so many screwups and incompetents, one just never knows what will go wrong at any given time. When everybody does their part and things go according to plan, one can barely wait for the next opportunity to arrive."

"You can be sure that my people in London are just as pleased," William replied. "From what I understand, Enrique Chupacabra is flying to Medellin to submit a proposal to his superiors. If he gets the go-ahead, he should be contacting his Montreal connections to finalize the deal. Here's the tidbit: if the Colombians go for it, I don't see any reason why they wouldn't agree to have you bring whatever product they decide to trade back to Montreal. You'd be able to charge them for that service as well."

"This deal just gets juicier as it goes along," Murra beamed. "You are a pleasure to do business with, and I am sure there are even greener pastures ahead of us."

"My people are banking on the fact that both your organization and ours are relatively new to the game," William revealed, both men pausing to thank the waitress as she brought their drinks. "It's never a question of whether or not the authorities can find you, rather of them knowing where to look. They wouldn't think that your outfit has become a major player in the smuggling game so suddenly, and I'm quite sure EUROPOL doesn't even know a European Mob Council exists. It'll be some time before they get wise, and by the time they do, we may have transported a significant amount of European bullion to our South American neighbors. At an enormous profit, I might add."

"Tell me, how would we go about applying for membership on this Council?" Murra asked.

"The Council is scheduled to convene again in about sixty days," William replied, sipping his orange pineapple juice. "I intend to personally report to my superiors in London to let them know what an efficient and disciplined outfit you are working with. I have no doubt that our representative will be able to present a forceful case on your behalf. As I told you before, we have no connection with either the Italian or Sicilian Mafias, so you would have an exclusive domain in overseeing our interests in Italy, Sicily and Sardinia."

"I tell you, William, with all the problems the Mafia has had with the FBI and EUROPOL, not to mention the dozens of other law enforcement agencies around the world, I think many of us would agree that their best days are behind them," Murra tilted his head. "The time has come for a younger and stronger organization to step forth and take control of the Mediterranean black market. Together you and I will make history, my friend."

"Yes we will, Emiliano," William grinned broadly. "We most certainly will."

Jack Gawain had also risen early and spent most of the morning on his Blackberry, which he had purchased shortly before leaving Yorktown. He did a considerable amount of research before heading out on the street with his MI6 cell phone and credit card, his fake ID, his $10,000 in cash and his Glock-17. He caught a cab and directed the reluctant cabbie to take him over to NW 15th Avenue, known as the Street of Death in Liberty City.

The Liberty City district had the highest crime rate in the city of Miami. Its Liberty Square apartment complex was the oldest housing project and the highest crime area in Miami, particularly along its North 15th Street border. The cabbie asked if Gawain was certain of what he was doing, and he not only assured the driver but gave him $10 for his troubles. The residents of the project watched from the graffiti-scrawled doorways as Gawain made his way down the street, figuring that he was probably another narc trying to play a different angle. He continued walking westward, crossing the street and coming to a dilapidated tenement where a strung-out gangster lounged about on the concrete staircase.

"Say, fellow, anywhere I can score hereabouts?" Gawain called over. He was dressed in a black blazer, T-shirt and jeans, the jacket covering the pistol in his waistband.

"You a cop?" the druggie looked around, puzzled that there were no vehicles anywhere in sight. He could not believe that a lone white man would have dared walk this far.

"Go way outta that!" Gawain scowled disdainfully, approaching the staircase. "I'm lookin' to do some business, anyone open around here today?"

"We open twenty-four seven around here," the black kid replied. "What you looking for?"

"I'm looking to pick up some weight," Gawain flashed five $100 bills that he had peeled loose from his billfold.

"Yeah, you lookin'," the gangster agreed. "Hold up."

He came off the steps and walked up to the corner, looking down the street for a moment before spotting someone and giving them gang signals. He stepped away from the curb just before a low-riding classic 1966 Thunderbird came squealing around the corner in reverse. The car burned rubber in a wide arc before screeching to a halt by the sidewalk by Gawain.

"What you lookin' for?" the driver, a Cuban gangbanger dressed like a pimp in a garish mint-green suit, barked at him.

"Well, fellow," Gawain sauntered over, pulling his jacket aside to flash his billfold at the dealer, the butt of his pistol visible in his belt. "I'm wanting to score some weight."

"You a cop?"

"Hell no."

"Go ahead and walk around the corner, go three houses down and I'll meet you there."

Once again the car's tires screamed as the car whizzed down the block and around the corner out of view. Gawain did as instructed and saw the car roaring around the corner down the block, burning rubber again as it came to a halt in front of the apartment building he had specified. The driver leaned on the car horn, blaring out a trombone riff from a salsa tune.

The driver was gunning the engine, which roared violently until three men emerged from the basement apartment.

"Man, what you doing on Fifteenth Street, you lost or something?" the leader, a heavily muscled Cuban kid dressed in a tan designer suit, swaggered over to Gawain. The two men in the background, also wearing suits, made a show of hooking their thumbs onto their waistlines.

"Actually I'm looking for work," Gawain announced. "My name's Jack Gain. Just come over from Canada. I'm a friend of a friend of Kenny Ray, he works with Ricky Chew."

"Where you know Kenny Ray? You must know his brother then," the Cuban challenged.

"Kenny's a big guy, about three hundred pounds, Big Kenny. Scar under his left eye. I met him and his brother Georgie. Georgie's a skinny guy, wears a goatee. Likes cleaning his nails with a pocket knife while he's talking."

"Well, sounds like he knows Kenny and Georgie," the Cuban looked back at his impassive gunmen. "I can bring you inside to talk to the boss, but you gonna have to let me hold your piece."

"Bollocks," Gawain sniffed. "There's three of you and one of me. If I make a move and you take me out, you get to keep the money I showed the black fellow back there. Why would I do something stupid unless I had to? Better yet, you can bring your man out and I'll wait right here."

At once he heard a feminine voice calling from the basement apartment at the wrought iron door under the staircase. He could hear it warbling in Spanish before the Cuban nodded and looked back at Gawain.

"Okay, bro, just follow my man there through that door, we're right behind you," the Cuban instructed him.

Gawain followed them into the dark corridor where the smell of mildew and marijuana smoke mingled with the aroma of *bistec*[1], black beans and rice. It led to an unlit hallway cluttered with garbage bags lined against the wall. The gangster led Gawain through a doorway to the left and into a small, brightly-lit apartment where a thin blond man stood wearing a white shirt, slacks and an apron.

"My cousin Kenny sent you here?" the man asked incredulously in a high-pitched voice.

"Not really," Gawain admitted. "As I told the fellows here, I met him up in Canada and told him I was planning to relocate to Florida. I've got a record in the UK and I didn't want the Mounties or whoever to be able to make me too easily. He told me he knew people in Miami and told me he'd put in a good word for me."

"Did he tell you I was his cousin?" the blond insisted.

"Well, he's Colombian and you seem to be Cuban, so I wouldn't have guessed."

"Very good," he smiled happily. "I'm Johnnie Sosa, and this is my brother Jimmy. My mother married his uncle. So, you want to do business with us?"

"Sure would," Gawain shook hands with both men, introducing himself. He had no doubt that Johnny was a faerie, while Jimmy, a handsome, dark-haired, green-eyed man, had the gape of a moron.

"How do you think you can help us?" Johnnie bade him to take a seat on the comfortable armchair facing the sofa in the paneled basement. It was across the small room from a cheap dinner table and chairs set alongside the small stove where Johnnie was preparing brunch.

"Well, I do all sorts of odd jobs," Gawain replied. "I'd prefer some sort of mid-management job for starters. I'm a bit long in the tooth and not quite the type to stand on the corner peddling, y'know."

1. beefsteak

"How about collections?" the faerie stared at him. Gawain found his voice to be peculiar, not having the typical near-lisp, but almost a bad Minnie Mouse imitation. Yet, he knew from his prison experience that these could be some of the most sadistic of psychotics and were not to be trifled with.

"That happens to be one of my areas of expertise," Gawain grinned.

"Wonderful," Johnnie gushed. "I've got one bad debt in particular I need taken care of. Tell you what, I'll have my man drive you home, and he'll come back for you at midnight. Where do you live?"

"I'm at the Shore Club on Collins."

"Ooh!" Johnny marveled. "That's Richie Rich! You must have brought a lot of money with you from Canada!"

"Well, I'm very good at what I do, and I get paid accordingly. I suppose you'll see for yourself."

"Splendid!" Johnny clapped his hands together. "Jimmy, go ahead and give Mr. Jack a ride back to his hotel. You just give Jimmy your number, and we will call you at midnight, and we will do business!"

"Looking forward to it," Gawain rose to shake his hand before following Jimmy out the door. He only hoped that Shanahan or his puppet masters did not have any impromptu shenanigans lined up to interrupt and spoil his fun. He fully intended to make this a week to remember.

Chapter Twelve

The city of Medellin was founded in 1616 by a Sephardic Jewish colony which had fled Spain to avoid the Inquisition. They remained clannish and secretive, partly because of their exclusive religious beliefs and partly to discourage outsiders from intruding upon their infrastructural industry and commerce. The industry thrived and prospered for three centuries as a fiercely independent rural community until the railroad companies arrived at the beginning of the 20th century. The Jews invested heavily in the burgeoning coffee industry, which provided a windfall profit that they used to industrialize their mining operations. This set off a financial explosion that allowed them to expand into the textile market, and by the end of the century Medellin was one of the richest metropolitan cities in South America.

The Antioquian tribes of aborigines began migrating into the cities, and when overpopulation became a problem, many of the rich landlords began expanding their fiefdoms further into the Cordillera Central of the Andes Mountains. The discovery of the coca plants proliferating in the area and their use in manufacturing cocaine resulted in the proliferation of *fincas*[1] throughout the region. The *campesinos*[2] were able to support their families and improve their standard of living, pledging their allegiance to the drug lords over the local govern-

---

1. plantations
2. peasant farmers

ment. The new criminal empires were able to arm and equip a peasant army that turned the jungles and mountain regions into paramilitary strongholds.

The War on Drugs of the 90's eventually turned the tide against the drug cartels. Some managed to survive by disappearing into the jungles and cutting back on production and distribution. Once the Colombian government was able to declare victory, the cartels gradually escalated their operations until they were able to recoup their losses and resume business on an international scale. They protected their interests and enforced their business standards by means of violence and murder, and Salvaje Pulga was the most vicious of the cartel leaders.

By the dawn of the War on Terror of the '00s, the drug trade experienced booming profits. America's military and law enforcement resources were being stretched thin against terror gangs as well as drug gangs in Mexico and El Salvador. The cartels were able to reestablish their trade routes by air and sea in bringing cocaine into the USA along the Southwest borders and the Southeastern seacoast. It seemed to be the perfect time to consider alternative means of converting their vast fortunes into legitimate wealth, but many of the old-school drug lords were skeptical and reluctant to change their ways.

"Look about you, Enrique," Salvaje gestured at the awe-inspiring landscape surrounding them as they sat in Pulga's multi-million dollar fortress. He had located the ruins of an Incan temple deep in the jungle outside Medellin, and paid a small fortune to have it rebuilt before having a mansion built alongside it. He then had it fortified as a paramilitary base before having the nearby jungle plowed into coca fields. The triple-canopied tropical forest provided excellent cover from surveillance aircraft, and when one sortie was flown to drop an Agent Orange defoliant on the treelines, Pulga purchased a few crates of RPG-7 missile launchers. After a few exchanges, the government planes never returned.

"This is a paradise, Pulga," Enrique glanced about as they sat in a glittering gazebo amidst an exotic flower garden which featured a granite walkway, marbled ledges and waterfalls.

"You are surrounded by history and tradition," Pulga rhapsodized. "This is the union of the history and culture of an ancient society, and the tradition of my own ancestors before me. Without our tradition, we are nothing. Without our history, we have no roots. We are like leaves being blown in the wind. The deeper our roots, the stronger we become, the longer we endure. Those who sprout up like weeds around us, when the storms and the floods come, they are torn up and swept away. Only those of the soil—like us—endure, Enrique. This is what you must learn This is what I want you to learn."

"This is a good deal, Pulga," Chupacabra insisted. "This European Council is going to change the ways of doing business in Europe. William Bruce speaks the truth. The Americans and EUROPOL are onto the Mafia. They're like pit bulls with their jaws locked into their prey. They will never let go. No one knows about the Council or the Sardinians. We can move billions worth of bullion into North America before they're discovered."

"We don't know who they are, Enrique!" Pulga slapped the top of the glass patio table, nearly upsetting the chicken broth and champagne they were enjoying at brunch. "We don't know their history! How do we know this isn't a setup by EUROPOL?"

"Salvaje, let us reason together," Enrique exhaled tautly. "They just moved seventy million dollars of gold from Belfast to Montreal. It has been redistributed to safe fortresses across Canada. Gold is untraceable, it has no serial numbers, no identifiable characteristics. In case of emergency, the gold can be melted down and remolded into bars of all shapes and sizes. Amschel Bauer has spent his entire life investing in gold, he is an expert in the field. If the Sardinians can bring the gold safely to Medellin, our only concern would be making the payment."

"Amschel Bauer, Nathan Schnaper," Pulga growled. "These are not the *paisas*[3] of Medellin. These are the Ashkenazis, the Asiatic Jews. These are the ones who nearly destroyed the colonies of the Medellin

---

3. Sephardic Jews

Jews. Instead of growing and harvesting coca and distributing it in traditional ways, they come in with their smoke and mirrors, daring the *gringos* to learn their tricks! They had more airplanes in the skies than El Dorado International, more boats in the water than the Colombian Navy! Greed is like a poison, my friend. It seeps into your system and slowly kills you. You look around, do you think all this was put together overnight? Do you think I had the land bulldozed, the temples restored, my mansion built and my fields planted in one week? There is no such thing as getting rich quick or building an empire overnight, Enrique, listen to me carefully!"

"Salvaje, I'm in a predicament here," Chupacabra weighed his words. "You sent me to represent you in Montreal and I told Bauer that we would take part in Operation Blackout. The plan was to buy up as much available bullion as possible before his Al Qaida connections could launch an attack against the gold supplies of the US and the EU. If we renege, not only do we risk offending these people but making me stink throughout the network!"

"Seventy million dollars, Enrique. Eighty million after I pay the Sardinians," Salvaje lifted the earthenware bowl and slurped down its contents before setting it aside. "I will have to notify the rest of the cartel before I give you my word, but rest assured it will be done. Just remember: as you detest offending *those people* and risking an odious reputation, so it is with me and my people. *Our* people, Enrique."

"You will not be sorry, *mi patron*," Chupacabra thanked him. "I am sure of Mr. Bauer. He stands like a rock behind this enterprise. This will be the first of many great transactions between us."

"He stands behind his enterprise just as I stand behind mine," Pulga said solemnly, "and I am standing behind you. Don't let me down, my son. Don't let me down."

Chupacabra nodded as the servants brought a smorgasbord of traditional Colombian dishes and platters of game meat which would be enjoyed by the bodyguards once the two of them finished their meal. He was relieved and exhilarated by Pulga's approval, yet had a queasy feeling over the remote possibility that Amschel Bauer's carefully laid plans might somehow go astray.

That next afternoon, nine days before the tournament, Bauer had contacted Shanahan and requested a video conference with him and Murra. Shanahan phoned Murra and arranged to have him come to his suite before having the necessary equipment brought in. Murra was staying at the Delano Hotel on Collins Avenue and was preparing to check out before getting the call from Shanahan. He extended his stay and took the short walk from the Delano to the Shore Club Hotel before calling Shanahan from the lobby.

"I hope this wasn't an inconvenience," Shanahan greeted Murra in the lobby with a handshake. "They called me on rather short notice, as you can imagine. He didn't give me much information. I imagine this 'Blackout' is coming sooner than expected."

They took the elevator up to Shanahan's suite, and Murra complimented him on the accommodations. He thanked Shanahan for a glass of mango juice just as room service arrived with the video equipment. The men waited patiently for the hotel technician to set everything in place as Shanahan contemplated their strange relationship.

Shanahan only regretted that things had not been different. He admired Murra for having asked for juice rather than alcohol, unlike Gawain who guzzled drinks at every opportunity. If only the Firm had approached Murra with the opportunity to act as a double agent rather than Gawain. He liked everything about the man: his style, his personality, his physical presence. In a different time and place, they might have been allies, even friends. He recalled a couple of times in Iraq and Afghanistan when he grew close to paramilitary leaders and tribal chieftains that he admired as persons, but none such as Murra.

William tipped the hotel tech before he took his leave, and sat at the PC station where he logged onto the website designated by Bauer. He stepped behind the professional video camera and made sure it was precisely focused on the sofa where he and Murra would sit. It was not long before the image of Amschel Bauer and Nathan Schnaper appeared on the wide-screen plasma TV as transmitted from Bauer's skyscraper suite.

"Good afternoon, gentlemen," Bauer greeted them. "It is great to see you, and I am very pleased to report that we are enjoying high-quality reception on our end."

The four men exchanged pleasantries before the videoconference came to order.

"We have received confirmation from Enrique Chupacabra that the Cartel has authorized the purchase of the bullion," Bauer revealed. "This gives Mr. Murra the green light to proceed with the transport from our location to Medellin. The Cartel has also agreed to pay ninety percent cash and ten percent product as suggested, so it will be arranged for Mr. Murra's people to safely deliver the merchandise here in Montreal."

"Excellent," Murra smiled. "I will have my ship en route at the earliest opportunity."

"As a matter of fact, we are so delighted with how things are working out that we are prepared to accept the next shipment from the European Council," Bauer announced. "Mr. Bruce, if your colleagues in Berlin can arrange another transport, we will be more than glad to make a purchase offer."

"On behalf of the Council, I want to express our thanks and appreciation for your cooperation and support in assisting us with this enterprise," William replied. "Of course, as you know, this is a joint project being supported by our own associates across the Continent. We would have to hold our own conference in order to determine the quantity and cost of our next delivery in order to give you a fair and accurate price."

"We will be waiting eagerly for further word from your organization," Bauer assured him.

"Mr. Murra, I just want to say that my people on the waterfront were very impressed by the professional efficiency of your transport crew," Schnaper spoke up, peering into the camera over his thick tortoiseshell glasses. "They had the containers ready to go as soon as the ship was docked, they helped our people hook the cables to our crane and made sure everything was secure on our trucks before they left the port. Considering the nature of our business and the serious risks involved, I would concur with our crew chief that your men were as cool as cucumbers. Most hijack teams try to unload as fast as possible, and they're twice as quick to leave."

"I will certainly convey your compliments to our crew and make certain they are rewarded," Murra nodded. "Rest assured that we will continue to provide the best quality of service available and guarantee the safety of each shipment at our own risk."

"Mr. Bruce, we will be contacting you shortly," Bauer said as he pointed a remote control at the video camera. "Good day, gentlemen. Montreal over and out."

"William," Murra smiled broadly, "I would suggest that this calls for a celebration of sorts. Let me take you to lunch, and afterwards we might possibly enjoy something a bit stronger than fruit drinks. A magnum of champagne, perhaps."

"My sentiments exactly," William replied.

Once again he repented of the fact that he would eventually betray Murra and that they were not working on the same side of the fence together.

It was several hours earlier when Jack Gawain was called on the phone at his suite by the Sosa Brothers. He brought his cell phone, credit card and the Glock with him, along with a 15" hunting knife he purchased earlier in the day. He took the elevator to the lobby, heading out to the front of the hotel. He got into the car where Jimmy Sosa and two of his crew members awaited.

"We going to see somebody," Jimmy spoke from the back seat with what seemed to be a speech impediment aggravated by a heavy accent. "If he no pay, we see what you do about it."

"Well, so will they," Gawain grinned into the rear view mirror from the passenger seat.

They drove over to the Liberty City district as the car slowed to a crawl and lowered its beams, finally switching them off as the low riding classic Impala rolled to a halt outside a three-story tenement building. The three men conversed in Spanish for a short time before pushing the car doors open. Gawain hopped out and followed them up to the building. There was a small group of teens out from, but they took one look at the quartet and hurriedly left the area.

Jimmy led the way up the front steps, the others trotting behind him as he shoved his way through the double doors to the second floor. He produced an oilcloth-wrapped object from inside his suit jacket which turned out to be a small crowbar. He went to the door of the rear apartment and hammered on it, waiting at length until a muffled voice responded in Spanish. There was a short exchange between Jimmy and the occupant before no further response came from within. Jimmy crooked a finger as one of his men joined him in smashing against the door with their shoulders. They busted it open with the third hit, only to find themselves impeded by a safety chain. Jimmy worked his crowbar onto it and ripped it off the doorframe.

The first man raced in, and they could hear commotion in the next room followed by crashing sounds and breaking glass. At once the gangster shoved a frightened, strung-out man wearing a dress shirt and slacks back out into the dilapidated living room. Jimmy began screaming at him, the words coming in an articulate torrent as the druggie cowered against the wall. As the man began crying in protest, Jimmy jerked a thumb at Gawain.

"Give the man a seat and tie 'em down, then," Gawain suggested. The Cubans retrieved a ragged kitchen chair, then produced a knife and began slashing upholstery and clothing until they had enough strips of cloth to tie the man to the chair.

"Now, then," Gawain stood before the man as the Cubans leaned up against the walls, one standing guard at the door. "I hope for your sake that you speak English."

"I no have nothing! I can get the money next week!" the swarthy man screamed.

"Well, I don't think these fellows are willing to wait that long. I think they think you can come up with something now," Gawain pulled the hunting knife from the sheath on his belt. "You'll have to work with me here, because they won't let me off until you make good."

"I no have anything! I have everything Monday!" he wept.

"You're not listening," Gawain replied in a singsong voice, starting to turn away before whipping around and slapping the man across the face with the flat of the blade. The man screamed as there was enough of a tilt on the blade to slice his cheek to the bone. The Cubans chuckled wryly and made clucking noises as Gawain glanced at the blood-spattered knife.

"Please!" the man begged. "No more! Please!"

"Come on, boyo, this is going to get messy," Gawain entreated him gently. "There's got to be something somewhere, these fellows can't be that stupid."

"I no having!" the man wailed. "I no having!"

"People is walking around downstairs," the guard at the door admonished the others.

"Now we're having a problem, fellow," Gawain tapped the blade impatiently on the palm of his hand. "One more time, are you gonna help me out here?"

"Please," the man sobbed as the blood ran down his cheek. "I no have anything."

"All right," Gawain sighed before lifting the knife overhead and driving it with all his might into the man's right thigh. The man screamed in agony but had his mouth covered by Gawain, who waited until his voice broke before wiping the spittle on the man's shirt. He then wrenched the knife out of the man's leg as the guard at the door gave another warning in Spanish. His voice was drowned out as the victim began screaming in Spanish, and at once Jimmy rushed into a back room. They heard a series of bangs and crashes, and suddenly Jimmy reappeared with a small valise in hand.

"*Vamonos!*" he yelled. The others rushed out the door past Gawain, and as he sheathed the blade, Jimmy calmly turned around and shot the man in the head.

"Okay," Jimmy smiled at him. "You one of us now."

Gawain wiped his blade on the dead man's trouser leg, sheathing it before trotting down the steps behind the gangsters, past the onlookers racing from the hallway. It wasn't quite Belfast, but life in Liberty City was proving most exciting indeed.

Chapter Thirteen

It was the Saturday before the game just a week away when MI6 contacted Shanahan with detailed instructions after he reported on the situation with Bauer and the Cartel. Shaughnessy was as optimistic as Shanahan but shared his apprehension about setting up another large shipment on such short notice. The CIA had been the suppliers of the bullion, and the question was whether they would be able to comply with Bauer's request.

"We've gotten the nod from our cousins in Langley," Shaughnessy and his peers at MI6 had grown fond of the euphemism. "They agreed to arrange the transport, but request that you stall as much as possible to give them sufficient time to get everything in order. They are shipping from an unspecified location along the Southeast US coast to Belfast once they've made the necessary arrangements on their end. The Firm is of the opinion that the most opportune time to make the delivery will be Thursday, two days before the game in Miami. That will give the Sardinians time to get the shipment to Medellin by Saturday at the latest. It would be perfect timing, in our opinion. Are you keeping Gawain out of trouble?"

"I—don't follow, sir."

"He's been checking in on schedule but I just want to make sure. I don't want him rotting in a Yankee jail at the time he's supposed to be facing off against Chupacabra at the championship game."

MI6 discovered that Chupacabra's passion was dominoes. It was a love he developed around the same time as Gawain while doing time in a Federal penitentiary in his early twenties. He, like so many other Hispanics, loved the game more than cards and was ecstatic to learn it had become an ESPN-sponsored pastime. He used his enormous influence to buy his way into the tournament, and when MI6 found out from the CIA (courtesy of Homeland Security), it seemed an opportune way to play another mind game on their target.

"Colonel, with all due respect, I have made it clear that it is not in my interests—or the Firm's interests—to have a senior agent fraternizing with this fellow. I told you already he was a drunkard and a lout, not to mention he's murdered five people on this operation. I know we've got support units in this area, I don't see why one could not be assigned to keep tabs on him."

"He's a lot more clever than you may think, that's why we picked him," Shaughnessy replied. "If he thought he was being followed he might take lethal action against our own people. We'll leave well enough alone, but I hope you might find time to make sure he is not checking in from a detention center."

"As you wish, Colonel. Shanahan out."

Shanahan stared out the window overlooking the Miami Beach shoreline for a long time, then decided to second-guess himself. He dressed in a forest green suit, light green polo shirt and black alligator shoes, wearing his shoulder holster with his Glock beneath his jacket. He took the elevator down to the seventh floor to check on Jack Gawain.

He knocked softly on the door and could hear the TV inside the room.

"Come on in."

Shanahan opened the door and saw Gawain sprawled out on the couch in front of the living room TV, munching on a plate of fish and chips and sipping a Guinness as he watched a porn movie.

"Little early for that?" Shanahan walked over to the well-stocked bar, finding some grapefruit juice.

"Nah, never too early for a pick-me-up," Gawain shrugged. "What's up for today?"

"Not much, just thought I'd stop by."

"Ever try that, DP?" Gawain pointed at the screen.

"What?"

"Double penetration, boyo. Sandwich job."

"Don't be a gobshite, fellow," Shanahan muttered as he popped the top on the juice can. "You pull the floozie out of the mix and what do you have? Two rump-roasters humping on each other."

"Well, the trick is to have one up front and one in back, so this way you're not rubbing on each other," Gawain finished the bottle of stout.

"Sounds like a couple of bowsies who can't get the job done on their own," Shanahan sipped his juice. "Is that what you have planned for Fianna?"

"No, she's a nice girl, that one," Gawain admitted. "You got the pick of the litter, you know. You get your finger wet yet?"

"Don't be an arse," Shanahan growled, walking over to stare out the sliding glass balcony door. "They're both nice girls, not the kind I'd expect you to keep calling on. Is that why you call them, more of your head games?"

"C'mon, boyo, I'm just doing you the favor."

"Bollocks."

"Now, don't you think I could just ask Fianna to come out on her lonesome?"

"I suppose so," Shanahan shrugged, wondering why he came down here in the first place.

"It really wouldn't do for someone of your station to get too deeply involved with a mere stewardess, would it?"

"Regardless of where you stroll about with a girl like that, it would hardly make a difference, wouldn't you think?"

"Aye, and so it is with Fianna," Gawain allowed. "She'd be a barrel of laughs wherever she'd go. And, of course, you never take women along on business, so there you go. Now, in your world, it's different.

You take your women everywhere, and if someone asked too many questions, they'd find you'd married beneath your station."

"Marriage?" Shanahan squinted at him. "What's that about?"

"That's why you wouldn't want to go steady with her or anything," Gawain popped a piece of flounder in his mouth. "It'd make you unavailable if that special someone came along. Of course, there's a way around that. You can always go over to the one you spot someplace when Morgana goes to have a piss, and drop a card. Women like stealing men off others, it boosts their ego, don't y'know."

"Not my style, Gawain," Shanahan took a big sip of his drink, getting annoyed with the porn soundtrack. "I'm not one for deception."

"Am I hearing proper?" Gawain made a show of digging his finger in his ear. "A government spy?"

"I'm talking about on a personal level," Shanahan was derisive. "Everybody plays the game professionally, even you."

"Nay, you're mistaken, fella," Gawain smirked back. "I'm sure you've seen my file. I did almost a year in solitary at Maghaberry before the screws decided to live and let live. I've survived attempts on my life both in and out of the can for taking shite off no one. I don't play games, fella, that's your line."

"Yet you've dealt yourself into this game, Gawain. How do you reconcile that?"

"Like I told you, I'm playing for my life. I know you bastards aren't going to let me go free after this, but at least I'm getting to walk about here rather than sitting in the can."

"So all that God and Country stuff doesn't really mean anything to you."

"I wouldn't say that," Gawain frowned. "Just because this Prime Minister and the Parliament is bent doesn't mean I've lost hope in the UK. Maybe they'll put me back in prison, but there'll be a new day ahead. I'll be around to testify as to what was offered and what was done instead."

"That doesn't make any sense," Shanahan argued. "Why do this just for a short time out? Why not just skip town and take your chances?"

"You don't like me," Gawain chuckled at him. "You're hoping I go on the lam so they can put another fella more like yourself in my place."

"I told you what the deal was back at the prison," Shanahan said flatly. "If you'd turned down the offer, I'd have worked my way down the list. Surely you don't think I'd found another more dignified fellow in a place like that."

"Certainly not one as capable. Probably not one who could've hooked you up with someone like Morgana."

"You're pretty full of yourself, aren't you?"

"Pot calling the kettle black, boyo."

"You're not going back to prison," Shanahan walked towards the door. "I can guarantee that. Not unless you go into the wind or compromise the mission. I am fairly certain that if Chupacabra loses that game Saturday with you at the table, it may be the straw that breaks the camel's back. If he goes into a meltdown and gets himself arrested or killed, I'm pretty sure that you and I will be on our way home."

"Y'know, you people are pretty gloopy at times," Gawain shook his head. "Why don't you just let me whack him before the game and be done with it?"

"Stick to the game plan," Shanahan admonished him. "There's a lot of things going on that you're unaware of. You saw the kind of people who were at that meeting in Montreal. Chupacabra's just a piece of the picture, but large enough to throw it entirely off-focus when our work is done here."

"Well, I'll be out and about," Gawain replied as Shanahan took his leave. "Do try and give me advance notice if we have to go out anytime soon."

"I'd expect the same courtesy if you invite the ladies to town," Shanahan replied, closing the door behind him.

Gawain decided to get dressed and pick up the rental car he had reserved for the week. As an afterthought, he turned the volume on the porn movie up full blast before he left. He was fairly certain the room service people and his next door neighbors would be impressed.

Prime 112 was one of the trendiest steakhouses in South Beach, and though most reservations had to be made a week in advance, the sight of Johnny Carmona and his entourage at the foyer guaranteed a table at the behest of any of the maîtres d'hotel on duty. The waiters quickly set a place for him in exchange for $100 tips for one and all. Soon he was joined at the table by MS-13 gang lord Tony Ramos.

"Nice place," Tony smiled as he admired the spacious yellow bricked dining area accentuated by its high ceilings and glass torch lamps set in niches along the walls. "I looked it up on the Internet. George Bush used to like coming here, so they say."

"When you taste the porterhouse steak, you'll know why," Carmona replied. He wore a white silk suit and a black shirt, a $10,000 gold chain around his neck, a diamond pinky ring of similar value, and a Masterpiece Rolex worth $90,000. Ramos, an old-school gangster, wore a dark green designer suit and tie with a tasteful Longines watch.

"You invite me to a place like this, I am expecting that we are having a celebration," Ramos sipped his champagne.

"Let's call it a pre-game celebration," Carmona raised a glass to Ramos. "I have everything arranged with Ernie Guzman in San Antonio. He is going to have his men in Houston Friday night to receive the shipment."

"This is bad business," Tony muttered as the waitress brought their Oysters Rockefeller appetizers. "I got a bad feeling about this job. I met with Salvaje Pulga a few days ago and gave him a pep talk, but now I'm having second thoughts. You met the Sheik last week, how did he come across to you?"

"He's a stand-up guy," Carmona reverted to their native Spanish. "He's paying a million dollars to everyone involved in the operation, and he's parceled it out so that no one is doing more work than the next guy. Hey, Tony, Al-Qaeda's been polishing up their act for over twenty years. They got this routine worked inside out. They've smuggled arms all over the world, they make the Communists look like amateurs. This is going to be a piece of cake. I got my best people on this, and so will you. My guys meet yours at Key West and we're both a mil richer."

"We're crossing the line with this shit, Carmona," Tony squeezed a lemon over an oyster. "It was bad enough risking twenty years for hauling coke. Now we're talking Guantanamo. This Administration's taken the kid gloves off. You get put there, you may never get out. Torture, murder, whatever they want. There are no rules, my friend. Not no more."

"C'mon, Tony," Carmona winced. "That's what Alberto Calix deals with every day. You get caught by the wrong people in Mexico, they hang you upside down and shoot pepper spray up your nose until your brains explode out your fricking eardrums. You smuggle your shit across another gang's territory, they nail you to a cactus in the desert, cut your balls off and leave you for the vultures. This is a rough game, my friend, it always has been. That's why we get paid so well. Besides, what's your problem? Do your smugglers have your address or your home number? I hope Homeland Security can't find you on Facebook."

"None of us are getting any younger," Ramos speared the oyster with a fork. "I've spent my whole life looking over my shoulder. Now all of a sudden, over the past ten years there are other people the Yankees want more than us. So here we are getting ready to join those people and put ourselves back on top of the list."

"Tell me, when has the money ever been better?" Carmona insisted. "When did you ever make a mil for hauling freight from Honduras to the Keys? Plus, Amschel Bauer's planning to start cutting us all in on that bullion pipeline with the European Council once the test runs with the Colombians are completed. We were once sitting on top of a mountain of coke. We are soon going to be standing on a mountain of gold. In a matter of months, we may all be able to retire as some of the richest men in the world."

"Nobody ever retires," Ramos waved his fork for emphasis. "Not even Pablo Escobar after he made *Forbes* Magazine. Too much is never enough. And that's how it happens. You go to the well once too often. We will all be caught or killed one day. The trick is to make it later than sooner. Smuggling weapons for Al-Qaeda can make it come much sooner."

"So is this what you told Pulga?"

"No, I spoke to Pulga the way you are speaking to me. I merely share my reservations with you. I am very much in favor of buying bullion and preparing for the conversion to the gold standard. My people who play with computers tell me that this is going to happen very soon. Smuggling weapons, though, may very well destroy everything we have worked for. We are on the verge of realizing our dreams, Carmona. I believe in Amschel Bauer. I believe that we may very soon become the richest men on the face of the earth. What I do not believe is that we should be smuggling any more weapons for Al-Qaeda."

"So what do we do, Tony?" Carmona asked bluntly. "Back out of the deal? You know this is a major part of the operation. Neither I nor Ernesto Guzman know who's getting the real shipment or the decoy. If one of us backs down, they'll need a new shipping route. It may be too late in the game for them to change plans. It may be more convenient for them to remove one of us instead. And, your gang provides the link between South and North America. You see what I'm saying?"

"That is also an ever-present danger," Ramos admitted. "Sometimes they look behind you to see if the next in line is going to be easier to deal with."

"Hey, Tony, I wouldn't be sitting here with you right now if the guy in front of me hadn't gotten clipped," Carmona reminded him. "Somebody blew Julio Cruz to hell in that parking garage in Montreal, and still no one knows who did it or why. Right away everybody looks at Chupacabra, but the reason why we haven't gone to war with the Colombians was because it's too easy. Our people all knew I was next in line, and my first instinct would have been to take them to war. That's when I looked before I leaped. If I'm at war with the Colombians, this Operation Blackout doesn't happen. Cruz was hot for the deal, he wasn't moved aside by Bauer and Schnaper. Somebody did it to sabotage the deal, and to show us all that any of us could be killed at any time."

"So you think it was an inside job? Somebody who is in on the operation?"

"Who else?" Carmona sat back, spreading his hands. "It's not going to be any of the smugglers. I snitch on you, you snitch on me, we both lose. Somebody else snitches on us after the fact, we're left holding the bag. Look, Cruz gets killed, everybody gives Chupacabra a pass for some reason or other. Maybe people are scared of the Colombians, maybe they don't want to see the operation go sideways, maybe people think I had something to do with it. They tested the frame, the infrastructure, and it held up, it stood fast. Now I'm the man, I'm bringing the box from Cuba to the Keys. If it works, fine, Bauer's plan continues to unfold. If it doesn't—that's the catch. Now it's the Cubans who brought the weapons over for Al Qaida."

"So you think it's somebody on the outside? Who?"

"Look at the map. Who is outside? The Montreal Mob, Al Qaida, and those new guys, the Council. If any of them wants to get any of us, they simply push one of us against the other. We try to go up against them, what are we going to do? Send our air force after them? No, we bought into this game, we have to stick it out. We go ahead and make the delivery, but once it's over, I'm going to find out who hit Cruz and why."

"Maybe we should start rebuilding our bridges, making sure we've got each other's backs if this thing falls apart. Every man for himself sounds more like divided we fall."

"That's why I didn't start looking for who whacked Cruz as soon as I took his place on top. I'm looking, but I'm not getting distracted. And I think I see something, but as I say, I'm waiting until this job gets done before I get onto the next order of business."

"What is that, Carmona?" Ramos buttered a slice of bread.

"One of my top guys in Liberty City has a guy from Canada who came in with him the other day and went out on a hit," Carmona revealed. "His hands got too dirty for him to be a cop. I think he may be a spy for the Montreal Mob. His name's Jack Wayne, some shit like that. They're gonna call him in tonight. I told my man Johnnie Sosa to find out what he can. Sosa's one of the best, he'll know if this guy's on the level or not."

"What the hell is a guy from Canada doing in Miami looking for work?" Ramos squinted.

"Good question," Carmona replied pointedly.

He was fully confident it was something that Johnny Sosa was going to find out.

Chapter Fourteen

It was shortly after midnight when Jack Gawain got a call from one of Johnnie Sosa's men, and within a half hour he was cruising in his rented black Lexus down to Liberty City. He pulled up in front of the Sosa Brothers' tenement building where three classic low riders were already parked. Patting the Glock in his waistband for reassurance, he switched off the engine, hopped out of the car and walked up to where three of Sosa's gunmen stood out front. He was recognized by Oscar Alfonso, who was on the hit the previous evening. He introduced the other men before they escorted Gawain into the building.

Once again, Johnnie Sosa was making a scrumptious dinner which included *pasteles*, black beans and rice with *lechon asado*. Gawain was invited to join the table along with Alfonso, Jimmy Sosa and Gilberto Echezabal, who was also on the hit last night.

"Here's your cut, my friend," Jimmy tossed a roll of bills over to Gawain. He counted it and frowned at Sosa disapprovingly.

"Two grand?"

"That's your weekly salary," Johnnie stood with hands on hips, once again wearing a designer shirt and slacks protected by a flowered apron. "That's not all that bad. If you keep up the good work, you end up getting raises and promotions. Plus, we don't take out taxes."

"Ah, what the hell," Gawain stuck the roll into his jacket pocket. "Y'know, the going rate on a hit is ten grand. If I do ten hits for you, which I'm suspecting I may be up to in a short time with you fellas, I'd have just about made my whole year's salary. Then again, after ten hits I may be the most wanted man in Florida, which'd mean I wouldn't be wise to stick around much longer."

"You're an unusual man, Jack," Johnnie began serving plates to his guests. "Tell me more about yourself."

"Not a whole lot to tell," he shrugged, thanking Johnnie for his plate. "I spent most of my life in the UK, worked for the Mob in Liverpool, did lots of smuggling out of Glasgow and Belfast. I know from experience what happens after you get too many notches on your gun. I relocated to Canada, made some connections, but eventually the Mounties started poking about so I came down here. Didn't think they'd be crazy about the weather."

"So you met Kenny Reyes in Montreal?" Johnnie licked the spoon after having served the last of the black beans.

"Kinda sorts," he replied. "There was this top secret meeting that I was asked to attend as backup for some big-shots from London. He was there with Ricky Chew and we got to talking, you know, wiseguy bullshite. He mentioned in passing that if I did wind up coming down here, just mention his name. Who knows if he'd even remember me if my name came up again, which would be a good thing for me, I suppose. Right after the meeting, one of the guys got car-bombed in a parking garage, and everyone in my crew took off straight to the airport."

"The guy who got killed was my ex-boss," Johnnie sat at the table across from him, searching his face. "A lot of people thought the man you call Ricky Chew was responsible, but that would've put my cousins and I at war with each other. Somebody tried to start that war, and I am going to find out who."

"Well, I'm sure y'have some idea," Jack said around a mouthful of pork roast. "Back home, we always say the guys who start the biggest fights are the ones who have most to gain."

"Who are you, Mr. Gain? How did you end up coming over here the way you did?" Johnny asked quietly.

"Oh, so now yer suspecting me?" he scoffed. "Y'know, if y'went down to the local library and found someone who could show you around computers, ye'd easily see that Liberty City's the worst crime area in town. If ye come down and ask to buy a ki from a street dealer, it's more than he's got the strength t'carry. He goes to his boss, and that's who y'make yer pitch to. That's who you ought to ask, why he introduced me in the first place."

"Hey, don't get me in the middle of this," Oscar held up a hand. "A man shows up in this neighborhood with a Glock and a roll of hundreds and tells me he's looking for work, hey, I don't make those calls."

"I seen him work, he okay," Jimmy spoke up, to everyone's surprise. "*Cojones*[1]."

"Well, you impressed my brother," Johnnie decided, "so now you have to impress me."

"And how do I go about doing that?" Jack scooped up a big forkful of *pastel.*

"Only half of the problem is people stealing from me," Johnnie frowned. "The other part is people stealing my business. Every time you turn around, somebody's setting up shop right on our doorstep somewhere. I have American blacks, Jamaican blacks, Haitian blacks, Dominicans, Salvadorans, Mexicans, you name them, I've got them. We have to set an example and show them what happens when they trespass in our neighborhood."

"All right, then," Jack poured himself a glass of rum and coke. "What'll it be then?"

"Go ahead and finish your meal, I spent a couple of hours on it," Johnnie insisted. "Afterwards, I want you to go over to Northwest 27th Street and do a drive-by. I don't want you to get out if you don't have to, but if we can begin and end this thing tonight we'll all be better off. You know how it is, you never want anyone coming back for revenge in this business."

---

1. balls

"Well, I'm just about done here, I don't like working on a full stomach," Gawain leaned back in his chair, taking a sip of water before going to work on his drink. "Soon as you fellas are ready, let's go out and get it done. I'd like to get some shuteye before dawn and not end up sleeping in all day."

Joe Bieber had called Shanahan earlier that afternoon, and William was more than glad to go out and meet him. He had resisted an impulse to ask Gawain to go out for a drink just to be sociable, perhaps build up a sense of camaraderie for the job ahead. After all, he had fraternized with more than his share of borderline psychos in Iraq and Afghanistan. When he rationalized things, he had to admit that Gawain was not much more different than they were. Post-traumatic stress was a reality, something that past generations had hid in closets like alcoholism, dyslexia, domestic violence and child abuse. Yet he couldn't dismiss the fault entirely. Men like himself and Shaughnessy had endured their own private hells and came through intact if not entirely unscathed.

It was what rankled him more than anything about Shaughnessy. It grew harder and harder to separate the myth from the man as time went by. He and MI6 seemed more like some aloof deities who withdrew from the real world at times, leaving their acolytes to their own devices to sort everything out. When Shaughnessy did not feel like coming down from his cloud, he had one of his flunkies take messages, if in fact Shanahan could reach a live person at all. Perhaps this was the test to see if he was worthy of Downing Street. Maybe they were trying to see if he was all action and no talk. Maybe they wanted to see how he was capable of dealing with their cousins from Langley.

He wasn't quite sure how much leverage Bieber had within the CIA, and Shaughnessy had not been of much help with it. He knew windows open and shut at random and of necessity in such agencies, and that you could be sitting with the Director one day and be unable to get past his assistant's secretary on the next. Bieber was obviously playing on Shanahan's level, but the question was whether whoever was pulling his strings was further along the food chain than Shaughnessy. Of course, that all depended on who Shaughnessy spoke for at any given time.

His mind was filled with such thoughts as he walked the short distance to the Nobu Restaurant on Collins Avenue, one of the best Japanese dining spots in the world. He got a call from Bieber shortly after leaving Gawain's suite, and agreed to meet him for a gourmet lunch. Shanahan enjoyed the spring breeze as he walked along, the exclusive shops, hustle and bustle reminded him as much of New York as anything. He decided he would spend at least one afternoon at the beach before he left, possibly work on his tan and see if he could find an eligible young lady to join him for a meal.

He met Bieber at the white-curtained Nobu Lounge, its dimly-lit interior and traditional Oriental décor giving it a regal atmosphere befitting the socialites and politicians who frequented the establishment. They took a table in the rear corner, and Shanahan idly wondered if Bieber was carrying a pistol in an ankle holster as he was dressed in an expensive ivory Guayabera shirt and mint-green designer slacks. The waitress took their orders and brought a bottle of Chateau D'Esclans rose wine as they sat back and exchanged pleasantries about the weather.

"Well, I can't say we're not all that anxious about what these narco-terrorists have up their sleeves," Bieber finally got around to business. "Still, things seem to be going along rather smoothly. We've got word that Al Qaida has a major shipment coming into North America in the next couple of weeks. We don't know if it's drugs or weapons from Africa, and whether it's coming in from Canada, the Caribbean or Mexico. We do know it's coming, though, and throwing everything we've got up against it. There's going to be a news conference at the White House in a couple of days, and the President's going to issue a general alert. Our biggest concern is inciting a backlash against the Arab-American community. It seems like every time there's a terrorist alert, it waves a red cape in front of every hate group in the country."

"We've got the same thing with the National Front back home," Shanahan sipped his wine as the waitress brought their lobster miso soup. "It's even worse in Ulster. It's the only time the IRA and the UDA sees things eye to eye."

"Actually, we're thinking some of this may work in our favor if push comes to shove," Bieber exhaled. "Homeland Security's been all over this, and one of the worst-case scenarios they're looking at has to do with the currency wars we're having with China and Russia. They're printing money like there's no tomorrow in order to devalue their currency and keep the international market in check. They're also hedging their bets and buying up all the gold they can get in case the nations revert to the gold standard like they're talking about. Our concern is that Al Qaida goes into the counterfeiting business and floods the borderlands with funny money. It'd take a while before the fakes start turning up, but by the time they did, chances are they'd be all over the South. With the recession being what it is, illegals'd be scrambling to take whatever they can and get all they can out of it. It'd be a Secret Service nightmare."

"The Nazis tried something like that against us in World War II, as I recall," Shanahan nodded. "Luckily our people caught onto the plot before they ever got the money in-country. I suppose you'll be counting on the same success."

"We're just hoping we're going to be able to plug up all the gaps when the flood comes," Bieber replied. "If we're going to have to count on all those activist groups jumping on the bandwagon, so be it. We've got the Colombian government leaning hard on the Medellin Cartel, we've got the California State Police all over the MS-13, and the Navy and the Coast Guard's doing some deep-sea fishing off the coasts of Honduras and Cuba. Plus the Mounties are working with Homeland Security to keep watch on our northern borders. As you can imagine, we're not looking forward to see any new players on the field here anytime soon."

"If anything unusual comes up on our radar during the course of our operation, you can be certain your people would be in on it," Shanahan assured him.

"Questions have been coming up as to Emiliano Murra of the Sardinian Mob being here in South Beach on business," Bieber revealed. "We've got an inkling of what's going on but we don't want to pry. Still, if the Sardinian Mob sets up camp Stateside, it's almost like having beaten AIDS and having a new virus turning up."

"You're a damned good poker player, Joe," Shanahan managed a chuckle. "You should have a go at Jack Gawain sometime. I'm not quite sure why our superiors aren't having this conversation."

"Maybe they're letting us work it out while the problem's still at our level."

"I suppose you're somewhat aware that we've got a sting operation of sorts going on," Shanahan lowered his voice. "Murra's bought into a European Mob Council that doesn't exist. We've got EUROPOL involved on the highest levels and even the Sicilian Mafia at the peak of its power couldn't compromise it. Murra's already helped us set up the Medellin Cartel, and we're just about to close the trap on our person of interest. If you want to nail Murra on a technicality and revoke his passport once we're done, we'll turn him over on a silver platter."

"What's the timeframe?" Bieber sipped a spoonful of broth.

"Our person of interest should be at the Magic City Casino for the domino tournament Friday," Shanahan disclosed. "We're going to need Murra to remain at large for at least a week after that. We've got a bigger sting going that may affect the entire infrastructure of the Medellin Cartel. Once we close that trap, I can fairly well assure you that Murra will be all yours."

"Any chance on you telling who the person of interest is?"

"Enrique Chupacabra. You telling me you didn't know that?"

"Oh, I just wanted to hear you say it," Bieber smiled softly. "Didn't you ever wonder why the Mounties weren't all over him after Julio Cruz got whacked? Homeland Security convinced them to let him come back to the States so either the Cubans or the Colombians could spare them the cost of a trial and incarceration. Plus, we knew that if the cartels dropped the ball, then you'd recover the fumble."

"We're pretty sure we will have found closure with the Chupacabra issue after Saturday," Shanahan reassured him. "We may be having our debriefing by the beginning of next week. Unless, of course, you might need—Gawain—for anything."

"Actually, unless something comes up right away, I think we'll be fine. The only other thing we might be interested in is if you came across any good intel on the Cuban Mob. The guy you took Julio Cruz's place on top of the volcano is a hardcase named Johnny Carmona. Carmona escaped prison in Cuba and made his way over here ten years ago. Since then, he's built a reputation on trafficking and murder. Most of the rival gangs were expecting Carmona to make a move on Cruz sooner or later, but somebody did him a favor in Montreal. His gang is stronger than ever now, and they are taking drastic measures to eliminate all their competition in Miami. Obviously this has no bearing on Company business, but since everybody's bunking up together on this one, it'd be all about my country owing yours a big one."

"Here's to cousins," Shanahan raised a glass as their orders of beef kushiyaki arrived.

"Family," Bieber toasted him back.

They could only imagine how severely those bonds would be tested in the days ahead.

It was several hours later when the classic '61 Chevy Impala cruised to a halt in front of a graffiti-scrawled apartment building along NW 27th Street. Oscar Alfonso had dimmed the lights as they passed the corner and switched them off as the car idled at the curb.

"So," Jimmy Sosa slammed a clip into his Uzi as his gunmen did likewise. "Everybody ready? It's the basement apartment, may be backup fire from the second floor. *Cuidado.*"

"All right, then, let me go upstairs before you start shooting. If I fire a round, you fellas start blasting," Jack Gawain suggested.

"Is your funeral," Jimmy shrugged.

Gawain got out of the car and immediately saw three gangsters sitting on the next door staircase take notice. He began a slow trot up the steps of the crack house as they began yelling at him. The front door on the second story opened, and Gawain barged his way in before the corridor flared as a shot was fired. Jimmy and his men popped out of the car and began hosing down the windows of the basement and second floors with automatic fire.

The gangsters on the staircase next door had drawn their pistols and began aiming at the Cubans as Gawain reappeared in the upper doorway. He was a crack marksman, firing calmly and deliberately as he scored head shots on each of the gangsters. He could hear screaming and commotion in the hallway, and he went back and shot three more people before galloping back down the stairs.

"Sons of bitches," Gawain growled. "You got a gas can?"

"Sure," Oscar replied.

"We gotta go!" Jimmy ordered. "*Vamonos!*"

"Pop the trunk!" Gawain insisted. Oscar did so as he gunned the engine, and Gawain unscrewed the cap while sticking a work rag into the spout.

"You smoke?"

Oscar held out his lighter and Gawain ignited the rag, bounding forth and tossing the can in an arc up through the second floor window. He rushed back to the car as the can exploded into flames, a fireball engulfing the entire glass frame. He hopped into the passenger seat as Oscar burned rubber, peeling away from the curb and down the street where they vanished around the corner.

"You my man!" Jimmy reached over the seat and patted Gawain on the shoulder. "You come on a hit wi' me anytime! You my man!"

"Well, now we know you don't smoke," Oscar managed to laugh, eyes darting back and forth between the rear view window and both side windows looking for the police.

Gawain vaguely considered the fact he had not lit up since he left Maghaberry. He remembered smoking in prison because it was one of the things inmates used to make them feel alive. Now that he was breathing free air, there was no desire for anything else.

"This was one of their best spots," Gilberto replied, staring out the window, decompressing from the hit. "Those damn Jamaicans won't be back anytime soon."

"They do, we be ready," Jimmy assured him.

"You got that right," Gawain chortled. He knew that the Cubans had only five more days to enjoy his services, and he would do everything he could to make it a time they would never forget.

Chapter Fifteen

It was Monday morning when Johnny Carmona and his top lieutenants flew out to Andros Island, the largest island in the Bahamas. They drove out to Swain's Cay Lodge in Mangrove Cay, where they were scheduled to meet Retired Colonel Vittorio Apollo. Brunch awaited them at the Reefside Restaurant, where the chef was more than happy to serve their dinner menu to their special guests. Steaks were served up to the six bodyguards, who sat at tables out of earshot of their charges. Carmona and Apollo enjoyed filet mignon and minced lobster as they admired the view of the white sand beaches, the aquamarine water and the palm-studded treeline bordering the resort area.

"I tell you, sometimes when I'm out here I feel like I'm back in Cuba," Johnny Carmona sipped his champagne as he looked out at the glorious West Indian sky. "Miami Beach is a great place, but this feels a little bit closer to home."

"Before Raul Castro got the power, I think your dreams and memories were not quite anchored in reality," Apollo smiled. He was dressed in a tasteful Navajo white designer suit, his curly black hair streaked with gray, his Valentino looks ever so slightly wrinkled in his mid-50's. He had fought in Angola during the 70's where over ten thousand Cubans had fallen in battle, and was one of the last troops to have been withdrawn from Africa in July 1991.He was one of the top operatives for the DI[1], Cuba's equivalent of the KGB, and was a main connection for the Cuban drug cartel in the campaign to undermine the American government.

"I agree, Colonel," Carmona took a bite of his black beans and rice. "I hear you have a French restaurant in Havana these days. You know, I don't know why they can't arrange a visitors' pass for me, just a couple of days or so. You know, we've moved a lot of coke into America and kicked a lot of money back. I should've built up some credit somewhere by now."

"Come on, Carmona," Apollo sipped his orange juice. "We go over this every time we get together, and it's not going to change. How much did you make last year? One hundred and fifty million? You've done a lot for Cuba, but so have I. I own a villa along the beach outside Havana City, I'm able to trade in my BMW for new one every year, and I've invested in a couple of *paladares*[2] over the last couple of years. I will never see a million dollars in my lifetime, and I know I will die and be buried in Cuba. Perhaps that's the tradeoff."

"I can't complain about the money, but sometimes it gets to you when you know you can never go home," Carmona said ruefully.

"Home is where the heart is," Apollo shrugged. "Your heart's in Miami, you know that. I told you, for many years I thought I would never see Cuba again. I spent the best years of my life in Africa, but after all was said and done, I wouldn't have traded it for anything. Neither would you."

"Right now everyone's looking at Ramiro Valdes," Carmona pointed out as he cut into his steak. "When he comes into power, the old regime comes to an end. Maybe then you can put in a good word for me."

"For all its faults, the old regime was always able to stand on its integrity," Apollo replied. "We've stood against the United States for over sixty years, a tiny island against the most powerful nation in the history of the world. We have maintained our reputation as the

---

1. Intelligence Directorate
2. private restaurants

purest Communist country of all time. We stood by our allies in Africa halfway around the planet for nearly twenty years. It is tradition that gives us our prestige, and that tradition is based on truth, liberty and justice. Tell me, Carmona, what happens to our system of justice when we allow a man who has been convicted of multiple murders to go free to walk our streets?"

"Come on, Colonel," Carmona scoffed. "I spent a year in prison before I escaped. Most of the people I did time with were political prisoners. Every one of them had a story to tell about a friend or family member who was killed in prison. Who goes after those guys, the killers? When do those guys ever see justice?"

"I don't make the rules, I enforce them," Apollo was curt. "You know that."

"Okay," Carmona relented. "So where we? I got shipments coming in from Honduras tonight and Wednesday. The big one's coming in Friday. The two small ones are about a half-ton, the routine runs. The big one, though, that one's Al-Qaeda. It's what they're calling a beta test. If we get this through, everybody wins, we turn a new corner, write a new chapter. This one may bring the Americans to their knees. Homeland Security is spending sixty billion this year. If this job gets done, all of a sudden they don't have sixty billion. All of a sudden they might not have shit. I don't know how you get the job on your end, but if I got to lose two out of these three, I'd rather lose a thousand ki's than this one shipment."

"It sounds like you're going to be drawing lots of heat," Apollo mused. "I don't know how much of that heat we can take. Especially if Homeland Security finds out that we helped Al-Qaeda set up an attack in the US. Our people are the best in the world, but we don't have the resources to take on the CIA in a clandestine war. Al-Qaeda tried it and they got reduced to a shambles. All their leaders were killed, even Bin Laden. With the transition of power and the world recession, we can't afford to go up against Homeland Security. We can guarantee security if you take a detour along our coastline, but when you cross international waters, you're on your own."

"With your permission, Colonel, here's the plan," Carmona put a Tablet PC on the table between them. "MS-13 has the shipments going out of the Gulf of Honduras. The first one's headed for the Isla de la Juventud tonight. The next one Wednesday and the big one's Friday. What we want to do is get the first one to Guanabacoa by tomorrow morning and ship it to Key West on Wednesday night. If it goes through without a hitch, we ship the second load from Cardenas on Thursday night to the Keys."

"Sounds like you're moving the big shipment from Santa Clara on Saturday night," Apollo surmised, looking at the map of Central America and the Caribbean on the Tablet.

"That's what we hope the Americans will think if they get wise," Carmona scooped up a forkful of minced lobster. "We're thinking more along the lines of a pincer movement. The big one goes right up the middle to Matanzas, and then we do what the Americans would call a draw play. It comes straight here, to Nassau. From here, we can get it to Jacksonville, and from there either Georgia or the Carolinas. Al-Qaeda's got sleeper units throughout the black communities all along the Southeast coast. Once they take possession, our work is done. If we make this happen for them, they'll start bringing regular shipments of heroin from East Africa to Morocco into Spain. From there it comes straight into the Caribbean. We are going to make big money, Colonel, bigger than we ever dreamed of."

"It sounds like a good plan, Carmona," Apollo agreed. "Excellent, as a matter of fact. The second shipment is a perfect set-up for the third. It might even do well for us to provide extra security for the first shipment to make them think it is the big one. If they are not fooled, they will most assuredly think that the second one is the prize. Intercepting two in a row would make them think it impossible for you to be so foolhardy as to ship from Matanzas instead of Santa Clara. Plus they would not think you would want to run the risk of being hijacked by pirates coming here to Nassau."

"Al-Qaeda's got that covered," Carmona smiled.

"Okay," Apollo decided. "We've got your back from the Honduras across Cuba, and we'll do what we can to distract the Coast Guard to get your shipments to the Keys and Nassau. One thing, though: if whatever Al-Qaeda has planned comes to pass and the Americans discover our connection, it may seriously damage our business relationship. Even the Russians won't be able to protect us if you're bringing a weapon of mass destruction across the Caribbean. That will mean we can no longer protect you."

"We're willing to take that risk, Colonel," Carmona said evenly. "It's a one-time shot, for all the marbles. If this works, we bring the giant to its knees and it will never rise again. Win or lose, we transfer an extra million dollars to your Swiss account this Saturday at midnight."

"I wish you all the best, Carmona," the Colonel raised a glass of champagne to him. "For your sake, and for all of ours."

With that, yet another fateful step towards Operation Blackout had been taken.

After the meeting, Johnny Carmona and his men took a Learjet from Andros back to South Beach where he returned to his mansion in the Estate Section of Palm Beach. He decided to rest until the evening when they would be heading out to the South Beach casino that evening. He was about ready to crash out when his top bodyguard, Ed Travieso, walked into the master bedroom with a cell phone.

"It's Sosa, there's a problem."

"Frickin' *maricon*," Carmona growled, beckoning Travieso. "*Damelo.*"

"Johnny, it's Johnnie," Sosa spoke up. "We took care of that problem last night, but I think we've got a bigger one now."

"Bigger problem? Like what?" Carmona had stripped down to his leopard-spotted briefs, padding across the shag-layered rug to the enormous sliding glass door leading to the marbled balcony overlooking the beach.

"The word on the street is that the Haitians and the Jamaicans are joining forces against us," Johnny informed him. "The Jamaicans convinced the Haitians that we're going to move against them next. They sent word that if they catch any of our people anywhere near 27th Street they're declaring war."

"So pull it back to 20th Street until the heat dies down," Carmona lit a cigarette. "We'll make the peace with the Haitians, and then we'll move on the Jamaicans again in a week to show them who's boss. If we pull back all the way to 20th Street, they'll move in heavy, they'll think they'll be picking up new customers and expanding their operations. They'll never know what hit them."

"20th Street? We can't do that!" Sosa was adamant. "We have five crack houses in that area, that's twenty thousand dollars a week, not counting the dealers we'll lose if they go in with the Jamaicans. Besides, if they cut the Haitians in, we end up going to war anyway, plus we have to take back all the lost territory. We have to win this fight now, or we'll end up having to fight twice as hard to get back what we'll lose."

"C'mon, Sosa, you always love a good fight, what're you, getting soft on me?" Carmona stepped behind the small bar to take a can of V8 from the fridge.

"Have you turned on the TV lately?" he insisted. "The media's all over this. You know how this is going to happen. The blacks'll lay low while the police and the sheriff's office step all over us, and when we're catching our breath they'll attack."

"Okay, lemme check this shit out and I'll call you back."

Carmona switched on his 70" large screen plasma TV across from his enormous California King Size bed and sat down to watch a live broadcast from WPLG Local 10 News where reporters were providing undated information on the Sosas' attack on the Jamaicans' crack house.

"Miami Beach Police Department officials are still gathering evidence this afternoon about a brutal massacre on Northwest 27th Street last night that left fifteen people dead and ten people injured, including a mother and two children," a lovely newscaster reported in front of a burned-out tenement. "This building you see behind me was the scene of a shootout between rival crack gangs during which a gas can was thrown through a second-story window. The can exploded and left the building in flames as terrified residents attempted to escape. The basement apartment was suspected of being used by local crack dealers who were attacked in a drive-by shooting by a rival gang. The dealers were reportedly part of a Jamaican posse competing for territory in the Liberty City district, which has one of the highest crimes rates in Miami. The perpetrators are suspected by MBPD to be connected to the Cuban drug cartel, whose control over Liberty City has been challenged by rival gangs as of late. This was a scene of chaos up until the wee hours of the morning as the Fire Department fought to take control of the blaze and rescue residents trapped in the building. In an even more senseless turn of events, there were rumors that firefighters and rescuers came under small arms fire as drug dealers were working desperately to salvage narcotics and weapons at the rear of the building. The community is outraged that not only such a ruthless attack could have been carried out in an urban neighborhood, but that dealers would turn their weapons on those already risking their lives to save others."

"The MBPD is prepared to take drastic measures to crack down on those who are attempting to turn our city into a war zone," the news team cut to a recorded statement by the Chief of Police. "We are working closely with the Palm Beach County Sheriff's Office and the DEA to coordinate efforts in breaking the stranglehold of crack dealers in the Liberty City district. The use of automatic weapons and incendiary objects in a residential area clearly demonstrates the total disregard for human life displayed by these perpetrators. Opening fire on city workers putting their lives on the line to rescue citizens is a despicable act we will not tolerate. We intend to pinpoint each and every crack house in Liberty City, we will obtain search warrants in order to invade these hideouts, and we will arrest and prosecute these people to the fullest extent of the law. Landlords who willingly and knowingly rent their properties to these people will be brought up on State and Federal charges. Those who possess automatic weapons and sell narcotics will also be arrested in State and Federal charges and face maximum prison sentences. Our message to these gangsters is simple: we are taking off the kid gloves, get out of this business before it's too late."

Carmona watched as ABC News switched to a special broadcast from the White House where the US Attorney General was holding a press conference.

"We have recently gotten reports of rumors that elements of Al-Qaeda have been discussing plans to stage an attack on American soil within the next couple of weeks," she said on the national telecast. "We are placing the Southern US coastal areas on a state of yellow alert as Homeland Security focuses its efforts on investigating these reports. Our sources indicate that Al-Qaeda is planning to extend its campaign of narco-terrorism across American borders, and we are taking preventive measures to ensure that this will not occur. While we are not trying to create an atmosphere of panic, we ask that citizens remain alert while in public and avoid any areas of suspicious or unusual activity. The State Department is holding discussions with the governments of Honduras and Colombia in taking measures to neutralize threats from the smuggling networks along our shores. The White House will be discussing options in negotiating the issue with Cuba and Venezuela within the next twenty-four hours. Once again, this yellow alert is cautioning all Americans as to potential threats to our security, but rest assured that we are taking strenuous measures to resolve these issues and will be notifying the media as to further developments."

"Hello. Johnnie."

"Carmona. Did you see the TV?"

"That's fuckin' hot, man. That's hot. What the fuck happened? Who went out on the hit?"

"Jimmy went with Oscar, Gilberto and the new guy, Jack Gain."

"The new guy," Carmona's mind was racing since he saw the broadcasts. "Jack Gain. I thought you were gonna check him out."

"I did," Johnnie insisted. "He's the one who threw the gas can. There were three gangsters sitting on the stoop next door when the shooting started, and they started shooting at our guys. Jack shot them, and he got another guy who was coming at our guys from the second floor. There were more guys in the second floor apartment, that's why he threw the can. He's good, Carmona, very good."

"Okay, here's what's gonna go down," Carmona insisted. "We go on the defensive. You don't do anything unless the Jamaicans or the Haitians come at us. Plus, I wanna meet this guy. I got some serious shit coming down between tonight and Saturday, but I wanna meet this guy Sunday. You got to keep him on the chain unless anything hits the fan, and even then you make sure Jimmy takes him out on a short leash. Very short. It sounds like this guy has some kind of military training. He's doing things out there that no street guy would dream of. You understand me, Johnnie?"

"*Seguro que si, mi Carmona.*"

"Lay low, stay on the defensive, keep the new guy on a leash. And I meet him Sunday."

"Certainly, *mi Carmona.*"

Johnny Carmona switched off the cell phone, staring out the frame window and wondered if his organization was going to be able to withstand the repercussions. He wondered if this risk was worth the cost.

And he wondered who the hell was Jack Gain.

Chapter Sixteen

Ozzy Barbosa left the Sam Gibbons Federal Courthouse on North Florida Avenue in Tampa shortly after noon that Wednesday after a grueling session with the DEA. He had been called in for an interview for the second time in as many weeks, and this time he felt as if he had narrowly escaped arrest. Even more disconcerting was the thought that they might have let him remain on the field as bait for bigger game.

Barbosa had been a tall, lanky kid, considered a bookworm throughout his school years in the Tampa Bay area. He graduated Alonso High School on Montague Street and got a part-time job as a computer repair tech in a local repair shop. There he made friends with other techs who enjoyed smoking marijuana as much as he did. They showed him how to double his income by selling weed, and his income nearly quadrupled when one of his friends devised a lucrative scheme. They began taking orders from students in upper-class neighborhoods, placing ounce bags inside PC's when they returned them to homes after servicing. The disposable income allowed Ozzy to realize a lifelong dream in purchasing a used yacht. He got to the point where he and his friends were buying serious weight, and eventually they made connections with a mid-level dealer in the Cuban Mob.

Ozzy was offered $2,000 to travel forty-five miles from Key West where an anchored float was left with ten hundred-pound waterproofed boxes. His instructions were to tow the float twenty miles before loading the boxes onto the yacht. He then continued on to a designated spot ten miles from shore where he was instructed to dump the boxes overboard. He was strictly ordered never to attempt to open the boxes. If intercepted by the Coast Guard, he was to say that he attempted to tow the float but decided to bring the boxes aboard to avoid losing them. He would claim to be on a scavenger hunt in hopes of finding items of value offshore. If caught dumping the boxes, he would claim he had been paid to dispose of them as waste materials.

Last week he returned to port at the Key West Yacht Club and was intercepted by a MSST[1] Coast Guard vessel. He was taken into custody and transported him by helicopter to District 7 headquarters at the Brickell Plaza Federal Building in Miami. It was there that he was turned over to Drug Enforcement Agency officials who questioned him for hours before releasing him. He was seen dumping boxes overboard from his yacht via telescopic surveillance by the MSST, but stuck by his story that he had been paid money by a trucker to dump what was said to be documents containing protected health information. He insisted that he did what he was told and never attempted to open the boxes. The DEA agents finally let him go but warned him that he might be contacted again in the very near future.

He had been requested to meet with agents for a follow-up interview, arriving at the Federal Courthouse at 10 AM. He was taken to a conference room by three DEA agents who informed him that they had come across a waterproof box similar to one that Ozzy had described in his initial interview.

"Did you see the news reports about the shark attack on that scuba diver along Key West the other day?" one of the agents asked.

"Yeah, it was all over TV," Ozzy wiped off his gold-rimmed glasses, sweat beading his brow beneath his close-cropped blond hair. "I didn't have anything to do with it. My yacht hasn't left the dock since you brought me in the last time."

---

1. Maritime Safety and Security Team

"The Coast Guard just managed to rescue the diver shortly before dawn," a second agent disclosed. "The man spoke almost no English. They saved his life even though he lost a leg. He had no explanation as to why he was scuba-diving in those waters that early in the morning other than that he wanted to join the Navy and try out for the SEALs."

"Well, that's kinda crazy to me, but you know how it is," Ozzy took a sip of the bottled water he had been provided. He sat at a narrow wooden table, one agent seated across from him while the other two stood in opposite corners. "People watch movies, they dream dreams, they try turning fantasy into reality."

"Like a computer repair guy from Tampa owning his own boat and having membership at the Key West Yacht Club?" the third agent growled.

"Hey, dude, we went over this," Ozzy insisted. "I got some big money clientele. Maybe you can accuse me of charging different rates for different people, but I pay my taxes and I have an accountant who keeps my financial records. I got nothing to hide."

"The Coast Guard sent their own divers down to take a look around the area where the scuba guy got attacked," the first agent stared across the table at him. "We found one of those boxes just like the ones you said you dumped overboard. What do you think we found?"

"Well, if it was exactly like the one you said I dumped, I suppose it was a bunch of soggy PHI docs," Barbosa shrugged.

"The box was waterproofed," the second agent retorted. "It turned out the Coast Guard retrieved forty ki's of cocaine."

"Dude, anyone who watches TV also knows that smugglers dump all kinds of containers off-shore," Ozzy put his glasses back on. "There's also all kinds of garbage, including industrial waste, confidential documents, defective merchandise and hazardous medical waste. I don't know what you're trying to hang on me, but ten boxes of paper doesn't equal one box of coke."

The agents left the room at what Ozzy perceived at fifteen minute intervals, browbeating him at random over how he made his money at Wizard Computer Service, how he joined the Yacht Club and how many other jobs he had taken dumping trash into the harbor. Eventually they turned him loose, once again reminding him that he could be called in for a follow-up interview at any time.

As he made his way towards the nearby parking lot, a black kid wearing a Tampa Bay Lightning hockey jersey came up to him.

"Hey, man, I got a home boy wanna talk to you," the kid peered over his sunglasses at Ozzy. "He sitting on that park bench in front of that Lincoln, it only take a minute."

Ozzy was reluctant but decided it would be best to comply lest they try to follow him on the highway. He heard of the Lightning Boys operating out of Tampa and was not looking forward to have them getting pissed off at him.

"Name's Choker. I'm with the Lightning posse in Hillsborough," the leader, wearing a Lightning cap and jersey, the sun glinting off his gold chains and rings. "Our home boys in Key West found out your boat got taken down by the Coast Guard. We checked your registration and found out you was from Tampa. We also found out you getting heat from the DEA. Everything going okay?"

"They got me mixed up with somebody else, homes," Ozzy replied. "They caught me dumping some shit off my boat and got all over my case for nothing."

"Check it out, man," the gangster handed him a business card. "Whatever you doing, it's gonna stop for a while because they're gonna be checking your boat, just like if they were scoping out your plates on the street. They can't be watching you forever, though. When you feel like making some real money, you call this number."

"Dude, I ain't gonna be doing shit after this," Ozzy insisted. "This shit's too heavy for me to carry around, you know what I'm sayin'?"

"Man, nobody gets out," Choker grinned at him with gold-capped teeth. "Whatchoo gonna do, give up your Yacht Club privileges? Move to a less expensive pad, start going to Mc Donald's for dinner? Look, you can keep your boat at the club, I'll put you on a Sunrise 45. We ship from Port Antonio in Jamaica to Great Inagua in the Bahamas. That shit goes straight to Andros Island, where we make the drop for you off Miami Beach. Our product comes in sealed metal containers, there's no way they can prove you know what you're dumping. The going rate's two grand per load, we'll pay you two and a half to work with us."

"I'm not sure I'm who you're looking for," Ozzy was hesitant.

"Naw, man," Choker chuckled. "You got busted by the Coast Guard, had two interviews with the DEA and you still walking around outside. You exactly who I'm looking for."

"Okay, Choker," Ozzy shook hands. "I'll call you in a couple of weeks when the heat dies down. "I'd like to come out and look at that Sunrise and we'll go from there."

"You got it, homes," he touched knuckles with Ozzy before the men parted ways.

Ozzy retrieved his BMW from the parking lot and headed out en route to Highway 92. As an afterthought, he pulled into a parking lot and auto-dialed a number.

"*Diga*," a voice replied.

"It's Ozzy for Johnny."

"Hey, man," there was a delay before Johnny Carmona got on the phone. "Whuzup?"

"It's hot down here," Ozzy replied. "The interview went okay, but I got approached by a Lightning Boy outside the courthouse. Guy named Choker."

"What the fuck did he want?"

"He gave me his number, wants me to call in a couple of weeks. He wants to hook me up with a luxury yacht to make runs from Andros to Miami."

"That's a Jamaican run," Carmona growled. "Fuck. They're coming at us from all sides. Look, you tear up that business card, and I'll fly you up to see me next week. That black piece of shit comes around looking for you, you let me know, I'll take care of him."

"Okay, Johnny, you da man."

"You're *my* man," Johnny replied. "Call me Monday."

After Carmona clicked off, he auto-dialed another number.

"Hello."

"Sosa. Carmona. What's going on with the Jamaicans?"

"They're taking baby steps in our direction," Johnnie replied. "Our people have seen some of their dealers crossing the streets. Mostly hustling the rich kids driving down from South Beach. I told our people to keep an eye out, but no confrontation."

"Okay, there's a change in plans," Carmona ordered. "You send Jimmy and a couple of hitters back down to Jamaican territory. We're gonna drive those motherfuckers right back across the county line back to Miramar, you got it?"

"Okay, Carmona, I'm on it," Johnnie replied before Carmona clicked out.

It was time for another call to Jack Gain.

Jack Gawain, like many others, was fascinated by the news accounts of the Miami drug wars and the Homeland Security yellow alert. He was wondering what effect one event was having on the other but spent little time dwelling on it. He was more concerned with the situation facing him this evening and how things were going down in Dade County. Johnny Sosa had called him and requested his presence at the meeting place before midnight. He told him he would be there, and strongly suspected there would be more gunplay on the agenda.

He took the ride out to Liberty City shortly after 11 PM and parked in the usual place behind the low riders in front of the tenement. He shook hands with Oscar Alfonso and Gilberto Echezabal out front, who escorted him inside as two gunmen stood guard out front.

"Hello, Jack," Johnnie was pleasant as Gawain shoot hands with the Sosa Brothers. He took a seat at the table as Sosa poured him a drink. "It looks like things are heating up with the Jamaicans. They want us to do another drive-by at one of their main crack houses."

"Well, y'know that last job got plastered all over the telly," Gawain leaned back in the rickety chair. "Most of the time the peelers maintain high visibility after such a thing to keep up appearances. It may be a whole lot harder to get out than to get in."

"We're going to try a little redirection before you make your move," Johnnie replied. "We're going to pull off another firebombing on Northwest 28th at one of their crack houses. While the police respond, you'll be making your move on Southwest 7th Street."

"Their base of operations is in the Kendall district, a traditionally Jamaican neighborhood," Oscar explained. Gawain was beginning to surmise that Alfonso was one of the brains behind this operation. "Since they began broadening their network, they've been making moves around Little Havana near the Airport out by the Blue Lagoon area. They've had their people bringing coke in on private flights and distributing it around the Lagoon and Lake Joanne. They're picking up more and more business from the yuppies at the Granada Golf Course in Coral Gables, and now they've got a couple of places on West Flagler Street, which had always been the traditional border line between us."

"That's why we needed to hit them when they showed up on the Northwest side," Johnny agreed. "They're trying to box us in, and they've made a deal with the Haitians to drive a wedge into our territory in Liberty City. If we can close them down on Southwest 7th, most likely they'll pull back to Kendall and quit screwing around near Little Havana. It's going to be the only way to avoid a gang war.'

"All right," Gawain relented. "I'll tell ye, if I do this, I'll want to lay low for the next couple of days after this. I didn't come out here to get pinched. D'ye have a couple of grenades I can use?"

"Sure do," Johnnie replied, giving orders to Gilberto in Spanish. Echezabal went through the ragged curtain into the bedroom, returning with a small sack containing three MK3A2 concussion grenades.

"Aw reet," Gawain put a grenade into each jacket pocket of his suit, and one in his right trouser pocket. "This should be a blast."

He accompanied Jimmy and the others to the Thunderbird outside, and they took off in the direction of Southeast 7th Street. Gilberto cruised down 8th Street so that they could enjoy the scenery which included cigar shops and restaurants situated alongside traditional bungalow architecture and historical buildings.

"You see," Oscar pointed out, "this is what we are fighting for. Miami is not all about exclusive resorts, business complexes and crack neighborhoods. This is the heart and soul of Miami, this is Little Havana. This is our own little slice of Cuba. Those Jamaicans will never be a part of this, and if they choose, they will die trying."

Gawain searched about, trying to figure out a game plan. He was getting more familiar with the area now, and was thinking of the best escape routes once the deed was done. They could probably hang a right on 27th Avenue and get lost in traffic en route to the Dolphin Expressway and the I-95.

"Aye, fella," Gawain pointed out the window as they turned north towards 7th Street. "Let's drive by and take a look at the target, then head down by 27th. I want to make sure we can get out of this in one piece."

"I don't normally like to have them see the car on the street twice, especially one as conspicuous as this," Gilberto was hesitant.

"Well, you're the one who brings it along," Gawain retorted. "You oughtta swipe one off the road sometime, it's the best way."

"Johnnie likes them to know who did the work," Jimmy informed him.

"When he's looking at twenty years on a murder conspiracy, he might not," Gawain replied wryly.

They drove down the residential street, appearing like most others with the tenement buildings sagging on each side of the gloomy street. Crackheads and drunks shuffled up and down the sidewalks, being hustled by whores trying to pick up an extra couple of bucks for their next score. One of the streetlights were flickering, about to go out which suited Gawain fine. At his behest, they circled the block and headed to 27th Street where Gawain urged him to stop at a corner gas station.

A gasoline delivery driver had pulled up to the station and routinely set out the danger signs as he prepared to unlock the gasoline pipelines to the underground tank. He was doing some paperwork as a man jumped up on the step leading to the passenger window across from him.

"You making your delivery?"

"Yeah, what's up?"

"Move over, mate, I need you to take the truck down the street."

"Are you out of your mind?' the man gasped as Jack Gawain trained a Glock on him, yanking open the door and sliding in alongside him. "This is a gasoline truck, you'll blow us to hell if that thing goes off!"

"No, but this might," Gawain pulled open his jacket so the driver could see the grenade in his pocket. "Cut the bullshite, let's move."

"Don't you see that cop car there?" the driver nodded towards the police vehicle parked outside the gas station. "He's gonna see I took off, he's gonna call it in!"

"Well, if he follows us, he'll be the one who gets blown to hell," Gawain replied. "You see that dark blue low rider there? Go ahead and follow it, we're going right on 7th, just before Beacom. You stop when I tell you."

"Look, buddy, I got a wife and kids," the driver pleaded.

"Good," Gawain replied. "Y'can tell 'em all about your adventure if you do as yer told."

The low rider turned on 7th and led the giant truck down the street, barely making it past the beat-up cars parked along both curbs. The T-Bird idled on the corner, switching on its emergency lights.

"Okay, boyo," Gawain ordered, "you get behind that piece of shite in front of that staircase where those kids are sitting, and push it up as far as y'can. You then back up, and put this thing on the sidewalk in front of the house as best y'can. Got it?"

"Mister, this thing's full of gasoline!" the driver whined.

"Well, then, ye'd best do as I say and run when I tell ye."

The crackheads and gangbangers watched in alarm as the gasoline truck pulled up behind the Chevy Spectrum at the curb and slowly began pushing it forward until it was in front of the building next door.

"Hey, man, what the fuck you doing?" a gangster got up, pulling back his button-down shirt to show the revolver tucked in his waistline. "You wanna die?"

"Don't be stupid, homes," a second gangster yelled. "That's a gasoline truck!"

"That shit empty!" the first kid yelled back. "It gotta be empty!"

The kids, six in all, were standing speechless as the truck backed up, then rolled onto the curb so that only its passenger side tires remained on the curb.

"All right, boyo, you haul your arse down the street. I'll count to ten," Gawain told the driver. He flung open the door, leaped from the vehicle and ran as fast as he could. The gangsters, sensing something was amiss, began racing up the street in the other direction where the T-Bird was parked on the corner. Gawain hopped out of the truck and pulled a grenade from his pocket. He pulled the pin and tossed it into the truck, slipping his Glock out of his waistline and carrying it at his side as he walked up the corner.

There was a great roar, then a secondary explosion as the 18-wheeler, carrying 9,000 gallons of gasoline, erupted into flames. The windows on all three floors of the crack house shattered as torrents of fire spilled over the brick façade. The gangsters inside and outside the T-Bird watched in awe as Gawain miraculously walked from amidst the flames, appearing as a gunman from Hell. Instead of drawing on the dark figure, they ran for their lives down Beacom Boulevard.

"Holy shit, Jack," Oscar stared at the spectacle as nearby residents evacuated the homes adjacent to the flaming crack house. "Holy shit!"

"You my man, Jack," Jimmy said gleefully, patting Gawain on the shoulder as the low rider squealed past the fleeing gangsters on Beacom, making a left on SW 25th and another left on SW 6th. They next hung a right on SW 27th and sped towards the Expressway. They watched as the patrol car parked at the gas station switched on its lights and pulled out of the service area, then breathed a collective sigh of relief as it hit the siren and proceeded towards the vicinity of the explosion.

"Well, I certainly hope that truck driver stuck around," Gawain eased back in his seat.

"Why's that?" Gilberto asked.

"He was carrying on about his wife and kid awaiting," Gawain replied airily. "I'm sure if the news trucks came around looking for an eyewitness, they could've got to see him on the telly."

"You a crazy sombitch," Jimmy cackled as the others roared with laughter.

Gawain considered the fact that William Shanahan would have readily agreed.

Chapter Seventeen

Spy Wednesday

Three days before the tournament, William Shanahan woke up at sunrise to take an early-morning swim after going for a run along the SoBe boardwalk. He saw the special news bulletin about the gasoline truck explosion just hours earlier and remembered his room shuddering sometime after midnight. He found it bewildering how such an affluent area as South Beach could be so close to violent areas such as Little Havana and Liberty City. Yet he considered how visitors to Belfast felt as they shopped downtown, blissfully unaware of the gang warfare between the IRA splinter groups and Protestant militants. Money could provide a buffer, he realized, but never a shield.

He had two important meetings on this day, one with Joe Bieber and afterward with Emiliano Murra. He knew that Bieber and the CIA were anxious over Homeland Security's yellow alert, especially after the media questioned whether the gang violence in the vicinity of Liberty City was actually acts of sabotage. He also knew that they were concerned over the increase of smuggling activity along the Keys, realizing that a WMD might very well have already found its way in-country. What he wasn't sure of was how Bieber thought Shanahan was going to be able to help. All they were doing was spinning their wheels and waiting for the tournament, wondering whether or not there might be another opportunity to compromise Operation Blackout in the meantime.

He had gotten a call from Shaughnessy late last night, advising him that the next shipment of bullion was being prepared for delivery to Montreal and that Murra should be placed on stand-by. He immediately contacted Amschel Bauer in Montreal, who in turn notified the Medellin Cartel that the next deal was ready to be made. It was now up to Shanahan to give Murra the go-ahead, and time for Murra to make the deal happen.

It was Bieber's concerns about the Sardinian Mob that had Shanahan second-guessing the Firm. It was entirely true that they may well have exposed the USA to a new criminal virus. The Sardinians had now established a new trade network from Belfast to Montreal, and from Montreal to Colombia. Their strategy and tactics were entirely unknown to MI6 or the CIA, and removing Murra from the game would not necessarily eliminate the threat.

He always felt at peace when near the water, as if it renewed his spiritual strength. It recharged his feelings and emotions, preparing him for the discourses ahead with Bieber and Murra. What he had to avoid was the desire to establish a bond with either man, both of whom he had respected as individuals. He knew that one of his flaws, his weaknesses, was his penchant to bring out the best in others. He would be making a fatal error in helping either man improve his organization's position, the Sardinian Mob or the CIA's, for that matter. Yet he had to avoid retreating too deeply into himself, not using his strict physical regimen as a way to maintain a distance from others. Perhaps he needed to spend a night carousing with one of the men. Perhaps he should take a chance and go drinking with Gawain.

That thought sobered him so that he was entirely focused when he called Bieber before Murra. He would meet Bieber for lunch at noon and Murra at brunch around three. It gave him plenty of time to get back to the room, have breakfast and possibly a short nap before setting out on the afternoon agenda.

It was right about that time when a luxury yacht dropped anchor along the southern coast of the Isla de la Juventud, having stopped short of the swamplands of the Cienaga de Lanier. The four-man crew climbed down from the yacht and unfastened a pontoon tied to the stern, towing it onto the white sand beach. They watched impassively as two Russian-made Volgodonsk gunships veered around a nearby reef and headed straight towards them.

"Good morning, my friends," the Honduran leader of the MS-13 crew greeted the Cuban Navy riflemen as they bounded into the surf. "Smooth sailing over here. I hope your people find their end of the journey just as peaceful."

"Is everything intact? Nothing missing?" Colonel Vittorio Apollo demanded, both he and the sailors dressed in camouflage fatigues. He detested having to deal with such vermin as the MS-13, but they virtually controlled the smuggling industry and could not be avoided in accepting transports from Colombia. He was almost wishing a box was missing so he could have the sailors cut them down like cordwood.

"Ten boxes, vacuum sealed and plastic wrapped," the leader assured him. "Plus the sealed metal container. As I said, there was no sign of the Americans anywhere. Smooth sailing."

"Good," Apollo growled, ordering the sailors to haul the pontoon over to one of the gunboats. "It would be most unfortunate if the Yankees observed your boat entering and leaving our territorial waters. We would have little choice but to seize your vessel or sink you so that the Americans don't get the wrong idea."

"Well, brother," the leader said nervously, "hopefully the relations between your country and ours will improve over the months ahead. You know, even with Chavez' passing, the Communist nations in our hemisphere grow stronger and stronger. The Venezuelans are more firmly resolved to stand up against American imperialism. Tony Ramos, along with so many other Hondurans, believes that Communism is the way of the future for our people. One day soon this charade will end, and Hondurans and Cubans will unite in our fight for freedom."

"You have thirty minutes to evacuate the area," Apollo lit a cigar, "or you will be in violation of our sovereignty."

"Say—uh—can I have one of those?" the Honduran smiled weakly as his men hastily made their way back towards the yacht.

"You are smugglers," Apollo blew smoke at him. "I'm sure you have more than enough."

"If the Beard was still in power, people like those would be rotting in prison," a Navy lieutenant came over as his men completed fastening the pontoon to the gunboat. "One has to wonder whether the Revolution can endure in times such as these."

"Great movements endure as its champions adapt and overcome," the Colonel's eyes narrowed as the Hondurans began lifting their anchor. "Castro was a visionary. He saw that the only way America could be defeated was to allow its decadence and greed take its effect, like a terminal cancer. It eats up its victims over time. When he exiled the criminals back in the 80's, they became the Marielitos that turned Florida into a snake pit. Although he might not have approved, we are now helping these gangsters pump narcotics into the veins of America. I am old school, Lieutenant. It makes me sick to be doing business with that Honduran scum. It turns my stomach to have to break bread with a thief and a murderer like Johnny Carmona. He asks me if there is ever going to be a chance for a pardon. I tell you this: if he is pardoned, I will personally guarantee that he is arrested and killed in prison before he sets one foot on Cuban soil as a free man."

"I agree, Colonel," the lieutenant concurred. "I watch the television and I see how the criminals are destroying Miami as we speak. Drugs and violence are spreading like a plague throughout their cities. Blessed will be the day when our Cuban brothers and sisters will be boarding ships and planes to return to their homeland to escape the lawlessness."

"It will never happen," Apollo said as he turned back and headed for the gunship. "It is like a house dog who has been allowed to run free across the fields. Once he has lost his domesticity, he can never come home again. He will shit and piss all over your house, he will swipe food from your table, he will snarl and bite when corrected. Even the Christians agree with us in saying that true peace and security is found in law and order. Unlimited freedom, in many cases for most people, eventually leads to anarchy and chaos. For the Marielitos—just like the Hondurans—freedom is a license to steal, a license to kill. America is learning this, and the final lessons will come to them far too late."

The Cubans returned to the gunships and languidly set off in the direction of the Honduran yacht, hoping that the smugglers would linger in their waters just a second too long.

They also wondered just what it was inside the large sealed canister.

Hours later and miles away, William Shanahan arrived for lunch at Joe's Stone Crab on Washington Avenue. The lines of customers waiting to be seated narrowed their eyes as Shanahan was escorted to a VIP table where Joe Bieber awaited. Bieber had flashed his CIA credentials and ordered a virtual smorgasbord of house specialties, including their hash browns, creamed spinach and seafood bisque. The appetizers primed their upscale clientele for their stone crab claws, which they claimed to have first discovered as a delicacy back in 1913.

Shanahan admired the buttercup yellow shading within the high-ceilinged restaurant, accentuated by chain-anchored chandeliers and contemporary paintings hanging above the elegantly-furnished dining area. He shook hands with Joe and took a seat, the waitress pouring him glasses of champagne and orange juice as Bieber encouraged him to try the bisque.

"I trust you saw the newscasts this morning," Bieber sipped his orange juice. Shanahan had taken a page from Joe's book, wearing a tasteful short-sleeve designer shirt in carrying his Glock in an ankle holster beneath his baggy-legged pants. "Homeland Security's starting to have a real problem with this. *Good Morning America* is starting to call it the dawn of narco-terrorism in the USA."

"Well, you know how manipulative the media can be," Shanahan greatly enjoyed the bisque, next sampling the creamed spinach with a piece of garlic toast. "If they can provoke enough of a public backlash, they might force the hand of local officials. Even though the violence has been limited to gang against gang, it simply won't do for gangsters to be blowing up gas trucks in residential areas on a regular basis."

"Right now, they've got the MBPD and the Sheriff's Department coming down on the crack houses like flies on crud," Bieber disclosed. "Arrests are being made and the streets are being cleared. The biggest problem they have is the danger of the violence affecting the tourist trade. With the economy being in the state it's in, Miami can't afford vacationers staying away because of the gang activity. This is the whole problem we're dealing with, the violence affecting our way of life. In a way the media's right: this is the essence of narco-terrorism."

"Aye, but you Yanks are known for your resiliency," Shanahan emphasized. "America's always come out on top because of its endurance. Those drug dealers have been in Liberty City for a long time, I researched it on the Internet. It hasn't stopped people from coming out here to South Beach before and it won't stop them now. Just as you say, they're going to make those streets too hot for those dealers after this. I've seen it in Belfast time and again. When the IRA and the UDA got too big for their britches, the police and the Army moved in and cut them down to size. There's a big difference between career criminals and suicide bombers. These people do not want to die. They're in it for money, and you can't enjoy your money when you're six feet under."

"This is what we have to ensure, that the suicide bombers never make it over here," Bieber nodded. "And we want to be sure that the Sardinians won't be the ones to help them get here."

"Is this what this is about," Shanahan chuckled. "You could've saved your Government a lot of money on this lunch. Rest assured, Joe, the Firm is accelerating our time table on this operation. They're planning to set Murra up a lot quicker than I thought. As a matter of fact, I'm scheduled to meet him later this afternoon."

"Why not bring me along?"

"You might call that a no-can-do," Shanahan was curt. "We have to keep the blinders on to make the trick work. We don't know the range or depth of his resources. His Mob is as opaque as we are making ourselves seem to be. Right now the only people he's met from our 'organization' is me and our 'smuggling crew' in Belfast. I'm kind of hard to find anywhere in the world, and I'm sure the 'smugglers' have been just as well-picked."

"Okay," Bieber relented. "So you say you'll be pretty close to a wrap by the weekend."

"Not entirely. I can fairly well guarantee that Mr. Ricky Chew is going to be in a predicament, though. I can also tell you that Mr. Murra and his people may also be in for the surprise of their lives."

"The problem on my end is that our operatives and informants in Europe and the Middle East are getting lots of buzz about impending activity. Word around the campfire is that something's up. The State Department wouldn't be issuing a yellow alert over a routine matter. William, we're very concerned about the possibility of another 9/11. Obviously, if it was being seen as an imminent threat, it would be far past you and me sitting here in a restaurant. I'm just hoping that you and I are doing everything on our level to keep it this way."

"Three days more, Joe," Shanahan reassured him. "Just three more days. Everything will be revealed to you and you'll find the results to be most pleasing."

Deep down, he was secretly hoping that this was not going to turn into a race against time.

A few hours later, a heavily-guarded Cuban Army truck roared across a dirt road outside the coastal city of Cardenas. Horse-drawn carriages were still a major means of travel in the quaint little town. It was known as the Banner City where Fidel Castro hoisted his first flag of independence during the Cuban Revolution. Many of the military fortresses of the 19th century still remained, now manned by soldiers of the 21st century Communist regime.

Colonel Vittorio Apollo had accompanied the military detachment across country to reach their destination. The Navy crew had brought the pontoon to a nearby port where it was unloaded and transported to an unmarked military truck for the journey to Cardenas. Upon arrival, the cargo was loaded onto separate pontoons to be shipped in different directions. Apollo repented of the fact that Cuban military personnel would be delivering these shipments to criminals. He reconciled himself with the knowledge that the ones who would pay the price would be the Americans.

He watched as each pontoon was fastened to separate gunships and towed away as tropical birds shrieked overhead from the jungle foliage. One gunship headed due north where its crew would dock the pontoon at a barge positioned five kilometers inside the Cuban international border. The second gunship was on its way westward to Matanzas. That vessel was towing the pontoon containing the mysterious container.

The Colonel had a sinking feeling about the container, but his was not to question. The DI had decided that the best course of action was to aid and abet the smugglers in transporting their goods to America as long as they understood that none of their products could ever make their way inland to Cuba. Substance abuse was rampant among a people who believed economic prosperity had become an impossible dream. Yet the government was fairly certain that the drugs were coming from the West Indies, and the sunken ships at the bottom of the harbor along with the dealers rotting in prison were proof of the fact.

There was something else going on with the container. Apollo strongly suspected that this was not an ordinary transport, and he sensed Al Qaeda was at the bottom of it. It was quite possible that a terrorist attack might well send America to the brink of chaos, but if it backfired, suspicion of Cuban involvement could have drastic repercussions. The Colonel turned his back on the dilemma as he trudged back through the tree line towards the waiting trucks. He would wash his hands of the disaster that loomed ahead. He knew that, like the smugglers, he was just a player in a game that was far beyond his control.

A couple of hours earlier, William Shanahan had finished his meeting with Joe Bieber and went ahead to meet Emiliano Murra for supper. He chided himself for indulging in all the rich food but resolved to make up for it on the beach tomorrow morning. They met at Osterio del Teatro, one of the area's classiest Italian restaurants, not far from Joe's Stone Crab on Washington. Shanahan gave himself enough time to take a brisk walk around two city blocks before returning to meet Murra.

The elegant, dimly-lit restaurant was decorated in soft pastels and Mediterranean furnishings. It was not quite as spacious as most of the restaurants in the area, giving it more of an intimate coziness. The men shook hands as Shanahan arrived, the waitress bringing grilled Portobello mushrooms as appetizers before the men ordered their entrees.

"I am pleased to announce that the Council has agreed to the next shipment," Shanahan announced after a brief exchange of small talk. "As a matter of fact, our people are going to be able to bring the shipment directly here to Florida, which will facilitate your own phase of the operation in getting the bullion to Colombia."

"Here? Florida?" Murra pondered. "If your people wanted to bring it into the States themselves, why not New York?"

"Too risky," Shanahan replied, taking time to order his veal scallopini while Murra opted for the black-ink tagliarini. "This yellow alert has the New York harbor cluttered with security vessels. We're thinking of bringing it in around Jacksonville, which will enable your people to get your trucks onto any major highway and bring it down here to Miami, or wherever you think best. Of course, this will be something you will want to work out with the Colombians."

"So you're shipping the entire load in one shot," Murra frowned. "Seventy tons of freight will be a tall order, especially with all the beefed -up security. If they do a random search at a weigh station, all hell will break loose."

"This is why we are paying you eight million, my friend," Shanahan grew sardonic. "Montreal has agreed to transfer the funds as soon as you take possession. We get paid for our bullion and you get your commission. After that, it is between you and Montreal and the Colombians. You don't necessarily have to take it over the highway, but I don't even want to begin that discussion. I am merely a middleman, I have no expertise in such things. Our people feel that you are among the best at what you do, and they feel confident that you will do whatever it takes to ensure a safe and timely delivery."

"Of course," Murra replied as the waitress brought them champagne. Shanahan was now able to detect a sudden change in the atmosphere as the deal was being adjusted somewhat. He perceived that it would be a loss of face for Murra to admit he did not have the authority to consent to the alteration. Emiliano's face was beginning to reflect the dissonance as he tried to adjust to the situation. He weighed the possibility that Shanahan might cut him out of the deal, something that he would not allow.

"Our biggest concern is if we shipped directly to Montreal, it would increase the possibility that Operation Blackout might be compromised," Shanahan prodded him subtly. "Consider the fact that the Bank of Montreal will have had to have reported a sizeable increase in bullion since the last shipment, even though the shipment was transported directly to Medellin. Bauer would not have dared let it go unreported lest the RCMP had come across the transfer of seventy million dollars from the Bank of Colombia. If we go that route again, there is a great risk that they might investigate the transfer of a total one hundred forty million in gold from Europe to Montreal in a matter of weeks."

Murra still knew very few details about the Operation. Shanahan told him that the participants were buying up gold in the event of a switch to the gold standard, but mentioned nothing about an attack against the G8's gold reserves. Still, Murra was shrewd enough to realize that the urgency with which the shipments were being accelerated indicated that something was in the wind.

"All right," he relented, sipping his champagne. "Only I am going to have to increase my fee to ten million dollars. We are taking great risk in transporting the bullion across Florida. I am going to be paying serious money to bail my people out of jail if something goes amiss, not to mention the problem I am going to have with Bauer."

"Ten million," Shanahan wrinkled his brow. "That's a twenty-five percent increase. I've got to run it by my people, not to mention the Colombians."

"I agree, I think we may be getting ahead of ourselves here," Murra smiled tautly. "I'll get in touch with my people and you go back to yours. We can resume this discussion during the weekend."

"Emiliano," Shanahan clasped his hands on the table, "I like you and I respect you. I have nothing but praise for the work you've done for us so far. I don't want to take our business elsewhere, I want to deal with you. Look, I'm going to stick my neck out and approve the increase. You have your people ready to go by the beginning of next week, and we'll let you know where and when we'll make the shipment."

It was the threat of taking the deal elsewhere that was the sinker. No matter how strong he was as a Sardinian Mob *capo*, he could not go home and tell them he had backed out of a twenty-million dollar deal. He would risk being intercepted and having the Florida highway turned into a river of blood before that happened.

"Okay, William," Murra reached over and shook his hand. "I want to do business with you, because I also trust and respect you as well. Let us make this deal and enjoy the harvest. Here's to many, many more profitable enterprises to come."

The men toasted each other, having deep reservations as if they had both made a deal with the Devil.

Chapter Eighteen

Holy Thursday

Ernesto Guzman took the long three-hour drive from San Antonio TX down to Brownsville, located along the Mexican border. It was a sun-drenched corner of Texas where humid Gulf breezes swept in over the white sand beach, stroking the palm trees and bougainvilleas flourishing across the countryside. Matamoros, considered its sister town, was walking distance across a footbridge into Mexico. It was a flashpoint for Border Patrol officers and agents who desperately sought to stem the tide of illegal aliens across the US border.

He brought five of his men with him to the meeting place along the border. They were armed to the teeth, and two of them would remain on alert in the van while two men guarded the doors and one man sat at the table with him. He had just endured a major war against Alberto Calix towards the end of last year, and was loathe to come to the table with this man again so soon. They had broken bread in Montreal at the Operation Blackout conference, but the car-bombing of Julio Cruz raised suspicions across the board. Even though it was an East Coast thing, there was the question of who was turning a blind eye to the conspiracy, and who might be next.

It had been a long-standing rivalry between the Mexican Mafia and the Mexico City Cartel. Many of their constituents were loyal to both groups and could cross over to either side, depending on what side of the border they were on. Although the gangs would cooperate with one another in joint operations, there were always accusations of skimming or double-dealing. Crossing the border and intruding on rival territory was another major problem, and mutilations and dismemberment were routine punishments for those caught offsides.

It sickened him that he had to tolerate a peer relationship with Calix. The gold-toothed, beer-bellied gang lord rose through the ranks as a scheming backstabber and a ruthless opportunist. He did not have to survive five years of hell in the penitentiary in Huntsville. Only his CIA training kept him alive, his martial arts skills enhanced by his ability to turn the most innocent items into deadly weapons. After he blinded a rival prison gang leader with a toothpick, Guzman became the leader of the Mexican Mafia in Huntsville. Once he was released, he traveled across Texas consolidating power until he stood alone on top of the volcano.

He and his men parked their van in front of the stucco-framed restaurant on the corner of the block. There were a few bungalows scattered along the area, separated by weed-covered lots featuring an occasional growth of cactus or a shrine to the Virgin Mary. They spotted two of Cruz' men standing outside and swaggered over, exchanging greetings before Ernie and one of his gunmen went inside.

"*Como estas*, Ernesto?" Calix stood up, coming around the table featuring a smorgasbord of Mexican cuisine. Two of his gunmen watched impassively as the three MM gangsters embraced Calix before coming over and exchanging handshakes. They took seats at the table, Guzman positioning himself so he had a view of the entrance while being able to sit face to face with Calix.

Ernie had an unusually fierce expression while concentrating. It often made those with whom he negotiated think he had nothing but bad intentions for entirely unknown reasons. Calix's men were somewhat edgy but Alberto was used to Guzman's demeanor and rambled on as usual while Ernie tried to focus on the fine points of his rival's rhapsodization.

"Ernesto, my friend," Calix cajoled him as he fixed himself a beef *fajita* from a sizzling hot platter. "We have to learn to let bygones be bygones. We all make mistakes, and you and I made a terrible one in putting our men up against each other. We must cut our losses and take advantage of this opportunity the Canadians are giving us. Now, I have made a lot of calls and gathered lots of information. I know for a fact that everyone who has taken part in this smuggling operation has received a million dollars for their efforts. Plus we are all getting the opportunity to buy bullion by the ton directly from Europe. I thought they were blowing smoke up our asses, but it's happening, right before our eyes! It's happening tonight!"

"My men will be in position on our side of the border waiting to accept the transport." The native Mexicans would later say that Ernie had the look on his face of one who had just eaten a plate of shit. "We are not crossing over to get anything or anyone. I am not risking my men if anyone shows up, the Border Patrol, the DEA, Homeland Security, the Federales, anyone. We will hold our position for as long as we can, but if you cannot get the transport across the border, all bets are off."

"*Calmate*, Ernie," Calix held out his palms. "Everything is going to be fine. I believe in the gold standard and I believe in Amschel Bauer. No one has ever come to us with these kinds of plans before. Who has ever come to us with an offer to make a million dollars for one shipment? Surely this is not the end of it. If we accomplish this, I am certain there will be many, many more jobs like it to come."

"Tell me, what is it you think they are giving us a million dollars apiece to deliver?" Guzman tried to control himself. "Suppose—now, just suppose—they are bringing over a quarter ton worth, let's say, worth twelve million. They've already paid either Colombians or their own people a million to get it to the Hondurans, and they are going to pay a million for you to get it to us. That leaves them with eight million even before I get it to my connection. This is not cocaine, Alberto, don't be simple. These are weapons. One weapon, a weapon that fits in a container."

"A weapon?" Calix wrinkled his brow. "What kind of weapon?"

"You know," Ernie threw his hand to the side, looking out the door in disgust. "What did you call me down here for, a science lesson? I drive all the way down from San Antonio in this friggin' heat, three hours' drive, and you don't have the first idea about anything."

"Come on, Ernie, we have to keep the peace," Calix pleaded. "You can't come all the way down here and disrespect me in public. All I wanted was for you to come down and tell me we were *compadres* again. *Hermano*, you got no idea the shit they planning on my end. I just wanna make sure you got your side of the line. What you said is fine, you can stay on your side of the line, but I got to know that if I get it over the line, you'll be there to take it. If I get it over the line and nobody is there to take it, I don't get paid. Ernesto, I am not going to walk through hell and not get paid."

"So what are you saying, Alberto?" Ernie leaned over the table towards him. He had not touched a bite of food though his gunman was well into his own plate as were his two counterparts. "We going back to war if my men can't accept delivery? Suppose the Border Patrol comes in from my side? They don't cross the border, they don't have jurisdiction, you know that."

"They come across if they have to, and I'm pretty sure they're going to have to," Calix insisted.

"How do you know that?" Ernie demanded.

"You see, this is what it is, we need to respect," Calix reasoned. "You know what you know, and I know what I know. I don't know about a weapon because I don't want to know. If anything goes wrong, you can't tell the cops what you don't know, *verdad?* Just like if your people don't know anything about the shitstorm we've got to deal with tonight, then there's no one for you to give up, *si o no?*"

"Let me ask you something. Is the rest of the Cartel in on this?" Ernie reluctantly accepted a glass of iced tea from the waitress.

"You see, *carnal*," Calix waved a hand. "Now you see why we don't know what we don't know. If one of your people mentioned any one of my associates, it would not be just you against me. You would be at war with the entire Cartel. What you don't know, you can't tell."

"All right," Ernie conceded. "If your people have to go through whatever shit you're talking, my people will hold their ground as long as they can. I'm not asking anyone to do time for a shipment they cannot see, though. Remember that."

"Excellent," Calix grinned. "Once this is over, you can come back down and tell me all about weapons, and I'll tell you about shitstorms."

"Great. Well..." Ernie seemed as if ready to leave.

"You aren't going to jump back into that van so quickly," Calix protested. "There is a cockfight scheduled in one hour. I have one of my prized roosters ready to go. Come, stay for a game or two, we'll have a few drinks before you leave."

Ernie was about to decline but saw the light in his bodyguard's eyes. He always allowed for his men's creature comforts when convenient. He knew from prison it was one of the best ways to strengthen their loyalty.

"Okay, call the guys in, tell them to come have something to eat," Ernie sat back. "Maybe they'd like to lose some money betting against Alberto's Super Chicken."

The men eagerly nodded, hoping that the cockfight would be the only violent action they would see on this day. Somehow they had a dark foreboding that their wishes would not be realized in the uncertain hours ahead.

The University of Texas at Brownsville was located at Fort Brown, traditionally listed as a historic landmark. Over ten thousand students from across the state came there to enjoy its diverse cultural influence in pursuing their four-year degrees. The subtropical climate provided the luxury of enjoying sunny days throughout the semester, and the Paseo coursing along the campus ran alongside *resacas* in which tropical fish resided and provided a watering hole for exotic birds frequenting the area.

The students particularly enjoyed the privilege of being able to cross the border into Matamoros and experience the thrill of interacting in a different society just miles from campus. By day, the citizens of Matamoros welcomed the visitors to visit their shops and restaurants in their commercial areas, eagerly catering to their extracurricular needs as college kids drove or walked over to hang out in the nightclubs and cantinas proliferating throughout the area.

It was the foreboding rust-colored wall outside the campus threatening to divide the Mexican-American border, as well as the warning posters all over the campus, that served as a reminder of the criminal element that threatened the safety of the American students. It was the triple threat of drug smugglers, illegal alien trafficking, and indigenous street crime that posed a constant danger to both students and local residents. Overworked law enforcement officials were backed up by US Customs and Border Protection officers and agents, as well Army and police units on the Mexican side. Together they united successfully to thwart the efforts of drug cartels, *coyotes*, thieves and murderers, but on this night their weaknesses were to be analyzed and exploited by the drug dealers.

It was shortly after midnight when Border Patrol reported a surge of over fifty individuals crossing the water on plastic rafts, propelling the devices with plastic oars of playground quality. They called for reinforcements but were still able to catch only a small percentage of the aliens. Many of them were shoving the rafts back in the general direction of the opposite shore before grabbing their bindles and charging for the treelines along the shore. The Border Patrol vehicles flashed their overhead lights and blared their sirens but it did little to deter the aliens from continuing a lemming-like procession into America.

Border Patrol contacted police and Federal officials, who proceeded to flood the area with reinforcements. Police trucks began setting up command posts at street intersections in the area, and DEA and Homeland Security personnel were on the scene in an advisory capacity though willing to call in additional support if needed. It was a drastic deviation from the aliens' standard method of operation, and officials were befuddled as to their motivation.

Their concerns were exacerbated as, out of nowhere, a mob of aliens appeared on the wooden bridge from Matamoros to Brownsville, and surged forth in mass to virtually overwhelm the outnumbered border guards. The guards began sounding alarms and brought down the gate. It was to no avail as the aliens began climbing over the rail and forcing their way over and around the human chain of border guards. They radioed for assistance, and suddenly the police and Border Patrol units were overstretched as they divided their forces to meet the new threat.

Students at the University got word of the commotion, and they contacted the media as they flocked to the wall to watch the event in progress. The Campus Police scurried around the college grounds warning students to stay indoors, but the incident had grown so widespread and boisterous that it was to no avail. Students began bringing video equipment to the fenceline in order to tape the clashes between Border Patrol officers and aliens. The illegals continued crossing the river in droves in a desperate attempt to capitalize on what would be called the Surge in tomorrow's paper.

An 'all-hazards' response to the invasion brought the Mexican Army into the fracas, which eventually escalated into gunplay as Border Patrol, the BPD and Campus Police began forming skirmish lines along the river. The Mexican Army cadre broke into battle formations as pockets of armed resistance began attacking with gunfire and grenades along the Mexican riverbank. Once again the defensive units were being stretched thin as the gunmen attempted to draw their forces away from the wooden crossing bridge. The Mexican police began using tear gas on their side of the border, but the fumes hampered efforts on the US side to contain the aliens staggering around and over the barricades.

The incident created a massive traffic jam as the police declared a state of emergency, setting up roadblocks along a ten-block radius on each side of the crossing area. It failed to stem the tide of aliens continuing to race towards the bridge, which made officials now suspect that this was a deliberately-staged assault that had been carefully planned and coordinated. It seemed almost as if the illegals had been told that they were being provided a window of opportunity that would be lost if they did not seize the moment. Border guards were being deeply affected by having to use physical force against women and children who were recklessly hurling themselves into the streams of people trying to cross into the US.

The combined Mexican and US forces seemed to be widening their perimeters in clearing the area around the bridge and the riverside. Yet after a short interlude, there was a great commotion as trucks and vans were being used as battering rams to crash through the roadblocks and come barreling across the bridge. The border guards watched in astonishment as the trucks smashed through the barricades, running over aliens and security forces alike before careening off the road on the US side to allow aliens to jump out and flee for their lives. There was sporadic fire from police officers which was returned by gunmen who were in the vans among the illegals.

Beneath the bridge, the Border Patrol had not noticed a black camouflaged Scarab AVS slowly making its way along the Mexican shoreline. It waited for an opportunity to drift alongside the international bridge, and coasted across until it reached the US side. It took advantage of the shadows and the commotion in reaching the shore, where four gunmen awaited with a Bobcat compact tractor and trailer also painted in black camouflage. The gunmen assisted the boaters in unloading a metal container from the motorboat onto the trailer. The gangsters then escorted the Bobcat as it slowly made its way across the riverside to where a black SUV awaited in the shadows at the top of a nearby slope. Once again they lifted the cylinder from the minitrailer and carried it to the Yukon XL where they loaded it before it sped off into the darkness, far away from the chaos surrounding the international bridge.

"We made the delivery," the leader of the four-man team made a call on his cell phone after the SUV disappeared from sight. "The shipment is on its way."

"Very good," Ernesto Guzman replied from his hotel room in Corpus Christi. He would be expecting the Yukon to be arriving within the next couple of hours, and from there the cylinder would be moved to a commercial 18-wheeler that would take it to San Antonio. From there it would be turned over to another crew. They would take it to the border city of Texarkana where the mission of the Mexican Mafia would end. From there it would be taken by people Ernesto believed belonged to Al-Qaeda.

Guzman had a gnawing feeling that something was terribly wrong, but dismissed the notion in crawling back into bed with his cell phone on the night table. He would adopt the perspective of Alberto Calix, deciding that what he did not know would not hurt him. His people had no idea what was in the cylinder, and he would do his best not to care.

All he could hope was that he was not participating in a terrorist attack against his adopted country. It was a guilt he could live without.

Chapter Nineteen

Good Friday

William Shanahan answered his cell phone early Friday morning after emerging from the shower. He had a good run on the beach and cut his time by five minutes. Running in the sand was always one of the best of cardiovascular exercises. To go five miles at a strong pace at a shorter time told him that he was on top of his game. The tournament was tomorrow night, and he knew all hell was going to break loose over the next seventy-two hours. He was in shape to go the distance no matter what came down.

"Morgana," he was surprised by her sultry voice. "How's it going?"

"Well, it's nice someone answers their cell phone," she replied. "Jack never picks up. I'm getting the impression you fellows found some other hangout pals."

"No, not quite," he tried to collect his thoughts. He was surprised at the effect her voice was having on him. All of a sudden it wasn't about Gawain doing him a favor by calling the girls to come out. Now it was him and Morgana, and he did not want this conversation to end on a cell phone.

"We've been rather busy. There's been some big deals going on our end and it's had me seriously tied up. I'm thinking we should have this wrapped up by Monday. Where are you staying? Perhaps I can come out and see you. My business with Jack may be done by then."

"I guess I'd better bring you up to speed," she replied tautly. "Fianna got a tremendous job offer from a private firm in Miami. They wanted her to start right away, they were paying a hundred thousand dollars. They transferred fifty thousand up front directly to her savings account. She paid off our lease for the year and let me pay my share back. She left two days ago, and after she arrived I haven't heard anything from her."

"Who was it she said she was going to work for?"

"It was some company out of Colombia. It had a name similar to your company's, some Colombiana Exports."

Shanahan broke a cold sweat as he quickly toweled himself off and stared out the window at Biscayne Bay in the distance. He knew it was Enrique Chupacabra. Somehow he found out that Gawain was in Miami and planned to turn the tables on him. Now there was a palmetto bug in the ointment and Shanahan had the unenviable task of cleansing it out.

"Uh, what are you doing this weekend? Are you particularly busy?"

"Well, they haven't given out our schedule yet, but I think I'll be working Monday."

"How'd you like to come out tonight?" he offered. "I'll make some calls and go looking for Jack. I'm pretty sure we'll be able to find Fianna."

"I'm just worried about her," Morgana was concerned. "It's not like her not to call at all. Her phone goes straight to voice mail and I'm not getting any e-mails either. I'm afraid something happened."

"All kinds of things may have happened," he replied gently. "She may be working in a facility where she can't get a signal. For fifty thousand, I doubt she'd walk away just because her cell phone's not working. It might have even involved travel. Look, I've got some big connections. I'll make some calls and have some people look into it. We'll find her. Maybe you can come out here and relax a bit while I'm on it."

"Okay, William," she agreed. "I'll be out there this evening. I'll call you when I get in."

After Morgana clicked off, Shanahan suddenly considered the fact he had not seen Gawain for six days. He had heard very little from MI6 other than updates on the bullion transport from Belfast, and assumed that they had given Gawain freer rein. Between mollifying Bieber and conning Murra, keeping track of Gawain had been a low priority until now. He called Gawain's cell phone, which went immediately to voice mail. He next called MI6.

"Hello," he went through the usual series of prompts and finally got a live person.

"Shanahan, Number 116.I need to speak to the Colonel."

"Shaughnessy," his voice came on after about three minutes.

"It's Shanahan. Has Gawain been checking in?"

"Like clockwork twice a day. First call comes between 11 and 12 noon US Eastern Time, last call same timeframe before midnight. I trust you haven't seen him."

"It's been a few days. I'm suspecting he may have taken a hand in some of the gang violence in the area over the past couple of days."

"We've considered it," Shaughnessy allowed. "Our only concern is that he doesn't get himself killed and jeopardize the mission. You have to take into account the fact he plans on being a free man in a week. He hasn't earned a shilling over the past five years. Most likely he's trying to set something aside for when we cut him loose. I wouldn't concern myself, William. You've got more important things to do tomorrow while he's playing at dominoes with Chupacabra. We need to you do what's necessary to keep Murra in the red zone."

"I'm on it, sir. Shanahan out."

Now things were beginning to crystallize, and he was starting to see the big picture more clearly. Drawing Chupacabra offside was just part of the big picture. Apparently MI6 was drawing both Bauer and the Medellin Cartel into the gold smuggling scheme, but they weren't letting him in on what trap lay ahead for the criminals. What he did know was that MI6 had already sold seventy million dollars' worth of bullion to the Cartel, and the sale went through without a hitch. Murra and the Sardinians were eight million dollars richer, and the

Cartel had bullion that could double in value in the months ahead. Up to now, he was seeing a whole lot of bait and not a lot of the trap. It was bigger than Chupacabra, and he could not see how the enforcer was figuring into the equation.

What he did know was that Fianna Hesher's life might be at stake. He had no way of knowing whether Gawain had heard from her, or what Chupacabra intended to gain by bringing her into the game. He must have taken into consideration the fact that Gawain was a sociopath who had little regard for human life. If he suspected, or knew, that Gawain was involved in the recent gang wars, it might have been an outside chance on his part to get some leverage on Gawain. Fianna was being used as a pawn by two people who cared less for her wellbeing. Even if Margana was not involved, Shanahan could not turn his back on the girl now.

He realized that it was his personal standards that were going to prove his greatest liability. He knew that if Murra was going to be allowed to walk off with sixteen million after the next shipment was completed, he was going to let Bieber in on the scheme whether the Firm planned to do so or not. He fully agreed with Bieber that letting the Sardinians secure a foothold in North America was going to be hazardous to the US in the long run. It would outweigh whatever short-term gain the Firm was enjoying, and he was willing to risk the repercussions if the trap did not chop Murra's legs off as he anticipated.

He also knew that his standards would require him to track down Fianna Hesher and find out what happened to her. He would use the information on Murra as a tradeoff with Bieber, in return for him using the CIA's resources to rescue Fianna from Chupacabra's power play. Cutting a side deal such as this might cost him his position with the Firm and his dreams of Downing Street. Yet he would never be able to live with himself if he let Murra walk away with the power and left Fianna at the mercy of Enrique Chupacabra.

It was late afternoon by the time Shanahan met Morgana at Miami International Airport. They picked up her bag and took a cab to the

Shore Club Hotel where he took care of her arrangements with a Superior King suite on the same floor with him. He fixed them both a glass of Bushmills on the rocks as she took her bag to the bedroom before coming out and joining Shanahan on the balcony of her suite overlooking the bay.

"I'm scheduled to see Jack tomorrow night," Shanahan told her as they sat at the patio table on the balcony. "I've got a business meeting with one fellow, but I'm sure we can get together afterwards. I'll find out if he's seen Fianna, and I should be getting some feedback from those connections of mine by Monday if we're needing it."

"You don't think Jack has anything to do with her disappearing, do you?" she wondered, her Bausch and Lomb turtle shell sunglasses shielding her eyes from the sun as her thick blonde mane was swept by the ocean breeze. "Even if they had eloped, she wouldn't have gone without telling me, I know her better than that."

"Did you think it was odd that she was flying out here to Miami to go to work with a Colombian company, with all the gang violence going on?"

"We had discussed that, and we did the research," Morgana replied. "They've got a website, and everything seemed to check out. They specialize in gold, silver and oil commodities. They're registered with the Medellin Chamber of Commerce for Antioquia."

"It could be a front company used for money laundering," Shanahan said gently.

"The whole thing boiled down to them transmitting the funds to her account," Morgana grew uneasy. "When she accepted the offer, she paid off our lease and the money went right through. She took care of all her bills and it convinced her it was legit. This is scaring me, William. You don't think this has something to do with drugs?"

"I don't know," he reached over and held her hand, the first time he had ever done so. "Listen, I'm sorry I wasn't there for you the way I could've been. This business deal has just taken up so much of my time. I wanted to get it out of the way before I started concentrating on my personal affairs. If I'd had known better, I would've let you know I was here for you."

"Thank you, William," she took her glasses off, her emerald eyes making his heart skip a beat. "I feel a lot better knowing you're able to help me through all this. You seem to know a lot about these things. It's nice to know you have someone in your corner when situations like this come up. My parents are dead and I'm an only child, so Fianna's all I have."

"Not anymore," he squeezed her hand. "Not anymore."

He was reassuring himself as much as he was reassuring her.

It was after midnight once again when Jack Gawain headed out to Liberty City to meet with the Sosa Brothers. They had agreed to lay low after the gasoline truck explosion, but Gawain had requested the meeting and the Sosas called him in.

He met Oscar Alfonso and Gilberto Echezabal outside the tenement, and they escorted him inside where Johnnie and Jimmy were seated on the cheap furniture in the living room. They stood to exchange handshakes with Gawain as he took a seat across from Johnnie in one of the work armchairs.

"Looks like they gave you the day off from the kitchen," Gawain teased.

"What did you want to see me about, Jack?" Johnnie assumed his serious demeanor.

"Look, I've got a deal," Gawain spread his hands. "I can move a ki tonight for thirty grand. I'll split the five grand with you. If this works out, I can turn it into a weekly buy."

"Jack, you're asking me to trust you with twenty-five thousand dollars' worth of merchandise," Johnnie stared at him. "If something were to happen, I would be out of enough product to cost me seventy-five thousand over a couple of months. The person I work for would be extremely upset if I came up short that kind of money in ninety days, and he would hold me accountable."

"Come on, John," Gawain reasoned. "You put the lives of your brother and two of your top guys in my hands, and I put mine in theirs twice. No questions asked. You didn't even tell me that first job was going t'turn into a hit, but did I complain? You made me an accomplice to a murder, and did I squawk? Plus I blew that place on 7th to hell, not to mention the place before that. I can't believe I'm sitting here listenin' t'you tell me you don't trust me."

"It's not like that, Jack, it's about dollars and cents," Johnnie explained. "Look at it from the street side. Somebody sees or knows you have a ki on you, that's worth one hundred thousand on the street. You could get ambushed, robbed or killed, and my boss will hold me responsible for the money. If an earthquake happened and swallowed this building, I would owe my boss one million dollars, no questions asked. It's different on my level. It's not who you trust or don't trust, it's how much you stand to make or lose."

"It's a quick five grand, John, and I could use the money. Look, you can have Jimmy come along with me if you like. I can turn this over in a couple of hours," Gawain insisted.

"Who are you going to sell it to, Jack? The competition? To some cowboy going to set up shop a few blocks from here?" Johnnie inquired. "Think about it. I make a quick twenty-five hundred and lose seventy-five thousand to my competitors."

"Come on, you're not talking to a duck on the pond," Gawain threw his elbow over the back of the armchair. "Your boss isn't giving the product to you at cost, and he's not holdin' you to the retail price. This is an Italian fellow who knows people. He says he can move it at profit and he's offerin' a kickback. If he does well, I'll sponsor him and I'll kickback to you. It's gonna be like a small business loan of sorts, you can see that."

"Well," Johnnie shook his head, then leaned forward and folded his hands as he rested his elbows on his knees. "I don't know what to make of this. You came in here like gangbusters. You come looking for a job, you retrieve fifty grand from one of my dealers who was getting ready to go into the wind. Next couple of days, you close down two rival crack houses and send our enemies running for cover. Now you're looking to set up your own dealership. You're moving kind of quick, and you're not afraid of anything. How can I know if you're looking to move past me?"

"And do what, have your boss lookin' for me?" Gawain was disdainful. "I told ye I know this business inside and out. Plus I told ye I was in Montreal when Julio Cruz got hit. I know how things work, and I know how to turn a buck. I'll take responsibility for the fella, and if he screws up I'll put him out of business and reclaim the consignment. If he does well, I'll put him under your flag. Like I said, you send Jimmy and the guys with me, I'll make the introductions and let him see who I'm with. You can't lose here, John."

Johnnie leaned over to Jimmy, who sat on the stringy sofa beside him. They conversed quietly in Spanish before Johnnie turned back to Gawain.

"Okay, we'll see how it works out," Johnnie gave in. "Jimmy will go with you along with Oscar and Gilberto. You will tell your man that you work for the Sosa Brothers. You will come back here with twenty-two five for me. We will split ten percent of everything he makes from the ki, which we would expect to be ten grand apiece. He can pay that off as he likes, but I get ten grand before he gets another ki."

"Aw reet," Gawain replied.

Jimmy went into the back room for a long while, and eventually emerged with a kilogram of pure cocaine in a plastic bag. He set it down on the scarred coffee table in the middle of the room between Johnnie and Jack.

"This is a major move," Johnnie exhaled tautly. "I only hope we are not moving too prematurely."

"No, I can assure you this is perfect timing," Gawain grinned. "Say, Oscar, can I have a cigarette?"

"Why, sure," Oscar replied, pulling a pack of Marlboros out of his jacket pocket and tapping one out for Gawain. "I thought you quit."

"Well, this is a special occasion," he replied, thanking Oscar as he gave Gawain a light. Gawain took a deep drag and then set it down on the kilo as if using it as an ashtray.

"Say, you know how expensive that stuff is," Johnnie whined.

"Sure do," Gawain replied.

At once he hopped up from his seat, drew and fired his Glock, hitting Johnny Sosa right between the eyes. He then whirled and shot Oscar, then Gilberto, square in the forehead. He rushed to Jimmy and grabbed him by the hair, putting the gun barrel against his temple.

"*No me mate,*" Jimmy pleaded. "Don't kill me, Jack."

"You think you're gonna make it without your brother?" Jack asked softly.

"*No me mate,*" Jimmy begged. "*No me mate,*"

"Aw reet," Gawain turned his head to the side, pressing the barrel into Jimmy's cheek. "I'll leave you to deliver the message. Tell them that Enrique Chupacabra sends his regards. Got it?"

"Yeah yeah yeah," Jimmy gasped.

"What's the message?" Gawain could hear commotion in the vestibule outside.

"Chupacabra say hi," Jimmy managed. "Chupacabra say hi."

"Good enough," Gawain replied, pulling the trigger. Jimmy nearly went into shock as the bullet ripped through his face, sending a spray of blood and teeth from the exit wound across the carpet. Gawain then shot the first gunman in the face as he barged through the entrance. He then fired into the wall in a tight pattern, hearing a body fall in the corridor as the rounds tore through the frame and plaster. He then picked up the kilo and calmly made his way out the door. Everyone in the streets ran for cover as he tossed the Glock and the kilo into his rental car before climbing in and cruising off into the night.

Chapter Twenty

Holy Saturday

The Magic City Casino was the site of the World Domino Championship being sponsored by ESPN. The million dollar grand prize, plus the prestige and fame accompanying it, made it the greatest domino competition in history. Hundreds of thousands had competed in auditoriums in the capitol cities of all fifty states, going on to qualifying round in neighboring states until it all boiled down to four regional champions. Ricky Chu was named the Southeast Champion, Jack Gain the Northeast Champion. Only the other two finalists required hotel accommodations, courtesy of the Casino. In order to fill up air time, ESPN showed videotapes of the qualifying games, giving viewers a tutorial on the rules and intricacies of the game as the contests progressed.

"Smashing," Jack Gawain marveled as the five men arrived at his suite that Saturday afternoon along with William Shanahan. One man walked up with a wide grin and handed Gawain his ID badge for the championship round. The man was almost an exact duplicate of Gawain and could have passed as a twin brother. "Where the hell did you get this fella?"

"That's classified," the leader of the four-man escort team spoke up with a Belfast accent. "You two wouldn't have remembered us, we were incognito. We were the ones who took care of that problem you had in Atlantic City."

"And y'did a great job, for sure," Gawain said admiringly.

"We just got in from setting up that deal in Jacksonville," the second-in-command led Shanahan over to the balcony, speaking in hushed tones. It indicated that Gawain was left out of the loop as regards that part of the operation. "We'll be expecting to hear from your boy at 0300. Things should really be moving along by then."

"Without a doubt," Shanahan replied. "I am certainly looking forward to how this all comes together. It should be a masterpiece."

The four men, dressed in black workout suits, left shortly afterwards with the Gawain lookalike. Gawain poured himself a shot of Jameson and offered one to Shanahan, who politely declined.

"So have you heard anything from Fianna as of late?"

"Nah, I've been keepin' myself busy somewhat," Gawain sipped his drink. "I figured I'd give the girls a buzz after the game, probably tomorrow. I'm figuring your people should be arranging my release, if in fact they intend to honor the commitment. That'd be something to celebrate, though unbeknownst to them."

"Have you been checking your voicemails?" Shanahan asked quizzically.

"Afraid not. I check in with your people twice a day, and that's all I have to do with cell phones. I carried one for emergencies when I was on the outside, and since I've been away I've had nothing to do with them at all."

"Morgana got here yesterday, I met her for breakfast this morning. She came looking for Fianna, she thought perhaps we'd seen her."

"What?" Gawain asked. Shanahan was almost startled to see Jack's wise-assed, arrogant veneer shattered for the first time since the two met. "How's that?"

"She got a fifty thousand dollar signing bonus on a hundred grand salary from a Colombian export company specializing in commodities," Shanahan replied coldly. "It sounds to me like Chupacabra set up a dummy company and lured Fianna in."

"How in the hell!" Gawain grew angry.

"I told you, Gawain," Shanahan snapped as he paced across the spacious living room. "I told you when we first started you had to approach this mission with an utter sense of paranoia. Chupacabra represents a multi-billion dollar organization. We have no idea how deeply they have corrupted any government agency on the planet. How can we possibly assume there is not one Homeland Security official somewhere who could be touched by these people? How could we not think there is not a bribe too great, an extortion too devious, or a computer security compromise too intricate for these people to attempt? The minute you called those girls on a cell phone might have placed them at risk. I shan't expect you to beat yourself up over this, but in moving forward we can piece things together and find out if she's safe."

Gawain wordlessly went into the bedroom and retrieved his cell phone. Shanahan went behind the bar to get a container of fruit juice from the fridge as he could hear Gawain retrieving his voice mail. After a long interval, he returned with a sour look on his face.

"She called Monday to tell me she got the offer and wanted me to call back to see what I thought," he grimaced. "She took the job Tuesday when she didn't hear back. She gave me a call Wednesday and said she'd call when she got here. That was the last message."

"Morgana didn't call until yesterday before she took the flight down," Shanahan replied. "Look, I don't think Chupacabra knows I'm here, or that we're working together. He must've caught on to you by researching the tournament. That ringer looks just like you, and the name Jack Gain isn't enough to toss off an imbecile. He would've gotten back to his people in Medellin who pushed a button to track your cell phone calls. I doubt they could've hacked into your MI6 phone but they could've worked backwards and tracked the calls to your number."

"The bastard probably suspects we had something to do with taking out that blonde of his," Gawain rubbed his chin thoughtfully.

"Thought *you* had something to do with it," Shanahan muttered. "That was a stupid move, Jack. We were supposed to get inside his head, not spit in his face. We were very lucky that your car bomb in Montreal worked in our favor, but killing that girl made it personal. Now another innocent girl's life is at stake."

"All right, boyo, you're the super-snoop James Bond character here," Gawain tried to retrieve his arrogance. "What can and should we do?"

"We have to stay well away from one another," Shanahan insisted. "Your game'll be held at the Amphitheater, and my meeting will be at Secada's Lounge. Under no circumstances should we meet anywhere near either place. You must not call me except in an extreme emergency. Fianna will not be an exception. Don't even think of mentioning her to MI6, it might have serious repercussions. We should have never gotten involved with civilians on this operation, and it was more my blunder than ours. If you see her, get all the information you can but do not compromise your position. Your pardon will depend on it, I guarantee you."

"Okay, fine," Gawain said resignedly. He considered the fact that if he had not killed Johnny Sosa, he could have reached out to him to help find Fianna. His best hope was that Chupacabra might be assassinated by the Cubans before tournament time, and that Fianna would be set free.

"Don't forget, Jack," Shanahan knocked down the mango juice before heading for the door. "Don't call me, I'll call you. And, good luck at the game."

It was the first time Shanahan could recall Gawain not having a parting wisecrack for him.

After leaving the suite, Shanahan headed straight to the lobby from where he phoned Morgana. She came downstairs to meet him, and he was pleasantly surprised to see her wearing a Hard Rock Café T-shirt and jeans. She looked like a beautiful aunt having borrowed clothes during an overnight stay, the denims fitting her marvelous hips and thighs like a second skin. She offered to go back and change when she saw Shanahan in a dark button-down silk shirt and dress pants, but he would not hear of it.

"I finally got hold of Jack," he revealed. "He's finishing up that deal tonight and he hasn't been taking calls. He finally checked his voicemail and he had messages from Fianna, on Monday, Tuesday and Wednesday. As I mentioned, I have a strong connection who can do some serious digging. I'll be able to get them on it tomorrow."

"I'm afraid for her, William," she said softly as they walked towards the downtown area towards the Brickell Bridge where the Capital Grille was located. He heard they served excellent porterhouse steaks, and also thought the walk would give them time to clear the air before lunch. "You don't think there's any way they could look into it sooner?"

"It's kind of complicated," he tried to explain. "The fellows I'm dealing with have limited connections with people in the State Department due to the nature of our business. If they waded into this, on a Saturday night, it might be taken in the wrong way by certain people. It'd be more likely that they would gather information tomorrow and be able to jump in with both feet Monday. That is, if we haven't heard from Fianna by then."

"Okay," she exhaled tautly. "This is getting a little bit over my head, and I'm sure you're more into this kind of thing so I'm going to trust you."

William held out his arm as they prepared to cross the street, and she slipped her arm through his. Both of them suddenly felt a deep sense of contentment that neither of them had experienced for a long time. They also had a feeling that somehow everything was going to work out right.

Hours later, the Amphitheater began filling up as the World Domino Championship was about to be taped before a live audience on ESPN. Jack Gawain reported to the Tournament Committee where he was given a badge and a rundown as to the tournament rules. It was to be one game that would decide the championship. They would be playing with a traditional twenty-eight tile set, and the tiles were to be set in brackets before each player. The players would wear headphones to eliminate any distractions, and the referee would call a play-by-play as the game proceeded. The player holding the double-six would play first. If no one could open they would continue calling double numbers up to the double-three. Should no one play there would be a reshuffle. In the event of three reshuffles the game would be declared a no-contest, and the player with the lowest number of spots on their tiles would be declared champion.

The players would be provided refreshment drinks with waitresses available for refills when a player tapped his drink. Elaborate gestures would be ruled an infraction, and three infractions would require the player to return their dominoes to the sleeper pile. If a player touched a tile on the rack they would be required to play the tile. Attempting any contact with anyone besides the waitress was an infraction subject to disqualification. The players would continue according to turn, and whoever played all the tiles on their rack would be the winner. If a player could not play, they would knock on the table indicating a pass to the next player. In the event the game was locked, the player with the lowest number of spots would be declared the winner.

The players were asked to sit in a restricted area while the game table was being prepared. Jack Gawain picked up a copy of *Sports Illustrated* and flipped through it idly, enthusiastically awaiting the sight of Enrique Chupacabra's face when the two men faced each other at the gaming table once again.

Johnny Carmona was surrounded by six of his most trusted bodyguards as he raved and ranted in the enormous living room of his Palm Beach estate. It was built in a concentric pattern featuring a ring of marble steps leading down to the carpeted and exquisitely furnished lounge area. He had been screaming and yelling from the moment his men arrived for the emergency meeting, and proved implacable regardless of whatever they proposed.

"They walked in there and killed Johnny Sosa, along with Alfonso, Echezabal and the two other guys!" he raged. "Plus they stole a ki! One ki! Fucking amateurs! There were nine other ki's in that bedroom they didn't even touch! They could've burned us for a million dollars' profit, but no! And why? Because they wanted us to know that Enrique Chupacabra set it up! Either they think I'm the stupidest motherfucka in Miami, or Chupacabra has finally lost his fucking mind!"

"Johnny, we have to calm down a bit and think things out," Ed Travieso insisted. "We cannot whack Chupacabra after that tournament tonight. Not only will we be at war with the Colombians, but the cops will come after us with everything they have. As it stands right now, we're fighting a war on two fronts against the Jamaicans and the Haitians. Think of the business we're losing. The rich kids are avoiding Liberty City like the plague, and even the junkies and the crackheads are heading across town to score shit. Besides, suppose someone is trying to set Chupacabra up. We have to hold off on this, Johnny."

"Fuck that!" Johnny screamed. "Fuck that! This is strike two! First Julio Cruz gets whacked, and now Johnnie Sosa. What are we gonna wait for, me to get whacked next? This is looking pretty good for you, not for me. I get hit next and you're the new boss. What's that about?"

"Don't talk to me like that, Johnny," Ed retorted. "That's bullshit and you know it."

"Look, have you gotten hold of Antonio or Heriberto yet?" Johnny snapped at the morbidly obese gunman hitting the automatic dial on his cell phone.

"I left messages, Johnny," he replied nervously. "You know we have instructions not to leave more than three calls in case they're being monitored. I also left messages for Dionicio, Tomas and Ramon. Three apiece, that's fifteen messages. There's no way they don't get back to us unless there's a problem somewhere else."

"A fucking problem," Johnny rolled his eyes, walking up the steps to the horseshoe bar that extended around a quarter length of the room. "What other problems do you think we might be having right now besides this?"

"Suppose your second guess was right?" a bony-faced man stared out the window overlooking the magnificent sunset over the harbor.

"Suppose someone is trying to get us to blame Chupacabra or the Colombians? They would have to have a lot of muscle, Johnny. If they're risking taking on both us and the Colombians, they need a lot of muscle. Who could that be?"

"Who the fuck knows?" Johnny sipped his rum and coke on top of the gold-chromed bar. "Maybe the MS-13, the fucking Hondurans. Those are some gun-crazy psychotic motherfuckers. That Tony Ramos sits down there on his banana plantation playing it so cool, blowing smoke up Alberto Calix's ass. He sat down with me at Prime 111 just a few days ago, looking me right in the eyes like he didn't have a clue. He knows something, that fat fuck. He knows something."

"Don't even start, Johnny," Ed admonished him. "Don't even think about making a move against Ramos. They've gotten too strong, it'd turn into a major war we couldn't win. He could easily get the Colombians to come in with them to bring a quick end to the fighting."

"I didn't say I was taking Tony Ramos to war," tony whirled towards him ferociously. "I said that fat fuck knows something. You know what? Get him on the phone, I wanna talk to him!"

"Come on, man!" the fat man whined. "Not Ramos, not right now. C'mon, Ed, why don't we take care of one thing at a time?"

"What the fuck, you think Ed's in charge around here?" Carmona snarled at him. "You think I died and left him boss already?"

Suddenly the cell phone went off and the fat man took the call immediately. He waddled off to the far corner and exchanged muted remarks before clicking off.

"What the fuck! You don't let me talk!" Carmona nearly went ballistic.

"The Cartel is in session," the fat man replied anxiously. "There is a bigger problem."

"What?" Carmona demanded. "Where? With who?"

"It's the DEA," the fat man said tersely. "They got the shipment. The big one."

The tournament game began with the four players drawing six tiles, four tiles going to the sleeper pile. Gawain played the double six, which automatically gave him a commanding lead. Chupacabra played a tile, as did the Southwest champion, whose tile at the other end of the double six closed out sixes play for the time being. The Northwest champion was forced to take a sleeper in order to play, leaving three in the sleeper pile.

Gawain had two more sixes to play along with two fours and the double blank. It was probably the best hand on the table. Only he did not have the required three or a two to play and would need to take a sleeper. He folded his hands and stared at the other players' racks, then the rack holding the sleepers, then glanced around at the crowd outside the guardrail surrounding the playing area. There was a five-minute time limit for each play, so Gawain decided to make the best of it.

He saw Chupacabra's dark eyes staring across the table to his left, and surreptitiously looked back at him while pretending to contemplate the rack before him. Chupacabra, who had his forefinger of his right hand set pensively against his headset, suddenly took it away and crooked it ever so slightly. At once there was a movement within the crowd behind him, and suddenly he saw her.

Fianna Hesher was resplendent in a silvery gown that not only enhanced her lovely features, but made her stand out like a beacon within Chupacabra's black tuxedoed entourage. She did not look out at the game, and most likely would not have recognized Gawain if she had spotted him. She did glance out to where Chupacabra was playing, and two of his men braced her and appeared to be giving her instructions. She nodded in understanding, then vanished into the crowd again.

He considered the notion of standing up and forfeiting the game to order to reclaim her from the Colombians. He would be fully covered by ESPN in doing so. Only then, the mission itself might be compromised as the media would jump all over it. Plus, he had no idea of knowing whether Fianna had willingly taken the job and was not going to go along with him at risk of $100 grand. He cursed his luck and played his double one, then realized his error in doing so. He should have played his five spot, and he could see a look of revelation in the eyes of the other players when he did not.

Luckily for him, Chupacabra played a tile, but the Southwest champion had to take a sleeper, as did the Northwest champion. There was only one sleeper tile left, and Gawain and Chupacabra stared at each other for the first time. Not only would one of them be faced with the prospect of taking that last one, but also who was going to end up with Fianna Hesher at the end of the night.

Emiliano Murra met with William Shanahan at Secada's, and things started going sour for him as their margaritas were served in plastic cups at the open air bar. He greeted Shanahan warmly as usual but was not overly enthused with the way things were going.

"Our people are in position in Jacksonville," Shanahan informed him. "We're going to bring the goods in ourselves. As soon as we take possession, we'll be able to make the payoff. The only thing is, there's another problem that has arisen that must be taken care of."

"What is that, William?" Murra stared at him.

"Enrique Chupacabra. I mentioned the problems we've been having with him in our network. It seems that his gang has been causing turmoil throughout Miami over the past week, and he may be about to initiate a gang war between our friends in Cuba and the Colombians. We think it is time to offer you the contract."

"You want me to take out Chupacabra," Murra stirred his drink.

"We intend to leave the existing bonus as is. We will pay you four million for bringing the shipment to Jacksonville. Afterwards, we will tell you exactly where Chupacabra can be located. We would suggest that you bring four of your best men in on the job. We believe he may be heading down to Texarkana, along the Texas-Arkansas border. There is a vital shipment coming through the area and we suspect he may be planning to compromise the operation in making a deal with the Feds. He may be expecting a hit from his people as we speak, and if so, he'll be looking at defecting into the Witness Protection Program."

"This is a radical change in plans," Murra sat pensively. "Tell the truth, I have done a bit of research on Chupacabra and he seems to be one of the top enforcers for the Medellin Cartel. I would not want to set my hand to such a thing unless I knew it was fully sanctioned by the Colombians."

"Obviously you are aware that we are in full contact with the Colombians," Shanahan was emphatic. "Your men brought one hundred forty million dollars of bullion just a week ago. You are about to deliver another seventy million. This is an enormous amount of money, and no one can afford to have this enterprise endangered. No one knows if Chupacabra is creating chaos throughout Miami in order to wreck the Cubans' operation and step into the vacuum. They may also be planning to usurp the Medellin Cartel's network along the East Coast and join forces with MS-13 to secure a lock on the entire region. The risks are too great and the possibilities too endless to allow Chupacabra go unchecked any longer."

"All right," Murra decided. "I will have him followed when he checks out of his hotel, and we will do this work for you. I expect that we will have both tasks accomplished by tomorrow evening, and afterwards we will expect payment of four million dollars. How much is the contract on Chupacabra?"

"That will be another million, which will bring your payment up to five million."

"Done."

The men shook hands, yet Shanahan realized the honeymoon was over. Murra was not eager to be taking a hand in what he perceived to be a looming gang war. All Shanahan could hope was that MI6's trap was set to close by midnight, and that the Sardinians would be at the end of what they perceived to be a long and lucrative relationship.

Enrique Chupacabra had been forced to take the last tile in the sleeping pile. He had a choice as to whether or not to play the three or the four tile, and knew that Gawain would most likely have to play his last six to win the game. The dilemma was that Southwest and Northwest also needed the three and the four, and it would give them a chance to play their last couple of tiles. He started to tap the three tile one time but considered it might be best to throw the four. Yet if he threw the four, it would open up the opportunity for Southwest and Northwest to break out the missing six that Gawain needed.

Chupacabra suddenly saw Gawain raise his hand slowly, majestically, propping his right hand alongside his head, his forefinger resting along his cheek. He stared and grinned triumphantly at Chupacabra before crooking his finger, as if slowly pulling the trigger of a gun. Chupacabra turned to look to his left, to see if anyone in his entourage was thrown offside by the gesture, and inadvertently brushed his finger against the tile rack.

"Southeast to play the four-six," the voice in the headphone announced.

Chupacabra was apoplectic in realizing that he had probably blown the game. He started to say something to the referee but realized that he, like everyone else, was wearing the damned headphones. The rules were the rules, and if they were broken, there was a penalty to pay. He did not know what rule he had broken to bring this man, Jack Gain, into his life. What he knew was that he was going to squeeze him out of his life, as slowly and painfully as possible.

Gawain watched as Chupacabra stood up and removed his headphones, tossing them onto the table and walking away. He realized that he could not possibly do likewise without blowing his cover, and had no choice but to finish the game. He looked on in frustration as Chupacabra's tiles were restored to the sleeper pile, ensuring at least four more rounds of play. Chupacabra returned to his entourage, and Gawain could see the silver dress in the group as it drifted away from the table.

He stared sightlessly at the dominoes on the rack, cursing himself for not asking Shanahan and his damned MI6 to have kept an eye on the table in case something like this occurred. He got caught totally off-guard, not expecting Chupacabra to have pulled something like this in front of ESPN and the nations of the world. What he did know was he would make no more slips, and that he would find Fianna Hesher. If anything happened to her, he would be bringing Hell into the world of Enrique Chupacabra.

The Cubans had brought the Hinckley H-64 Ketch into the port shortly after dark, having navigated their way through a small fleet of ships en route to the Florida Keys for a boat show. They had experienced smooth sailing as they crossed over from Andros Island to the private dock in Jacksonville. They saw the four Jamaicans waiting as scheduled with an eighteen-wheeler parked in the background next to a small shack. One of the Cubans climbed up a ladder to the dock and walked over to the Jamaicans.

"You got a crane?" he asked. "This shit heavy."

"You pull up right there near the ramp so we have room to work, man," the Jamaican insisted. "We give you straps, you cinch it up fuckin' tight, man. We got instructions this shit no bounce around."

The Cubans backed the fiberglass yacht up to the ramp before unlocking the huge storage trunk in the stern of the ship. They opened the hatch and gathered around the large metal cylinder packed in along a number of metal cans of similar size containing fishing chum. They stood on the cans and carefully hoisted the cylinder out of the load, then handed it off until they had it propped on the deck. They next took hold of the straps of the crane that had been lowered, fixing them tightly around the cylinder before guiding it gently as the crane was raised.

"You bring this in from Andros, man?" the Jamaican came up to the leader again.

"Yep, smooth sailing, no problems."

"They brought this over from Matanzas?"

"Yeah, that's what I heard."

"Fuckin' hot tonight, man," the Jamaican opened his button-down shirt. The Cuban watched, his face twisting in horror as he saw a recorder taped to the man's chest.

"DEA! Freeze!" the other three Jamaicans roared, whipping out .38 revolvers and fanning out across the dock. The Cubans raised their hands in surrender as other agents jumped from the eighteen-wheeler and flooded the dock in boarding the yacht. The smugglers were dragged off the boat as the agents used a carbide-tipped sabre saw blade to pare the top off the cylinder sitting atop the dock.

"Sons of bitches!" the Jamaican agent yelled, now speaking perfect English.

"What's going on?" another agent asked after cuffing the four Cubans who laid face down on the deck.

"It's a fucking engine! They pulled a switch on us!"

Yet another agent stepped forth and dragged the leader of the Cubans off the deck.

"Take these other bastards down to Duval County," he ordered. "This piece of shit here goes to Dade County. Homeland Security wants to have a word with him."

The Cuban had no idea that he was soon about to meet Jack Gawain.

PART THREE: The Prestige

Chapter Twenty One

Emiliano Murra took a private flight on a Learjet from Miami International Airport to Jacksonville International Airport shortly after his meeting with the man called William Bruce. He took a cab out to Jacksonville Harbor, which ran along the St. Johns River onto the Atlantic Ocean. The marine terminals along the waterfront were fairly deserted at that time of night, and he assured the cabbie he had made arrangements before tipping him handsomely and dismissing him.

Murra waited until the cabbie disappeared before walking down to the end of the dock and descending a concrete staircase to one of the loading ramps. The cargo ship from Belfast was at the dock as expected, but there was a heated debate going on between the crew and Murra's gangsters who were waiting to take possession of the scheduled delivery.

"They say there's a problem with the shipment," one of Murra's gunmen cursed in Italian. "They're telling us the deal's off."

"What the hell is going on?" he asked Jimmy Burke, who was accompanied by the same three smugglers he met in Belfast several days ago. "You know the kind of money we're dealing with here."

"We got a call from our people in Belfast," the red-haired Irishman replied tautly. "The Colombians called off the deal. They said they got ripped off on the last shipment and they won't go into details just yet. They're talking nasty shite right now, and we're hearing that Amschel Bauer is on the frying pan. They're holding him responsible to find out who screwed them over. Right now, as we speak, the Montreal Mob is on the line with Mr. Bruce trying to find out if the problem was on our end. I'll tell ye, Mr. Murra, our hands are clean on this, and we'll travel around the world to kill any bastard who says otherwise."

"This is impossible," Murra stared out at the darkness encompassing the river, dimly illuminated by the silvery moon. "We never even opened the crates, they were nailed shut when we took possession in Belfast. We brought them straight to Montreal, and once they were unloaded and processed they were repackaged and reloaded onto our ship. They were nailed shut when we got them, and we took them straight to Medellin unopened. We have to get more information on this. What are you going to do with the shipment?"

"The Council's made contingency arrangements," Burke narrowed his eyes. Murra was getting a distinct impression that Burke was suspicious of him, but he was not going to call the man on it at this place and time. He had seen enough in Belfast to indicate that these Irishmen would just as soon pull a gun as engage in discussion. "We'll take the merchandise to a holding area and wait for further instructions. In the meantime, Mr. Bruce wants you to give him a call. He's pretty sure he knows what the problem is and says you can probably help sort it out."

"You told me you go back with the Council a couple of years," Murra said as his men retreated back to the eighteen-wheeler parked on the dock, opening one of the overhead doors at a nearby warehouse in order to return the mobile crane they were to use to unload the cargo. "Have you ever run into a problem like this before? Maybe someone tampered with the shipment before it was passed onto you."

"Think about this, fella," Burke said moodily. "You brought the merchandise to Montreal where it was unloaded and sent to the Bank of Montreal. After they made the purchase, they gave it back t'you to haul down to Medellin. How in bloody hell could a national bank have processed such a transaction if the load came up short? I'm suspectin' those bloody frogs lifted some of the load before they handed it back off t'you. It's none of my business, but if it were my way, I know you're dead sound, so I'd be goin' frog hunting for the missing bullion. All I know is, if our name comes up, we'll cover the earth to find the man who would accuse us in this matter."

"Let us continue to watch each other's backs, my friend," Murra shook his hand. "I too will stand against anyone who accuses you, just as I know you will do for me. Let us just hope that these thieves are discovered and dealt with so we can get on with this most profitable enterprise."

"That's our way in Belfast," Burke assured him. "We clean up our house before we suggest to others how to clean up theirs."

Murra smiled wordlessly, thinking of the many ways he might be able to assist others in their own housecleaning.

Salvaje Pulga sat in the tropical garden of his jungle fortress along the outskirts of Medellin enjoying the evening breeze along with a late-night margarita. He was pleased with the way things were going as of late, and was expecting to get word from the Europeans shortly as to how the next shipment of bullion was proceeding. His train of thought was interrupted by a call on his cell phone, and he was immediately agitated in knowing that it could only be a matter of dire importance at this time of night.

"Pulga."

"Someone tampered with the last gold shipment," a voice spoke in a crisp Castilian dialect. "Check the bars before you transfer the next payment."

"Who is this?" he demanded.

"A friend. Maybe your only friend. And don't forget who supervised the shipment," the voice replied before the line went dead.

Pulga resisted the urge to throw the cell phone out into the night. He set it down on the marble table and thought things through before making a call.

"*Si, mi Salvaje.*"

"I want you to call Fortress #7 and have them check three of the gold bars," he ordered. "Tell them to cut each bar in half, make sure they are solid, and analyze them for any impurities. Take a bar from the top of the stack, one from the middle and one from the bottom. I want this done immediately, and I want them to call me with the results in one hour. Do you hear me? One hour."

"*Si, mi Salvaje.*"

The biggest problem he had with this situation was the insinuation that Enrique Chupacabra was at fault. He had been going to bat for Enrique on several occasions as of late. The rumor that Chupacabra had sanctioned the hit on Julio Cruz in Montreal was just the start of the troubles. Next there was the formal complaint from the Cuban cartel that Enrique was behind the hit on Johnny Carmona's lieutenant in Liberty City. Pulga was irked that Chupacabra was participating in a televised game of dominoes at such a time as this, but dismissed it as just another idiosyncrasy of one of his favorite captains. The issue at hand, however, was something that someone would be held accountable for if a problem did indeed exist.

A call came back in about forty-five minutes, and Pulga could tell by the tone of the man's voice that something was amiss.

"*Mi Pulga,*" the man on the line was distraught. "This is Andrade at the Fortress. Before I report, I want you to know that when I accepted the shipment, I personally X-rayed the bars with our standard equipment, weighed the bars, and checked the serial numbers with our Swiss bank. Everything checked out, *mi Senor.*"

"If it did, then what the hell are you trying to tell me!" Pulga snapped.

"I just had one of my experts drill into three of the bars, just as you instructed," the man's voice quavered. "Your hunch was correct, sir, and I curse myself for not having just a tiny bit of your shrewdness. The bars were filled with tungsten. Somehow it seems that they were able to hollow the bars along the side and insert the tungsten ingots. From there it was a matter of resealing and polishing the bars. Tungsten has the same exact weight as gold, it would have been impossible to detect by anyone involved with the shipment."

"I want you," Pulga managed to control his voice, "to drill into every single bar and determine how much money we are losing on this deal.

I don't care how long it takes, as long as it is done as soon as possible. I don't want a word of this to leak out or someone will be killed. You call me as soon as you have a figure."

Pulga set the cell phone back on the table before pacing anxiously up and down the terrace. He knew he was going to be held accountable before the Cartel. Despite the fact that he could easily refund their investment, it would still leave him in the hole for the better part of one hundred forty million dollars. He could do the math and rationalize that the imminent conversion to the gold standard would more than recoup his loss even though the bullion was only worth a third of what he paid. Yet someone had ripped him off big time, and somebody had to pay. Even worse, Enrique Chupacabra was given full responsibility for making sure things like this did not happen. Chupacabra, as it turned out, was playing dominoes in Miami.

This situation had to be resolved immediately, even if it meant pulling out of Operation Blackout. There were calls to make, issues to be resolved, and people to be killed. He only hoped that his most trusted enforcer would not become one of them.

William Shanahan got a call from MI6 at midnight, shortly after his meeting with Murra at the Magic City Casino and a late-night cocktail with Morgana. He found that Gawain had lost the championship game, coming in second in points to the Southwest contender. Gawain called him to disclose that he had seen Fianna at the game, and they mutually agreed that MI6 would most likely make arrangements to have her situation confirmed in short order.

"The Colonel wanted you to know that the first phase of the operation has proved successful," the voice informed him. "The bullion shipments were loaded with bars filled with tungsten. When you contact Murra, you are to tell him the Colombians contacted the Council and cancelled the deal. You don't know anything about the fake bars, and it's important that you remember that. We're only letting you in on it so you don't get caught unawares when the word gets out. It's possible that the Colombians may report their findings to the Montreal Mob or the Sardinians before they get back to you, or us. This may be the most dangerous part of the operation at this juncture. The Colombians are going to be looking hard for the double-cross, and they will be using every lie and subterfuge at their disposal to trick someone into giving up the scam. You have to be on your guard, and do not do anything or meet anyone until you check in with us."

"There's another problem," Shanahan reported. "There were a couple of American girls who Gawain befriended. Somehow Chupacabra became aware of the connection. I believe that he suspected Gawain was moving against him, and may have compromised the girl to get inside Gawain's head. There is a moral obligation to protect this girl, and the Firm must be made aware that this is an urgent matter."

"I'll inform the Colonel immediately. I strongly urge you not to take any action in this matter until you receive further instructions. You know the Americans do not take such things lightly, and this entire operation could be compromised if Chupacabra is forced to leave the country for whatever reason."

Suddenly it occurred to Shanahan that Fianna might be used as a shield by Chupacabra for more than one reason. He could be thinking that if the FBI or the DEA were on him, they would be less likely to make a move on him if an innocent girl were in his entourage. Plus, if a member of the criminal network planned to act against him, they would also risk taking major heat if the girl was compromised in the event.

"All right," Shanahan reluctantly agreed. "I need to have a word from the Colonel on this matter at the earliest opportunity. Also, what is the situation with Gawain? Has he been scheduled for debriefing?"

"Gawain has been dispatched on a special mission as we speak," the voice replied, startling Shanahan with the news. "There was an arrangement with the CIA which I'm sure you're aware of. The DEA has taken a smuggling team into custody which was acting as a decoy for a group we suspect is affiliated with Al Qaeda. We have been acting on unconfirmed reports that North Korea has recently sold a small nuclear device to the terrorists. The smugglers were caught bringing a sealed metal cylinder in-country. As it turned out, the cylinder contained a small vehicle engine. The CIA is convinced that the cylinder was being used as a diversion for the genuine item which we fear is in the US at this very time."

"How does Gawain fit in?"

"The CIA has no time to transport the terrorists to Guantanamo Bay for questioning," the voice was curt. "We have agreed to have Gawain taken to an undisclosed location to expedite the matter. You'll be updated as we obtain further information. Six out."

Shanahan sat staring at the cell phone in disbelief. He was appalled by the thought of MI6 having agreed to such a thing, and equally astounded that the CIA would have made such a request. He tried to rationalize the situation by considering the possible danger of a nuclear attack. Yet he could not overlook the consequences of government agencies sinking to the level of those who had no scruples or sense of decency.

He could not abide by the notion that, in the near future, there might be no standards at all.

Gawain was picked up at the hotel shortly after midnight, and driven to the airport where he met up with Jimmy Burke and his partners. They boarded a Learjet and were flown to a secluded property in Key Largo which belonged to the CIA. They had used their time-tested tactic of moving their captives and operatives around in random patterns that anyone outside the loop would find impossible to track.

The Irishmen were escorted to the soundproofed mansion that was surrounded by miles of deserted beachfront, preventing any outside interference with activity on the property. There were a dozen riflemen posted around the house, with a fire team on guard at a spotlight situated further along the beach alongside a commercial-sized garage where a fleet of trucks and cars were parked. There was a squad gathered around the garage area, leading the Irishmen to believe there was a unit of platoon strength assigned to the property.

Gawain and the others were greeted by the agents on the patio, and Gawain shook hands with Joe Bieber. He led them inside to the spacious living room area, where Gawain was given a meat processor's frock.

"You're kiddin'," Gawain chuckled.

"It has a psychological effect, not to mention the more practical purposes," another agent assured him.

Bieber took them downstairs where the captive was being held. It was a finished basement occupied by a small refrigerator, a sofa, a pool table, a poker table and some folding chairs. In the middle of the room sat a tightly bound, heavily sweating Cuban, whose eyes bulged with terror at the sight of the grim-faced Irishmen.

"We told the gentleman that we need to know where the other shipment landed," Bieber said as he stood in front of the Cuban. "If he doesn't give that up, then we need to know who gave him the job and where he can be located. It'll be much easier for him and for us if he just tells us where the second cylinder went."

"Oh, he'll tell us everything," Gawain walked over and patted the Cuban's chubby face, glancing over at the surgical instruments set out on the pool table. He spotted the machete in the corner, certain that it was all he would need.

"I'll be upstairs, I'll come back and check on you in a bit if you're not done," Bieber told him, beckoning the three CIA agents to follow him back upstairs.

Bieber tried to remain calm, though realizing they were in a frantic race against time. The Company had determined that the bomb sold to Al Qaeda was, in fact, a 15-kiloton device that would decimate an area of one square mile. If they were able to detonate the bomb next to a truckload of radioactive waste material, it would create a 'dirty bomb' effect that could possibly irradiate an area of up to ten square miles. In a heavily populated area, the effects would be catastrophic. If the bomb was already in-country, the government would have to take drastic steps to search all vehicles capable of transporting hazardous materials. Such a scenario would create major traffic congestions, and possibly create further diversions for the terrorist to use to their advantage.

Like Shanahan, it made him sick that they had to resort to extreme measures to obtain information from these suspects. Nonetheless, a nuke attack inside the US was unthinkable. Such a catastrophe could cost the lives of hundreds of thousands of innocent Americans. He could not disregard the fact that the man being interrogated downstairs had knowingly and willingly brought a cylinder into the country that quite possibly contained a weapon of mass destruction. Even if he knew he was carrying a decoy, he knew what was going on and was now facing the consequences of his actions. Yet, Bieber believed in the Constitution, believed in America as a land of righteousness and justice. There had to be a better way than this, but there was no time in figuring out what it was.

Bieber was just about to go down and check on Gawain at the half-hour mark, but he heard footsteps on the staircase. At length Gawain came up and walked over to him, smirking as he took off his blood-smeared smock and tossed it in a ball onto the parquet floor.

"Well, we got the name of the person who sent him out, as well as all the details of his own part in the deal," Gawain revealed. "The other cylinder landed in Brownsville, Texas about a day ago. He says it's probably in the possession of the Mexican Mafia, if they haven't passed it off to Al Qaeda already."

"So the Mexican Mafia's in on it," Bieber shook his head. "Holy shit. I need to get in touch with my people right away. Listen, we've already discussed contingency plans with your people. Go ahead and give them a call. We've made arrangements for you and your team to be flown to the hot spot in case we intercept any more terrorists. I'm thinking they're going to want to get you out to Houston, but give your people a call and clear it with them first."

"You've got to be kiddin'," Gawain arched his eyebrows, turning to Jimmy Burke. "Did you know about this?"

"Well, it had come up in conversation," Burke admitted.

"Thanks a million for sharin', boyo," Gawain sneered. "Okay, I'm off to the patio to give them a buzz. Do you know if Captain Gummo—erm, Shanahan—is on his way in here, if you don't mind my askin'?"

"He's got some urgent matters of his own to attend to," Bieber assured him. "Go on and make your call, we're going to have to be moving fast on this."

Gawain headed out to the patio, realizing that the plot was getting thicker and the risks would doubtlessly increase as well. He knew his freedom would come at a price, but he was starting to wonder just how high a price he might have to pay.

Chapter Twenty Two

It was around that time that the world found out how Amschel Bauer's plans were being complemented by those of Al-Qaeda.

Shortly after midnight, the State Department announced that a coup had been staged in Pakistan by a radical faction headed by Islamic extremists. Though the military dictator had been rescued by loyalist troops, the Prime Minister's residential building had been taken by rebels who announced plans to install a caretaker administration. Federal and provincial governments across the nation were under siege by insurgent forces, and Al Qaeda announced on Al Jazeera that it was governing the Islamic state of Pakistan by proxy.

Shanahan had been tossing and turning throughout a sleepless night, and was available when his cell phone went off once again.

"Six," the voice said. "Have you heard the news?"

"It's the middle of the night here," he grumbled, switching on the lamp on the nightstand.

"There's been an attempted coup in Islamabad. British and US troops have been deployed. We're seriously compromised at this juncture. We've already got a significant number of special operations forces tied up in Iraq and Afghanistan. We're going to need you on a black op mission, we don't have anyone else with your qualifications available."

"You've got to be kidding," Shanahan slid up to a sitting position at the edge of the bed. "What happens to this operation?"

"We want you to finish your business with Murra. Have him locate Chupacabra and let us know as soon as you've got a fix on him. Gawain has been reassigned to the backup unit which is working as our liaison with the CIA. This operation's just about wrapped up, we're needing you on this new assignment as soon as possible. Contact Murra at the earliest opportunity and let us know when you're ready to proceed."

"What about the girl?" he pressed.

"The Colonel has been made aware of the situation and it is being addressed as we speak. We expect to hear from you at your earliest convenience. Six out."

Shanahan snatched the remote control off the nightstand and switched on the plasma TV. He tuned in to the BBC network, which was buzzing with the latest developments from Islamabad. Their Parliament had been besieged by rumors of an impending insurgent attack for months. Yet their ongoing problems with elements of the Taliban operating on the Afghanistan border had distracted them from the extremist rallies in the capitol city. The rallies had acted as a subterfuge for the terrorists, who smuggled their weapons into the city during the demonstrations. They had troops stationed near key government buildings, ready for action once a signal for action was given. Rioters pressed close enough to the buildings for the gunmen to stage their attack. It was now estimated that twenty percent of government buildings across the country had been seized by the rebels.

He was not clear as to what MI6 was planning to do about Operation Blackout. He had reported that Amschel Bauer was planning to disrupt the international gold standard, and it was obvious that the smuggling of the WMD's were integral to the plot. They could not possibly think that killing Chupacabra was going to derail the operation. If anything, the entire episode was posing a distraction to the criminal network at best. He was certain that the sting operation involving Murra had done enormous damage, but now the focus was shifting back towards Chupacabra and it made no sense to him.

He checked his cell phone and saw that Murra had called, and undoubtedly he was already planning his own moves in light of the latest developments. He would have to meet with Murra and pin the blame on Chupacabra in order to put this final phase of the operation into effect.

He fell backwards into the king-size bed, hoping to get at least a couple of hours of REM sleep before sunrise. He doubted very much that there would be time for a morning workout. The spit was about to hit the fan, and now all of a sudden Shanahan was facing the prospect of being in uniform in South Asia once again.

He tossed and turned until the sun began peeking through the blinds. He decided to call Murra, knowing that he must have gotten word about the cancelled shipment by now.

"Murra."

"It's Bruce."

"William. What happened?"

"We're still trying to sort it out. Apparently there was a problem with the shipments."

"Your smuggling team told me what happened. They said someone tampered with the shipments. They said you were in contact with Montreal to find out what happened."

"I can meet you in the lobby in a half hour."

"I'll be there."

Shanahan dressed quickly and took the elevator down to Terraza, then made a reservation for a table on the terrace. He bought a newspaper and skimmed through it, frowning at the news of the Pakistani insurgency before Murra came through the glass doors. He walked over and they shook hands before heading to Terraza and being seated by a waitress. She took orders for coffee, orange juice and toast before leaving them with a menu.

"Have you gotten any word from your people yet?" Murra's normally grim countenance smoldered with tension.

"The word was that they found bars that were filled with tungsten," Shanahan revealed. "It weighs just as much as gold and is impossible to detect by X-ray. The bars obviously passed inspection at the Bank of Montreal. The Colombians didn't find out about it until last night. Everyone's being secretive at this point, even my people. The higher-ups have been in communication since word came back from Colombia. They're trying to find out where the switch was made."

"Your people from Belfast appear to be very upset," Murra noted dourly. "My people are very upset at the prospect of losing our commission on this pending shipment. Have you checked the merchandise at Jacksonville to see if it's been tampered with?"

"Right now I'm completely in the dark," Shanahan admitted. "The reason why they wanted me to meet with you is Chupacabra. He was the one who was supposed to have arranged security for the entire operation. He was responsible for the gold to have been transported from the Montreal harbor to the Bank of Montreal, then back to the dock where it was turned over to your people. They are certain the switch was not made in Belfast, and your people are considered beyond reproach. Right now, it looks like Chupacabra is being left holding the bag."

"So he is going to be the scapegoat," Murra glanced out at the downtown skyline.

"So it appears," Shanahan replied. "It's not only this, but the other things. From all reports, Liberty City has turned into a war zone. He's suspected of having killed two of the Cuban cartel's top dealers in a joint effort with the Jamaicans to take over the drug trade in Miami. Right now it looks like the Jamaicans and the Haitians moving against the Cubans, but the smart money says it's Chupacabra. He's been communicating regularly with the Montreal Mob and people think he's getting ready to go independent."

"How do you want to handle this?"

"My people are working with the Colombians to get their approval for the work. Once they do, we'll expect them to set it up somewhere in West Florida to make it look less obvious. The overriding concern is to make it clear that the Cubans have nothing to do with it. At the same time, we don't want to risk offending Montreal and compromise any future enterprises. I am fairly certain we should be able to get this going sometime this evening."

"Very well," Murra exhaled. "I'll notify my people in Sardinia there's been a change in plans. I am hoping that this issue can be resolved as soon as possible. My people are going to be very upset to find that we left eight million dollars on the table."

"Everything will be resolved very shortly," Shanahan assured him. "You have my word."

Morgana McLaren had played a hunch. She contacted one of her friends from Aer Lingus, Lakeesha Washington, who worked for Airport Security with the airline. She had recently accepted a job with Homeland Security but promised to keep in touch with Morgana in exchanging phone numbers. Morgana gave her a call and asked if she could use her new connections to check on some names for her. Lakeesha was glad to help and called Morgana back that morning.

"First off, I have nothing on Fianna," Lakeesha reported, sitting in her new office in Washington DC. "All I have on Colombiana Exports is just what you told me. They deal with commodities out of the home office in Medellin. She must have taken a private jet from New York. She definitely hasn't left the country, and I can let you know if anything comes up. Bear in mind that if they're flying around in a private jet, it's going to be hard to pinpoint her."

"I understand."

"Now, this guy William Shanahan," Lakeesha continued. "I've got him as a Captain in the British Army. He served in Iraq and Afghanistan with the Special Air Service and the Special Boat Service. Almost all of his information is classified, which means it's a safe bet that he's still involved in counter-intelligence. I'm not getting much on Universal Exports, which makes it look a whole lot like Colombiana Exports. They both look a whole lot like dummy corporations, but that's just a guess on my past."

"Okay," Morgana's tummy was churning with trepidation.

"As for this other guy, Jack Gawain," Lakeesha's tone softened. "I've got a John Oliver Cromwell Gawain, five-foot-nine, one hundred eighty pounds, black hair, dark brown eyes, currently serving a triple life sentence for thirteen murders and twenty-seven attempted murders, plus crimes of insurrection, terrorism, drug dealing, extortion, robbery, you name it. According to what I have here, he's doing his time at Maghaberry HMP. That stands for Her Majesty's Prison."

"So that's not the Jack Gawain who's out here," Morgana murmured.

"What kind of stuff you got yourself into, girl?" Lakeesha asked. "Why you looking at people like this? Is Fianna in some kind of trouble?"

"No, no," Morgana insisted. "We met these guys while we were in New York and I was just wondering about them. It doesn't sound like these are the guys you came up with. I'm betting they're from Europe or Australia. They probably made up that Universal Exports thing. I just haven't heard from Fianna and I got curious. I sure appreciate you, Keesh."

"Sure, honey, no problem. Next time you're in Washington give me a call, we'll have lunch, okay?"

"Thanks so much. Talk to you soon."

Almost as an afterthought, Lakeesha decided to pass the information along to her supervisor. She figured it might come in handy in light of the turbulence of recent events.

On the other end of the line, Morgana sat down on the balcony of her suite and sipped her coffee pensively. She wasn't fooling Lakeesha any more than she was fooling herself. Maybe they were barking up the wrong tree with Jack, though the physical description was creepily familiar. As far as William and Universal Exports, that was too much to ignore. He was involved with something other than international commerce, and Fianna's disappearance was making her think he probably knew more than she was letting on.

She decided she was going to wait until tomorrow morning and see if William came up with anything. She resolved herself not to call him, and if she did not hear from him she would not tell him she was checking out. She would go back to New York and file a missing persons report and let the police handle it. She greatly disliked the idea of severing ties with William, but if he had lied to her, then there was no point in pursuing the relationship any further. She had seen countless women in her life hurt by relationships based on deception, and she was not about to become one of them.

Miles away, Ernesto Guzman was arrested on the Riverwalk in San Antonio by Federal agents and transported to Homeland Security's field office on Fourwinds Drive. Guzman grew suspicious when the unmarked car headed north on the I-35 instead of going towards the Bexar County Jail on North Comal. He figured that it was some kind of Federal rap, and only hoped it had nothing to do with Alberto Calix. If one of his people had snitched, the last war between the Mexican Mafia and the Mexican Cartel would be as a paintball game compared to this one.

Ernie was taken down to the basement of the building, remaining in cuffs as he was seated in a metal folding chair in the middle of a small yellow-painted room. The agents left him alone for about twenty minutes before three of them returned. One stood before him as the other two stood slightly behind him on either side of the chair.

"You gonna take these cuffs off?" Guzman demanded. "They're starting to cut my circulation."

"*Something's* gotta cut your circulation, home boy," the tall agent to his left chuckled.

"I'm Kelly Stone," the tall, solidly-built young man with the thick coiffured mane stood before him. "I'm here to figure out what your people did with the item you smuggled in from Brownsville during that border incident a few nights ago."

"Brownsville?" Ernie squinted. "I'm up here in San Antonio, how the fuck do I have anything to do with Brownsville?"

The husky agent to his right shifted his weight before hauling off with a roundhouse right cross that nearly knocked Guzman out of his chair.

"Brownsville, Ernie," Stone set back on the small table sitting against the wall. "Your coyotes in Matamoros let loose a human wave of refugees near the campus at UT that night. They drew all our Border

Patrol units out of position so that your gangbangers in Matamoros could storm the bridge with their trucks and catch Cameron County's law enforcement officers off-guard. We knew it wasn't just a half-assed attempt to force all those illegals over the border, but we couldn't really figure what was up."

"What the fuck you hitting me for?" Ernie asked groggily. "I want my fucking lawyer."

"We intercepted a vessel in Key West that came over from Andros Island by way of Cuba," the tall agent informed him. "We caught four smugglers from the Cuban Mob bringing a sealed metal cylinder in on a boat full of chum barrels. We know Al Qaeda's made plans to smuggle an WMD onto American soil, and it was obvious they were using the cylinder as a decoy to make the traffickers think they were moving the real Mc Coy. Since the Cubans we caught were aliens without Constitutional rights, we shipped them off to Guantanamo."

"Our people in Guantanamo can get away with a lot more shit than we can," the husky agent slapped Ernie across the back of the head. "It didn't take long before they gave up everything. We know about Brownsville and obviously we know about you. Now we need to know where the second cylinder went."

"Look, man, I don't know what the fuck..."

The husky man swung again, a solid right cross smashing Ernie's jaw and sending him to the concrete floor, the metal chair clattering alongside him.

"Watch your language," the agent snarled through the mist. "And don't lie to us."

"I know you've got your green card, and your wife and kids are citizens," he could see Stone 's shoes as he came over to stand by Ernie's head. "Too bad your mistress and your two bastard kids aren't. They're doing pretty good up there in Austin. The youngest is getting all A's in middle school and the oldest is in the National Honor Society, doing pretty good on the football team. I think it'd be pretty shitty for them to get flown down to Guantanamo."

"You get your Jew lawyers in on this and it gets worse," the husky agent kicked him lightly in the back. "We'll move the bitch and her kids back to Brownsville, put her in County and the kids in Juvie[1].When your lawyers find out where they are, we send them right back to Guantanamo. I think after a few trips back and forth, when your little bastards go back to school, *in Mexico*, their grades are going to turn to shit."

"Don't fuck with my kids," Guzman managed. "If you do, you might as well kill me right here. I don't give a fuck who you are, I'll find you and I'll find your family. You can do whatever you want to me, but don't fuck with my kids."

"Okay, tough guy," the husky agent grabbed him by the back of his white silk guayabera, ripping the collar as he dragged Ernie to a sitting position against the wall. "All we need to know is where that cylinder went after Brownsville. We think it's a small nuclear weapon from North Korea. We think your shitbag connections from the Mexican Cartel brought the nuke up from Central America and handed it off to your guys in Brownsville. We know you scumbags aren't going to set off a nuke in Texas. So now, dickhead, who got the nuke and where's it going?"

"Look, Stone, you know how the game's played, unless you just got out of law school like I'm starting to think," Guzman snarled at him. "They never tell you what they're shipping and where it's going! You just move it along your end of the pipeline and collect your money!"

"You think we're bluffing, don't you?" Stone wiggled a cell phone at him.

"None of us knew it was a bomb!" Ernie yelled at him. "Bring some of your fucking sodium pentothal[2] in here, and a lie detector! You think they're going to seal a container and tell us what's inside it?"

"Where'd it go, Ernie?" Stone insisted. "Where did you send it?"

---

1. juvenile detention
2. truth serum

"Houston," he gave in, defeated by the thought of his mistress and their kids being taken into custody. "I didn't have anything to do with the details, I only gave my consent. Our people picked it up in Brownsville and drove it up to Houston. I don't know anything about WMD's, Al Qaeda, or any of that shit."

"We didn't say Al Qaeda," the husky agent growled. "You just did."

"Fuck you," Guzman hawked and spat bloody mucus onto the concrete floor. "That son of a bitch right there said Al Qaeda a minute ago."

The tall agent walked over and patted Ernie's head.

"Okay, get him cleaned up, get him something to eat," Stone got up off the table. "We're going to send you to Huntsville for a couple of days until this boils over. The ragheads'll either set off the bomb or go underground in the next forty-eight hours, so it won't matter whether you're back on the street or not. You might as well save yourself some money and sit this one out. By the time your lawyer files for habeas corpus and requests bail, you'll be back in circulation."

"Who's gonna pay for my shirt?" Guzman sneered as they stood him up and uncuffed him.

"Send it to my boss," Stone shot back as he opened the metal door in leaving the room. "He's in the big white house on Pennsylvania Avenue in Washington."

Ernie pulled a handkerchief from his back pocket and spat more blood.

He wished that Al Qaeda was sending the metal cylinder to the big white house on Pennsylvania Avenue.

Chapter Twenty Three

Salvaje Pulga sat in the tropical garden of his fortress stronghold that afternoon, waiting impatiently for his computer technicians to complete their set-up of the monitors and speakers for the videoconference scheduled in a half hour from now. He greatly disliked having to fiddle with electronic devices and equipment, relegating the duties whenever possible. It got to the point where his overseers were requiring the household staff to have basic PC skills in order to facilitate Pulga's daily communications.

He was faced with a major crisis in dealing with the bullion ripoff, and hopefully this conference would resolve all issues. He spoke to the other members of the Cartel shortly after midnight, and they agreed to postpone their decision on the matter until he had conferred with Bauer and William Bruce. They had done a great deal of research on the mitigating facts and evidence surrounding Operation Blackout, and determined that it was truly an ingenious plan. They did not want to withdraw from the operation unless absolutely necessary, and would leave it to Pulga to get everything sorted out.

He had finally gotten in touch with Enrique Chupacabra this morning, and after a heated exchange simmered to a slow boil, he was fairly certain that someone might have been trying to set Pulga's golden boy up. He gave Pulga a detailed narrative of how his men met Murra's smugglers at the Montreal harbor, loaded the crates onto eighteen-wheelers and drove them directly to the Bank of Montreal. They stayed in local motels until the funds from Medellin were transferred to the bank, and promptly recovered the bullion and brought it back to the dock where it was loaded back onto the Sardinian cargo ship bound for Colombia.

"Come on, *mi patron*, use your head," Chupacabra railed to the point of disrespect. "You can check the records and see when the Sardinians came into port, and you can check to see when our guys arrived at the bank. At the very least, the security guards at both places would have logged the dates and times when my guys showed up. Where the hell do we get the time to unload all that shit and switch out good gold for fakes? We're talking about sixty tons of metal! Who are my guys, supermen? Same goes for the delivery time from the bank to the dock. Besides, we're talking one hundred and thirty four million dollars here. Sure it's a lot of money, but you and I have made that kind of money dozens of times over through the years. Do you really believe I would screw you over for that amount?"

"Okay, I'm going to go to bat for you," Pulga finally relented. "Let's talk about something else. What in hell is going on up there in Liberty City?"

"I talked that into the ground with Johnny Carmona," Chupacabra said impatiently. "Some cowboy named Jack Gain got into Johnnie Sosa'a crew in Miami and stirred up some major shit with the Jamaicans before killing Johnnie over a fucking ki. He shot Jimmy Sosa in the face but let him live to deliver the message. He tried to pin it on me, the fucking prick. He mentioned something to Johnnie about having been at the meeting in Montreal, and my guys remembered some Limey bastard telling a bunch of jokes and cutting up out in the hallway that day. I'm thinking he came in with that crew from Europe, those Council guys."

"Those Europeans," Pulga growled. "It's bad enough dealing with those Ashkenazi Jews from Montreal, let alone the English and those other sons of bitches. How can we know whether they all got together to burn us for the hundred-forty mil? They've sold *mi compadres* on the deal, but I'd just as soon damn the whole operation to hell!"

Pulga felt much better after having ironed everything out with Chupacabra. He trusted his enforcer implicitly, and just needed to hear his side of the story for peace of mind. Now it was a question of getting things squared away with Montreal and the Europeans, and find out whether anyone was going to make good on the one hundred forty mil. His people had determined that the tungsten inserts comprised about thirty-three percent of the weight of each bar, so he had been burned for somewhere around forty-eight million dollars. It was not chump change by any means, but it was far more sustainable. It was the first number he would throw on the table when the videoconference began.

"It certainly is a significant amount, and by no means are we considering this a trifling issue," Amschel Bauer appeared with Nathan Schnaper on the left side of the enormous plasma screen his crew had set up on one of the marble tables in the garden. On the right hand side was the image of William Bruce. "Our people are investigating the matter thoroughly, and we intend to deal with this as expediently as possible."

"So what the hell happens to my money?" Pulga demanded. "You know I represent the entire Cartel. It is not just Salvaje Pulga who got burned, but the entire Medellin Cartel. I don't want this profitable enterprise to degenerate into a bloodbath."

"We certainly do not want the Medellin Cartel to be placed at an inconvenience by any means," Bauer assured him. "Your organization is far too important to us to compromise our relationship over such a trifling sum. I have made some calls, and I believe we can file an insurance claim over the bullion having been embezzled. As a matter of fact, since our people virtually control the bank, we will go ahead and transfer the forty million back to you and await the settlement for our reimbursement."

"The obvious question is, how are you going to make sure that we are not burned again?" Salvaje demanded.

"I think we are going to start this part of the conversation with Mr. Bruce," Bauer decided. "So far he has vouched for the Sardinian team that has delivered the shipments from Belfast to Montreal, and from Montreal to Medellin. The fact of the matter is that the Sardinians have been in possession of the items for longer than anyone else involved in the transport. I think it would go without saying that a bank such as ours would not be knowingly processing bogus commodities. Without placing blame, I think Mr. Bruce may continue speaking comfortably on behalf of the Sardinians."

"Not too comfortably," William played his trump card. "Unfortunately we have just begun dealing with the Sardinians in an effort to expand our own network. I can and will vouch for Emiliano Murra, with whom I have been dealing directly here in Miami. As for his people, I am starting to think that this is where the problem may lie. I am quite certain that the Sardinian Mob would hardly risk the possibility of having their ties severed with the Council over such an amount. However, one overly ambitious smuggler in his crew might well think that several million dollars would well be worth a gamble."

"Very well, gentlemen," Bauer continued. "What we will also guarantee is that we will conduct a random check of every shipment from here on to verify the purity of the bullion. Furthermore, we will send word to our insurers that we have confirmed notice that there are bogus commodities being traded on the open market. This will facilitate any further claims we may have to file on the behalf of Colombiana Exports."

"And let me add to that by saying that if we find out who's trying to screw this deal, my crew guarantees we will sever their heads off and throw them out in the street," Nathan Schnaper assured one and all.

"I'll be meeting with Mr. Murra in a few hours," William informed them. "I'll express our concerns and let you all know what preventive measures he plans to take to avoid a recurrence in the near future."

"It's been a pleasure, gentlemen," Bauer concluded the videoconference. "I will contact you both individually so we can reschedule the shipment on hold in Florida."

Salvaje Pulga ordered his servants to take the video equipment away. He considered his options in remaining in business with the Canadians and the Europeans. It sounded very much like Bauer remained in control, and Pulga was fairly certain that his money would be returned.

He also firmly resolved that blood would run in torrents before he got burned again.

Shortly after the videoconference, Shanahan called Morgana's room and got no response. He next phoned the front desk and was told she was scheduled to check out at 11 AM. He threw on a short-sleeved dress shirt and slacks, then rushed to the elevator to see if he could catch her. He hastened to her suite and found the door wide open as if room service had arrived, but when he approached he saw her sitting on the bed near her packed luggage.

"What's going on, love?" he walked over to where she sat forlornly, looking down at the thick shag carpet. "You mean you weren't even going to call me to say goodbye?"

"I—really thought things were going good between us, William," she said quietly. "I was just about to go down to the lobby but decided to wait to see if you called."

"So it's not about Fianna," he determined. "Listen. Why don't you let me call down and get your reservation reset. Let's talk about whatever's bothering you."

"I have a friend at the airport who has a few connections, and they did some checking around," she admitted, her beautiful eyes misty. "There is no Universal Exports, is there?"

"I'm going to close the door," he said, taking the Do Not Disturb sign and fixing it to the outer handle before closing it gently. "There is a Universal Exports, but it's not what it seems. I'm actually working for the British Government as an investigator of sorts. I can't tell you everything because it's highly classified. I haven't been trying to hide anything from you, lass. There are just some things that I'm tending to here that is far better for you not to know about."

"Is that what happened to Fianna?" a tear escaped from her emerald eyes. "Did Jack tell her something she wasn't supposed to know?"

"I don't think so," he said, sitting down alongside her. She was wearing a dress as was her fashion, and his heart skipped a beat as her legs were crossed alongside him. "I can fairly well assure you that Jack is very much concerned about Fianna. We had a discussion about her a day or so ago, and I saw a side of him I had not seen before."

"Has he—has he been in trouble with the law?" she asked softly.

"Well, let me say this," he cleared his throat. "You know we're both from Northern Ireland. Unfortunately we're from different sides of the track, so to speak. What is seen as patriotic duty on one side, and doing the right thing for one's family and friends, can be seen as a criminal act by the other side. To tell the truth, Jack was on the right side, and you can say that I was born on the wrong side. Somehow in this crazy world we live in, the roles got reversed. I end up the hero and he ends up being someone's scapegoat somewhere. What I can tell you is that, as we both can see, he is walking about as a free man. If he were a bad man, or a dangerous one, surely he would not be walking around free, wouldn't you say?"

"Is he the man that they say is in that prison in Ireland?"

"He's not in prison, Morgana," Shanahan put his arm around her for the first time, her hair nestled against his cheek so he could smell the fragrance of her perfume. "He is free."

"I just need you to tell me Fianna's going to be okay," she managed.

"I've got some very powerful people looking into it," he assured her. "I am fairly certain I will have some good information by this evening."

"If you can promise me you'll never lie to me," she sniffed, "I'll stay."

"As long as you understand that there are things I cannot share, for your protection, I will tell you I would not lie to you."

She took his hand in hers, and they sat in peace for a long while. Finally she called the front desk and told the clerk she would be renewing her reservation.

Both she and William realized that their relationship had quite a long way to go.

Morgana and William spent the afternoon together walking along the beach and wandering around the boardwalk, checking out the stores and chit-chatting with the shopkeepers and tourists. Shanahan decided that he was going to set the day aside for Morgana and took on a different personality in doing so. He found himself closely resembling the bright-eyed, bushy-tailed young pup that was first deployed to Iraq during Operation Desert Storm when he first volunteered for the military. It was before he got his first taste of the battlefield, before he ever saw a man killed on the field, before he ever killed a man. It was a time when he was happy-go-lucky and carefree, light years before MI6. Now he knew why it took this long to find a woman like Morgana. He would not have known what to do with her.

It was a perfect day for them, both having changed into T-shirts, shorts and sandals. He could not remember the last time he had laughed so much, and she brought joy to his heart with her tinkling laughter, her dazzling eyes and her mischievous smile. She held onto her arm as they walked up and down the thoroughfare, and he could not help but burst with pride as he caught other men staring with envy on his peripherals. She took a childlike delight with the simplest of things, inspecting every novelty shop and souvenir stand. Somewhere along the way he lost his core values about saving himself for a woman of the manor born. He was not sure that he would ever again find a woman so beautiful with this unique spirit, for up until this time in his life he had not ever seen one like her.

"William, I've had a wonderful time," he brought her back to her suite after they had a seafood dinner at the Yuca Restaurant. Morgana tried their Cuban Paella and Shanahan ordered the Mahi Mahi, both of them finishing half of their meals before exchanging plates. They finished off a bottle of white wine before heading back as the sun began setting along the harbor.

"So have I, love," he smoothed a lock of hair away from her face. "I'll call you for breakfast in the morning unless something comes up. Now, promise me you won't get upset if I'm not on the dot. I've got some things to attend to, but it doesn't mean I've forgotten about you. I don't think I'll ever be able to do that."

"Okay," she gazed into his eyes. "I trust you."

At once it was if he lost control of himself for the first time since he could remember. He took her into his arms and crushed his lips against hers, his tongue swirling into her mouth as if a magic portal to ecstasy. She responded feverishly, kissing him as if they were never to see each other forevermore. He pulled him tightly to him and could feel her luscious melons pressing against his chest. He buried his hand in her golden mane, holding her head next to hers as if it were the most precious thing in existence...

"Let's go inside," she said huskily, licking her lips ever so lightly.

"No," he managed weakly. "Oh, my gosh, no. I have to go to this meeting, there is no way around it. You'll be the death of me, lass. Let me call you tomorrow morning, darling."

"Okay, big guy," she unlocked the door to her suite. "Don't say I didn't offer."

"You're very special to me, Morgana," he embraced her once again, kissing her on the lips. "Very special."

"You're not too easy to forget either, sexy boy," she winked before closing the door behind her.

At once it dawned on him that regardless of how this mission ended up, for him and Morgana, it was only the beginning.

Shanahan waited in front of the hotel later that evening, dressed in his black jogging suit as Murra's black SUV arrived. One of his men was driving the Ford Escape, and Murra sat beside the driver with a third man alongside him as they pulled up to the curb alongside Shanahan.

"Beautiful weather we're having," Murra greeted him with a handshake. "Hop in."

Shanahan climbed into the passenger seat as they headed for the airport. Murra's rented Learjet awaited as they planned to fly to Panama City where they got word that Chupacabra and his men had been spotted.

"So everything has been cleared with the Colombians?" Murra asked as they sped along the highway, the magnificent sunset fading to midnight blue along the vast horizon.

"Yes," Shanahan lied. "I had a videoconference with the Cartel and the sponsors of the enterprise. They mutually agreed that Chupacabra was a risk that could no longer be tolerated. I gave you and your people my full endorsement, and they assured me that if this job was done according to plan, you would be the best candidate to oversee and supervise our operations as this venture moves forward."

"Excellent," Murra smiled, looking out the window pensively. "Excellent."

Shanahan assessed the gunmen as Murra had introduced them before they engaged in small talk to pass the time. Napolitano was a tall, stocky man with a hint of an accent. Pellegrino was a runt of a man but had a wicked glint in his eye, the kind of man who would slit a throat at a moment's notice. They seemed friendly enough, but shared the deadly aura of their master in making Shanahan feel as if he sat in a pit of vipers.

"So," Shanahan asked matter-of-factly. "What'd you think about the fellows from Belfast? They came across as dead sound on our end. We've been thinking that having you and them connecting on the harbor is the tightest link in the chain."

"I agree," Murra nodded sagely. "That Jimmy Burke and the O'Connor Brothers are the genuine gem. If they weren't so Irish, I'd swear they were Sardinian."

"They're out on a job with one of my people," Shanahan joined the others in sharing a laugh. "I'm glad to hear he's in good company."

"Yes, he is," Murra peered into Shanahan's eyes from the rear view mirror. "I met them in Belfast when I traveled there to arrange the first shipment. They took me carousing all along West Belfast. Let me tell you, it was one of the more unforgettable moments of my life. Those Irishmen certainly know how to party."

"East Belfast, you mean," Shanahan gently corrected him.

"No, it was West Belfast," Murra replied pointedly. "We drove down to Falls Road, to what they said was an IRA stronghold back in the day. I met quite a few strong men who told me they were IRA veterans. Of course, the Continuity IRA is still quite active, as is the Real IRA. I believe Jimmy and his men are with the Continuity group, but I can't be sure."

Shanahan's stomach began churning as he realized the situation Jack Gawain was in. If Jimmy Burke and his men were with any of the splinter Irish Republican Army groups, there would be little doubt that they would know who Jack the Hacker was. He broke a cold sweat as he considered the fact that MI6 had knowingly sent Gawain on a one-way ride with those killers.

"Well," Shanahan managed, "I'm glad that you fellows were able to connect in such a way. It is so important that we establish trust and confidence in one another as we travel these roads of destiny together."

"I trust them," Murra's powerful hand reached over and squeezed Shanahan's shoulder reassuringly. "I trust them as much as I trust you."

Shanahan stared out the window into the shadowy landscape, hoping that MI6 was just as trustworthy in their dealings with Jack Gawain.

Chapter Twenty Four

Hours earlier, Joe Bieber and his men were monitoring their electronic communications from several different Federal, State and local agencies as the search for the terrorists continued throughout South Texas. They had a clandestine office set up in Galveston from which they were coordinating efforts with Homeland Security. The DHS, in turn, was working in conjunction with the FBI, the DEA and the Bureau of Alcohol, Tobacco and Firearms and Explosives to track down the mysterious cylinder from Brownsville. They were feverishly compiling information and putting together a game plan, knowing that they were in a race against time.

The first step they took was a racial profiling of all persons of Arabic descent in the region, both Arab-Americans and immigrants, and compiled the information into a database which they proceeded to weed out in a cursory qualification process. Their first step was to divide the database into categories, separating males over eighteen years of age from minors, women and the elderly. They next eliminated the infirm and the sickly from the list. They then removed all who had claimed mixed descent or denied Islam as their religion on public record. Moving towards more positive identification, they narrowed it down to all those having criminal records, licenses for any purpose or field of endeavor, traffic violations and interaction with public media.

They ended up with a handful of individuals, but the one that attracted Bieber's attention was a man named Mohammed Hassan. He had been detained shortly after 9/11 for questioning, and the incident seemed to have pushed him over the edge. He had a Facebook page advocating radical Islam philosophies, was a subscriber to Al-Jazeera, and attended a militant mosque in the area as well as Islamic study groups who were on record with the FBI as potential agitators and subversives. After a short discussion with his team, Bieber put in a call to Jack Gawain.

Gawain, along with Jimmy Burke and the O'Connors, had been on stand-by at a motel in Houston when he received the call. He was given detailed instructions as to Hassan's home address, the address of his mosque, and those of his study group partners. After a brief meeting with Burke and the Connors, the five men piled into their rented Ford Explorer and headed out to the home of Mohammed Hassan in West Houston.

Hassan was on the Internet when he heard the knock on the door. The person on the other side had a thick Irish accent, announcing he was with the FBI. Hassan replied that he wanted to call the Police Department and notify them before he opened the door. There was a brief pause before the man outside the door began kicking violently against it, destroying the door jamb. They next wedged a small crowbar into the door and wrenched the safety chain off the door frame before four man came barreling through the entrance.

Hassan had retrieved a meat cleaver from the kitchen, but the sight of the Glock in Jack Gawain's hand caused him to hesitate. Gawain smashed the cleaver out of his hand before bashing him across the face, sending him sprawling across the sofa in the small apartment. Outside, the O'Connors were showing tenants fake ID and identifying themselves as FBI, warning them to go back to their apartments.

"Okay, boyo," Gawain grabbed him by the front of the shirt and shoving him against the sofa, sticking the pistol under his bloody nose. "I've not a whole lot of time to spare here. Somebody in your particular circle is planning to strike a hard blow for Allah very shortly. I need to know who, what, when and where, or I'm going to smash all the teeth out of your mouth just for starters."

"Fuck you," Hassan mumbled. "I want to speak to my lawyer."

"I'm afraid I just don't have that kind of time," Gawain said, standing up and kicking the man as hard as he could in the groin. Jimmy Burke giggled and mockingly winced at the ferocity of the kick.

"That's a goal from mid-field, fella," he kidded.

"Aw reet," Gawain grabbed Hassan by the hair. "Are you gonna help me out?"

"Ah, I think he'll need another swift one," Burke climbed up on the sofa above Hassan and began reaching down for his pants legs.

"No, don't," he begged. "Don't hit me there again."

"Now listen," Gawain lowered his face next to Hassan's ear, pressing the pistol against Hassan's groin. "If ye don't help me out, I'm goin' t'put one in yer balls. It won't kill ye, fer sure, but you'll wish it did."

"Please," Hassan gasped. "There's only one person who might be doing something. Samir Farhat has a booth at Traders Village on Eldridge. He's the only one with connections. I don't know anything about anyone planning anything, I swear to Allah."

"I think that means 'no bullshit' in Arab," Kevin O'Connor came in from the hallway.

"Okay, yer comin' with us," Gawain dragged him off the floor by the collar, spinning him around and cuffing his wrists behind his back. "That'd better be yer best bet, because if we come up with nothin', there'll be a little bag of mush hangin' beneath your Arabmaker."

They proceeded to shove Hassan out into the hallway and off into the street before the small crowd gathered in the lobby. Edward and Danny warned them to back off, but the tenants began taking pictures on their cell phones and dialing 911. Unbeknownst to them, both the police and the Sheriff's Office had been notified by the FBI of the situation and were asked to delay their response until the operatives had left the scene.

"Okay, Aladdin, down on the magic carpet ye go," Edward grabbed Hassan and shoved him into the back seat of the Explorer, where the O'Connors forced him down onto the floorboards before using him as a footstool.

"Aw reet," Gawain told Burke, "G'wan and look that Traders Village up on the GPS, let's get goin'."

"What, this thing?" Burke pulled the device over. "How d'ye turn it on?"

"C'mon, don't feck about, give it here," Gawain grunted, yanking it back and punching commands into the interface. Within a couple of minutes the Explorer was on its way back towards the I-10 en route to Eldridge Road.

"You guys aren't the FBI," Hassan gurgled.

"Neither are you," Danny replied, stepping on Hassan's face.

"You got to loosen the handcuffs!" he cried. "I can't feel my hands!"

"I can't feel 'em either," Edward laughed. "Raise 'em up here where I can reach 'em."

Gawain stepped on the gas and the Explorer zipped down the highway, and at length they reached the Eldridge exit. They turned north and drove about eight miles, turning left along Highway 6 just short of the Sam Houston Tollway. Hassan continued to moan and plead but was kicked into silence by the O'Connors. Gawain rolled up to the front gate to where the security guard came over and informed them the facility was closed.

"Go on out and babysit this fella," Burke asked Danny, who hopped out of the truck and shoved a gun in the guard's face. He forced the guard to open the gate as Gawain drove the Explorer towards the rear of the facility. Edward took advantage of the extra space to pull Hassan by the hair to a sitting position where he could see out the window.

"Okay, now tell us where yer friend's place is," he was ordered.

Gawain followed Hassan's instructions and pulled up to a stall located in the far northeast corner of the lot. He saw the lights on in a narrow white trailer parked slightly to the rear of a vendor's booth and a small storage barn. They warned Hassan to keep quiet as they yanked him out of the Explorer and pushed him forward towards the trailer.

"Who is it?" they heard a muffled voice after Gawain knocked softly on the door.

"It's Hassan," he gasped. "It's an emergency."

The Irishmen heard the man shouting in Arabic before the occupants could be heard scrambling around the trailer. Gawain kicked in the door and fired at one of the Arabs, who was reaching for an Uzi behind a couch. Another Arab yanked open a drawer to retrieve a pistol before Gawain shot him in the back of the head. The third man bolted out of the rear door and Kevin chased after him, firing a shot after which only silence was heard. Edward rushed over and stuck his pistol into the last man's ear.

"Okay," Burke asked him, shoving Hassan into the trailer. "Where's the feckin' bomb?"

"Bomb?" the Arab whined. "What bomb?"

Gawain stepped from behind him and wordlessly shot Hassan between the eyes.

"As ye can see, we're not feckin' around," Burke stood before the Arab, who was forced down on the couch by Edward. "One more time: where's th' bomb?"

"What bomb?" the Arab insisted. With that, Burke impatiently drew his pistol and shot the Arab through the kneecap. The man screamed in agony as Gawain stepped forth and jammed his Glock against the man's cheek.

"Now, I'll tell ye," Gawain leaned over him, "I shot a fella through the teeth a couple of days ago and he didn't like it one bit. Either you tell us where the box is or I'll shoot ye in th' face."

"Shite," Kevin looked out towards the front of the market where a number of police and government vehicles had converged on the entrance with their emergency lights flashing. "We got company."

"I've got a lot ridin' on this job," Gawain muttered. "Stall 'em if ye can, I need to get this taken care of."

"It's back in the shed!" the Arab cried, realizing that not only was the game over, but he might be spared another bullet at the hands of these wild men.

"That's a good boy," Gawain patted his head before jumping out of the trailer onto the ground, racing towards the shed with Burke right behind him. He scowled at the lock on the door, blowing it off with a bullet from the Glock before shoving his way through the entrance. He groped around for the cord from the overhead light, switching it on to reveal a large washing machine positioned at the back of the shed. Gawain opened the lid, peering inside to where the apparatus had been removed in order to house a large metal cylinder appearing as a giant bullet.

"Now there ye go," Gawain grinned in satisfaction, sticking his pistol back in his waistband as patrol cars began slamming their brakes in front of the trailer outside. "That's a sight ye won't see but once a lifetime. If it's not a nuclear warhead, what?"

"Y'think if we put a bullet in it, we'd send all Houston t'bloody hell?" Burke chuckled.

"FBI!" two agents dressed in flak jackets stormed the door behind them. "Freeze!"

"Relax, fella," Gawain nodded towards the washing machine. "We just found yer damned bomb for ye."

"Okay, you two, come out slowly, and let me see your hands," the FBI riflemen trained their weapons on the Irishman.

"Begorra," Burke stepped forth with his hands at waist level as the agents took his pistol and guided him through the door. "Ye'd think yer the ones doin' us the favor."

"Begorra?" Gawain squinted at him. "Bad choice of a word, ye might be mistaken for a damned Fenian."

"Slip of the lip," Burke grinned back.

"Look, I don't know what you guys make of this, but we're taking these perps downtown," a police officer argued. "This is a massacre!"

"Bullshit," a deputy sheriff was adamant. "We got here first. They're going straight to County."

"I got news for both you gentlemen," one of the FBI agents stepped forth as Gawain and Burke were prodded over to where the O'Connors were herded and disarmed. "This is part of a Federal investigation. We're going to be taking over here."

"Hey!" the sergeant in charge of the Houston Police units stormed over. "I've got four dead bodies here, all of them shot at close range. One guy's in handcuffs and another guy got it in the back of the head. Your people don't have a mark on them. This looks like an execution in my book!"

"Let me help you with something here," the agent confronted him. "I'm pretty sure we've got a WMD on premises. You guys can file all the paperwork you want, but if you do anything to obstruct this investigation, chances are Homeland Security's going to have your badge."

"C'mon, quit feckin' about, these fellas are kinda pissed," Burke elbowed Gawain, who was flapping his lips in mockery of the police officers.

"They should be pissed over bein' so feckin' stupid," Gawain said it loud enough for the police and the agents to hear. "If we hadn't nailed these bastards, chances are this whole feckin' city'd have gone up in a mushroom cloud, with their women and children to boot."

"He's got a point there, cowboys," one of the FBI agents admitted. "We'll have the bomb squad here in a couple of minutes, but that's a nasty-looking mother in there. Those guys might've saved the whole city."

"I'm Agent Starkey," the leader of the unit came over to where the Irishmen had been gathered. "I don't know what you guys did to get the job done, but the bottom line is, you probably saved thousands of lives. There's gonna be a shitstorm once word of this gets out, though, unless your people can wave a magic wand somewhere."

"We just got word from the CIA," another agent said quietly. "They want you guys to report to the Galveston rendezvous as soon as possible. They said that James Burke has all the details."

"Sounds good," Burke replied. "I take it we can get back on the I-10 right down the road here."

"Yeah, like yer gonna drive," Gawain grunted. "Gimme the address and I'll set up th' GPS. Hopefully we can get debriefed so I can get on me way back home."

"Aye," Edward exhaled. "America's a nice place t'visit, but I sure wouldn't want t'live here."

They climbed back into the Explorer, joined by Danny who had been brought up from the front gate by the FBI agents. The five of them drove off amidst the convoy of Federal and law enforcement vehicles, on to the next stop on their date with destiny.

Chapter Twenty Five

William Shanahan stared out the window of the Learjet as it came to a gliding halt along the tarmac at the airstrip in Panama City. He knew that they had a lead on Enrique Chupacabra's whereabouts, and now it came to this. It was an assassination, the first one that he had ever been ordered to undertake. He had killed over thirty men on the field, but it was in combat between armed troops and hostile forces. He remembered having killed his first man, his soul torn between the macho thrill of taking out an enemy soldier and remorse over having ended a human life. Eventually the call to duty won out, but the dissonance returned when he killed his first insurgent, an armed civilian. Again his troubled spirit endured the moral conflict, and once again, duty to God and country prevailed. Now he was asked to serve as judge, jury and executioner for this drug dealer, this killer. Who was it who decided who had rights and who did not? In this case, it was MI6. And who would pass judgment upon them?

"It looks like we're here, William," Murra peered past Shanahan out the window before unhooking his seat belt and rising to his feet. "Time to go to work."

"Do you have a vehicle waiting?" he asked, waiting for two of Murra's bodyguards to slip past them along the aisle.

"Yes, we do," he replied. "It's a Ford Expedition. Nice big ride. It'll take us in and get us out of anywhere we need to go."

Murra informed Shanahan that his people had made contact with Chupacabra's crew and told them that they wanted to meet near the Bay Dunes Golf Course near the Panama City Mall near Highway 231. They explained to them that they had a shipment compromised off the Keys and needed to move it as soon as possible in order to avoid the DEA dragnet sweeping the area. They also informed the Colombians that Shanahan and his people had been unable to help them as their own connections were limited in the States.

"I think we've got a perfect set-up," Murra assured him as the two of them headed for the Expedition where his men were waiting. "The area's wide open. We checked it out on the Internet, there shouldn't be anyone in the vicinity at this time of night. We convinced the Colombians that it'd be a perfect place to exchange the cash for the product. Of course, all we are bringing is a suitcase full of newspapers. We gave them the latitude and longitude, told them we'd meet them inside the fence line by the fifth hole. I doubt he'll have more than four men with him, it should be a piece of cake."

"Did you tell him I was coming along?"

"Sure, no problem. He hasn't seen you since the conference in Montreal. He knows his people have been talking to yours, and he knows you and I have been meeting almost daily. He'll be thinking this is a chance to strengthen ties between his crew and yours. He'll never expect us to be cutting him out of the picture."

For some strange reason he began thinking about Morgana, and a wave of guilt swept over him. He knew that if she ever found out about this part of his life, about him becoming a paid assassin, there would be a possibility she would end the relationship. She would be looking at it from the same perspective that he was, wondering what lay deep in the heart of a man who could take a life of another outside of a war zone. He knew that they were here to mess with Chupacabra's head, but the notion of murdering him had never come to the forefront. Obviously they needed to derail Murra as well, and this would literally kill two birds with one stone, but he had not thought this far ahead.

"So have you figured out how we are going to do this?" Shanahan asked.

"You will go forward when they recognize us, and greet Chupacabra," Murra revealed. "You would introduce me, and I will come forward, most likely at the same time as Chupacabra. I will say when, and you will drop to the ground as I shoot him. I will then drop down alongside you and my men will finish off his men."

"Sounds like a plan," William allowed.

They cruised down the highway towards the mall, and Shanahan could not help but consider how his heart had changed over the course of this mission. What he was now realizing to be blind ambition had been quenched in allowing himself to see things outside his box. The desperate need to succeed was being replaced by a stronger and less superficial sense of right and wrong than he had known before. It was if his standards had been adjusted and rectified. He was seeing Morgana for more than the beautiful woman she was, as if he was letting himself see what a wonderful person she was deep down. Once this work was done, he would take time off and go somewhere far away with her, where they would explore each other and determine whether they were destined to stay the course together.

The Expedition eventually pulled up in view of the golf course, and they slowed down as they cruised along the deserted street. They noticed that the treeline along the fence covered the area with shadows, making it easier for them to access the property without being noticed. The driver cruised to a halt and they parked the car, then clambered out of the SUV and looked about for a long while before heading towards the fence. One of his men produced a pair of titanium wire cutters. Shanahan was greatly impressed by the gangster's vise-like grip as he swiftly cut out a large hole for them to access.

The five men slipped through the fenceline and moved briskly across the green towards the fifth hole. The three gunmen quietly exchanged comments in Italian, leading the way as Murra and Shanahan followed closely behind them. The course was fairly well-lit, though the clusters of trees and bushes growing intermittently along the range provided them with enough cover to proceed without fear of being spotted from afar.

Knowing that Murra was going to kill Chupacabra made it easier, though the commission of the act made it all the same. The dealers were being lured onto the killing field to slaughter, and the result would be the same no matter who pulled the trigger. MI6 had decided that Chupacabra was expendable now that the bullion sting had been completed. It was not clear as to how they would settle accounts with Murra, or what they were going to do about Fianna. What was certain was that these Colombians would never return to her. Was she in a place where no one would ever find her? It was a thought that filled him with apprehension.

The Sardinians signaled Murra and Shanahan to a halt, and they crept closer to a nearby tree as one of the men stepped forth boldly towards the dimly lit clearing. They detected motion about thirty yards ahead, and they watched and waited until a lone figure came forth from a stand of bushes alongside the perfectly manicured thruway.

"*Hola!*" the man called out.

The Sardinians stepped away from the trees and walked forward nearly in unison. Every step was cautious and deliberate as they fanned out and came to a halt ten yards apart from one another. They saw figures from the bushes ahead moving likewise, spreading out so as to appear as a mirror image of their counterparts. Only there were four of them in their skirmish line, with a lone person coming forth to meet the Sardinians.

"Now," Murra nudged Shanahan with his backhand. "Let's go."

"Enrique," Shanahan called out, walking forward with Murra accompanying him to his left. Murra stopped short at twenty paces, leaving Shanahan to walk ahead as he approached who he could now recognize as Chupacabra.

"Mr. Bruce," he called out, his face barely visible in the distance. "We meet again."

"I believe this is where the game ends, William," he heard Murra call quietly from behind him.

"What?" he asked, turning his head slightly yet not turning his back on the Colombians.

"I took the liberty of reaching out to Mr. Chupacabra myself," Murra raised his voice loud enough for Chupacabra to hear. "It didn't take us long to figure out where the tampered bullion came from, or what steps your people took to turn the Colombians and the Sardinians against one another."

"And now you are caught in the middle!" Chupacabra snarled, yanking a pistol from a shoulder holster beneath his suit jacket.

The Colombians in the firing line whipped automatic pistols from their own jackets and began pouring fire down on Shanahan. The Kevlar jacket beneath his black workout suit absorbed the brutal impacts though Shanahan's body was jolted by each shot. He staggered backwards, but at once he could hear shots ringing out from behind him. He felt a bullet hammer into his left shoulder blade, turning him sideways so that a second shot grazed his right bicep before he dropped backwards onto the grass.

He heard orders being given on either side, and eventually a gunman from each side crept forward to check on Shanahan as he laid flat on his back on the grass. William was assessing his position as best he could, determining that he was in at the bottom of a slope not far from where the two groups stood. He was fairly covered by shadow, and they would have to come close to see where he had fallen.

He had managed to draw his weapon as he fell, a tactic he had practice for hours on end during training and practice drills throughout his career. He held his right arm at his side, concealing it as best he could, his other limbs spread-eagled as one who was mortally wounded. The impacts to his torso were as if having taken a hammering from a heavyweight champion, and he was having trouble catching his breath. His back, his arm and his right leg were somewhat numb, and he knew that time was of the essence. He knew that the numbness would soon be replaced by searing pain. A steady flow of blood would soon weaken him and make him groggy. He had to formulate a plan of escape before they finished him off, and his career come to an end on this foreign golf course over a thousand miles from home.

"*Alli esta*," one of the Colombians called upon spotting Shanahan. "*Esta muerto.*"

The Colombian and the Sardinian converged from either side of him. Shanahan waited for a couple of seconds before tightening himself into a ball, firing at both targets and putting bullets in their heads with precise shots. He then began rolling eastward to another depression on the field where a drainage ditch was situated. He heard the two groups yelling and giving orders, spreading along the north and south on either side of him.

"William, it is useless," Murra called. "Give yourself up and I will hold you for ransom. I will let your people bargain for your life. You know I am a businessman, I would not want this thing to end at no profit to anyone."

Shanahan knew that there were three Sardinians and four Colombians left. He decided he had to even the score even further. He crawled on his elbows, spreading his legs in staying as low to the ground as possible as he made his way towards the ditch. He was pleased to find it dropped to a slope so as to accommodate running water, and rolled twice in order to reach the slope.

"*Alli! Alli!*" one of the Colombians yelled as he spotted Shanahan. He began firing at Shanahan, who was nearly upside down as he laid on his back. Yet it was but another familiar position for an expertly-trained SAS marksman, whose shots tore off the forehead of the attacker before he dropped backwards out of sight.

"Turn your gun on yourself, Bruce!" Chupacabra yelled from afar. "End it now! If you run out of bullets, and I get you, you will wish you were never born!"

Shanahan chuckled grimly as he considered that the Glock 17 held just as many rounds in its clip, and he had only fired four shots thus far. He had thirteen bullets left, more than enough to take out six men. Plus, if he could make his way over to any of the fallen gunmen, he would be able to retrieve their weapons. This game was far from over.

Yet he could feel the throbbing aches in his arm, shoulder and leg, and knew they would be able to hold their ground longer than he. Still, as daylight approached, the enemy would have far less time to procrastinate.

He could discern movement along either side of him, and knew they were trying to encircle him. He could see a greenside bunker amidst a stretch of smooth stones aligned by the ditch as part of the landscape design, and decided to avail himself of its cover. He rolled and crawled over towards the white stones, and suddenly the field erupted with slugs ricocheting off the rocks all around him. He began rolling again just as another shot tore into his bulletproof vest. This particular one was able to make its way through so as to cause a sticky wetness to spread across his chest. He saw one of the Sardinians rushing towards his position, and dropped the gunman with two shots left of center below the shoulder.

He knew that this was a serious hit, and could feel it interfering with his breathing. Almost as an afterthought, he grabbed a few rocks and shoved them into his pocket, hoping they might come in handy in the next few minutes. He knew the enemy had to end this as soon as possible to avoid detection by the property owners as well any further losses. He could hear them calling back and forth, cautious not to expose themselves as they now realized that Shanahan was an expert shot.

"William, let us reason together," Murra called from the darkness. "This is to no avail. This gunfire will draw attraction, and if the police arrive the situation will be beyond control."

"All right," Shanahan yelled back. "You tell the Colombians to clear out, and send your men over here to help me out. I've been hit in the leg, I can't stand up. If the Colombians leave, I'll let you bring me back so I can call my people in London. They'll pay good money to get me back, you know that."

"Enrique," Murra's voice cut across the range. "This seems reasonable. If you and your men leave, I will take Mr. Bruce back with us. I will settle matters with his Council and have him sent back to Europe."

"Very well, Mr. Bruce," Chupacabra's voice echoed. "Let us hope to never see each other again."

Shanahan pulled himself up to his elbows and could see the silhouettes of the Colombians as they came forth from the shadowy bushes. They lingered in discussion as the Sardinians slowly emerged from the treeline from the opposite direction. Murra made a hand signal and the Colombians gradually began moving off the field. Shanahan realized that they were probably coordinating their efforts via cell phone and adjusted their plans to accommodate his gambit.

Shanahan counted to three, and marshaled all his strength before springing to his feet and firing four shots at the Colombians before spinning and firing at the Sardinians. He slipped and fell to the ground as bullets came flying at him from both directions. He rolled away from the greenside bunker, back towards the slope where he had originally fallen.

"You are a dead man, William," Murra's voice was filled with wrath. "You will wish you were dead when I get you."

Shanahan knew it was now just between him, Chupacabra and Murra. Yet he had no doubt that these were the deadliest of all his enemies. Both these men were seasoned killers who would take great pleasure in ending William's life. This was the end game, and he would have to play it as he had never played before.

"Okay, it's just the three of us," he called out. "I think we should just cut our losses and walk away now. I've done what I came here for. I'll go back to Europe and you'll never see me again."

"You fucked up, Bruce!' Chupacabra yelled, the voice coming from the northwest to his left. "Now it is too late for you!"

Shanahan took one of the rocks from his pocket and threw it to his right due southeast. The stone clattered along the greenside bunker, and the sound drew a couple of shots from Murra. He could now tell that Murra was approaching from the south, and they planned to converge on Shanahan as he lay in the decline along the slope. He began crawling ever so slightly to his left, moving west, the pain in his arm, shoulder, chest and leg now searing as if slowly catching fire.

He could hear Chupacabra's voice echoing ever so faintly from the north about twenty yards from him as he communicated with Murra via cell phone. He knew they were closing in on him, and his next move would determine the outcome of this showdown. He took another rock from his pocket, and waited until he could guess Murra's position before springing again.

He rolled up into a crouch, tossing the stone as best he could in Chupacabra's direction while firing wildly towards Murra. He hurtled forward and rolled once, then twice, the movement barely visible from the cover of the slope. He was gambling all his hopes on them seeing his silhouette coursing along the slope towards the treeline just twenty yards to the west ahead of him.

It was then that both Murra and Chupacabra determined that William was making a desperate break for the treeline and safety. They both rushed the slopeline, spotting the figure before them and firing a volley of shots at the moving target. There was a resounding exchange of gunfire that at once faded into an eerie silence.

Shanahan rolled into a crouch and looked to either side as Murra and Chupacabra stood staring at each other in disbelief, reeling from shock as they beheld each other's bullet-riddled torsos. Blood spewed from their chests as they weaved drunkenly, trying to keep their balance, standing twenty yards apart from one another. After a long moment, Enrique Chupacabra dropped his pistol before his knees buckled and he sagged to the grass. Emiliano Murra saw Shanahan rise in a crouch with the Glock pointed at him. Murra lifted his hand but his pistol slipped from his fingers before he fell dead to the ground.

Shanahan barely managed to holster his pistol as pain seared through his body from his shoulders to his calves. He staggered over to where Murra's gunmen laid, digging into the pocket of the man he recognized as the driver of the Expedition. He tore the keys of the SUV from the man's pocket and began lurching back towards the fenceline, instinctively making his way back to where they had cut their way in. He could hear police sirens in the distance as they had been dispatched to the gold course in response to reports of gunfire.

He slipped out through the aperture, tottering back to the Expedition, and managed to climb inside. He gunned the motor and cruised away from the scene, hoping to find a secluded place where he could try and keep himself alive.

Chapter Twenty Six

The Ford Explorer zipped along the I-10 on the way to Galveston, the three brothers cramped in the back attempting to get a little shut-eye as they neared their destination. They were directed to a RV park on Port Bolivar where a Winnebago had been left for them. There they would find provisions, necessary items and directions with which they could wrap up their business with MI6 and catch a flight back to Belfast.

"Okay, fellas, look sharp," Jimmy Burke called, rousing the O'Connors from their snoozing. "Here's that Highway 87 on the map."

Jack Gawain eyeballed the GPS screen, noticing that State Highway 87 was the only major thoroughfare in the vicinity. He noticed that there was a bridge at Rollover Pass undergoing repairs, and that the entire area was still being inspected by the Texas Department of Transportation for hurricane damage. At this time of night, the area was deserted but danger signs and warning lights were visible everywhere.

Gawain was still considering the ramifications and pondering the implications of what was accomplished this evening. It reminded him of a Yank movie called 'The Dirty Dozen' where convicted military inmates were offered parole in exchange for participating in a sabotage mission. They never showed what happened after the convicts were released. He wondered how the government was going to justify putting him back on the streets as a free man. If they publicized what he had done, he would become a national hero but the government would fall under severe criticism as to how the mission had been ac-complished. If he ever let on what he had done in Liberty City, who knows what it would cause. Tricky business.

"I'll tell ye, Mr. Gain, that was remarkable work you did back there, just remarkable," Jimmy Burke relaxed in his seat as a drizzle rain be-gan to fall. "I'd never dreamed those ragheads would spill the beans as quickly as they did. You certainly have a gift for persuasion."

"Well, when you're working under a deadline, sometimes you have to know exactly what makes a fellow more persuasive than the next," Jack smiled, switching the radio on. He fiddled with the dial until he found a death metal station, keeping the volume just loud enough to be able to discern the vocals and the melody.

"What the hell ye playin' that bloody squalor for?" Danny playfully slapped the headrest on the driver's seat.

"Keep ye awake, fella," Jack replied. "Never know if we come across another roadblock or checkpoint. It won't do if yer half asleep and we have to shoot our way out of a mess."

"Well, maybe we'll just sit back here and let you chop our way through," Edward teased.

"I may be handy with a blade, but not bulletproof," Jack peered at the three brothers through the rearview mirror, all of whom appeared wide awake now.

"Aye," Kevin grinned broadly. "Y'know, it reminds me of a fella who used to play the game a while back. They said that if you went under the blade on his watch, there wasn't a thing you'd hold back, not even details about how your Mum and Da made the beast. When I sat there admiring yer work last night, I couldn't help thinkin' of that. The way ye slapped that bastard with the flat of the blade, there was just no way to tell when ye were goin' t'flip the edge on him. Hell, when ye did lay down the cuttin' edge, I could tell he would have told any tale ye liked just to get himself outta there."

"And it's best he did, it could've been much worse," Jack pressed the master lock on the armrest beneath the window, making sure the doors were all locked.

"Who was that fellow, now?" Danny asked quizzically. "I know they had him up in Maghaberry. Some of the fellas who got released spoke of him. He was in the Proddy[1] section, in maximum security. I think he got busted for computer fraud, wasn't it?"

Jack switched on the windshield wipers, noticing the detour sign about twenty meters ahead. He smiled grimly as the others joined Danny in boisterous laughter.

"That was quite the joke," Kevin cackled. "The Hacker, wasn't it?"

"Say, I've got a great one for ye," Gawain broke in cheerily. "You remember that place over there on Glen Road? Didn't one of you fellas go there at one time, that grade school?"

"Yep, St. Mary's," Danny replied.

"That's what I thought," Gawain grinned.

At once, he simultaneously opened his window, cranked up the car stereo to full blast, and slammed the gas pedal to the floor. The brothers began yelling as Gawain unbuckled his seat belt, snatching a pen off the console between the front seats and stabbing Jimmy Burke in the eye with it. Burke let out an anguished scream as the Expedition smashed through the blockades, bouncing across the potholes on the bridge and crashing through the guardrails into the blackness over Galveston Bay. Gawain scrambled up and out of the car window as the SUV plunged downwards, the O'Connors screaming and yelling as they clawed at the doorlocks and their seatbelts. Jimmy Burke was in a paroxysm of agony, clutching feebly at his torn eyeball, nothing else in the world being of the slightest concern to him. No one was in position to do anything as Jack Gawain jumped free of the Explorer, just before it created an enormous splash in plunging head-on into the bay.

William Shanahan cruised into the Allanton section of Panama City and spotted a twenty-four hour pharmacy along a sparsely populated area. Once again he mustered up all his strength in dragging himself

1. Protestant

into the store and making his way to the rear counter. A pharmacy tech was reading a magazine while the pharmacist busied in the rear area filling orders for early-morning pickup. Shanahan asked if he could avail himself of the walk-in clinic as he had cut his arm and thought he might need an antibiotic. He explained he had taken a tumble on his bicycle and could barely move his arms. The female tech took pity on him as he asked if she could help him with his jacket, seeing the blood smeared all over his right hand.

When she activated the buzzer to open the back door, Shanahan barged his way in and drew his gun on the workers. He made them lay face down on the linoleum floor, binding their hands lightly behind their back before grabbing a couple of large bags and filling them full of medical supplies.

"You're hurt pretty bad, guy," the pharmacist called from the floor as he saw the drops of blood sprinkling from Shanahan's sneakers. "Let us up, and I'll treat you. We'll give you time to drive off before we call anyone."

"Aye, one good shot of morphine'd do, wouldn't it?" Shanahan smiled weakly. "Say, I hate to be a bastard, but I'm going to take your jacket. I'll mail you the money in a couple of days."

"No problem," the pharmacist rolled onto his side. "Those are gunshot wounds. You're losing too much blood."

"Well, that's the reason I stopped by," he replied. "A stitch in time saves nine."

"Look, you may not even make it down the street."

"If you'd be so kind as to give me that time to drive off, I'll bet I can," Shanahan said as he fled out the door and away from the pharmacy, back to the SUV and on down the street.

He had felt as if he was driving drunk, a feeling he had not experienced since his last days in Afghanistan. He remembered his last night out with his SBS teammates before he was shipped back to the UK, and he was the designated driver as his fellow commandos could barely walk after having nearly consumed a case of whiskey. His vision was blurred and he was having trouble keeping his eyes open, having to gnaw on his inner cheeks and tongue to stay awake. He kept going until he spotted a seedy-looking motel just outside the city limits, veering off the exit and coming to a stop in the nearly-vacant parking lot.

He managed to pull the tattered, blood-drenched warm-up jacket off, replacing it with the pharmacist's off-the-rack Wal-Mart fleece jacket. He entered the office of the fleabag motel and signed for a room at the rear of the property, paying for it with the cash he had in his wallet. He knew that either the CIA or MI6 were probably monitoring all electronic transactions for the credit card he was given by the Firm. The Indian manager gave him the card key, and he got back in the Explorer and parked it around the back.

Morgana McLaren was unable to sleep, fraught with concern over Fianna as well as her relationship with William. She was certain that William was going to make inquiries on Fianna's behalf, but was filled with apprehension over what he might find. As she pondered her conversation with Lakeesha, she ruefully considered the possibility that Fianna was, in fact, on a private jet that might have taken her anywhere in the world. She might be in some remote jungle area of Colombia, never to be heard of again.

It filled her with even greater speculation as to how the Colombians had taken an interest in Fianna, and what either William or Jack had to do with it. She knew that the Colombians were the biggest drug dealers in the world, and that William said he was doing some sort of investigative work for the British Government. It might well have been some very dangerous business, and if Jack Gawain was anything like the person who was supposed to be in prison in Northern Ireland, it was something that neither she nor Fianna should ever have gotten involved in. She needed to have a serious discussion with William and find out where all this was taking her.

The ringing of the phone jolted her awake, and she sat up in bed before rolling over towards her cell phone on the night stand.

"Hello?"

"Morgana."

"William. Where are you?"

"I'm in West Florida, outside Panama City."

"You don't sound good. Are you okay?"

"Actually I'm in a bit of a situation right now. I wouldn't have called you, but you're the only one I can trust right now. Is there any way you can come out here?"

"Are you hurt?" she switched on the light, noticing that it was almost daybreak. "Are you in some kind of trouble?"

"I'm not in tip top shape right now," he managed. "Let me give you the address where I'm at. If you can bring breakfast and some cold drinks it'd be greatly appreciated."

She jotted down the directions before calling the airport and making a stand-by reservation. He dressed hurriedly, throwing on a black sweatshirt, jeans and sneakers before packing a carry-on bag with a change of clothes and personal items. Suddenly she realized just how smitten she was by William. She didn't really know him at all, though she knew she would have probably had sex with him last night. They had found kindred spirits within each other, and she knew that was why he had called her and she was going to him. She had not had a relationship for a long time, but she knew this was right for her, and she did not want to leave him by himself in whatever predicament he was in.

She took the elevator down to the lobby, and walked out to the front entrance where she hailed a cab. It sailed off down the road on the way to the airport, and she said a prayer that she would be on time to help. She prayed that everything would be all right when all was said and done. Most of all, she prayed that William was not involved in something that she would be powerless to help him out of.

Shanahan had stripped down to his underwear and turned on the shower as hot as he could stand it. He then released the bathtub stopper and just sat down for a long while, letting the water revive him as best it could. He had been grazed in three places on his right leg, and managed to stop the bleeding before tending to the gash in his right arm. His Kevlar vest was ready for the dumpster, though he managed to pull the slug meshed into the Kevlar out of the hole in his chest. The volley from the Colombians' pistols had torn the vest to hell, and it was a miracle that it had enough resilience to keep the last shot from killing him. He could not reach the slug that was embedded in his shoulder blade, and all he could do was pray that Morgana would arrive in time.

He left the door unlocked, knowing that he might not be able to answer if she arrived by the time he got any weaker. He watched the bloody water streaming down to the drain and managed a grim chuckle, considering how it reminded him of a scene in *Psycho*. His left shoulder was entirely numb and his arm was nearly useless. His right arm was aching and he could barely use it to shift himself around. He had left his briefs on because he knew there was a distinct possibility that he would not be able to get up to cover himself when and if Morgana arrived. He had taken a couple of painkillers but did not dare medicate himself any further. If she came in and found him unconscious, she would most likely call an ambulance. From there it would be a matter of time before everyone knew where he was.

He was in and out of it for a long while, fading to black before a sharp stabbing pain would wake him back up. His left leg was his only good limb, and he pushed against it to redistribute his weight to keep his battered frame at ease as best he could. He had no idea what time it was, and felt hunger pangs due to his high metabolism. He was also very thirsty and could barely scoop water from the tub to bring up to sip from his hand. The loss of blood had dehydrated him somewhat, and he was thankful that he only pissed himself but once.

He could hear a knocking at the door, a pause, then knocking again. He knew this was the moment of truth. If it was room service, a thief, or if someone found who they were looking for, it was all over. The hot water had revived his limbs somewhat, and he was able to move his arms with great effort to shift his weight and turn onto his right side, facing the door. He anchored his left foot against the corner of the tub and shoved himself up so that he could rest his chest on the side of the tub.

"William!" he heard Morgana's lovely voice, like an angel calling from heaven. "Oh, my god, what is going on here!"

"Morgana!" he cried out.

"Oh my god!" she gasped as she appeared in the doorway, her eyes wide as saucers. "William, don't move, I'm calling an ambulance!"

"No!" he insisted. "No cops, no doctors! I need you to help me! Come over and help me out of here!"

She came into the steamy bathroom, trying as best she could to avoid seeing his nakedness. She slipped her hand under the streaming water and turned off the water, then stared in horror as he hoisted himself up with newfound strength.

"William! What happened here!"

"Go on and put that towel around your shoulders so you don't get all wet," he told her, forcing himself to his feet, trying not to put weight on his right leg. "See if you can help me keep my balance, we'll go to the bedroom, I've got some supplies in there."

All of a sudden it dawned on him that God had put Jack Gawain in his life for this moment. The mission would have brought him to this place and time regardless of Gawain, as Jack had no knowledge of it. He and Morgana, however, would have never met had Gawain not broken all the rules. He had never been so glad to see a woman in his life. There was no angel in heaven who could have been more beautiful to him, or more desperately needed.

"William, listen to me," she said fervently, her eyes misty. "There is a hole in your back. There are gashes in your leg. You've got a tear in your chest and both your arms. If they get infected you are going to die!"

"How about my butt?" he hobbled painfully, reaching out to her for support. "Around the swimming pool, some of the ladies have said it was not too shabby."

"I hope you don't think this is funny," she grabbed another towel, attempting to pat him dry while helping him into the next room. "What are you planning to do?"

"We've got to get the bullet out of my back," he groaned as they continued on to the bedroom where he had tossed the shopping bags with the medical supplies. "The other ones went in and out, this one has to go next."

"Oh my gosh," she managed as he slipped away from her and fell onto his face on the bed. "You were shot? Who shot you? Did someone try to rob you? Is that your Expedition outside? Why can't you go to the police?"

"I told you I was working for the British government," he gasped, forcing himself up to a sitting position as he began rummaging through the shopping bags. "I was involved in a sting operation that went sideways. One of the persons of interest in the case made a false move on us. There was some gunplay involved, and I got hit."

"Are these all gunshot wounds?" she stared aghast at the oozing wound in his shoulder blade, surrounded by black and blue skin.

"Unfortunately," he murmured, taking things out of the bags. "I was wearing a bullet-proof vest, or so it is called. Things could have been much worse. Plus, I was fortunate that they were not the best shots in the world, either."

"William, let me see that chest wound," she insisted.

"Morgana, my darling, listen to me carefully," he turned to her. "I'm not sure how much those friends of yours told you, but I spent ten years in Iraq and five years in Afghanistan. This hurts like hell but it's old hat to me at this stage of the game. Now I know this looks bad to you, but it's not what it seems. Bad is when I'm lying on my back not breathing and my eyes won't close anymore. What you have to do is get this slug out of my shoulder blade."

"I can't!" she wailed. "I'm not a nurse, I barely know CPR!"

"Listen," he handed her a few items. "This is a local anesthetic, you just stick it in and inject it, about an inch from the hole. Give it a few seconds, then start daubing the wound with the antiseptic. From there you'll have to take these forceps and find the slug. You'll get a decent grip on it and wiggle it loose as best you can, then pull it out. Use the cotton swabs to wipe any residue or bone fragments away. You don't want to leave them in there."

"I can't, I can't," she wept. "Suppose you pass out?"

"Then it won't matter one way or another," he stared into her eyes. "Either that or we can just sit here until I pass out. I'm at your tender mercies, love."

"Turn around," she winced. "Now, are we going to have to do the same thing with the other ones?"

"No, the other ones were in and out. The chest shot got caught up in what was left of the vest. All we have to do is clean the other ones and stitch them up."

"Stitch them up!" she demanded. "What do you mean by stitch them up!'

"Well, we can't just leave them gaping, I might catch a death of gangrene. I can pretty well do the leg ones, but I'll need help with the arm and the chest shots. Sorry to say, I'm not a contortionist and we don't have lots of mirrors to work with. I'm afraid that leaves you having to open and close the one you're on."

Thus began one of the most harrowing experiences of Morgana McLaren's life.

Chapter Twenty Seven

Jack Gawain had swum back beneath the bridge and made it back to shore, moving quickly to avoid detection before the police arrived. He saw no motion from the SUV as the water obviously rushed into the truck and sank it to the depths. He took off his jacket, then his shirt and socks, wringing them out as best he could before making his way along the shoreline. He saw a group of homeless men huddled under an overpass as he made his way eastward, and made his way over to them.

"Say, there," he called to them. "I'd like to see if I could trade for a couple of items."

"Trade what?" one of the bums challenged.

"Well, I've got a couple of bucks here," Gawain made a show of pulling back his jacket to reveal his Glock as he went for his wallet. "Perhaps I can buy a towel or blanket off you. Would five dollars suffice?"

"How about a ten?" another vagrant asked.

"Well, that'd come with a leftover bottle of whiskey, wouldn't it?" Gawain busied himself peeling a bill from the soggy wad in his sopping billfold.

"What'd you do, go for a moonlight swim?" another hobo chortled.

"Aye, with some silly bastards who couldn't swim," he handed the bill over to the bum. "I'd prefer a towel if you've got one, and don't forget the whiskey. I've a bit of a hike ahead."

They could hear the police sirens as a convoy of emergency vehicles arrived to reports of a truck having lost control and driven off the Rollover Pass crossway. The vagrant reached into a shopping cart and came up with a ragged towel and a quarter-full bottle of whiskey, handing it to Gawain in exchange for ten dollars.

"Aw reet," Gawain uncorked the bottle and chugged down its contents, setting it aside as he wiped his hair with the towel. "Look, if the peelers come through, you haven't seen hide nor hair of me, okay?"

"Well, now, I think that'd be worth another ten bucks," the hobo decided.

"Then let's try this," Gawain replied. "If they happen across me, I'll tell 'em a group of homeless men showed me a knife and made me hand over a soaking wet ten dollar bill. How'd that be?"

"You're cool, dude," the bum waved him off.

Gawain walked about a half mile before the police sirens grew distant, then made his way back up to the highway. He decided that he would go on to the rendezvous at Port Bolivar. It would take the police until daybreak to locate the Explorer and make arrangements to haul it to surface. He could find the RV park and break into the Winnebago in a couple of hours, then swipe everything those IRA bastards had been provided to get back to the UK.

It chapped his arse to think that the government had set him up like that. They must have picked him out precisely because they knew he could get information out of suspects like no other. Their value system would not allow them to accept the collateral damage in Liberty City, and rather than doing so, they decided to rub him out and pretend it all never happened. He would set the record straight, as well as settle scores, one way or another.

All he needed was a ride.

Darcy Callahan sat in her battered 2000 Volkswagen Beetle, wiping a tear of frustration from her cheek. She and her boyfriend had been invited to a friend's house for a party where most of their crowd showed up. There had been plenty of liquor and drugs, and everyone was wandering around the girl's three story house and finished basement as her parents were away on vacation. They were blasting music on every floor and the lights were dimmed or turned off, giving it a surrealistic atmosphere as the night progressed. She had knocked down a few mixed concoctions that, along with a few big hits off a big bong pipe, nearly put her lights out. She was snoozing for a while, and when she awoke, her boyfriend had disappeared.

She searched far and wide for him, then grew desperate in searching the bedrooms that the friend had declared off-limits to the partygoers. When she intruded upon the master bedroom, she found her boyfriend and the hostess screwing each others' brains out. She hadn't put it past the hostess, but she had caught her boyfriend messing around one too many times. This, she decided, was the last straw.

The problem now was that she was cruising on fumes and dared not hit the highway with the gauge needle on the red line. The bastard had all their money on the pretext that he was going to score an ounce while they were at the party. She decided that she would crash out until the sun rose, then bum some change from customers at the gas station where she was parked. Hopefully she could get enough to make her way home, or at least make a phone call and have someone come help her out.

"Say, Miss, I've a bit of a problem and could use a lift," the dark-haired, ruggedly handsome man stuck his head in the passenger window.

"Sorry, dude, out of gas," she replied curtly.

"Well, I'll tell ye, I've got no trouble payin'," he replied, opening his suit jacket to show his Glock in his waistband while pulling a soggy $100 from his pocket.

"You don't have to do that," she grimaced.

"Well, if I told ye I was havin' t'drive, I might," he replied. "Go on and scoot over, I'll get us filled up. Don't do anything silly, I'm pretty much out of sorts right now and might do something desperate."

"Are you carjacking me?"

"Kinda hirin' ye at this point," he replied. "I've got a couple more big bills on me and lots more waitin' where I'm going. Judgin' from the look of this vehicle, I'm pretty sure you can use the money."

"Hey, if you don't like it, you can go carjack somebody else," she shot back.

"Y'know, that may not be the worst idea," he mused. "Look, gimme the key and I'll fill her up. Ye'd best move over and not get any funny ideas. G'wan and take the $100 for now, I'll give ye some more later."

"Are you a drug dealer?" she wondered as she stuffed the bill down the front of her T-shirt into her large-cupped bra.

"Nay, but I've put a couple out of business as of late," he replied, fishing his credit card out of his wallet before going around to the driver's side. He gunned the engine and drove the VW over to the gas pump before switching it back off to fill the tank up. She watched moodily as he got back into the car, heading back towards the highway.

"So are you a cop?"

"Not in the strictest sense of the word," he cruised onto the access road towards the highway entrance. "What do you do? How d'you put gas in the tank?"

"I'm unemployed right now, I get my checks," she replied. He glanced over and saw she was an attractive woman in her twenties. She wore her hair in a spiked shoulder-length punk style, though her thick Goth makeup and nose piercing were not to his liking. Her hourglass figure and generous bosom, however, were more than sufficient compensation.

"I'm Jack, by the way," he cruised onto the highway and could see emergency vehicles all over the road in the distance where he just sent Jimmy Burke and the O'Connor brothers to the briny deep. That meant that neither MI6 nor the CIA had any way of knowing their plans to dispose of Jack Gawain had gone astray.

"I'm Darcy," she replied. "So where we headed?"

"Over the bridge to the ferry. I need to pick up some money, then I'll have to get us out to the airport. I might need to rent a room in the meantime to get my bearings. If I get as much as I'm expecting at

Port Bolivar, I'll probably be able t'give ye enough t'get this piece of shite tuned up."

"Hey, fuck you. I didn't see you cruising up in a limousine, dude."

"Y'got some mouth on ye, missy," he smirked.

"Glad you like it. Where you from anyway, Germany?"

"Now that'll get ye a bullet in yer arse," he chuckled. "I'm from Norn Iron."

"*Where?*"

"Nor-thern Ire-land, ye silly twit."

"Don't blame me, you sound like you just got off a boat."

They slowed to a crawl as the police diverted traffic to the right lane, emergency vehicles filling the area where he ran the Explorer off into the bay. He could see patrol boats down below, indicating they had not made much progress in getting the SUV out of the water. He smiled and waved at a lady cop as she waved him through the bottleneck.

"Wonder what happened?" Darcy peered out the rear window.

"Ah, some silly bastards making rude remarks about the Protestants in Belfast."

"Yeah, how do you know?"

"Well, I just put 'em in there, don't y'know."

"Bullshit."

"Feel me pants leg, if ye like. I got soaked to the gills."

"So you walked to the gas station, then carjacked me...holy shit," Darcy realized.

"That's why you're carrying a gun and your money's soaking wet."

"Y'know, yer pretty bright. Y'oughtta think of goin' back t'school while your dole holds up," he said airily.

"And maybe you should go back and take some English lessons, you son of a bitch."

"Language, child," he chided as they continued down the highway. At length they came in sight of the ferry to Port Bolivar. Gawain's luck continued to hold out as they arrived right on time to pull onto the boat before it left the dock.

"So how come you didn't stick around for the cops?"

"To tell the truth, the bastards were plannin' t'do me in, but it didn't go well for them."

"Dude, this is some deep shit," she shook her head. "You're not going to kill me so I don't talk, are you?"

"And y'think they'd believe ye for one minute, with that shit stickin' outta yer nose and all?"

"Fuck you," she snapped.

The ferry let them off at Port Bolivar, and they drove to the nearest gas station to ask directions to the Port Bolivar RV Park. The Winnebago was parked in the rear just as they had been instructed by Six at the MI6 phone number. Gawain left Darcy in the VW as he accessed the truck, using the combination he had been given to unlock the door. Darcy felt a thrill rush through her body, feeling as if she had woke up in the middle of a *Mission Impossible* movie.

At length he returned to the Beetle and got back in, gunning the engine and heading back towards the ferry.

"Okay, here's the deal," he explained. "We're going to take a room on Galveston Beach while I get things sorted out. I need to get on the Internet and make some calls. I may need you to ride me around for a bit longer, but I assure you I'll make it well worth your while."

"Hey, if you have another one of those soggy hundreds to spare, it's all good by me."

They caught the ferry back to Galveston, heading southeast on Highway 87 en route to the beach. It was just before daybreak by the time they reached the Galveston Inn, where Gawain checked them into a room on the upper level at the rear of the motel. They made their way up the steps, and they were both glad to find a clean and neat arrangement in the double-bed room.

"I've got to use the bathroom," she insisted. "I'm about to bust."

"Have at it, Missy," he replied. "I need t'check me messages."

He switched on the air conditioner, setting it to warm before laying his shirt, jacket and socks over it. He then dialed into his voicemail and listened intently to the messages from MI6. He was very much annoyed by what he heard but blew it off as soon as Darcy came back into the room. He had turned on the TV to a news program so that she did not inadvertently hear his messages, and paid no mind to the exclusive reports coming in from different parts of the nation and around the globe.

"Okay, lass," he opened the pillowcase full of items he brought out of the Winnebago, plucking a stack of bills out and tossing it to Darcy. "Here's your cut in advance so's y'know I'm a right fellow. Don't try and bail out on me, though. I've got your plate number and I'm liable t'come lookin' for ye if y'leave me in the lurch."

"Holy shit," she was aghast. "This must be like ten thousand dollars!"

"Aye," he nodded. "As y'can imagine, it's of no use to the fella it was intended for. As for me, I've got as much as I can carry. Maybe ye can replace that piece of shite outside with a new car now."

"Omigod, omigod!" she ran over to him and hugged his neck as tight as she could. "You're wonderful, you're wonderful!"

"Okay, missy," he squeezed her back lightly, greatly conscious of her huge breasts pressing against his chest. "Now, you wouldn't want me t'get carried away here."

"Let me tell you something, mister," she brought her face to within an inch of him, "you've just become the sexiest man in Galveston."

"And yer the hottest item I've seen in this part of the country, lass, I'll guarantee ye. Now, I'll warn ye, I haven't had a woman probably since you were in high school, so I may be making up for a lot of lost time."

"Go for it, Norn Iron."

She plunged her tongue into his mouth as he moved her back towards the bed, dropping on top of her as they ran their hands along each other's bodies. They pulled each others' shirts and pants off, rolling towards the middle of the bed, greedily feeding off each others' lust in a feast that would last for over an hour.

They were blissfully unaware of the exclusive newscast reporting that a nuclear device had just been discovered and deactivated in London, and that Al-Qaeda had announced that it was preparing to launch another nuclear attack on Europe within the next forty-eight hours.

Jack and Darcy were in another world.

Chapter Twenty Eight

Mark Shaughnessy sat in his office with Lieutenant Bill Masterson, his former teammate and closest friend in MI6. They had served together for over a decade with the SAS, and were reunited after the Good Friday Agreement of 1998 in Northern Ireland upon being transferred to the Secret Service. Shaughnessy was completely disconcerted by the series of events transpiring as of late, and turned to the one man he could confide in.

"Damn it to hell, Bill, this whole deal's gone sideways," Shaughnessy snarled as he paced the room, wincing as he attempted to ignore the pressure in his hip. "What in hell is the Chief and MI5[1] thinking of, to have allowed this to have gotten so screwed up? How in hell am I supposed to clean up this damned train wreck they've gotten me into?"

"It's the same crap we've been dealing with since we got into this business, one branch competing with the other," Masterson was unusually coarse. "It's like you've been preaching to me since we first met: look before you leap. This looks like it's going to be a big leap, Mark."

"Who in hell would have given the order to have Gawain terminated?" Shaughnessy fumed. "The man saved the city of Houston from a nuclear attack. I don't care whether he instigated a gang war in Miami, he was doing it to set up Chupacabra. Now Enrique Chupacabra is

---

1. Security Intelligence

dead, and William Shanahan's an MIA[2]. Nobody's able to get in touch with him, the man's gone into the wind and he's virtually irreplaceable. I've got my best men in Pakistan putting down a revolutionary coup, and there's no way in hell I'm sending rookies on the field with this much at stake!"

"Colonel, I understand perfectly where you're coming from, but you can't just throw on a uniform and expect to be able to go out there and do it yourself. You haven't been on the field for almost twenty years, and you've had a hip replacement. We both know—*everybody* knows—you're one of the best who's ever played this game. There's just too much at stake here, just as you say, to let your ego become a factor. For god's sake, if push comes to shove, let me go out instead. I may be rusty but my parts work just fine."

"This isn't about ego, Lieutenant," Shaughnessy's tone let Masterson know he was close to overstepping. "If we deploy a team to Iran to sabotage a nuclear facility, the team's going to have little to no information on what they're up against. They're going to be relying heavily on sheer instinct, and—at the risk of sounding egotistical—there's no one in the Firm whose instincts I trust as much than my own, other than William Shanahan and about six other men who are in Pakistan as we speak."

"I take it I'm not on that list," Masterson said quietly.

"I need you here to watch my back, Bill. I don't want to live the rest of my life knowing that hundreds of thousands of people were killed and there was something I could've done about it. Neither do I want to regret having gotten one in the back from some pogue when I could have had one of my best men over here watching it."

"I've known you too long to think anyone's going to change your mind on this," Masterson exhaled tautly, rising from the chair facing Shaughnessy's desk. "I'll stay home and mind the shop, but I want you to make sure I've got a hot line to the Chief in case anything

---

2. missing in action

goes wrong. I don't want to live the rest of *my* life thinking there was something that should have been done that was not."

"Let's get the job done, Bill. Who dares wins."

Masterson could only hope that the venerated SAS motto would hold true in the fateful hours to come.

"Jack, I'm hungry."

"Aye, I could do with a bite meself, I figure."

"There's a Mickey D's across the street. I can get us a few Egg Mc-Muffins and some coffee."

They had screwed each others' brains out for about an hour before passing into slumber, but the novelty of the relationship had not allowed them to stay asleep for long. She laid in bed with the sheet only covering her from the waist down, and he was greatly tempted to dive in for seconds but there was too much work to be done.

"Aw reet, let me go on over with ye," he decided.

"So what's up, you just fucked me and you still don't trust me?" she seemed disappointed.

"I don't trust anybody," he snickered, "but since you put it that way. Go on, I've got some calls t'make anyway. Plus, we need to hit a library on the way out. We can get a room closer to th'airport so I can figure out what to do next."

"So you're going on a trip?" she asked, getting up to find her clothes before she headed to the bathroom for a quick shower. He shook his head, coming to another erection at the sight of her.

"I don't know, lass. I'll probably come up with a plan after I make these calls."

He plopped back on the bed and watched with interest at the newscast as it gave the details about the aborted nuke attack in London. A group of four Islamic students with extensive Al-Qaeda connections had driven a car containing a rigged nuclear warhead into the Financial District. It was a tipoff by a Muslim immigrant that resulted in Scotland Yard intercepting the bombers before they could activate the crude device. Early reports suggested that the bomb may have been smuggled out of Pakistan by the insurgent forces, but more details were still to come.

"Okay, hot stuff, I'll be back," she said as she headed out the door, looking younger and prettier with the makeup scrubbed off her face. "We're going to have to go to a store so I can buy a change of clothes if you plan to keep me around for a couple of days longer."

He waited until she left before picking his cell phone up off the night stand to check his messages and find out just what MI6 had to say for themselves...

...just as the phone rang.

"Gawain."

"Well, well, well. How now, Gummo? I'll be long gone by the time you trace the call, you know that."

"I'm not in position to trace the call," Shanahan's voice sounded weak but Gawain was not readily buying into it.

"Well, rest assured I'll find you, boyo, sooner or later. I can fairly well guarantee you I'll be paying you back in spades."

"I don't care if you believe it or not, but I had nothing to do with double-crossing you. I think I got set up too. There's another branch of the government that may have gotten involved. Chupacabra and Murra are dead, and I got hit pretty bad."

"Well, I suppose that somebody decided to let me finish the job."

"Listen, Gawain. I know they sent you out with those fellows from Belfast to interrogate those smugglers. I know they wouldn't have made a move on you if you hadn't got the job done. Scotland Yard just caught a team trying to set off a nuke in London. I got a message from MI6. They think there's a third nuke getting set to launch from Iran on a target in Europe."

"And ye think I'm so feckin' stupid I'll go along with some half-arsed plan to invade Iran and save the day, is that it, boyo?" Gawain laughed.

"We've got all our best SAS and SBS troops tied up in Pakistan trying to crush the rebellion," Shanahan gasped in pain. "They patched together a commando team for a mission to take out the Iranian missile site. I can't make it, Jack. I took five bullets a few hours ago. You're the only one who can stand in for me."

"You've gotta be feckin' kiddin, fella," Gawain snorted. "After you bastards sent me off for a one-way ride with that IRA hit squad? How dumb do you think I am?"

"Look, just hear me out. I've got the account number for a safety deposit box back in Miami. You can send someone else to pick the item up for you. It contains a packet with a passport and a ticket to Baghdad. There will be instructions as to who to call when you get there. They'll pick you up and you'll stand in for me. You've been carrying on about God and country, how everything you've ever done was for the Crown. Well, this is the real thing, Gawain. The Iranians are set to launch, and we don't know where the missile's headed. You saved lives in Houston, Gawain. You can save a lot more and I swear to God I'll tell the whole world about it."

"So the last one was just another game of dominoes."

"I have no idea why they covered it up, or why they screwed you over. Maybe the Yanks didn't want Al-Qaeda to know just how close they came. I'm not going to make excuses for them. What I do know is that I can't make this run. It's up to you, Gawain. They're expecting me to pick up the packet before the bank closes this evening. When you hang up I'll text you the info."

"Erm...anything on Fianna?"

"We've got the CIA, Homeland Security and the FBI on it. They're already on the Colombians like flies on shite for their part in smuggling the nuke into the US. We're quite certain they'll be wagging their tails to give up Fianna in exchange for a deal or two."

"Be sure and give her my regards," Gawain said before clicking off. He then watched as Shanahan texted the instructions to him.

His only question was whether he should trust the Last Boy Scout just one more time.

On the other end of the line, Morgana McLaren was beside herself with nervous exhaustion as she lay in the double bed, barely listening to Shanahan as he tried to bargain with Gawain. She had sewn him up like a human rag doll, her stomach churning as she put the sewing needle through his bleeding flesh in closing his wounds. She was astonished at how he was able to deal with the pain after the Novocaine shots wore off. She was greatly relieved to hear the news from the CIA that they were going all out to find Fianna, but it wasn't enough to take her mind off having put nearly forty stitches in Shanahan's body.

"William, this whole thing is driving me insane," she managed as he finally set the phone down and fell onto the bed alongside her, laying his head on her tummy. "What was all that about going to Iran? What did you mean about a nuclear attack on Europe? Is this some kind of code language you people use?"

"You remember what I told you about Jack and me working with the government?" he explained, wearing her sweatshirt after she changed to a chiffon blouse. "Well, we were investigating reports of Al Qaeda smuggling weapons into the US and the UK. The British Government got word that the terrorists were planning an attack in an effort to destabilize the global economy. They were sending a bomb to Fort Knox and one to the Financial District in London. North Korea and Pakistan donated a couple of outdated warheads to the cause, but we got to them in time. What we're hearing now is that Iran has a test missile that they may be launching against Zurich."

"Switzerland?" she gasped. "Why?"

"It has the third largest gold supply on Earth outside of Fort Knox and London," he managed, wincing as his weight strained the stitching in his shoulder. "Al Qaeda's plan is to knock out a portion of the world's bullion to cause an economic depression. They're involved with a criminal network that has been stockpiling gold for over a year now. If they bankrupt the governments of the Free World, the nations will be defenseless against the terrorists. Plus the criminal network will be the richest organization on the face of the earth."

"This is unreal," she murmured, trying to piece it all together. "And you were supposed to go on a mission to Iran?"

"The Iranians know that once they launch their only missile, they'll be considered defenseless against a counterattack. They also know that the G8 nations will never drop a nuke on Iran and wipe a whole nation off the planet. There's nothing to stop them. Our people have a good idea where the missile is located, and they are pretty certain an elite unit can move in and take it out."

"So you sent Gawain to take your place on the team?"

"I don't trust him enough, Morgana," he pulled himself up and gazed into her eyes. "You've helped me get myself back together. You can help me further. You can help me get on a plane and get to Iraq to join the team."

"William, are you crazy?" she insisted. "You could have died a few hours ago. I just stitched you up. You're not fit to walk around the block. You can't go on a mission."

"They need another pair of eyes, someone who knows how to read defenses and find weaknesses. If I go along I can direct traffic, tell others where to go and what to do. Morgana, hundreds of thousands of lives may be depending on it."

"This is insane," she wiped tears from her eyes.

"Please," he implored her.

"All right," she sniffed. "What do you want me to do?"

"You want me to do *what*?"

"I want you to chill out at the hotel for a couple of days after I book us a room," Gawain replied as he returned to where Darcy Callahan awaited in the parking lot at the Galveston Public Library. "If I'm not back in forty-eight hours and you don't hear from me, I want you to take this letter to the Houston Chronicle. It's all about where I went and what I did."

"So where are you going?" she asked quietly as he got in behind the wheel.

"I'm going to go bail some dumbarse out of trouble," he replied, heading out to the San Luis Resort on Seawall Boulevard. "We'll stop off at a store and pick up some clothes. I'll need some stuff for carry-on and I'm sure you can use a change of clothes. I'd really like seeing you in women's clothes before I go."

"Hey, this is my style, dude," she said defensively. She wore a black T-shirt with a silver anarchy sign, tight black jeans and Harley-Davidson boots. Her raven hair was flowing naturally without her mousse, her violet eyes sparkling without her makeup. She was the exact opposite of Fianna, and though she made his heart skip a beat, he knew that they were worlds apart and Fianna was more of the type of woman he could go the distance with. Still, he had grown very fond of this girl and was resolved to do her right when all was said and done.

"You're a winner, Darcy," he assured her. "Forget about that piece of shite boyfriend ye told me about. You've got a good bit of change now, just make yourself comfortable and get yourself fixed up. With a trip to the beauty parlor and a nice boutique, you'd look like a movie star. You owe it to yourself, lass. It's your time, girl, make the best of it."

"What are you talking about?" she insisted. "You're coming back, aren't you? What is all this about? Is this about that car that fell into the bay last night? Is somebody looking for you?"

"No, that's all over," he said as he cruised onto Highway 87 towards the 61st Street exit. "I'll be catching a flight overseas. It's some government business, that's what the gun's about. They need me t'make sure some bad people don't plan on doing something very stupid."

"Can't I come with you?" she asked plaintively.

"I need you to deliver that letter if I don't come back. Now, ye can be sure I fully intend t'come back. Don't ye think I'd do anything to spend one more night with ye?"

"If I buy some girly clothes and get real sexy, you promise to come back?"

"You do that, lass, and I'll go through heaven and hell to come back for ye."

"Promise?"

"Promise."

It was a promise that Jack Gawain was determined he would keep.

Chapter Twenty Nine

Nearly twenty-four hours after Colonel Mark Shaughnessy had flown to Baghdad, he met with an elite unit of SAS commandos in a small bungalow on the outskirts of town. He had his left hip shot full of Novocaine and had an entire pouchful in his rucksack to help him get through the next day. He had gone to the gym faithfully over the past few years and kept a strict diet, but he knew that his cardiovascular conditioning was nowhere near where it had been a decade ago. He would be going through hell to stay this course but he was determined to pull it off or die trying.

"Okay, gentlemen, here's the deal," he stood before the lean, mean fighting machines that had been selected for this perilous assignment. "You've all been briefed on the mission individually and gotten detailed instructions as to your roles in the operation. We're here for a last-minute review and an opportunity to ask questions and share ideas before we hit the lights."

"We're almost eight hundred kilometers out from the target area, which is the missile silo outside Isfahan," Shaughnessy pointed to a map posted on a board at the front of the room. "The tricky part will be invading Iranian air space without getting shot down. The Iraqis have agreed to stage an incident that will justify a sortie along the Iranian border. We'll be flown in by chopper to a rendezvous point west of the silo. Our double agents in Iran have military trucks waiting for us, and they should allow us to get as far as the checkpoint at the main gate."

"What happens if we get intercepted before the gate?" a commando asked.

"It's a wash," the Colonel replied. "We take out the interceptors and avail ourselves of whatever equipment we can salvage in continuing along the mission. This one is no surrender, no retreat, gentlemen. The only way out of this is by destroying the target and returning to the rendezvous. If we are discovered in the middle of the desert, surrounded by hostiles, you've got two options: death, or a fate worse than death."

"Life in prison eating Iranian food and listening to Iranian music," a soldier joked. "Sounds like hell on earth to me."

"When we get to the gate, we will leave two men at the check-point to block traffic through the facility. Fire teams will then proceed east and west from the checkpoint while the sabotage team will head directly north towards the silo itself. The fire teams will be on seek and destroy runs, creating a distraction for the two-man team moving against the target. Once the fire teams have reached midfield on the campgrounds, they will split into two-man teams, the first of which will continue in an attempt to reach the rear of the facility. The second team will split off towards the silo as backup for the sabotage team."

The commando team looked abruptly towards the door as it opened and closed, a lone soldier making his way through the entrance as Shaughnessy stared at him balefully.

"Sorry I'm late, fellas," he smiled apologetically.

"You missed the meet and greet," the Colonel said tersely.

"Well, I'm Captain William Shanahan," the compact, muscular man announced. "Pleased t'meet ye fellas."

"Our pleasure, Captain Shanahan," Shaughnessy narrowed his eyes. "Have a seat.

"Thank you," replied Jack Gawain.

The Colonel went on to explain that the purpose of the mission was to gain access to the silo and sabotage the launching system so as to make the missile inoperable. The nature of the search and destroy imperative was such that, unless the entire base surrendered, they would be required to kill as many enemy troops as possible. They would also destroy as much of the base as they could before deactivating the missile and retreating to the rendezvous point for extraction.

"I assume you were briefed on the way in, Captain Shanahan," Shaughnessy inquired as he brought the meeting to a close.

"The plan seems dead sound t'me," Gawain grinned. "Oughtta be a piece of cake."

As the team prepared to board the helicopter on the landing pad outside, one of the soldiers sidled over towards Gawain.

"Were you with the Black Watch Regiment in Scotland?" he asked.

"Nah," he shook his head. "3rd Battalion of the UFF."

"UFF?"

"Aye. We're always lookin' for a few good men. Look me up when y'get discharged."

The young man stared at him as a deer in the headlights.

Just as the commandos began climbing into the chopper, a jeep cruised up to the takeoff area and stopped alongside Shaughnessy.

"Colonel Shaughnessy," the tall, strapping man stepped gingerly from the passenger side of the vehicle. "Sorry I'm late. I was getting last-minute instructions."

"Your name, soldier," the Colonel suppressed a smile.

"Sergeant Jack Gawain."

"Glad you could make it," Shaughnessy stepped aside to allow William Shanahan passage to the transport helicopter.

"Wouldn't have missed it for the world."

Miles away, Colonel Mahmood Akbar sat in his command headquarters at the missile base in Isfahan. He and his men were on red alert in anticipation of the launch scheduled at 1500. His stomach churned with apprehension at the scenario which lay just hours ahead. He had a wife and five kids at home on Tehran, and he knew that a retaliatory strike by NATO would wipe his family and his people off the face of the earth. The Supreme Leader had assured the military that the UN would never tolerate a nuclear strike against a defenseless nation such as Iran, but there was not one of his colleagues who believed it. They would annihilate Iran as an example to rogue nations such as North Korea and Pakistan, who had already been accused of supplying WMDs to Al Qaeda. The fate of an entire nation was at stake, though if he refused to obey orders, he would be executed and a phalanx of officers would be available to take his place.

At about 0600 he received notice that Iraq was under attack by Al Qaeda operatives in western Baghdad, and was responding to enemy activity along its eastern border. The Army and Air Force were scrambling in the area, but the overriding concern was that the Iraqis, or their American counterparts, might detect the missile being activated and launch their own pre-emptive strike.

"What are those idiots doing!" Akbar raged as the communication was relayed. "Don't they know that we are preparing a strike against the infidels! Why are they compromising this sacred mission!"

"We have no control over those bandits," his lieutenant grimaced. "I doubt that our superiors have shared such confidential information with them. Let us hope the Americans do not send their damned drones into this vicinity and find out what we are doing."

The Iraqis sent sorties of recon planes and attack helicopters along the Iranian border, along with armored units on standby in case of armed intervention by the Iranians. The Iranian diplomatic corps were quick to contact the Iraqis, the Americans and the United Nations in attempt to stall for time. There was now a heated debate in progress between the Guardian Council and the Council of Ministers as to whether the strike against Zurich was worth the risk of having their entire nation annihilated. With just hours to go before the scheduled attack, Colonel Akbar could only hope that the light of reason might dawn on the religious and political leadership.

Sunlight had barely broken over the desert horizon when Akbar was alerted over a disturbance at the front gate. The sentries reported that an unmarked military vehicle had arrived with top secret information from Tehran that had to be relayed exclusively to the Colonel. It was reported there was a squad of riflemen in the truck, led by an emissary of lieutenant rank insisting this was an extremely urgent matter.

"Did you get any passwords or clearance codes?" Akbar demanded as he accessed his command console, sending word to military headquarters in Tehran.

At once the line went dead.

The colonel sounded the alarm, which put his forty-man platoon on full alert. The soldiers raced from their barracks onto the field, and suddenly there was a series of explosions along the fence line followed by automatic rifle fire. The Colonel immediately notified the 28th Mechanized Division stationed in Kerman for backup support as he patched in his platoon sergeants for on-base intercommunication.

"First Squad has located enemy riflemen along the storage area west of the main gate!" the sergeant reported. At once the communication was garbled by static, then cut out completely. Akbar tried to contact Second Squad and Third Squad and experienced similar communication failure. He finally was able to get through to the sergeant of the Fourth Squad, though the line was garbled by the background explosions.

"Sergeant, you are to hold the line in front of the silo at all costs!" Akbar ordered. "Let's get a machine gun out there and some sandbags, put a barricade up and keep those dogs out!"

Jack Gawain was assigned alongside SAS Sergeant Cena to drive a wedge through the Iranian front line. The fire team deployed to their right had caught the Iranians by surprise and used grenades to destroy nearby storehouses, setting a couple of them on fire. The team to their left had killed a number of Iranians but was pinned down by rifle fire due to the scarcity of buildings and objects behind which to take cover. The Iranians were at a disadvantage due to their reluctance to blow up their own buildings on base, while the invaders had no such constraints.

"Okay, listen," Jack called over, both he and Cena hiding behind a large delivery truck parked twenty meters from the gate. "If one of us can get inside this thing and get it started, the other can rig it to blow before we drive it right into 'em."

"So I take it that's not your job description," Cena replied wryly. It did not take long for the commandos to figure out that Shanahan and Gawain had switched names, and that Gawain was not a member of the SAS. Most of them had heard of Shanahan but had no clue as to who Gawain was.

"Well, I'll tell ye, boyo, I'm not too shabby with a knife and I'm pretty hot with a heater, but acrobatics is not somethin' I'm well known for," Gawain admitted.

"Like they say, one should never volunteer, but there's not much of a choice here," Cena managed a grin. The commando rose to his haunches, and Gawain could see that the man had already caught a slug in his left side which was bleeding profusely down his camouflage fatigues. He duckwalked around to the passenger side and tossed a grenade, causing a lull in return fire from the defenders positioned twenty meters ahead of them. He then hopped up and began firing as Gawain jumped out and clambered into the driver's side. He gunned the engine as the key had been left in the ignition, and pulled the pin on a grenade before slamming his foot on the accelerator and diving back out. As he did, he could see Cena lying face down on the ground alongside the passenger side of the truck.

The defenders fired wildly at the truck as it rolled toward them, either unaware that Gawain had jumped free or thinking he was crouched down inside. It plowed into their midst within ten yards of a loading dock leading to the complex surrounding the silo before the grenade went off. It caused a secondary explosion as the gas tank was full, resulting in the entire area erupting as a gigantic fireball spewed into the sky. Gawain rolled to his feet and crept towards the loading dock, soon realizing that the Iranian riflemen were either dead or wounded.

He ran towards the dock and rushed up the steps, perceiving that he was well inside the red zone. He rushed towards the metal door and yanked it open, only to have one of the Iranians fire a round which hit him in the right thigh. He cursed as he shot back, hitting the Iranian lying on the ground below the dock right between the eyes. He slipped through the door and halted momentarily to adjust his vision to the dimly lit area.

He then crouched and sprang through the vestibule leading to the warehouse area, which had been converted it a command center controlling not only the military installation but the missile launching system as well. He could see a dozen technicians busy over their monitors, and when they saw Gawain they began yelling and reaching for handguns. Gawain began spraying them with rifle fire long enough to force them to duck for cover. It gave him time to toss a grenade into the opposite corner of the facility, destroying the equipment and killing the personnel as it detonated.

Gawain spotted the emergency booth, painted in red, to the right of where he stood on a platform surrounding the control center. He knew that it contained an emergency lever which would fill the silo full of concrete and neutralize the warhead and the rocket if necessary. He started towards the booth, then spotted Colonel Akbar on the other side of the platform from him. Akbar aimed and fired, catching Gawain in his left shoulder and driving him into the wall. Gawain managed to pull his last grenade and hurl it at Akbar, causing the Colonel to disappear in an exploding cloud of concrete dust.

The bullet in his thigh hurt like a bitch and his shoulder did not feel much better. He hobbled painfully along the platform, staggering to his left though his right leg could barely support him. He limped along the platform, training his rifle on the ground level though all the technicians lay dead or dying amidst the rubble and smashed equipment. He finally made to the control room and tossed the door open, propping his rifle against the wall to his right.

As once he was slammed against the wall, and reflexively shoved himself off so as to push his attacker away. He spun around and confronted Colonel Akbar, who was bleeding profusely from a gaping head wound but was inches from plunging a bayonet into Gawain's face. The Colonel was taller and heavier that Gawain, but Jack was far more powerful. He rammed Akbar backwards into the guardrail, but the pain in his shoulder was unbearable. He spun in the opposite direction away from Akbar, hoping to lock himself in the control room while he flipped the lever and submerged the missile. To his chagrin, the Colonel tackled him through the doorway onto his back, sending a bolt of pain through his shoulder and thigh as Akbar tried to slit his throat.

Gawain drove his knee upwards, delivering a vicious blow to the Colonel's midsection. The Iranian gasped with pain as the wind was knocked out of him. Gawain tried to wriggle away from him but Akbar proved relentless, hanging onto Jack's collar while forcing the blade towards his face. Gawain began firing punches at Akbar's head but the bayonet cut into his wrist, causing blood to pour over both of them. Jack then grabbed the Colonel's arm with both hands, trying desperately to keep the cold steel away from his face. Akbar was able to anchor his feet against the door frame and was now driving the knife at Gawain with all his body weight.

At once there was a twin blast that reverberated in the small room, and suddenly Akbar's forward motion came to an end as the Colonel fell lifeless against his chest. He was completely exhausted as he looked up and saw William Shanahan tottering in thorough the doorway.

"Now, I hope that makes us even," Shanahan managed, trying to maintain his balance. He had ran at full speed across the base to the silo after Gawain had blown up the truck, and shot his way past the remaining defenders who were retreating before the team of commandos encircling them. He had bounded across the loading dock into the control center, but tore so many of his stitches open and lost so much blood and energy that he had nothing left. He weaved dizzily before his knees buckled, dropping him to the floor alongside Gawain.

"Getting kinda crowded in here, don't y'think?" Jack grimaced, shoving Akbar's body off to his right, pulling his legs up into a crouch.

"You should see the pile out front," Shanahan managed, the wounds in his shoulder, arm, chest and leg burning like fire.

"Well, it looks like you gentlemen are finally getting on," the massive figure of Mark Shaughnessy filled the doorway above Shanahan and Gawain. He had followed Shanahan across the square and up onto the dock, straining his hip joint beyond endurance. It was all he could do to force himself across the control center to where the operatives lay. "Do either of you gentlemen care to do the honors?'

"Be my guest," they exhaled in unison, too exhausted to move.

Shaughnessy limped up to the red closet and threw the door open, reaching in and pulling the lever down with a mighty yank. At once there was a groaning roar as an avalanche of concrete began pouring into the silo from an outside container. The smell of concrete permeated the center as the adjacent tower was slowly flooded.

"Well, so much for nuclear aspirations," Shaughnessy was drained as he fell backwards against the wall.

"Say, fella," Gawain managed, "d'ye think y'can get this curry arsed butt smell off me, then?"

"Let's put it this way," Shaughnessy grimaced. "I feel as if I've got a rocket in my socket. I think we're best off waiting for the younger fellows to help us out of here."

"How are they going to get us back across the desert to the rendezvous point?" Shanahan wondered. "I don't think there's a truck out there they didn't blow up."

"The Yanks made contact with the Israelis and told them we'd come across a WMD that was set to launch," Shaughnessy revealed. "The Israelis agreed not to launch a retaliatory strike against Tehran provided they allowed our boys to send in a ride to get us out of here."

"Now, I think the Crown and country owes me a bit of a favor at this point," Gawain managed to shove Akbar's body away with his boots. "You seem to be the head honcho here. Am I going to be walking around Belfast any time soon, or are you going to stick me in another car full of Taigs?"

"That was MI5," Shaughnessy admitted dourly. "They had jurisdiction over you and the IRA men since you were technically prisoners of the Realm. They offered the Burke and the O'Connors the same deal you got to help us set up the sting operation with the Sardinians and the Colombians. We had no idea they were going to sub them out with our disposal team until after the fact. The disposal fellows were SAS men who got shipped off to Pakistan. We had no choice but to split you and William up when the CIA captured those Al Qaeda agents at the same time we were getting ready to close the trap on Chupacabra."

"One hand not knowin' what the other's up to," Gawain smirked. "Lovely, lovely. So those bastards thought they'd do me in and score one for the West Side."

"Sad but true," Shanahan managed.

Outside the room they could hear the surviving SAS commandos storming into the center, calling out for the Colonel and the Captain, intent on making sure that the area was secure and the nuclear threat to Europe had come to an end.

William Shanahan and Jack Gawain had come to realize that their wishes just might come true at last.

Chapter Thirty

Amschel Bauer stood before the Board of Directors at the monthly executive meeting in the main building of the Bank of Montreal. It was the day after the failed launch, reported as an aborted missile test by the world press, proved to be a rebuke and a disgrace to the nation of Iran. The combined might of the UN Peacekeeping Forces, led by the US and the UK, had crushed the rebellion against Pakistan. The military regime was reinstalled, and they promised the world that the presence of Al Qaeda inside their borders would no longer be tolerated. In addition, North Korea faced new sanctions by the UN and was more isolated than ever. It appeared that Operation Blackout was doomed to failure, but Bauer and his confederates were determined to recoup their losses.

"Although the Americans and the Europeans appear to be having second thoughts about converting to the gold standard, our bank's recent investments in bullion makes us stronger than ever. Furthermore, our clients throughout Latin America are continuing to invest in commodities and will rely exclusively on our bank to cater to their needs. The nations of the world plunge deeper into debt, yet the business associates in our network grow more prosperous as we continue to explore new and innovative ventures in an ever-changing global economy," Bauer was resplendent in a $1,000 bronze-colored suit, standing before a display of charts and graphs documenting the surge in the Bank's annual profit margins.

"Our next project," he paced before the enormous conference table, seating twenty-four executives including Nathan Schnaper, "will focus on the African diamond industry, as we lend a hand in offering stability to the war-torn nations in that poverty-stricken continent. We have been negotiating with several of the private security firms that have been protecting and serving investors throughout the Middle East. We have no doubt that, with our direction, we will not only be able to help defend and protect our prospective clients in the region, but establish our bank and our associates as the leaders of commerce and industry on the continent."

At once the door flew open, and a squad of Royal Canadian Mounted Police officers stormed into the room. Bauer was astonished as a police sergeant confronted him with a legal document.

"Amschel Bauer, this is a warrant for your arrest on charges of insurance fraud, securities fraud and violations of Federal, provincial and territorial banking statutes. You have the right to remain silent; anything you say can and will be held against you in a court of law..."

"This is a fuckin' Board meeting," Schnaper popped out of his chair. "What the fuck do you sons of bitches think you're doing?"

"You're coming too, smart guy," a Mountie grabbed Schnaper and threw him face first against the wall.

"Well, you know what they say," one of the officers said as he led Bauer out.

"What could that be?" Bauer muttered.

"We always get our man," the trooper smiled broadly.

The arrest and indictment of Amschel Bauer had a domino effect on the members of the criminal network participating in Operation Blackout. The United States of America, though quashing all reports of WMDs having been smuggled into its borders, brought intense pressure against the nations that were harboring the conspirators. As a result, Salvaje Pulga and three other drug lords of the Medellin Cartel were arrested by the Colombian government for multiple counts of narcotics possession and distribution, smuggling, racketeering and extortion. Pulga, in turn, turned State witness against the Honduran smuggling ring that was the cornerstone of Tony Ramos' MS-13 criminal empire. The Honduran government issued a warrant for Ramos' arrest, forcing him to flee to Europe to escape prosecution.

The Mexican Cartel was next to feel the wrath of the renewed US War on Drugs. In order to alleviate pressure from the DEA and the Mexican government, Alberto Calix was abducted and tortured, his body chopped in pieces and left on the border between Matamoros and Brownsville. Ernesto Guzman was arrested by the FBI on charges of conspiring against the American government and immediately requested an interview with the CIA. In exchange for amnesty, he and his family were sent to the Philippines where he was rehired as a double agent to infiltrate Al Qaeda cells in the region.

Johnny Carmona, beleaguered by hostile drug gangs throughout South Florida, declared open warfare against his Jamaican and Honduran competitors. As a result, gang activity heated up to the point that the National Guard was sent into hot spots such as Liberty City to restore order. Facing life sentences in some cases, many gang leaders turned State witnesses which led to the arrest and indictment of a number of drug lords. Johnny Carmona was one of them, and he eventually fled to South America to escape prosecution.

Morgana McLaren was phoned by an anonymous caller who said they knew the whereabouts of Fianna Hesher and asked where she could be reached. Morgana was hesitant but gave the person the address of the hotel where she was staying. It was hours later when she was summoned to come down to the lobby to meet a visitor. She rode the elevator to the lobby and was exhilarated to see Fianna awaiting her.

"Oh my gosh," Morgana exchanged hugs with her, both girls on the verge of tears. "Where have you been? I was so worried about you!"

"These last couple of weeks have just been crazy," Fianna insisted. "That company, Colombiana Exports, hired me as a social consultant for Ricky Chew, the CEO. They flew me out to Andros Island, and we had no Internet and couldn't receive phone signals. The only time we left was one night when Ricky had a domino tournament. We went right back to the Island and spent all our time at this resort hotel. It was like being in a fairy tale castle on a desert island."

"What kind of work were you doing?" Morgana wondered as she brought Fianna back to her suite with her.

"They gave me a book of fabrics full of patterns and colors," Fianna explained. "I had to help put together designs for his tailor. Sometimes he was real nice and complimented me for helping me put together the best wardrobe in Florida. Other times he'd get mad and say, 'That's not the color I like!' and throw the book across the room. I'd get real sad and then he'd apologize."

"So what happened?"

"His guys just came in last night and said Ricky didn't need me anymore. They transferred the balance of my salary to my bank account and flew me back here to Florida."

The girls had no way of knowing that Enrique Chupacabra had been killed in the shootout at the Bay Dunes Golf Course. The identities of the perpetrators were remaining confidential pending a Federal investigation. Salvaje Pulga had named Enrique Chupacabra and Emiliano Murra as co-conspirators as part of a plea bargain, since both men were dead and dead men told no tales.

A ceremony was scheduled at Buckingham Palace that weekend as Captain William Shanahan and John Oliver Cromwell Gawain were to be decorated with the Distinguished Conduct Medal. The awards were to be given for extraordinary gallantry in Her Majesty's service. Gawain was given honorary status as an enlisted man in order to make him eligible for the award. The ceremony was closed to the public so as not to compromise Shanahan's position as an undercover operative, or to disclose Gawain's history as a convicted terrorist.

It was a magnificent occasion, and the Prince of Wales was in attendance to lend his prestige to the occasion. The Palace Guard was ubiquitous throughout the ancient halls, and the massive red-carpeted, scarlet-draped chambers were as in legends past. Portraits of venerated English kings seemed to peer down magnanimously at every turn, and all in attendance shared the feeling that they had become part of something bigger than life at this moment in time.

There was a reception after the event, and chamber music was played in different areas of the great hall as champagne and caviar served as appetizers for the delicacies provided in the elaborate smorgasbords. The nobility and other dignitaries socialized as special guests roamed about, delighted to exchange pleasantries with important people while taking in the sights along the hallowed ground.

"So tell me," an acclaimed novelist stopped by to chat with Gawain, who was walking around with a cane after being treated for his injuries in Baghdad just days ago. "How does it feel to be a national hero?"

"Well, there'd be a lot more to it if people found out about it," Gawain frowned. "Unfortunately this top-secret stuff doesn't do much to enhance one's braggin' rights. Besides, if I told people about it they wouldn't believe it anyway."

"Try me," the novelist encouraged him.

"Well, I thwarted two nuclear attacks, started a drug war in Florida, killed four IRA assassins and nearly won the World Domino Championship over the past couple of weeks. How's that grab ye?"

"Sure you did," the novelist shook his head and moved on.

Shanahan and Gawain had Morgana McLaren, Fianna Hesher and Darcy Callahan flown over to London for the event, and they were so stunningly beautiful that they were mistaken for royalty. They played their roles as best they could, and both men were beaming with pride over the way the women were being treated. Only Fianna and Darcy were miffed that they had both been invited as Gawain's special guests, and though they had made each other's acquaintance, they were not very happy with their escort for that afternoon.

"Say, love, won't ye get us a plate of that caviar and some champagne," Gawain called to Fianna as she passed by, resplendent in a glittery white evening gown. Her auburn hair had been combed back, held in place by a diamond tiara with matching earrings that Gawain had bought for the occasion. He had sold the kilo of cocaine he had stolen from the Sosas when he went back to Florida and came back $50,000 richer for his efforts. "I'm havin' t'rest the damned leg with the bullet holes and all."

"Go ask your daughter, big shot," she snapped at him. "You did fine without me while I was tied up with that drug dealer friend of yours, didn't you?"

"Well, it's not like I asked him to kidnap ye while I was busy savin' th' feckin' world," Gawain called out after her, causing a couple of the honored guests to raise an eyebrow. She shot him the finger, which caused the nobility even greater consternation.

"Not doing so hot with the ladies today, eh, Gawain?" Shanahan came over, dressed in a tuxedo as was Gawain, also hobbling around with a cane with his own gunshot wounds.

"Fair to middlin'," Gawain admitted. "Of course, I've still got two to yer one, but I'd be willin' to consider a fair trade if ye like."

"I wonder if that medal's going to eventually rub off on you, or you're going to rub off on that medal," Shanahan grinned.

"Well, if it goes the other way, I'd like to see a box of 'em shipped to my comrades back in Belfast. God and country, y'know."

"God and country," Shanahan replied softly, finding it inside himself to pat Gawain on the shoulder before moving on.

"Say, precious," Gawain called to Darcy, who was passing by in her dark blue gown with a pearl comb in her hair and matching earrings that he purchased for her. "What say ye fetch us some of that champagne and caviar so we can sit together out on the terrace?"

"I thought you just asked your wife," she narrowed her eyes at him, jerking a thumb at Fianna who was still within earshot.

"Well, she's not my wife," he managed. "She's a friend."

"And what am I, chopped liver?" she demanded.

"You know," Fianna came over to Darcy, "I had a couple of really hot guys over there who were asking if I'd like to go check out Carnaby Street after this. I'll betcha they'd be more than glad to make room for one more."

"Sounds like a plan, girlfriend," Darcy agreed.

"Well, yer gonna go hang out with those losers instead of someone who's got *this*?" he mockingly dangled his medal at her.

"Yeah? Well, you got that and I got *this*," she grabbed her crotch. "And you're not getting any." With that the girls turned and walked off arm in arm.

He started to laugh but winced at the stabbing pain in his thigh, wondering if this was going to be a lifelong problem. He also wondered if he would be able to go back to Belfast and find girls like those two again someday.

"Enjoying yourself?" Shanahan made his way over to where Morgana was admiring a portrait of King Henry on a far wall. She was stunning in an emerald satin gown, and many of the other women came up to compliment her on how lovely she looked.

"This is like a dream," she gushed. "I can't thank you enough for inviting me."

"It's the least I could do for you saving my life," he reached into his pocket. "Say, by the way, you know some of these airports have some shops you just wouldn't expect to see in a terminal. I happened by one of them, and came across the cutest little item and thought you might like it."

Shanahan handed her a small velvet box, and her eyes widened as she beheld a $10,000 diamond ring set in platinum.

"Oh my gosh, William," she managed. "It's fantastic."

"So are you, Morgana. You're the kind of girl I want to spend the rest of my days with."

They fell into each others' arms, and it became the highlight of the first day of the rest of their lives together.

About the Author

I began my so-called career at the age of six, writing dialogue for my stick-figure cartoons. I actually began reading at the age of three, a God-given talent that my parents attested to. Upon entering first grade I refined the technique of expressing words in print, and from there it progressed. By sixth grade I wrote my first novella, a James Bond ripoff called *Enemy Ace*. It was about a WWII German pilot, Fritz Hammer, recruited by the CIA to thwart a negriphile named Blackman. Umm... yeah. Well, guess what? Fritz Hammer appeared in *Tiara* a half century later, and the plot morphed into *The Standard* shortly thereafter. Hmm.

I continued writing through high school, spending one summer writing a 1,000-page epic about the USA turning fascist and starting WWIII. I pulled it in a tad and wrote a second spy novel featuring Fritz Hammer. I lent both of them to two of my teachers and never got them back. At this stage of my life, I am certain that none of us will ever profit from those long-lost treasures.

It really kicked in during my twenties while I was masterminding my punk band, the Spoiler. I wrote a ten-novel series on Richard Mc Cain, a Special Forces superhero in Vietnam. They were action-packed, well-researched classics that never saw the light of day in the pre-Internet days. Mc Cain became the hero of *Bloody Sunday*, an apocalyptic Northern Ireland saga. Again, an awesome piece of work that never went anywhere. Mc Cain became the protagonist of my Christian novel *Abaddon (Destroyer)*, so it wasn't all in vain. I also wrote a half-dozen sci-fi space novels, great action tales that never got published.

When I relocated to Texas, I went through another writing phase which sowed some major fields. I wrote *Hezbollah*, which got published a quarter-century later, as did *The Bat* and *Both Sides Now*. There was also *Tiara*, which was an offshoot of a sci-fi novel I wrote back in NYC. I was really gearing up to make something happen, but that didn't progress until I moved to Missouri.

I ended up going to bed with Publish America, a vanity press rip-off that ended up with some of my best work. They got *Tiara*, then *Wolfsangel*, followed by *Cyclops* and *Penny Flame*. It took four years before I realized they weren't paying me a dime and never would. I decided I had to make a last-ditch effort to make something of my so-called career, and 2013 was the year.

I devoted myself full-time to getting published and put thirty novels on the market. Some were self-published, and many others went to indie lit publishers. I've had over two hundred reviews of my work posted on Amazon. Over eighty percent are five-star reviews. I haven't made any decent money yet, but my readers have made it worthwhile.

What keeps me going? The great, incomparable stories, the awesome characters, and the satisfaction of knowing you are writing things that people will appreciate long after you're gone. I can pick up one of my novels after years of not having read it, and become absorbed by it all over again. I wonder why they never reached the heights that so many farce novels find in Hollywood. I'm not gonna worry about it. My readers know and I know. 'Nuff said.

All I can say is: pick up a JRD novel and see what you think. If you really think it sucks, just write me an e-mail and tell me why. Odds are I'll send you your money back. Or if you're in Kansas City, I'll buy you a beer.

Oh, yeah, and I give all the credit and glory to my Lord Jesus Christ. He put the spirit and the vision inside me. If He didn't like what I was doing, He would've taken it away a half century ago.

And I'm glad He hasn't.

Also by the Author

- The Nightcrawler Series
    - Nightcrawler
    - Tryzub
    - The Plague
- Generations
- King of the Hoboes
- Strange Tales
- Penny Flame
- The Test
- Tiara
- Vampir
- Wolfsangel

Printed in Great Britain
by Amazon